Time and Chance

by

Teresa Davis

The Lake City Series

Publishing History
First Edition, 2025
Trade Paperback ISBN 978-1-5092-6312-7
Digital ISBN 978-1-5092-6313-4

The Lake City Series
Published in the United States of America

Dedication

Without my husband Don, I'm not sure I would've focused and dedicated the time to complete this story. Over the fifty-three years of our marriage, he's encouraged me to follow my dreams of publication and appreciates the hard work and long hours it takes for my manuscripts to reach the publisher.

Thank you to the team at The Wild Rose Press, for again, giving me the opportunity to share my stories. You're an awesome group!

Thank you to my daughters, sons-in-law, grandchildren, and our new great-granddaughter, Stiorra, for inspiring me to keep creating.

Above all, thank you to my Lord and Savior for this amazing life!

Chapter One

"Miss Austin!" Mindy hurried from behind the reception desk. "We've all been worried! I'll let Ms. Russo and Mr. Walters know you're back."

Chloe wanted nothing more than to reach her private office and close the door, but the concern in Mindy's dark eyes made her pause. "Thank you, Mindy. Please let Ms. Russo know I'd like to meet right away."

"Of course." Mindy returned to her desk and lifted the intercom phone.

Chloe slipped into her downtown Sacramento office and closed the door. What. A. Day. And it wasn't over. She could still lose the Billings design account.

She set her computer case on her desk and the tote holding her tools of the design trade on the credenza. For a moment, she paused to gaze through the large window overlooking the city's downtown core. *Ah.* Back in her element. No more snow-covered roads or listening to the ringing of Hallie's phone. Still...

"You're back!" Gina swept into the room carrying a fully outfitted tea tray. "Mindy wanted to bring this, but I waylaid her. Fill me in—how did the drive and the Billingses' home consultation go?"

Chloe met Gina at the midcentury modern sideboard. "I might need your human resource skills and, as my best friend, your advice."

"O-k-a-y…" Gina cringed. "Start at the beginning while I pour tea. I almost went after you when Mindy informed me that Juanita canceled the plan to drive you."

Chloe scoffed. "Believe me, I almost rescheduled." She blew a breath through pursed lips. "But I didn't. I forged on with the appointment, and even my car performed well on the snow-covered road."

"I keep telling you to get all-season tires. They work better in the rain, too. But go on." Gina set a cup of tea on Chloe's desk.

"I survived the road conditions, but that doesn't mean I want to venture from town anytime soon." Chloe moved to her desk, picked up the teacup, and flinched. "Yikes, too hot." She set the cup on the matching saucer. Okay—here's where I need your HR help."

"When I arrived at the Billingses house, a car sat outside the garage. The security system was disabled, and the house was unlocked. Juanita had warned me to expect a cold house, but when I entered, the furnace hummed, and the great room was toasty warm."

"Hold up." Gina raised a palm. "Don't tell me Juanita decided to meet you, or I'll call her right now and chew her out. She's already adding unneeded pressure to this project. Did she tell you she mailed the invitations for two, instead of one, senate campaign parties?" Gina shook her head. "Why can't she host them downtown? I'm sure they belong to a country club."

"What?" Chloe gripped the back of her chair. "No, she didn't tell me. What's the date of the first party?"

"Well in advance of the primaries in March and

soon enough to put a rush on the design work." Gina dropped into a chair on the client side of the desk.

"Ah, that explains the added fee." Chloe attempted a sip of tea, but her hands trembled from the lingering angst. "But hey, after this afternoon—nothing should surprise me." Her favorite tea blend of lavender and honey bush began to soothe her ragged nerves.

"Okay, so I get the sense something's coming that I won't like to hear." Gina smoothed her hands over the magenta twill of her slim-cut skirt and raised a dark brow.

Chloe sank into the soft, buttery, leather of her office chair. "So, I set up a workstation on the glass coffee table in the great room. With the snow falling, I wanted to complete the work and get the heck out of the mountains." She sank her teeth into her lower lip. Her chest was still tight, and her thoughts kept jumping ahead. She needed to be methodical with her account of the afternoon.

Restless, she pushed her teacup to one side and unloaded the colorful file folders from her computer case. "Bear with me. What happened next might prompt a call from Bruce Billings. He's likely to demand that Keith remove me from the account."

Gina narrowed her dark eyes, crossed her legs, and rested her hands on the polished armrests of the chair. "I can't imagine Keith would agree with Bruce but go on."

Chloe shivered with nervous energy. "I'd finished the measurements for the furniture groupings in the great room when a gasp came from behind me."

Gina uncrossed her legs and scooted forward on the chair. "Yikes! Well, you did say a car was parked

3

out front. Who was it?"

Chloe smirked. "Hallie Smith, the lead paralegal at the Billings Law Firm. Get this; Bruce burst from the hallway, ranting about how she'd walked away while he made an important point. At first, he didn't seem to notice me." She raised a forefinger. "The house has three bedrooms and bathrooms, but Bruce and Juanita each have home offices. The *work* premise might have flown if Bruce's shirt hadn't been untucked and Hallie's blouse wrinkled."

"What a circus!" Gina raised a brow. "Now, I understand why you look so frazzled."

Chloe shrugged one shoulder. "When Bruce calmed down enough to notice me, he began to frantically button up and tuck in. Hallie turned beet red. You tell me."

"If Juanita hadn't canceled—wow—I can just imagine what that scene would have looked like." Gina's dark brown eyes widened, and both eyebrows shot up.

"Well, I informed Bruce Juanita had planned to come. He blustered, then turned a bit sheepish." She'd almost felt sorry for him—but not quite.

Gina glanced at her wristwatch. "You were gone for hours so you must have stayed and finished the work."

"After a ninety-minute drive with thirty minutes of terrifyingly slick roads? You'd better believe I stayed. Bruce gruffly permitted me to continue with whatever I needed to do but to stay out of the office. They were working with sensitive information." She arched a brow and waved a hand. "Believe me, I had no desire to see their sensitive information.

"They returned to the office, and I continued with the purpose of my trip. I took photos and sketched the subject rooms. Juanita will be here at ten thirty sharp tomorrow morning. She expects to see a complete presentation."

Gina rose to refresh her tea. "Well, your meeting will be awkward, but you can't say anything about what transpired today." She clicked her tongue.

"Oh, my story doesn't end there. I'd begun to wrap up the essentials for my initial proposal, and Hallie reappeared with Bruce at her heels. She wore her suit jacket, but her hair was still mussed, and she looked on the edge of tears. She demanded Bruce immediately take her to town, or she'd walk."

"What did Bruce say?" Gina gripped the back of a chair.

"He begged her to stay until after the storm let up and to stop acting ridiculous. I witnessed the scene, feeling like I was part of some old soap opera. In the meantime, the snow had continued to fall, and the temperatures were well below freezing."

"Yikes." Gina sank into her chair. "I'm still unhappy with Juanita's change of plans. You made clear you have no winter driving experience."

"Well, I do now. Hallie persisted about leaving, grabbed her coat, and left the house. Bruce glared. What could I do? I packed my supplies and hurried to my car. By that time, Hallie had reached the main road—slipping and sliding in her leather pumps."

"Wow." Gina shook her head. "This is unacceptable. You don't want to lose this account, but Juanita needs to guarantee Bruce won't work at the house until after the remodel. Otherwise, they need to

5

find another design firm."

Chloe drank her tepid tea in one gulp. "After what I went through today, I deserve this commission *and* the rush fee. I refuse to let this account go." She drew a breath. "But back to Hallie. She agreed to ride with me but probably regretted it about the second time the car almost slid off the road. To make it worse, her phone kept ringing, ringing, ringing. She refused to answer and let the calls go to voice mail. I assume Bruce was the caller. He finally gave up."

"Oh, boy." Gina pursed her lips. "Keith will hear about this, but first from me. You did everything right. I doubt Bruce will complain to Keith or Juanita. He'd be exposing his affair with Hallie."

Chloe straightened her shoulders and lifted her spread fingers. "I don't know what to expect. The man has a lot on the line. He's deep into the run for the California State Senate, and he can't afford a scandal."

"Well, he's not doing a good job at preventing one! I'm so sorry you had to deal with such an ugly scene." Gina pushed from the chair. "I'll catch Keith before he leaves for the weekend. I don't want him to be blindsided if Bruce calls."

"Please assure Keith I have everything I need to consult with Juanita and with her approval, complete the plans." She swallowed hard.

Gina set her empty teacup on the sideboard. "Where did you leave Hallie?"

"At the Crazy Bean. She didn't want to face the office until Monday morning. Honestly, I didn't want to leave her on the curb, but what else could I do? She insisted, and after the way my day had gone, I just wanted to get here." Chloe set aside her cup and saucer and began to sort through the willy-nilly packed file folders. "I swear, Juanita's more dedicated to Bruce's election win than he is. Can you imagine? Having an affair in their vacation home?"

Gina ran her manicured hands over the fabric of her fitted magenta jacket. "Keith will defend how you handled the situation. He's a consummate professional, and so are you." She leaned into the desk and tapped a file with the tip of her long, red-polished nail. "When did you start using generic file folders?"

Chloe blinked and picked up the odd duck. "What? I haven't switched. Where did this come from?" She grappled to recall where— "Oh, no. This is just great!"

"What? What is it?" Gina rounded the desk.

"When I arrived, this file was lying on the Billingses' coffee table." She moaned and leaned into the leather upholstered chair. "In my haste to get out of there, I scooped it in with my folders." She pressed a hand to her forehead. "Bruce will explode when he finds it missing."

Gina frowned. "Maybe it's Juanita's or Hallie's. Open it."

Chloe gazed at the folder. "I'm afraid to. It's not even labeled." She slowly shook her head. "Maybe I should call Hallie first. She gave me her business card. Would you believe she asked me to meet for coffee? Not likely, after what happened today." The pressure in her chest increased.

Gina snapped the folder from under Chloe's hands and flipped it open. "I'll take the responsibility for identifying the file and for calling the owner." She ran her dark gaze over the top page.

"What is it?" Chloe struggled to breathe.

Gina clamped her white teeth on a corner of her full bottom lip. "This belongs to Bruce. Oh, Chloe, when you do something, you do it big."

Chloe shot out of her chair and angled to read the spreadsheet—with dates, names, and dollar amounts. On the far left were handwritten notes. "Oh, my gosh. Is this what I think it is?"

"If you think it's a shadow campaign donor file, you're right. I need to meet with Keith and right away." She fished her sleek cell phone from her jacket pocket and thumbed in a text. "Bruce will be calling."

Chloe gripped the edge of the desk. "How could I have done this? I take pride in protecting my client's information." She opened and closed her mouth. "This confirms why Bruce called Hallie at least five times. He discovered it was missing and suspected her of taking it." She paced between the door and the large window behind her desk. She paused. "Did Keith answer your text?"

"Yes, just now, and he wants to meet me in his office. Keith will handle this, Chloe. Hang tight, I'll be right back. I assume you plan to work late?" Gina moved toward the door.

Chloe nodded. "Regardless of how the file dilemma ends, I'm committed to follow through with the design plans." She repositioned her chair and opened her laptop. Job security might become the least of her worries. It had been an accident, but she'd taken a highly sensitive file filled with enough information to sink the careers of numerous large businesspeople and Bruce's campaign.

"Wait." She hurried toward Gina. "Before you go, I need the file. Please." She snapped the folder from

Gina's hand.

"What are you doing?" Gina dropped her jaw.

"Creating an insurance policy." She fed the pages through the top feed of the copier. "Keith will stand by me, but Bruce is in a very awkward position. He won't back off. He might accuse me of theft and sue the design firm. The Billingses are powerful attorneys."

Gina planted her hands on her hips. "And how does making a copy of a highly sensitive file prevent a lawsuit?

Chloe gathered the warm pages from the tray and retrieved the original document. "Because when Bruce learns I have a copy of the file, he'll back off."

"You're not thinking straight." Gina ran a hand over the top of her long, dark brown hair. "You're traumatized from the hazardous drive and the drama at the house. Your phobia about leaving the city limits has pushed you over the top. Take a breath and think this over."

Chloe stuffed the copies into an emerald-green folder. "I thought about the situation every mile back to town. And that was before I discovered this." She held up the folder.

"Okay, at least lock the copies in your desk. I'll be right back." Gina waved both hands. "And for heaven's sake, don't call Juanita or Hallie."

Chloe surrendered the generic folder. "I'll be here, trying to focus on the design plan." The moment Gina left, Chloe sank to her chair and set the emerald folder on her desk. The file seemed to taunt her. *In for a penny.* She flipped open the cover and ran her gaze over the first page. Names, she recognized from the business section of the *Sacramento Times,* leaped off the page.

The top name on the list sent a chill over her shoulders.

Drew King. King owned one of the most powerful software businesses in San Jose. Rumor had it, if anything interfered with his expansion plans, he could be ruthless. According to a recent article in the *Times*, he'd filed a challenge to the Department of Interior over a parcel adjacent to King Enterprises' main software plant. The parcel belonged to a local native tribe, but King didn't care.

She glanced at the next three names. All belonged to tech giants—worth billions—and who were after more power. She closed the folder and braced her elbows against the edge of the desk. She'd been right to copy this file. She blew a frustrated breath and opened her laptop—time to accomplish the report for Juanita.

Twenty minutes later, Gina returned. "Any progress on the design plan?"

Chloe glanced at her best friend. "Some. What did Keith say?"

"As I anticipated, he has your back." Gina reclaimed her chair. "He tried to reach Bruce, but no answer on Bruce's cell or office number." She glanced at her watch. "It is after five on a Friday night. For now, the file is locked in Keith's safe. He'll follow this situation until Bruce arranges to pick it up." She took a breath. "Keith agrees the file is a record of over-limit contributions to Bruce's campaign. A shadow file with earmarks written in the margin."

Chloe shook her head. "Shadow file? Earmarks? Where did you learn that lingo?"

Gina shrugged. "Throughout the years, I attended several political fundraisers with my dad. You learn the terms—legal limits, campaign promises, earmarks."

She drummed her long, red fingernails against the glass protector on Chloe's desk. "Dad belonged to a PAC—Political Action Committee—and after he'd return from a meeting, we'd stay up late and discuss the status of an upcoming election."

Chloe lifted a brow. "Well, while you were gone, I read the first few names on the list. Did you notice, Drew King is listed first?"

Gina retrieved her phone and typed something into the browser. "Like I said, girlfriend, you do it big. Here's the website for King Enterprises. Headquartered in San Jose. Satellite offices in various locations across the West. Numerous links to articles regarding King's zoning infringements." She set her phone on the desk and leaned forward. "Brace yourself—Bruce has too much to lose to take this lightly."

Her empty stomach roiled. She hadn't eaten since early morning, and then only a bagel smothered in cream cheese. "What now?"

Gina stood. "We wait until Bruce responds to Keith."

"Ugh—you know I'm not the patient type. I could still call Hallie. She might know how to slip it into Bruce's desk."

Gina bobbed her head. "Bruce knows he had the file with him."

Chloe snapped up her cell phone and Hallie's card. "Speaking of earmarks, I have plans for the commission from this job. Help with Mom's cancer care expenses. The investment in your winery." The call rang, and she scooted to the edge of her chair.

Hallie's chipper voice mail message announced she wasn't available.

"Hallie, it's Chloe Austin. When you have a moment, could you please call? Thank you." She disconnected and set her phone on the desk. "I feel like I need to warn her. Bruce might think she took the file to spite him."

"That could end badly for her." Gina tapped her fingernails on the desktop.

Chloe trusted Gina with her life. Through the college years, and the ten years since, they'd shared fun times and weathered storms. Among those storms, was the death of Gina's dad and Chloe's mom's cancer diagnosis. As her dear friend, and the skilled HR director for the top design firm in the city, Gina would stand by her.

"Gina, tomorrow's Saturday and your day off, but would you mind meeting me here—not to sit in on my meeting with Juanita, but to be close by in case she brings up the file?"

"Of course, I will. Don't forget we made lunch plans with Diane for eleven thirty at Luigi's." She cringed. "Keeping this information from Diane won't be easy, but Keith requested we keep the file between the three of us."

"Ugh, I'm not good at lying." Chloe returned to her software and gazed at the furniture layout for the Billingses' great room. "Wait, that won't work. Diane coordinates our appointments. She's aware I drove to the Billings house. She'll ask how it went."

"I'll help distract her." Gina moved toward the door. "I'm going home, and I'll lock the outer office door on my way out. Don't work too late."

After Gina left, Chloe forced her exhausted mind to focus on the new design and not the illegal campaign file. "Austin, you can handle whatever Bruce dishes out." She spoke the words out loud, and the sound of her voice emphasized the quiet of her office and the outer office.

She shivered, suddenly reminded of life after her father left. He'd taken their safe, middle-class lifestyle and his income, forcing them out of their home and into a series of low-income apartments. During Chloe's teen years, she spent hours alone, while her mom often worked two jobs, and listened to domestic disputes through the thin walls. Zach Austin had saved them in so many ways.

Three hours later, she stretched and flexed her fingers. The initial report and the new furnishing choices were ready for Juanita's approval. Barring supply-chain issues, the deliveries would arrive in time to complete the work before the first campaign party. The glitch in her schedule appeared when her wall covering expert, Louise, couldn't take the job right now.

She sighed, closed the numerous open vendor sites and powered off her computer. She'd take her laptop home in case Juanita responded to her email yet tonight.

The drama of the day had wiped her out. Thank goodness, she lived a short drive from the office. Reaching her fifth-floor apartment, she unlocked the door and slipped inside the warm foyer. The Himalayan salt lamp, Gina gave her on her recent birthday, cast just enough light to see where to place her purse on the credenza. She toed off the three-inch heels and wiggled her aching toes. Reaching past the bull-nosed corner to turn on the overhead can lights in the living room, she had her fingers on the rocker switch when the sharp screech of wood against wood ripped through the apartment. Chloe froze. A thud, then heavy footsteps rang against the metal treads of the fire escape outside her bedroom window.

She stifled a scream and pressed against the wall until the footsteps faded away. What good would it do to scream? Her apartment was soundproof. Sluggish with fear, she relocated the rocker switch and flexed her fingers. The can lights illuminated. Chloe gasped and pressed a hand to her throat.

Her home—her refuge—lay in utter shambles. She stumbled into the living room and picked her way around the shredded cushions from her white, designer-label linen couch. Her toes encountered a piece of the ceramic dish she kept on the glass-topped coffee table.

"Ouch!" She hopped on one foot while she removed the shard from her big toe. A drop of blood bloomed over her coral nail polish. Tears threatened, but she blinked them away. She'd have time to weep later. She needed to see the rest of her apartment and call Paul. No, first she needed a weapon in case someone hid in her bedroom or bathroom. She reached the sofa table and wrapped her fingers around the brass candelabra before she continued toward her bedroom door. The destruction of her home almost overwhelmed her.

Just inside the bedroom, the open window caught her attention. Backlit by the streetlights below, the sheer curtains lifted on the evening breeze. She shivered—more from fear of the intruder's return than the chilly night air. She moved toward the window that doubled as an emergency escape. She'd never succeeded at breaking the layers of enamel paint the previous renters had applied, but out of precaution, she'd installed a lock. The lock now dangled from the wood frame.

She reached the Art Deco floor lamp and clicked on the switch. The soft glow illuminated the slashed cushion on her Louis IV reproduction chair. She set the heavy candelabra on the windowsill and used all her strength to close the window. She pulled the curtains and turned to take in the full extent of the damage.

The bedding had been stripped, and the mattress slashed in several places. The closet doors hung open, and her clothes lay in a tangled heap of fabric and hangers.

A whirlwind of fear, outrage, and disbelief tumbled through her. Everything she'd worked so hard to build—the symbols of her success as a designer and as a shrewd businessperson—was ruined. She might lose the largest account of her career and her job.

She sank to the edge of her bed. The presence of strangers seemed to hang in the air, stealing her sanctuary. She sniffed. Time to call Paul and Gina.

Chapter Two

Detective Paul DeMers, and the two officers who accompanied him, assessed the damage and collected evidence.

Hopefully, they'd find enough to convict the intruder.

Gina, who'd arrived ten minutes after Paul and his officers, helped her sweep up the remnants of her teapot collection.

Chloe picked up the spout of the cobalt-blue teapot her parents had brought her from their second honeymoon in Belgium. No sense in trying to fix it. She gently set it in one of the paper grocery bags she'd lined up on the floor. Tears welled. Of all the things she'd valued most, her teapot collection had been her prized procession.

"You poor thing." Gina leaned the broom handle against the granite-topped island. "What happened to your stellar building security?" She turned toward Paul, who'd moved his inspection team into the dining area. "Paul, you need to find whoever did this."

Paul planted both hands at his lean waist. "I intend to." He turned to assess the damage and tightened his mouth. "We've taken prints and pictures, but I'm puzzled. Chloe, are you sure nothing is missing?"

"I don't think so." Still in shock, Chloe turned in one spot.

Paul examined the framed reproduction of a famous impressionist painting of water lilies. "At first glance, the damage looks like pure vandalism. Like someone has a vendetta against you or possibly broke into the wrong apartment." He turned over the painting. "They sliced the paper backing on every print, but didn't damage the artwork. The cushions are slashed, and some stuffing is removed." He clicked his tongue. "The damage is consistent throughout the apartment."

"Except for my teapot collection." She compressed her lips and fought fresh tears.

Gina planted her hands on the curve of her hips, located under the loose-fitting loungewear. "Paul, what does that tell you? Why would they break teapots?"

"Maybe they're looking for something small. But the other damage isn't consistent with that idea." He made more notes in the small notebook he carried. "Overall, the evidence supports the intruder searched for something flat."

Her stomach lurched, and she turned to grasp at Gina's velour sleeve. "Something flat?"

Gina shook her head.

"Yes." Paul glanced around the room. "I'll need full access to the apartment to finish my investigation. Your insurance adjustor will also need access."

Chloe glanced over the room, and her heart broke all over again. Part of her wanted to stand firm and fight for her privacy—the other part wanted to pack the salvageable personal belongings and never return.

"One thing is for sure." Gina pressed a hand against her forehead. "You'll go home with me tonight. Paul, Chloe and I are under strict orders from Keith not to mention a situation from work, but you have a right to know what might have caused this vandalism."

Chloe's chest tightened, and she swayed on her feet. "Gina."

"I know." Gina clasped her arm. "But this is over the top."

"Okay, ladies. Out with it. How could a workplace situation cause someone to break into Chloe's apartment?" Paul lifted his chin toward the two officers waiting for further instructions. "Hey, guys. Go ahead and take the evidence to the precinct. I'll see you in a few." He turned and pinned Chloe and Gina with his blue gaze.

Gina straightened her shoulders. "If Keith agrees, I'll tell you everything."

Paul flung out his arms. "I'm a detective with the Sacramento Police Department. The law's been broken, and if Chloe had arrived two minutes earlier, she could have been hurt or worse. Why do we need Keith's permission?"

"Paul." Chloe rested a hand on his arm. "Let Gina call Keith. Something happened today that might explain this." She gestured toward her home with a sweep of a hand.

Gina pulled her phone out. "Keith, sorry for the late call but I'm at Chloe's apartment. Detective Paul DeMers is with us. I'll put you on speaker so we can discuss a situation."

"Of course. What happened?" Keith's voice boomed through the heavy silence.

Very clearly, Gina relayed the sequence of events since Chloe arrived at her apartment.

"Wow." Keith's shock and concern carried through the phone speaker. "Wow. Yes, tell Paul everything."

Exhausted, Chloe slumped against her damaged couch. She'd thought her workday had been bad—it didn't compare with this.

****

"This isn't good." Paul shoved his fingers through his short blond hair. "Uh, in light of what you've shared, I need to break protocol and alert you to something. A 9-1-1 call." He paused and drew a breath that lifted his broad shoulders. "At five this evening, a young woman, identifying herself as Hallie Smith, called dispatch for help." He held Chloe's gaze. "She'd caught a ride with someone called 'Steve' who shoved her from the car along the Interstate."

"Did the police rush to help her?" Chloe crossed her arms and braced for a blow

"They did." He rolled and released his lips with a smack. "While dispatch ordered officers on the scene, she heard a loud thump."

"Are you saying a car struck Hallie?" Her knees wobbled, and she sank to the floor. "Is she at the hospital?"

Paul took a knee and lifted her to her feet. "Chloe, I'm so sorry. Hallie died at the scene."

Her vision blurred. She clutched Paul's arms. "No! I left her at the Crazy Bean at four fifteen! She planned to grab a coffee and go home."

Paul's dark blue eyes were shadowed. "We have the closed-circuit TV footage from in front of the Bean. Once reviewed, we'll confirm whether someone forced Hallie into the car, or if she knew the driver." He pulled her close. "None of this is your fault."

Chloe shoved her fingers through her hair and tugged a curl loose from the large clip. "Someone murdered her." Anger bubbled from deep inside. "On the way back to town, someone repeatedly called her. She refused to answer. I'm sure Bruce was the caller."

"We have her cell phone." Paul drew a breath. "Once we crack her security code, we'll review the recent call log and the voice mails." He looked away. "Full disclosure—my police chief will try to keep Bruce Billings out of this investigation. The Billingses are friends with the mayor."

"You can't mean an officer of the law will squash a murder investigation." Chloe waved her hands in the air. "Paul, you can't let that happen."

"I'll do my best. I'm just warning you, politics play a role in the city. Even the police department." He ran a hand over his mouth, his expression grim. "This investigation won't be prioritized. In the meantime, stay with Gina. Tomorrow, call your insurance agent." He met Chloe's gaze. "For the next few days, your apartment is a crime scene."

Gina touched Chloe's arm. "Let's gather whatever you need for a few days."

Chloe traced her fingertips over the arm of the linen couch. "All I can think about is Hallie." Her lungs seemed to deflate. "She made a huge mistake by becoming romantically involved with her boss." She choked on the words. "Huge. But to murder her…"

"Until we have more facts, we can't call it murder." Paul cleared his throat. "Be prepared for the case to be ruled as a hit-and-run." He turned to leave and paused. "Everything I've shared must remain confidential. Even from Diane."

Chloe exchanged a glance with Gina. "Once Diane hears about this mess, she'll demand details." She lifted her hands and pressed her fingertips against her eyelids. She couldn't erase the images of Hallie's final moments.

****

At noon on Saturday, Chloe saw Juanita Billings to the outer office door and thanked her again, before she locked the door and leaned against it. The past two hours had been torture.

Not once had Juanita mentioned Hallie, and Paul had forbidden Chloe to ask questions.

Hallie worked for Billings Law Firm. Her photo and the sad details of her death had hit the front page of every newspaper in the city. The papers described Hallie as an up-and-coming paralegal, who worked for one of the largest law firms in California. Juanita had to know about Hallie's death.

Paul had been accurate about the department calling the tragedy a random hit-and-run. Even though the CCTV footage in front of the Crazy Bean showed the car, and Hallie getting into it, the driver's photo had been blacked out.

Chloe scoffed. *The Times* journalist called the driver a person of interest. What an understatement. The driver had taken Hallie from town and left her along the interstate to be struck down. A prearranged hit? Or a fluke?

She returned to her office and sank into her chair. Despite the security of Gina's suburban home, she'd barely slept last night. At least she'd made it through the meeting with Juanita. Now to call her insurance agent. Would the insurance adjustor notice the pattern in the damage to her furnishings? How would she answer their questions?

Gina stepped into the office and sank into the chair Juanita had occupied. She planted her elbows on the edge of the desk, and the sleeves of her tan linen jacket retracted to reveal the silver bangles on her tanned wrists. "I assume Juanita didn't mention Hallie."

"Not even once." Chloe braced an elbow on the desktop. "How can she not mention it when she knows we all saw the article?"

"Think about it." Gina leaned against the curved back of the chair and smoothed her hands over her linen trousers. "She's managing the law firm, and she's in the middle of a remodel. She's arranging campaign parties for her undeserving husband, and I suspect in the not-too-far back of her mind, she knows Bruce is unfaithful. She might suspect he'd dallied with Hallie."

"Dallied?" Chloe blinked. "Such a charming old-fashioned term for something so ugly. Why hasn't Paul called? He must have listened to Hallie's voice messages. I'm dying to know if Bruce mentioned the file." She broke her cardinal rule about protecting her complexion and scrubbed at her face with both hands.

"Speaking of Bruce." Gina crossed her long legs and smirked. "At ten thirty this morning, he sent a courier to meet with Keith, but this situation won't end quietly. I called an acquaintance at *The Times,* and the newspaper obtained the footage from the CCTV at the Bean."

"Are you kidding? The crime just happened yesterday afternoon!" She wanted a cup of tea, but they didn't have time to make tea before they left to meet Diane for lunch.

Gina smacked her lips. "Oh, Chloe. It's painful and it boggles your caring mind, but when Hallie tangled with Bruce Billings, she made a terrible choice. She probably made a chain of bad choices. She became a victim of unscrupulous politics and an affair gone bad, but she played a part in the outcome."

"Maybe, but—"

"Wait," Gina said. "During the 9-1-1 call, Hallie mentioned her purse. Do you remember, if her purse could hold the file?"

"Let me think." Chloe struggled to recall Hallie's accessories. "A beige leather bag about the size of the purse you're using today. Yes, the file could have easily fit inside."

Gina pushed from the chair and braced the flats of her hands against the glass desktop protector. "If Steve, whoever he is, tossed the purse when he shoved Hallie from his car, the police should have it. Paul could tie the size of the purse with the file." She straightened and cocked a dark brow. "How are we going to keep this from Diane? She's too good at reading expressions, and frankly, you're a train wreck."

Chloe tried to keep up with Gina, but she couldn't. "I am a wreck. We must tell Diane about my apartment. She's our good friend, and she's very sharp. She'll guess something is wrong." She smoothed her hair with both hands. "Give me a minute to freshen up."

Gina glanced at her smartwatch. "I'll call Diane and tell her we're on our way. Please make sure your bottom desk drawer is locked. I'd rather you shred those copies, but I know you won't."

"You're right. I won't. If Bruce tries to pull a fast one and accuses me of theft, then I need an insurance policy." Chloe double-checked her desk lock system. She hadn't mentioned the copies to Paul. He'd probably blow his top and demand she hand them over.

Chloe's thoughts reverted to the design account. "This probably sounds frivolous but did Keith mention anything about Bruce demanding a new designer?"

"Keith is still furious over what happened yesterday, but he's not upset with you. We agreed—Bruce doesn't dare draw attention to you, or Juanita will demand the reason why. From there, it would snowball, and all explanations would lead to Hallie."

Out of habit, Chloe took one final look at her office—all looked secure. With her mind in such a mess, she wouldn't put it past herself to leave something lying out. "I get what you're saying. I'd like to rail against Bruce for what I suspect he did—like cheat on Juanita—but I'll trust Paul to find whoever's responsible for both Hallie's death and the destruction of my home."

She slipped a black raincoat over her sage-green suit jacket and matching slacks. So, Bruce had the file again. Maybe he'd back off—assume his career would survive, and he'd win the upcoming election. She gathered her purse and laptop bag. For Hallie, it was too little, too late.

****

By one o'clock that afternoon, Luigi's spacious parking lot was full. Chloe had to make several passes before a car backed out of the far row facing the boulevard. She turned off the engine, slid from the warm interior, and slipped the straps of her leather cross-body purse over her shoulder.

Mouthwatering aromas drew her and Gina through three long rows of cars and toward the entrance to the famous *ristorante*. She could already taste Luigi's marinara. Her stomach growled. She pressed a hand against her middle. "I'm starving."

Gina looped her arm through Chloe's. "Good. I couldn't believe it when you declined my delicious cheese omelet this morning." She tugged Chloe's arm against her side. "The past twenty-four hours have been horrendous, but don't let Hallie's situation get too far inside your head. You shouldn't carry the burden for something you didn't create."

Chloe paused in front of a blue sedan. "Maybe not, but I took the file and I left her at the Crazy Bean." Her whisper came out on a hiss. "That file started this entire chain of events."

Gina turned toward the busy entrance. "Okay, enough about the file and the break-in. Paul doesn't want Diane to know yet."

"Got it, but we both know the file is intrinsically tied to both crimes." Chloe stepped into the lane preceding the entrance.

Tires screeched from down the aisle, and an engine roared. A dark sedan raced toward them.

Chloe and Gina stepped back and flanked the hood of the parked blue sedan.

The speeding black sedan came to a screeching halt and cut off their path to the restaurant entrance.

The back car door flung open, and a tall man dressed all in black and wearing sunglasses, exited the backseat and grabbed Chloe's arm.

"What are you doing? Release her!" Gina ran toward Chloe and grabbed her other arm.

Chloe pulled against the man's firm grip and like a rope in a game of tug-of-war, she see-sawed between Gina and the stranger. A pain shot through her right shoulder. "Let go of me!" Chloe dug her three-inch heels against the asphalt and pulled from Gina's hold. She swung her purse and connected with the man's face.

"Release her!" Gina's shout projected over the combined traffic noise.

Warnings she'd learned over the years raced through Chloe's mind. Never get into the car. Draw the attention of others. She gripped the car door frame with her free hand.

Hallie had climbed into a dark sedan.

She kicked out, and her pointy-toed shoe connected with his shin.

He grunted and arched his back to put distance between his body and hers. His grip on her arm didn't ease.

Gina appeared behind him and swung her large leather purse with enough force to impact the back of his head.

His biting finger-hold on Chloe's arm eased. She kicked out again. This time, the pointed toe of her pump connected with his groin.

He grunted and bent forward.

She released her grip on the doorframe and swung an arm in a self-defense move she'd learned years ago. The edge of her hand connected with the back of his neck.

He lurched against the open car door, his head down.

Chloe grunted and slammed her right knee against his face.

The driver raced the car engine, and the man dropped into the backseat and slammed the door. The sedan squealed away and barely navigated the tight corner at the end of the parking lot. The car disappeared down the boulevard.

Chloe stumbled toward the parked blue sedan and collapsed against it. She pressed a hand against her chest and blinked to clear her vision.

Several diners had gathered at the entrance to Luigi's and gazed toward her, their mouths open.

A kid wearing striped pants and a hoodie held up his phone, videoing the scene.

"I called the police!" a woman yelled. "They're on their way."

Chloe raised a hand and nodded, but her voice wouldn't work. From blocks away, sirens wailed.

In minutes, three police cars entered the parking lot and took over the scene. They split the bystanders into two groups for questioning.

An officer who appeared to outrank the others pulled Chloe aside. "Miss, did you recognize the man? Did you have any previous dealings?"

Chloe's jaw dropped. "Previous dealings? What do you mean?"

Gina wedged between Chloe and the officer. "Detective Paul DeMers has arrived. Chloe will answer his questions."

Paul parked his unmarked car behind a patrol car and strode toward her.

Chloe glanced at Gina with a raised brow.

"Yes, I called him when the thug jumped into the car."

Paul reached them. "Officer Jones, I'll take over from here. Thank you for your quick response."

"This is outrageous." Gina waved toward the spot

where the black sedan had stopped. "That man almost abducted Chloe! This can't be a coincidence."

Paul looked Chloe over from head to foot. "Are you hurt? Should I call an ambulance?"

Her chest tightened, and she struggled to breathe…let alone speak.

Gina gave her a gentle shake and ran her hand over Chloe's back. "Are you hurt?"

Paul gently took hold of Chloe's right arm and escorted her into the restaurant. "You need a glass of wine. I see Diane's waiting at a booth. We'll have to let her into the circle of trust."

Chloe nodded but did well to put one foot in front of the other.

They reached the booth.

Diane took one look at Chloe and gasped. "Oh, my gosh! I heard noise out front, but it didn't occur to me you were involved!" She guided Chloe into the booth.

Paul recounted the situation with the would-be assailant.

Gina filled in the blanks.

"I'll be okay." Chloe finally made her voice work. She rotated her wrist and shoulder. She'd be okay, but she'd have some ugly bruises and would need to use a heating pad tonight.

A server arrived.

Paul ordered himself a cup of coffee and wine for the three women.

The server left.

Paul slid along the vinyl upholstered bench to sit closer to Chloe. "Do you recall anything the man said?"

Diane glanced between them, and her almond-shaped eyes narrowed. "Okay, out with it. There's more to this story. Why would someone want to abduct Chloe?"

Other diners glanced their way.

"Paul, should we discuss this here?" Gina leaned past Chloe. "Shouldn't we take this conversation somewhere private?"

Paul followed Gina's visual sweep of the dining room. "Yes, we should, but the longer we wait to form a plan, the more likely Chloe remains in danger. I'll lower my voice."

Chloe quietly recounted the episode, beginning with the moment she heard the screeching of tires and ending when she and Gina managed to fight off the abductor, and the car raced away. She reached for the rain jacket she'd laid on the bench and fished out a travel packet of tissues. An ivory-colored business card fell on her lap. She picked it up. "Where did this come from?"

"What?" Paul leaned into her side and gazed at the card. "You didn't put it in your pocket?

"No, I've never seen it before." In the dim lighting of the dining room, she couldn't read the black type.

Paul took the card and held the edges carefully between his forefinger and thumb. "Most unusual business card I've seen. No name, no logos, only a phone number. I suspect your would-be abductor shoved it into your pocket." He pulled out his phone and punched in the number.

Chloe watched Paul's expressions while he waited for someone to answer.

His mouth tightened, and he disconnected. "No answer. Just a voice message."

"Did the message mention a name?" Chloe huffed

a breath. "Is it safe for me to leave Luigi's?" She caught an exchange of glances between Paul and Diane.

Diane shook her head.

Not subtle enough because Chloe caught it. She clutched the sleeve of Paul's suit jacket. "Do you think they'll try to grab me again?"

"I don't know, but I don't like this sequence of events." Again, he glanced at Diane. "They'll fill you in after I leave." He zeroed his gaze on Chloe. "Until further notice, no late nights and no solo trips. Park your car in the Walters Design garage or in Gina's garage. Until I trace this number." He held up the business card. "Your life is on hold."

"Hold?" Chloe choked on the word and lifted her wine glass to take a long drink of the red wine. She swallowed hard. "It's already on hold. Remember, my home has been destroyed!"

"What?" Diane squawked the word. "Okay, what else don't I know about?"

Gina patted Diane's hand. "We didn't mean to exclude you, but Paul asked us to keep the information under wraps. Chloe's close call could be tied to Hallie Smith's death. We'll fill you in, soon."

Paul nodded. "After what happened out front, Diane needs to know for her protection. Anyone close to Chloe could be in danger." He directed his gaze to Chloe. "Which makes me revise my original order for you to stay with Gina. The department owns a safe house, and it's available. After lunch, return to Gina's to pack. I'll pick you up by three."

"A safe house?" She waved a hand. "Paul, I'll go stark raving mad!" Chloe's world shifted and spun out of her control. "A hotel close to Walters will be safe."

His mouth tightened. "A hotel isn't secure enough. People come and go at all hours. The safe house is the only way I can offer twenty-four-seven protection." He ran a hand over his mouth. "Work with me, Chloe. The investigations into Hallie's death and your apartment will take time. Like I said last night, the mayor is a close friend of Bruce Billings." He blew a breath, his cheeks inflating. "To add another layer, the mayor and the police chief are dating."

Chloe blinked. "So, politics will dictate which case is pursued first." Her life had been upended—still—she'd do everything possible to keep her friends safe. Even if it meant staying in a generic safe house.

An idea occurred. "What about the Portland Walters Design office? There's an executive apartment. I could move in for a week or so. Long enough for you to arrest the thugs."

Paul's blue gaze became intent. "Is the Portland office listed on the Walters website?"

"Yes," Diane said. "It's been on our main website since it opened two years ago. I just updated the photos of the exterior and introduced a new designer to the office." She cringed. "Anyone researching the Walters site will see it."

Paul shook his head. "In that case, the safe house is your only option."

Chloe glanced at the neighboring diners. They seemed to have lost interest in the woman who'd nearly been abducted in front of Luigi's. She drew a deep breath. "One condition. Please don't let my case, and Hallie's, get stuffed into a cardboard box and placed in an evidence room with the lights turned off."

Paul placed a hand over hers. "I'll do my best to

work around the current situation at the department."

If possible, her chest tightened more. "I won't stop working. Can we three video chat?" She didn't mean to sound shallow, but the life she loved was in jeopardy. "My mom is still receiving cancer treatments. I refuse to worry her and Dad."

Paul folded his hands on the table. "Since they live in San Diego, we should be able to keep your involvement quiet. Look, I'll post a patrol outside Gina's house for a few days." He clicked his tongue. "If I had a copy of the file, the investigation could move faster."

Chloe cleared her throat. "I copied the file."

Paul's eyes went wide. "You what?"

"My career is on the line, and now, so is my life. I'll make you a copy, but you have to promise to keep it away from the corrupt PD."

Paul slowly nodded. "Deal. Where is it?"

"Locked in my office. We can meet there after lunch." Her mind reeled. "The first name on the list is Drew King. The names are listed in the order of the dollar amount they contributed. It won't surprise me if the phone number on the business card belongs to Drew King."

Paul blinked hard. "Guess it makes sense he'd be involved in the Billings campaign." He fiddled with the spoon resting on the saucer next to his coffee cup. "Would King murder Hallie to keep the file out of the public eye?"

Chloe drew a sharp breath. "After the way she died, I believe they'll do anything to protect their corrupt dealings." She tried to keep her voice low, but the position that file placed them all in enraged her.

"I'll look into King and work down the list." Paul shook his head. "He's in San Jose, so out of my jurisdiction, but I have a contact at the San Jose City PD." He rolled his lips in and out and released them with a smack. "A wrong word or a careless probe into any of the donors, and the case could be botched. Please practice caution in everything you do and say."

"So, if you can't solve this within two days, I'm stuck with moving to a safe house." She clutched her head with both hands, her gaze locked with Paul's.

He cracked a smile. "Hey, the safe house has secure Internet with a pile of firewalls. You can work behind the scenes. After the initial home consultation, how often do you meet with your clients?"

"Not often." She shook her head. "The follow-up meetings are usually electronic and over the phone. Until the final stages of the work. If Juanita agrees to keep Bruce away from the project, then can I perform the final inspection on their mountain house?"

"No. A hired thug could pose as a construction worker. Someone else will need to do the in-person appointments." He pressed a hand against the table and slid from the booth. "I'm going back to work. Call me when you reach the office."

"Wait!" Diane yelled, then grimaced. "Sorry, I just thought of something that might work for Chloe."

Chloe moaned. "Please tell me it's not another safe house."

Chapter Three

Four months later, Coeur d'Alene, Idaho

Chloe hesitated and glanced left, then right, before she opened the ground-level entry door to the historic early-century building. The quiet, just off downtown neighborhood remained safe. She lifted her gaze and took a moment to enjoy the sight of the freshly mounted sign over the carved wooden door.

Jacque Taylor Designs.

Paul had created the alias before she left Sacramento in January. It looked foreign over the design studio entrance, but when she'd opened the doors in February, she couldn't use Chloe Austin Designs. She still couldn't—even after four months of living in a strange town, in a different state, over eight hundred miles from home.

After the near-abduction, Diane had suggested this town. Friends had moved here a year ago and raved about the beauty and, most important, the low crime rate. Coeur d'Alene had been the refuge Chloe hoped for and offered a bustling resort town set on the northwest shore of Lake Coeur d'Alene. Within an hour's drive were two ski resorts and countless summer sports.

Chloe had no desire to play in the snow, and she didn't plan to stay through the summer, but a newcomer could blend with the flow of tourists without question.

She spent two weeks in the beautiful resort hotel before she went stir-crazy. With no progress on the case at home, one day in late January, she struck out to find a place to live. She yearned to nest, design, and settle in, until Paul okayed her return to Sacramento. She found the solution to her restlessness in this two-story, Spanish Revival-style building, with an apartment on the second floor, and a commercial space on the street-facing ground floor.

She turned the key in the old-fashioned lock and entered the studio. A quick jiggle of the knob confirmed the door had locked behind her. Another precaution she'd practiced since January. Life could be worse—right? She could be counting the minutes, and days, from a hotel room or worse yet, a safe house. In the meantime, Sacramento politics continued as usual.

She breathed in the blended scents of her happy place. The spicy essential oil from the diffuser, the new fabric smell from the drapery samples she'd hung from a rod along the wall. The faint tinge of coffee, from early this morning before she walked to Tracie Woodward's midcentury-modern investment home.

"Woof!"

"I'm coming, Scotty!" She set her leather tote on the desk and raced up the interior stairs to open the apartment door. "How are you?" She knelt to pet the black Scottish Terrier, the first pet she'd ever owned. As a child, she'd longed to have a dog, but her mother could barely afford to feed them without adding dog food to the list. Funny, how being forced from her hometown, and her friends, had reawakened her old dream.

Maybe because she'd grown tired of talking to herself. With the no-kill animal shelter only a few miles away, she'd stopped by and found Scotty. He'd instantly stolen her heart. "Come on, boy. I'll let you outside while I make a smoothie. Tracie will be here in about thirty minutes, and as you know, she's allergic to pet dander."

Scotty beat her to the exterior apartment door that opened onto a square, metal-grated landing. He raced down the metal stairs and into the enclosed yard to do his business. Mostly, he sniffed the perimeter of the fence.

The studio and Scotty had helped her build this temporary life. She gripped the door handle, gazed over the yard below, and toward the single-car garage. A black wrought iron fence followed the boundaries of the lot and created an attractive barrier between her yard and the quiet street separating her place from the Clarks—her closest neighbors.

Yes, things could be far worse. She had a lovely home and an adorable pet. She lived in a beautiful and quiet neighborhood with mature gardens and towering, deciduous trees.

The Grind, a downtown coffee shop, was only a fifteen-minute walk away. There she'd met her first design client. Tracie Woodward had been poring over design magazines, her brows drawn and her mouth tight. Chloe had casually commented on the popular designs and Tracie had insisted she join her for coffee. Out of that meeting came a working relationship—and Chloe had to acknowledge—a friendship.

When she shared her excitement over the studio with Paul and Gina, they'd freaked out. She'd assured them she'd keep a low profile. No social media and only word-of-mouth advertising. She'd use local vendors. They'd calmed down but warned her the visibility could be dangerous.

Scotty yipped and tore around the yard.

Chloe ambled halfway down the stairs, one hand on the cool metal rail. "I'll be right back, buddy. Hey, Rachel should be here soon. She finished the cottages."

Rachel had become another big surprise in Chloe's move to Idaho. They'd met shortly after Chloe opened a vendor account at Lake City Furniture. Working with head designer, Ted Finney, Chloe noticed how he kept his assistant, Rachel Banks, in the background. Rachel's talent far outshone Ted's.

A week later, Rachel visited the studio and proposed a way for Chloe to hire her.

Ted Finney wasn't happy about Rachel's defection.

Chloe didn't care. She liked Rachel, and she wanted to help her spread her wings.

Chloe turned to climb the stairs. Life in Coeur d'Alene had turned out well, with her only concern being to continue to avoid a meeting with Diane's friends, Mike and Melissa Parker.

They'd relocated to Coeur d'Alene to live closer to Melissa's mother and were how Diane knew about the area. Mike's career as contributing journalist to the *Sacramento Times,* concerned her. He also worked as editorial assistant to the *Coeur d'Alene Press*. If he learned the truth, he could expose her.

While Paul knew and liked the Parkers, he'd forbidden Chloe to meet them. Sharp and ambitious, Mike might see Chloe as a ticket to an award-winning *exposé*.

She'd already had a close call. In early April, during a meeting with Tracie at The Grind, she noticed as the Parkers entered the coffee shop and sat at a table near the entrance. Chloe immediately recognized them from a social media post. She became so distracted by their appearance, she'd barely heard Tracie's suggestions about the current project. The Parkers seemed oblivious to her presence and set up their laptops and ordered coffee. She'd made some excuse to Tracie about why she wanted to change tables and positioned her back toward the Parkers. When her meeting ended, she left through a side door.

Ugh, enough reminiscing. Time to make her smoothie or she'd go hungry. Two steps from the square metal landing, she froze. A huge floral arrangement sat in the far corner. Far enough from the swing of the door, she'd missed it in her rush to keep up with Scotty. Now, the pungent fragrance of the large pink lilies and long-stemmed pink roses hit her senses. Sprigs of baby's breath and ornamental ferns filled any gaps between the larger flowers. The arrangement was beautiful, but big and overdone. Not something she'd order, nor would anyone who knew her send such a ginormous, pink arrangement.

She gripped the handrail and pivoted toward the Clarks' house across the street. They'd begun a remodel of their nineteen seventies rancher, and a small green garbage receptacle sat in their driveway. Had they noticed the delivery van?

She climbed two steps and crouched next to the arrangement. A clear plastic cardholder protruded from between the flowers. She took a deep breath and grabbed the small envelope. The cardstock inside held a message that chilled her.

It's time to talk.

Nothing more. No greeting—no signature. She grabbed at the metal railing, closed her eyes, and forced her lungs to work. Someone had sent a clear message. She'd been discovered.

Scotty yipped from the bottom of the stairs.

She opened her eyes and scanned the street. They might be watching her right now. Somehow, they'd found her studio and knew she lived upstairs. She stuffed the note into her sweater pocket. "Come on, Scotty. Time to go inside."

He darted away and began another circuit of the yard.

"Scotty, come here." Her voice broke, and panic surged through her chest.

Scotty ran up the stairs and sniffed at the floral arrangement.

"Can you believe this, boy? Who would have sent them?" She glanced over the yard and the street, then opened the door and shooed Scotty inside. Breathing became difficult. Rachel would return from her brother's ranch, and she'd notice something was wrong. Chloe couldn't allow her to see the flowers. She needed to dispose of them soon, which meant going outside before Rachel returned.

She double-checked the vintage filigree lock. Charming but not completely secure. How had she missed that? She'd call a locksmith and have a modern system installed. She'd save the old ones from the apartment entrance and the street entrance to the studio, just in case her landlord wanted them.

Through the square paned window in the door, she

caught a glimpse of the flowers. A harbinger of what might come.

She hurried to freshen Scotty's water and added kibble to his dish, then started to prepare a smoothie. Her hands were unsteady, and she slopped the coconut milk onto the laminate counter. Next, she accidentally scattered dried lavender blossoms on the floor. "Great! Get your act together." To the mix, she added a tablespoon of peanut butter and half of a frozen banana. She turned on the blender, and the racket added to the cacophony of thoughts running through her head.

The message on the flowers might mark the end of her time in Coeur d'Alene. Paul would arrange another location. Not back to Sacramento but to a town without this marvelous building, the studio, and her new friends.

She crouched to pat Scotty's back. "Wherever I go, Boy, you're going with me."

The feel of his soft fur against her fingers calmed her heart. "Okay, think logically. I'll take a photo of the flowers and the note and text them to Paul." Yeah, and her newly constructed world would come crashing down, like the frozen banana, struggling against the merciless strokes of the blender blades.

She blew a breath and stood. Why, after four months, would Bruce or Drew King contact her? Why send the flowers with the cryptic note? If they'd found her, why hadn't they grabbed her? Like the thug had tried to accomplish in front of Luigi's. She turned off the blender and pulled the floral card from her sweater pocket to re-read the message. Her heart lodged in her throat. In an instant, everything had changed, but nothing had changed. Hallie's murderer lived in freedom. No arrests had been made in connection with Chloe's apartment break-in.

She glanced at the clock on the dining room wall. Ten minutes until Tracie arrived. If only she could confide in Tracie, she wouldn't have to face this alone. Or Rachel.

Even Rachel's brother, Levi Banks. From the set of his broad shoulders to his steady amber gaze, the man exuded strength and security. A quintessential cowboy turned rancher, he'd spent his former career conquering bulls and broncs. Now, he owned a large ranch located an hour from Coeur d'Alene—too far from town to help.

She poured the smoothie into her favorite purple glass, stuck in a lavender straw, and took a sip. She barely knew Levi, and he might feel obligated to inform the police. According to Paul, he hadn't notified the local police of her presence or situation, out of concern they'd notify his chief.

She took another sip, and the cold, creamy blend of flavors slid over her tongue and cooled the burn of anxiety in her stomach.

Levi was very caring. Soon after the studio open house in March, he'd begun to stop by every Friday late afternoon to visit Rachel. Chloe stayed in the background and allowed Rachel the fun of sharing her accomplishments with her brother.

Not to say, Chloe hadn't noticed how fine Levi looked in his black, Western-cut pants and how his freshly ironed white shirt framed his broad shoulders. Chloe tucked the card back in her pocket, pressed her hand to her stomach, and took another draw on the lavender straw. After Tracie's consultation, she'd call

Everblooming Floral, the name on the tiny card.

Now, to change out of the dusty jeans and T-shirt she'd worn to inspect Tracie's new job site. She exchanged the work clothes for an olive-green, knit skirt, a black, short-sleeved top, and the tennis shoes for cream-colored, three-inch heel pumps. As a designer, she'd adopted a style and just because she lived in a smaller town, she wouldn't compromise her image.

At the interior door leading downstairs to the studio, she turned toward Scotty. "After Tracie leaves, I'll open the door, and you can have the run of the building."

Reaching the beverage cabinet separating the seating area from the desks, she turned on the electric water pot. In case Tracie preferred coffee, she touched the power button on the single-cup coffee brewer.

Pillows fluffed on the loveseat, she centered the pair of armless chairs and stood back to assess the furniture situated against the exposed brick wall. Client consultations were held away from the desks and computers.

She tented her fingers in front of her mouth and smiled. Despite it not being in Sacramento, she loved her studio.

She hurried to her desk, close to the interior stairs to the apartment, and straightened the paperwork. Rachel's desk sat eight feet from the consultation area. Everything just as it'd been before she found the flowers—yet nothing seemed the same.

The water in the kettle boiled and clicked off. She filled a stainless-steel ball with leaves and hooked it on the mouth of the china teapot to steep. The fragrance of Bergamot filled the space and soothed the insidious fear in her gut. She had to solve this mystery soon. Before the sender of the flowers sent a more dire warning.

With only five minutes before Tracie arrived, Chloe sank to her desk chair and removed the emerald-green file folder from her bottom left drawer. For months, she'd resisted the shadow file, but soon, she'd dive deep into the list of names. On top of the spreadsheet sat the printout of the Sunday *Sacramento Times* online article reminding the people Hallie's death had not been solved. The author of the piece accused law enforcement of dancing to the tune of the local politicians and big-money interests, instead of bringing Hallie's killer to justice. She added the floral note to the file and slipped it back into the drawer. Later after Tracie left and she'd completed the calls to the florist, the locksmith, and Paul, she'd read the entire file.

She slammed the drawer shut. Bruce had swept the March primary election and his numbers led for the general election in November. Why threaten her now? Unless he'd noticed the *Times* article and panicked.

Or maybe, Drew King had ordered the flowers. If Hallie's murder investigation became a focus of the police department—which it should—King could have a lot to lose.

She returned to the narrow beverage cabinet and filled a teacup. For a moment, she forced her mind to calm and ran a thumb over the curved handle on the china teapot. One of several new-to-her pieces since she signed the lease on the building and started a new collection.

The studio door rattled.

Chloe jumped and spilled the tea over her hand.

From upstairs, Scotty barked, and his nails tapped

across the dark hardwood floor.

"Jacque, are you in there?"

She pressed a palm to her chest and breathed deeply. "Coming!" She hurried toward the door and opened it for Tracie. "I'm so sorry! I forgot to unlock it after I returned from the job site."

Tracie Woodward swept inside, the real estate investor a force to be reckoned with—a force for good.

"Jacque, you've only lived here for a few months so you're still adjusting, but you don't have to lock your door every time you go upstairs or take Scotty outside. This isn't the big city. Besides, this neighborhood is in the safest part of town."

Tracie moved directly toward the cozy seating area. "Ah, Earl Grey. You're amazing. I don't know how you accomplish so much and never forget the details. Mind if I pour a cup? I spent most of the morning haggling with Ted Finney, over the outrageous prices on the furniture we're buying for the downtown house."

"Please, help yourself." Chloe grabbed her laptop and Tracie's file off her desk. She juggled her cup and joined Tracie in the area.

Tracie chose one of the bright-teal armless chairs and sipped her hot tea.

Chloe knew her well enough to see under the calm exterior. Tracie's mind raced with her next brilliant idea. They made a fabulous team, which made not sharing her entire story even more difficult. Instead, she sipped tea and restored her composure. "Old habits die hard, and I'm used to locking my doors." She set the cup and saucer on the table.

Tracie chuckled. "Point taken. Now, what are your

impressions of our new project so far?" She crossed her legs, and the khaki fabric of her slacks stretched over her long, lean legs. Her cream, short-sleeved pullover showed off her trim waist.

The confident and vibrant woman stayed for another hour, and her presence almost made Chloe forget about the large floral arrangement on the landing. *Ugh*—and the ominous note. She escaped into the details of the demo crew at the project and how she'd like to salvage the midcentury modern built-ins to repurpose for the butler's pantry.

Tracie liked Chloe's ideas and promised to go directly to the job site and revise her instructions to the contractor. An hour later, Tracie hugged Chloe and walked to the door. Her hand on the antique knob, she paused. "I almost forgot. A colleague of my husband's is moving to Coeur d'Alene next month. His wife's eager to meet with you about a home they plan to buy."

"Wonderful." Chloe smiled. "Where are they from?"

"The Bay Area, but specifically, San Jose. You'll like them." Tracie fluttered her fingers at Chloe. "Ta-ta!"

Chloe closed and locked the door. "Of course, they're from The Bay Area."

Chapter Four

Before Chloe returned to her desk, she grabbed the leftover lavender peanut butter smoothie from the fridge and tapped in the number for Everblooming Floral. Rachel could return from the ranch anytime, and Chloe wasn't ready for her protégée to hear this conversation.

The proprietor, Edna Bloom, answered. "Oh, dear, I'm so sorry the arrangement didn't bring you pleasure. I knew something was off when he added such an ominous message."

"Edna, I have no idea who ordered the flowers. Can you share the name on the credit card?"

"No idea? Oh my! Well, the credit card reads, Bay City Investigations."

Chloe gripped the edge of her desk. Bay City. A name for the cities encompassing the San Francisco Bay. Drew King, and many other tech moguls, had offices in San Jose. Even Tracie's new referral came from the area. She glanced at the closed desk drawer where she'd stashed the folder. "Edna, I'm so grateful for the information. Rest assured—I won't tell anyone you shared it."

She disconnected the call and lifted the file from the drawer to reread the *Sacramento Times* article. The floral card was another clue. The lavender smoothie churned in her stomach. She'd been discovered. Her head went light, and her vision blurred. She blinked and focused on the list of names. "Okay, start at the top with Drew King." She coached herself out loud.

She and Gina had read the software mogul's name, but they'd stopped there. Now, the names of several contributors leaped off the page. Lawyers, business owners, and even the owners of the Northern and Central California newspapers. She set the top page aside and scanned the second one. More professionals from the tech world were listed. Halfway down page three, she blinked and shivered. This had to be a coincidence.

"William Mathers, Mathers Engineering." It couldn't be. Her biological father's name was William Mathers. Her stomach churned. He'd left on her eleventh birthday. Software engineering? She hummed a sigh. Well, he had attended night school to earn his degree in engineering. Huh—guess he finished his education and went on to own a company.

"Wow." She huffed a breath. Her mom had worked two jobs to maintain a humble roof over their heads and put food on the table. She set the file aside and opened the browser on her laptop. "William Mathers." She typed the name into the search bar. She'd made it to thirty-four years old without searching for her father. Zach Austin had become her real dad—the man who loved her mother and happily took on a teenage daughter. On Chloe's sixteenth birthday, Zach handed her the signed adoption papers formalizing their relationship. Had William Mathers given Zach his permission? Wasn't protocol in an adoption to notify the biological parent? She'd never asked.

Her search connected with a business website, and

an older version of her father appeared on the screen. The image sent a flurry of emotions through her gut. From early childhood memories, she recalled his vivid green eyes. Eye color like her own. His features were strong, and his dark, curling hair trimmed into a professional, yet trendy, style.

Memories of her eleventh birthday party emerged. She'd invited four school friends to her suburban home. Her mom had provided hotdogs, pizza, and root beer floats. After lunch, they'd played games and cheered over the three-tiered chocolate cake with pink frosting roses. Like it happened yesterday, Chloe remembered the flavor and texture of the pink frosting roses, how she'd dipped her finger into the center of the largest rose, and stuck it in her mouth. Her friends had giggled, and her mom had smiled and shook her head.

Right after Mom cut the cake, her dad left and didn't return until long after the party ended.

She had to give him credit for waiting until her friends left before he made his big announcement. He'd send for the rest of his belongings.

Her mother had begged him to stay—to try to talk it out.

Her mother remained elusive about what had ended their twelve-year marriage and why he didn't visit or call.

After moving from the comfortable middle-class home to a series of low-income apartments, Chloe began to realize her father didn't send money. Their total support relied on her mom's jobs—usually two—which meant long hours away from Chloe.

The website description of his company proved her father had gone far with his engineering degree. Chloe hissed a breath of frustration. She'd almost managed to bury the bad memories from those days. As a grown woman, she experienced a pang of regret on her mother's behalf. Samantha Mathers had worked hard to maintain a stable life for Chloe.

She sniffed and swiped at her damp eyes. Time to get it together and dispose of the flowers before Rachel returned. She stashed the file in the drawer and locked it. Did Will Mathers personally know Bruce Billings or Drew King? He'd contributed to Bruce's campaign—Drew King was a competitor in the software engineering business.

A bone-chilling thought crept into her mind. Had Bruce alerted Will Mathers about the missing file? Her thoughts splintered and her head swam. She hurried up the stairs and opened the door connecting the apartment.

Scotty wagged his tail and followed her to the outside door. Her hand on the knob, she paused. She had to find out what Will Mathers knew.

She hurried downstairs and slid into her desk chair. First, she'd create a new email account using her childhood nickname, Loy Mathers. Feeling like a genealogy enthusiast who'd found a DNA match, she typed a quick missive.

—*It's been forever, but I'm curious to know if you ever think about me. Are you willing to communicate?*—

If not for Zach Austin, no telling what would have happened to Chloe and her mom. Her mom met Zach during one of her evening shifts at a local restaurant. Zach had been in town for a conference of union plumbers. He and Mom had fallen in love, hard and fast.

Within two months, Chloe stood next to her mom in a small wedding chapel, and their futures were rewritten. Afterward, Zach helped them move to his beautiful home in Mission Hills, a suburb of San Diego.

She reread the email that might change her life. Strange. No, *Dear Dad*. No greeting at all. She settled deeper into the leather upholstered office chair and stared at the email before she clicked on Send. The swishing sound of the email leaving her inbox made the action irreversible.

She exited Will Mathers' website and opened the *Times* to check for any follow-ups to the Sunday article. The front page of the digital version held a photo of Marla Yates, the anchor of a local Sacramento television station. Dressed in her usual pencil skirt and fitted jacket, Marla stood in front of the Billings Law Firm. Chloe's goose bumps tripled. She clicked on the video link.

Marla came to life. "I have on a good source, Bruce Billings, one of Sacramento's leading attorneys and nominee for the upcoming U.S. Senate race, should soon exit this building. If I'm successful, then you, the viewers, will learn firsthand what he knows about the ongoing investigation into the unsolved and tragic death of Hallie Smith, a paralegal employed at Billings Law Firm."

Bruce exited the building and stopped short. Seeing the reporter hurry toward him, he froze. In a split second, he recovered and flashed a bleached-white smile.

Chloe snorted. The consummate politician.

"Marla, are you waiting to pounce?" He bobbled

his head, and the bright smile widened.

"Mr. Billings, it's been four months since your lovely assistant, Hallie Smith's life tragically ended when a motorist struck her. The initial reports were vague, but by now, more information must be available. Don't you want this situation put to rest before the general election?"

"Marla, while Ms. Smith worked as a Paralegal with the Billings Law Firm, I know nothing about her personal life or why someone would want to hurt her." He faced the camera. "The police department needs to find whoever drove Hallie to the spot where she died. They've ruled her death hit-and-run." His brows lifted. "She obviously caught a ride with the wrong person. Now, if you'll excuse me." He touched Marla's shoulder and passed through the crowd.

The camera angled to follow him to a black town car waiting at curbside.

"What?" Chloe shrieked the word. "Is he referring to me?" She crossed her arms and rubbed her shoulders to erase the chill. Bruce knew darned well she'd given Hallie a ride to town. She propped her elbows on the edge of the desk and read the date below the video. Monday. Two days ago. After the *Times* article. Were the flowers and the note his way of dropping breadcrumbs?

She exited the newspaper website. Mike Parker had written the article. Why would he be interested in Hallie's case? Besides human decency and his familiarity with Sacramento, why would a journalist who'd moved over eight hundred miles away try to shake things up?

She ran her hands over her hair, unconcerned when

her fingers tugged and loosened several strands from the tortoiseshell clip. Diane had assured Chloe and Gina, she hadn't shared anything confidential with the Parkers. Still…they could have learned another way and know what happened on that day in January.

She drew a breath. She'd rather spackle an old wall, than to figure out the motivations of powerful, and greedy businessmen—but she had no choice. What had led Bruce and King to Coeur d'Alene? The article hadn't mentioned her connection to Hallie Smith, but if Mike discovered she was Chloe Austin, and somehow determined she'd visited the Billingses' home that day… She clamped her teeth on her bottom lip. She'd recognized the Parkers at The Grind, so why not assume they'd recognized her from the Walters website?

She glanced toward the front entrance. The locks. "Stay focused," she murmured. "Call the landlord, then a locksmith."

The landlord consented to her idea and only asked her to save the old locks-sets and knobs. He'd collect them later. Next, she arranged for the locksmith to change the locks.

Now, to explain her sudden decision to change locks to Rachel.

But first, the flowers.

Back in her apartment, she opened the door to step onto the metal-grated landing.

Scotty trotted downstairs to his yard.

Chloe assessed the humongous floral arrangement. Her garbage can wasn't nearly large enough to hold the arrangement and her usual garbage. Besides, Rachel might carry out her trash and find it.

The green receptacle in the Clarks' driveway caught her eye. Even better. But what if Jim or Pam Clark saw her tossing the flowers into their container? She propped her hands at the waistband of her olive-green skirt. She could always use the ex in San Diego story. She cringed at the idea of perpetuating the lie she'd told Rachel about her sudden move to Coeur d'Alene. She picked up the large vase and descended the stairs. Juggling the gate latch, she assured Scotty she'd be right back and crossed the street. Thankfully, no one drove by, and the Clarks appeared to be gone. She lifted the lid and launched the entire thing into the half-empty container and onto a stack of sheetrock scraps.

From across the street in his fenced yard, Scotty yipped and raced from the garage wall to the exterior stairs and back.

Chloe hurried to her side of the street and entered through the wrought iron gate. She called Scotty while she brushed the white sheetrock dust from her skirt and blouse. Back inside of her apartment, she locked the door.

"Hello?" Rachel's voice carried up the interior stairs.

Chloe's heart skipped a beat, and she grabbed at the back of a dining chair. Had Rachel seen her scurrying across the street and back? Surely, she'd have seen Rachel's small station wagon. "I'll be right down!" She hesitated at the top of the stairs to collect her wonky emotions. A breath and she descended to the studio.

Rachel was already at her desk. "I loved working on the cottages and spending time at the ranch, but it's good to be back." She sent Chloe a raised-brow glance. "I'd planned to finish the cottages and return to town last night, but yesterday, when Lake City delivered the furniture, they didn't remove the heavy plastic and industrial-strength staples! I enlisted Riley and Levi to help. Can you believe wire cutters were needed to remove the bands and staples?"

Chloe shook her head. Thank goodness, Rachel hadn't noticed her unease.

Rachel continued to describe how the furniture fit. "The cottages are ready for guests."

Chloe cringed. "I'm afraid Ted Finney still hasn't forgiven me for your departure from Lake City Furniture." Never mind he'd chased Rachel away with his refusal to let her become a designer in her own right. Chloe went to her desk. "Glad you're back. When do you expect the first vacationers?" She opened Tracie's new file.

"This weekend. Can you believe it? I uploaded the advert into a popular site, and two parties have booked. I wish you'd visit the ranch and tour the cottages."

A subject they'd discussed several times, but Chloe wasn't ready to drive an hour into the countryside. "Before I forget to mention it, I ordered new lock systems for the entry doors. The locksmith will install them at about three this afternoon."

Rachel's dark eyes widened. "Really? Did we have an unwanted entry while I was gone?"

"No, I just suddenly realized the current knobs are very old, and it's possible previous tenants still have keys. I should have done it before I moved in."

"I get it." Rachel slowly nodded. I'll dig out my key before I forget."

"I've ordered the keyless entry systems, so no more keys to worry about, but I'll save them with the hardware for the landlord." She pushed a breath through pursed lips. Leave it to Rachel to accept her decision without question. "One of these days, I'll venture to the ranch to see the cottages and the dining hall you've told me so much about."

"It's a beautiful drive, and I could ride with you. Besides, over the past day and a half, Levi asked about you several times." Rachel's smile turned mischievous. "He mentioned he couldn't find you online." She toyed with the gold hoop in her right earlobe. "Don't ask me why he did an online search, but he's puzzled over your lack of a website and social media. I couldn't give him a good reason—I've wondered the same thing. Someone with your talent should be listed everywhere." She shook her head, and her long, dark hair brushed her shoulders. "It's almost as if you lived under a rock before you came to Coeur d'Alene."

Chloe swallowed hard. "Remember I explained I don't want my ex to find me. I closed everything."

"Huh." Rachel pulled her lower lip between her teeth. "Still…I don't know how you could have closed the online history. It usually follows the owner, even if your name is simply listed on a design ad." She pulled an open file close to her laptop. "Maybe, it's time to face the guy. Stop giving him the power to control your life. He lives almost fifteen hundred miles away. You could file for a restraining order."

"Maybe. We'll see." Chloe's stomach roiled with regret. The lies wouldn't stop until Paul cleared her to tell the truth.

Rachel turned her attention to the file. "Hey, on the

drive back, I got a call from a prospective new client, Janelle Meeker. A previous client referred her. She and her husband, Cain, live on Riverview Drive."

"Great news! Where's Riverview Drive?" Chloe hadn't ventured past the city limits since she'd fled to Coeur d'Alene.

"Off Highway 95 South. I've never been on that road, but it winds up a mountain to a development where several multi-million-dollar lake-view homes were built a few years ago."

"Uh-huh." Chloe typed the dimensions for Tracie's midcentury modern into her design software. She'd promised Tracie a basic presentation by tomorrow. "How does Levi feel about the vacation renters, now that both cottages are booked for this weekend?"

"He's still not thrilled about strangers staying on the ranch, but he'll adjust. Good heavens, a new group of his rodeo students arrive every three weeks, and he doesn't know them." Rachel's phone rang. She answered, listened for a moment, then her expression went from happy to indecisive to contemplative. "Yes, I'll see you, then." She disconnected and leaned into her desk chair. "That was Janelle Meeker. They're only available for the home consult at two on Friday. I've already scheduled the brake repair for my car. It's at noon on Friday. I'll never make it to the Meekers' house by two."

"I didn't realize your car had brake issues." Chloe adjusted the dimensions of the design and added an island in the kitchen.

"Yes, and the check oil light came on. The mechanic needs to keep my car over the weekend, so I'll call a ride-share."

Chloe glanced at her protégée. "Hey, no worry. You can borrow my car."

"Drive your car? Your baby?" Rachel's dark eyes went wide. "Are you sure?"

"It's a car, Rachel. Like any other." She smiled. "You're welcome to use it. Friday afternoon, I'm working with Tracie on her new project, and it's only three blocks away." She brushed her hands together. If only everything could be solved so easily!

Chapter Five

Levi ran a chambray fabric shirtsleeve over his sweat-damp forehead and leaned against the split rail corral to study another bull rider. The final afternoon of this rodeo school session had arrived.

His new bull twisted, bucked, and snorted, trying its best to unseat the rider. The buzzer sounded, and the student jumped from the bull's broad back. Already in a cloud of dust, his boots hit the ground and sent up more.

Tomorrow, they'd review team roping techniques and mark the end of this three-week session. Sunday evening, about fifty area residents would arrive for the mini rodeo he'd started hosting two years ago—the chance for the students to show off their new skills.

Another rank bull and another cowboy. A combination of twist and arch and the cowboy hit the ground hard. The buzzer sounded. No points.

Levi had never become immune to seeing a rider hit the ground with bone-jarring force. He'd been there—many times. All while a snorting bull danced around him. He raised a hand at Riley.

Riley lifted his chin in response.

They'd talked about Levi leaving earlier than usual for his weekly trip to town. His day to conduct business at the bank and the local feed store. He'd begun to incorporate a stop at the design studio to check on

Rachel. He knocked his hat against his thigh, and dust rose, testifying to the amount of corral dust filling the air during practices. He tried to brush the dust off his wash-worn jeans but made little impact. Time to hit the shower and change into town clothes.

If she wasn't up to her elbows in a design, then he'd invite Rachel to join him for dinner at the resort. He could already taste Chef Dakyn's mouth-watering rib eye steak. He chuckled. Yeah, it'd be fun to share the evening with his little sister, although, he should stop thinking of Rachel as his *little* sister. She might be twelve years his junior, but she was an adult and a very accomplished young woman. By age twenty-two, she'd graduated with honors from the University of Montana in Missoula, and she'd achieved a certificate in Interior Design. Last March, just two months ago, she'd advanced from assistant designer at Lake City Furniture to a full designer position at Jacque Taylor Designs.

He clicked his tongue. She'd also worked hard to finish the guest cabins in time for their first vacation guests this weekend. His stomach rumbled. He'd missed lunch, and breakfast was eight hours ago. He'd swing through the kitchen and grab a coffee and one of Janice's famous cinnamon rolls to hold him over. He'd reached the outside kitchen entrance when the door swung open. Levi stepped back.

Janice stood in the open doorway, her blue eyes wide and filled with tears. She held Levi's cell phone.

"Janice, what's happened?"

"Levi!" Her voice quavered. "Rachel's been in a car accident!"

His insides seized. The ground seemed to buck beneath his boots. He grabbed at the cedar plank siding.

"What?" He'd heard the words, but his mind refused to consider them.

Janice grasped his right hand and folded his fingers over the phone. "The hospital couldn't reach you, so they called the house phone. I've set up the call. Just push the button. The emergency room nurse assured me—Rachel's injuries aren't life-threatening."

Memories of a snowy winter night and the call from the Idaho State Police flooded him. He blinked to clear the brain fog and touched the green button. Hearing the ER desk nurse confirm Rachel's life wasn't in danger, his legs went weak. The break in her left arm did require surgery. His doctor, Greg Princeton, was the on-duty doc. Trapped air rushed from his lungs. He swallowed hard. "Janice, I'll call when I have an update." He turned to leave. "Uh, Riley needs to know."

"I'll tell Riley." Janice pushed him in the direction of the machine shed. "Go see Rachel, and for heaven's sake, drive carefully!"

"I will." He half ran and half strode across the graveled area between the house and the outbuildings. The drive to Coeur d'Alene usually took an hour. Somehow, he needed to get there sooner. See Rachel in person. Calm his mind. He gunned the three-quarter-ton pickup and, within minutes, turned onto the highway. "Ah, Rachel. Hang in there."

Rachel lived in Coeur d'Alene because of him. Two years ago, she'd declined a lucrative job offer in Missoula and relocated to help him dig out of the twelve-month-long depression after Lucy's death. He'd tried to talk her out of passing up the job, but Rachel was a stubborn Banks and wouldn't change her mind.

He tightened his grip on the steering wheel. Thanks to Jacque, Rachel had opportunities she wouldn't have had at Lake City Furniture. Jacque had even smoothed things over with Rachel's former boss, Ted Finney, who hadn't made Rachel's departure easy. Jacque talked him into opening a vendor account for her studio.

Levi blew a breath and struggled to keep his mind on driving safely and not racing to town. Jacque's image floated through his mind. His opposite in many ways, the thirty-something classy designer had broken through the wall around his heart and stirred something he hadn't experienced since losing Lucy.

He lifted a hand from the steering wheel and forked his fingers through his dusty, sweaty hair. The call from the hospital illustrated how fast life could change. How plans fell by the wayside.

He should call his parents, but he'd wait until he confirmed Rachel's condition. They'd have a four-hour drive from their ranch just outside Missoula.

Up ahead, three Whitetail deer meandered across the highway. He slowed to let them safely reach the other side before he gunned the engine and pushed the speed limit. Five minutes after he reached the city limits and navigated the Friday afternoon traffic, he reached Kootenai Health. He took another five minutes looking for a parking space large enough for his pickup. By the time he reached the wide electric doors, his blood pressure had to be over the top.

No bull rider was immune to an emergency room, but the sharp tang of antiseptic cleaners hit his senses like a wall. He strode across the tiled lobby toward the staffed reception desk.

The professionally dressed woman sitting behind

the desk glanced up and smiled. "May I help you?"

"My sister. Rachel Banks. She was in a car accident." The words left his mouth like they were edged with glass.

Her smile softened, and her brow creased. "I'm so sorry. Please have a seat. May I see your ID? I'm sorry to keep you waiting, but I'll need a few pieces of information before I call the doctor."

Levi wanted to demand to see his sister. Immediately. The gold name tag pinned to the woman's navy-blue jacket read, *Judy*, and Judy was just doing her job. But every tap of her red-polished nails against the keyboard frayed Levi's nerves like an old rope.

She handed back his driver's license. "Thank you, Mr. Banks. Dr. Greg Princeton is overseeing your sister's care. I've messaged his coordinator. He should be here very soon."

He nodded his thanks. Whenever a cowboy hit the dust at the wrong angle, Princeton was his go-to. He left the reception desk and moved toward a small group of brightly colored, molded plastic chairs. But he couldn't sit. He paced from one end of the room to the other. With every slide of the electric doors, and every announcement over the PA system, his nerves threatened to snap.

"Levi?"

Startled, Levi turned toward the feminine voice. "Jacque?" Rachel's beautiful employer placed her manicured hand on his sleeve.

"Oh, Levi, please tell me Rachel will be okay!"

He half nodded and half shook his head. "That's what they say. She's in surgery to repair a couple of breaks in her left arm. I'm waiting to see Doc

Princeton."

The sparkle in Jacque's jewel-green eyes dimmed, and after a long second, she closed them.

He studied her gold-flecked eye shadow and long, dark, lashes. Her appearance surprised and pleased him.

She opened her eyes. "So, we wait." Her chest rose and fell with a sigh. Tears balanced on her lower lids.

A strong instinct to hold her fired deep within his being. Levi placed a hand over hers, where it rested on the dusty sleeve of his blue chambray shirt. The perfectly shaped, coral-polished nails were in complete contrast to the faded fabric of his work shirt and his much-larger hand. "She'll get through this, Jacque. Rachel's strong and determined."

Everything about Jacque's cream silk perfection, contrasted with his rough-and-tough ranch life and persona. The filmy sleeve of her blouse had slipped back to show the sparkly diamond bracelet on her slender wrist.

He removed his hand from hers and stepped back, then ran it through his hat-creased hair. "Did you say the police called you? Are you listed as an emergency contact?"

She pressed her fingertips to her eyelids. "No, not as an emergency contact." Her voice broke. "Rachel was driving my car."

He couldn't quite grasp the situation. "What? Why would she drive your car?"

She folded her arms over her slender middle and angled to glance behind him. "Is that the doctor?"

Levi pivoted on a worn boot heel to follow Jacque's line of sight.

Dr. Greg Princeton stood at the reception desk an

open file in his hands.

Levi clasped Jacque's arm and moved toward Doc.

Princeton glanced up. "Levi, glad you're here." The tall doctor clamped his hand on Levi's shoulder. "How are you holding up?"

"How's Rachel? The receptionist said she's in surgery." The need for answers precluded polite conversation.

Doc nodded. "Let's sit over there. Step away from this Friday afternoon traffic."

Levi guided Jacque toward the indicated seating arrangement.

Reaching the chairs, Doc turned and shook Jacque's hand. "I don't think we've met. I'm Dr. Greg Princeton."

Her chest rose with a breath. "Yes, Levi mentioned you're Rachel's doctor. I'm Jacque Taylor, Rachel's employer."

Doc maintained his clasp on Jacque's hand and angled toward Levi. "Do I have your permission to include Ms. Taylor in sharing Rachel's condition? We can sign the forms later."

"Yes, of course. Rachel will want Jacque to be informed. Doc, how's my sister?" Levi lifted his right hand and clamped it on the back of his neck.

Doc sank to the orange plastic chair and motioned toward two turquoise ones. "Levi, sit down and take a breath. You're pale as my lab coat. Rachel's in the care of the best orthopedic surgeon in the region." He touched his arm in three places. "The breaks are in the humerus, the ulna, and the radius. The surgeon will place pins as needed to aid the healing process. We're fortunate. The surgeon happened to be in the hospital for a post op consultation when Rachel arrived in the ambulance."

Levi's brain hurt, and he struggled to absorb the medical details. "The breaks in her left arm are her only injuries?"

"The most complex injuries." Doc rested his forearms on his thighs. "She also has two cracked ribs. We'll make sure they don't pose a danger to her internal organs. From what I gather about the collision, the impact slammed her against the center console of the car. Thankfully, she drove a quality car with reinforced steel doors."

Jacque wilted against the hard plastic chair, her arms still clutched across her middle.

Doc leaned to touch her arm. "Ms. Taylor, it's difficult to see beyond the shock and worry, but Rachel has youth and good health on her side. She needs time to heal, but she will heal."

Jacque's lips quivered. "He hit her that hard..." Her words tapered, and her throat flexed with a hard swallow.

Levi frowned. "He? Am I missing something?"

Her gaze shot to his. "I just assumed a man drove the pickup."

Levi shifted to the edge of the chair. He needed more answers. Now. "Why was Rachel driving your car?"

Jacque blinked and unfolded her arms. She shifted on the hard plastic chair and placed her clenched hands on her lap. "Rachel had a car repair appointment scheduled for noon today. A new client needed to meet at two p.m., so I loaned her my car." Her voice caught on the words, *my car*.

Levi frowned. "Are you more upset over Rachel being involved in a collision or about the damage to your expensive car?"

Jacque's green eyes went wide. She opened and closed her mouth. "Of course, my entire focus is on Rachel's well-being! I-I just wish I'd driven her to the appointment."

"Sorry." He swallowed hard. "I'm not thinking straight." He scrubbed at his face with both hands.

Back down and breathe. Rachel held Jacque in high esteem—he'd seen them interact. He couldn't allow his fear of losing another loved one to cloud his judgment. But something didn't seem right about Jacque's body language. He shifted on the hard chair and mentally reset his composure.

"I understand." She grimaced and attempted to slip two curls that'd escaped the large clip back into place. "You're very worried about Rachel, but please be assured, so am I. I'd never intentionally place her in danger."

Levi exhaled. Something still didn't seem right, but Doc said Rachel would be okay. He needed to cling to that. He closed his eyes. When he opened them, he caught Doc eyeing him like a bug under a microscope.

"Levi, when did you last eat?"

He lifted a shoulder. "Breakfast."

"Well, your adrenaline just ran through the last of your reserves. Rachel will be in surgery for another hour, then in recovery for maybe two. I'll approve a late-night visit but not before you refuel and collect your emotions. She's been through a trauma and needs your strength and support." He glanced at Jacque. "You, too, young lady."

Jacque's lips lifted into a wistful smile. "I'll grab something to eat."

"Good." Doc tapped the edge of the file folder against Levi's knee. "You two have plenty of time to eat at the Bistro down the street, but if you don't want to leave the hospital, the cafeteria isn't half bad."

Levi pushed from the hard chair and glanced at the front of his dusty work clothes. "Guess, we'll check out the cafeteria." A thought occurred. "Wait. The other driver. What happened to him?"

Doc stood and smoothed the tails of his lab coat. "From the police report, he immediately left the scene."

"How?" Levi gazed at his doctor. "Wasn't his pickup damaged?"

Doc lifted his chin toward someone across the room. "There's Officer Carson Haynes. He's probably here as the lead officer for the accident. I'll check in on Rachel's surgery, and if anything changes, I'll call you." Doc glanced at his gold wristwatch. "Plan on her being in recovery until seven thirty."

Levi retrieved his pocket watch from the small pocket in his dirty jeans. Five o'clock. Somehow, it seemed later. Two and a half hours to wait before he could see his sister. "Thanks, Doc."

Jacque tugged the strap of her leather purse over her delicate shoulder.

She probably stood five-eight, but the large bag seemed out of proportion with her slender frame. A wave of compassion hit him. Levi slid his fingers around Jacque's arm and led her toward the officer, who waited just inside the electric doors, his uniform issue hat in his hand. He'd wait a bit longer to call his parents. Gather more information. He didn't look forward to that call. No doubt, they'd make the four-hour drive tonight.

As they neared the thirty-something-year-old officer, Levi observed the precision-pressed khaki uniform and the nametag fastened to the left breast pocket of his shirt. *Coeur d'Alene City Police, Detective Carson Haynes.*

Jacque stepped forward. "Officer Haynes, I'm Jacque Taylor. Thank you again for notifying me about the accident."

Levi angled to face them both. "I'm Levi Banks, Rachel's brother. I understand the other driver left the scene. Do you have any additional information?"

Officer Haynes raised a palm. "Let's move to the seating area and out of this traffic."

The electric doors slid open and closed, as if proving Haynes right. Levi clamped his molars and followed the officer and Jacque back to where they'd met with Doc.

Jacque sank to the same chair she'd previously occupied.

Haynes claimed Doc's chair. He leaned forward and clamped his hands together between his knees. "Mr. Banks, I'm happy to supply you with as much information as possible. According to witness statements, the black pickup that T-boned the car your sister was driving had a lift kit and an aftermarket brush guard. The height difference of the two vehicles and the guard on the front of the truck prevented it from sustaining major damage. The driver sped from the scene right after the impact." Officer Haynes gazed at Jacque. "I know this information is upsetting, but I have questions."

Jacque's gaze darted between Haynes and Levi. "I wasn't there. I don't have any additional information." She blinked rapidly.

"According to pedestrians waiting to cross both lanes of traffic; the northbound light was red. They were waiting in the median for the southbound light to turn, when the black pickup ran the red light and picked up speed." He lifted a shoulder. "Not unusual to speed while running a red light, but the witnesses indicated that while Rachel made the left-hand turn, the truck seemed to aim at your car. My job is to exhaust all possibilities. Are you aware of anyone who'd want to hurt you?"

Jacque opened and closed her mouth. Her bright-green eyes went wide, and her delicate nostrils flared with the quick intake of a breath. "I, uh, of course not! Why would someone in Coeur d'Alene want to hurt me?"

"Exactly what we need to rule out." Haynes cleared his throat. "Can you recall any unusual situation since you moved to town that might have led to an angry reaction?"

She smoothed her hands over the gold fabric of her skirt and drew a breath.

The hint of something Levi couldn't define passed through her expressive green eyes. A sick feeling settled in his empty stomach.

Haynes withdrew a packet from his shirt and handed it to Jacque. "I retrieved your registration and proof of insurance. Everything appears in order. There are other personal items in the car—a blanket and a dog bed. You can arrange to collect them when you're ready. The car is likely totaled." His mouth tightened.

"It can be difficult to see your vehicle after it's been involved in a collision. Especially, when someone you care about is involved."

Jacque trapped her bottom lip between her teeth. "Thank you." She accepted the packet of paperwork and glanced at Levi. "I'm in no hurry to visit my car."

Levi flinched, catching the way she punctuated the statement and pinning him with a raised brow. What had possessed him to ask if she valued her car more than his sister's life?

"Ms. Taylor, would you like a bottle of water?" Haynes gestured toward a beverage cart tucked in an alcove.

"No, thank you. I'm fine." She swept another escaped curl off her temple.

Levi moaned under his breath. She didn't look fine. Oh, she looked mighty fine in a womanly way, but Haynes was right. She looked ready to faint and had lost the usual cool, self-confident, polished designer image he'd seen since they met in March.

Jacque pulled a tissue from her oversized bag, dabbed at her eyes, and delicately blew her nose. "Officer, please continue with whatever you need to ask. I don't want my discomfort to slow the investigation."

Levi agreed. He wouldn't allow law enforcement to drag their feet on this accident. Not like they had with Lucy's. They'd accepted road conditions as the only cause. A jackknifed semi-truck on a snowy mountain pass. Okay, so it turned out they were right, but today—the collision involving Rachel, in Jacque's car—seemed different. The pickup reportedly aimed at Jacque's car. He couldn't get the image out of his mind.

Haynes' lips tightened and released. "One more question. Could someone, maybe from wherever you moved from, want to hurt you?"

Levi sat straight and fixed his gaze on Jacque. "Officer Haynes, I—"

Her green eyes glazed. "Not that I'm aware of."

Levi shifted to the edge of the chair. "Officer Haynes." He didn't want to go down this path, but if the officer thought it was a possibility, then he needed to know. "Is there a way to investigate the current location of someone from out of state? A way to determine if they're in Coeur d'Alene?"

Jacque closed her eyes. Tears escaped and splashed against her pale cheeks.

Haynes switched his gaze from Levi to Jacque and back. "Yes, with the right information to get us started. Ms. Taylor, would someone from your past want to harm you?"

Her sigh turned to a moan. "If I'd even suspected this could happen, I never would have loaned Rachel my car."

"Officer Haynes, has an alert been issued on the pickup?" Levi didn't want to rip Jacque to shreds, but he needed answers. Somewhere out there, someone could still intend to hurt her, and Rachel had already been caught in one attempt.

"All area law enforcement has been notified, including the Spokane County Sheriff's office and the Bonner County Sheriff's Department to the north." Haynes nodded.

Jacque's delicate throat flexed with a swallow. She clutched at the edges of the plastic chair. "Good, I hope they catch him." Her jaw clenched.

Haynes made notes in his small spiral notebook and returned it to the breast pocket of his khaki uniform shirt. "We'll drop the questions for now. Here's a card with my contact information. Day or night, please call if you remember anything that might impact the case."

Levi ran his gaze over the woman his sister adored—the woman who'd opened doors for her. Had they both misjudged her? She'd moved here in January, the coldest and snowiest month of the winter. According to Rachel, Jacque moved from San Diego to escape an ex-boyfriend who wouldn't leave her alone. Wow—would he be angry enough to want to hurt her?"

Haynes stood and turned his hat in his hands. "Camera footage from the intersection has been transferred to the PD. We'll analyze the footage and get back to you."

The setting sun streamed through the floor-to-ceiling windows of the ER and caught the reds and golds in Jacque's hair.

She resembled a terrified bird torn between fight or flight. Levi's chest tightened. The way her voice quavered when she said, *no one in Coeur d'Alene* had a reason to hurt her, haunted him. Why not inform Haynes about the ex? He extended his hand to the officer. "Please keep me informed. If the truck intentionally hit Jacque's car, she could still be in danger."

Jacque blinked rapidly.

Interesting. Hadn't she thought of the possibility? Levi tapped his hat against the side of his knee.

"It's something we need to consider." Haynes nodded. "I'll keep you posted, and please return the courtesy. Sometimes, observant citizens are the department's best assets." He moved toward the exit.

Jacque gripped the back of the bright-orange plastic chair. Her lips quivered, and fresh tears welled and poised on her bottom eyelids.

Levi pinched the bridge of his nose between his thumb and forefinger. "Doc's right. Let's regroup before we visit Rachel. Get something to eat."

She pressed a hand to her throat. "My car isn't the only white foreign model in the area. It could be a mistake to think the other driver targeted me."

He touched her slender arm, and his calloused fingertips caught on the filmy fabric of her blouse. "Look, I won't stop searching for answers or allow the police to file this away as a fluke accident. Rachel deserves answers, and so do you." He propped a hand at his waist. "Let's at least grab coffee."

Jacque swiped at her tears. "Rachel is so dear to me. I would never place her in danger."

Doc approached, the tails of his white medical coat fluttering with his movement. "I figured you'd still be here. Great news. Rachel's out of surgery. Her ulna and radius are pinned. Her vitals are good, but she's in recovery until she wakes up. Give her a couple of hours, then check in with the second-floor medical desk."

"Thanks, Doc." As if he'd just heard the eight-second bell, relief rushed through Levi. He shoved a hand through his dusty hair and was reminded of his mad dash from the ranch. He could run to Rachel's cottage and shower, but he didn't have clean clothes. He glanced at Jacque. Besides, he needed to stay and wait with her until they could see Rachel. He took a breath and slowly let it out.

Doc narrowed one eye. "I'm serious, Levi. Take care of yourself, or you'll be no good to your sister."

Levi nodded and shook Doc Princeton's hand.

Jacque seemed to cave. She grabbed at Doc's arm.

From early childhood training, Mom's voice echoed through Levi's mind. *Take care of those who can't take care of themselves.* He wrapped his fingers around Jacque's left arm. "Let's grab dinner in the cafeteria." She'd steadied under his touch but still looked lost and weak.

"Scotty's home alone. I should wait with him."

Levi understood Jacque's concern over her black Scottish Terrier. He loved animals, too. "Has he only been alone since you came here?"

She nodded. "Yes, but—"

"In that case, he should be fine. We'll only be allowed to spend a few minutes with Rachel."

"But, that's two hours from now." Her gaze darted between his and the exit doors.

Strange, but through his frazzled nerves, sinking blood sugar, and unavoidable suspicions, her beauty still struck him. Creamy complexion and light-red hair she always wore up in a clip. The curl he'd touched earlier beckoned him, but he resisted the urge.

She clutched her large purse like a shield, and her expressive green eyes flickered with something he aimed to learn more about.

Chapter Six

Chloe's equilibrium threatened to fail. Someone had intentionally struck her car, and Rachel had been caught in the middle. She should have responded to the message on the flowers. Called Bruce Billings and—and what? Order him to back off? Tell him, if he didn't, she had the information to topple his political campaign and take a few big businessmen with him? She swayed and grabbed at Levi's arm.

"Jacque?" Levi grasped both of her shoulders. "You're pale. Are you okay?"

Levi's touch seemed to drag her from the dark thoughts threatening to suck her under. "Coffee sounds good." She pushed the "what-ifs" to the back of her mind where later she'd unpack them when she called Paul and reached out to Gina. "Let's check out the cafeteria."

Her losses—the apartment in Sacramento, her freedom, and her beautiful car—meant nothing. A weight settled on her chest. If her suspicions about the collision were proven correct, she'd personally hold Bruce Billings to the fire. Building anger revived her strength. She moved toward the reception desk, where she asked a woman named Judy for directions to the cafeteria.

Levi waited next to the molded plastic chairs, cowboy hat in hand, and his amber eyes radiating deep worry and exhaustion. No wonder he'd rushed to town in his work clothes, instead of the usual dress slacks and crisp white shirt. A vicious attack had injured his sister and might have killed her. Chloe moaned and returned to his side. "Levi, let's go."

The Friday afternoon ER rush reflected the growing population in Coeur d'Alene. More people meant more vehicles and more traffic injuries. Luckily, none of the patients appeared to be critically injured— like Rachel had been.

A vision of what it must have looked like when the ambulance pulled under the portico, and attendants rushed outside to unload the gurney holding Rachel, made Chloe's stomach churn. She hurried toward the hallway and the cafeteria.

The large cafeteria teemed with medical staff either coming on shift or taking a much-deserved dinner break. Glass-fronted refrigerators held bottled drinks, premade sandwiches, and salads. A long buffet held a variety of hot foods. The smiling staff wore disposable gauze hair covers and clear plastic gloves.

Chloe gravitated toward the stacks of wax-coated paper cups and filled one of the largest sizes with strong black coffee. On second thought, she grabbed a couple of creamer pods and a foil-wrapped hamburger.

Levi huffed a chuckle. "Funny how life happens when you're making plans. I'd planned to treat Rachel to dinner at Beverly's. A far stretch from hospital cafeteria food." He followed suit with a large coffee and a hamburger.

"She always looks forward to your late Friday afternoon visits." Chloe sighed.

"Yeah, the hospital called before I had a chance to

hit the shower." He glanced at the front of his dusty ranch clothes.

Her heart ached for him. The call from the hospital had sent him on a stressful race to be with his sister. She pressed her fingertips to right above her collarbone where a lump of emotion had lodged. Where would this all end?

Levi added a cardboard container of French fries to his tray, then grabbed a precut slice of apple pie.

Chloe eyed the large slice of pie, tempted by the cinnamon-coated apples encased in a flaky crust, but she resisted, and instead, grabbed a small side salad.

The brightly colored, laminate-topped tables, and molded plastic chairs, matched the furniture in the ER. She supposed bright colors were used to make the institutional setting cheerful. She settled in a turquoise chair and tugged at the hem of her burnished gold skirt.

Levi sat across the table and arranged his plates and silverware. "Not Chef Dakyn's fare, but..." He glanced at his hands. "Uh, be right back."

As he crossed the room toward the double doors, Chloe watched him, then glanced at his unwrapped burger and reached across the table to rewrap it. Her stomach knotted with regret. By association, Rachel had become a victim of the file debacle. Levi or Tracie could be next.

Her hands trembling, she drizzled balsamic vinaigrette over the dinner salad. But why had her nemesis waited four months before he decided to strike?

Someone had shared the contents of her police file. The one Paul created for her break-in. It might contain her account from the Billingses home consult and how she'd given Hallie a ride back to town. It probably contained the details of her near abduction at Luigi's. Had Paul added her alias and location to the police file?

Levi returned from washing his hands and unwrapped his burger. He took a large bite, and for a moment, he chewed with his eyes closed. "Doc was right about needing to eat."

His gaze seemed to reach beyond her protective shell. Funny, how they'd never been together without Rachel present. "Have you called your parents?" She stabbed the tines of her fork into a slice of radish and brought it to her lips.

Levi set down his burger and finished chewing. "Not yet. I'll call now." His broad chest lifted with a deep breath. He wiped his hands on a paper napkin and started to push from the chair.

She reached across the table and touched his big hand. "Why not finish your dinner first? Waiting a few more minutes won't change the outcome of the call. Take time to gather your strength and your thoughts."

"Yeah, I guess you're right." He settled on the chair. "A few more minutes won't make much difference to their drive."

Chloe bit back a moan of regret. Levi's parents would drive four hours to reach their daughter's bedside. Oh. My. Gosh. Somehow, when she and Levi visited the Intensive Care Unit, she needed to hold it together—not turn into a blubbering mess at the sight of Rachel in a hospital bed hooked up to monitors and IVs.

Levi finished his hamburger and fries before he excused himself to call his parents. He headed toward the corridor behind the noisy cafeteria.

Chloe leaned into the hard chair and covered her face with both hands. She could imagine his conversation with his parents. Tears. Frustration. Helplessness. She'd taken the file, but Hallie and Rachel had paid the price. Hallie had paid the ultimate price. Hopefully, Rachel would recover.

Lost in her misery, she suddenly perceived a movement at the table. She lowered her hands from her eyes.

Levi had reclaimed his chair and rested folded hands on the tabletop.

His intense amber gaze seemed to see right through her front as Jacque Taylor. Seemed to read her guilt over exposing Rachel to danger. The same expression she'd seen when Officer Haynes asked who would want to hurt her. As if she'd hid something serious enough to lead to the collision. Okay, so she had, but Paul hadn't given her a choice. He'd warned her that if she returned to Sacramento, or made any attempt to contact Billings, she'd be putting Gina and Diane in danger.

He broke their locked gaze. "My parents will head this way in about thirty minutes." He took out his pocket watch and studied the face. "How about we check with the medical desk early? See if Rachel's awake."

"Has it been long enough?" Chloe glanced at her wristwatch. "Dr. Princeton mentioned about two hours in recovery."

"You're right." His lips tightened. "We probably have another hour."

He spoke the words as if he didn't believe he could make it through another hour of waiting. She got it.

The flow of medical staff through the cafeteria had

slowed, and the room seemed cavernous and far too quiet.

Chloe pushed to her feet and ambled to the large coffee urn to refill their cups. Had Levi added sugar to his coffee? To be safe, she added a teaspoon to his cup and a dash of cream to hers. Something she rarely did, but tonight, she needed all the sustenance she could get. Back at their table, Levi had cleared the plates and trash."Let's take our coffee to the ICU waiting room."

He accepted the fresh cup and murmured his thanks.

Twenty minutes later, the ICU Nurse led them to Rachel's room.

Stepping through the wide doorway, Chloe froze. Rachel lay in the hospital bed, her face as white as the bright sheets tucked over her shoulders. Her dark hair was captured under a green gauze surgical cap, and she lay so still that Chloe could barely breathe.

"Rach?" Levi approached the bed and touched his sister's shoulder. "Can you hear me? It's Levi."

Chloe remembered last Christmas and Mom's breast cancer surgery. She'd spent a week in San Diego, alternating between Mom's bedside and helping Dad with meals and housework. Thankfully, Mom's cancer was in remission, but she'd never forget the sinking panic of nearly losing her.

The beeps and whirs of the medical equipment that monitored Rachel's vitals and administered medication from the IV bag that was suspended over the bed. The scene made Chloe's dinner churn. *Oh, Rachel. This should never have happened.* She moved to the other side of the bed, careful not to disturb the tubes and wires.

Rachel's heavily bandaged left arm lay at an angle.

Chloe moaned. The side of impact.

Rachel's eyelids fluttered, and her mouth worked. She licked her lips.

From a tray on the nightstand, the attending nurse retrieved a plastic cup with a bendable straw. "Here, Miss Rachel. Let's moisten your mouth. Your brother and sister-in-law are here to see you. Can you open your eyes?"

Chloe glanced at Levi and opened her mouth to correct the nurse.

He flashed her a glance, then settled his attention on his sister.

Her eyes still closed, Rachel fastened her lips on the straw. She took two sips, then pulled away and licked her lips. Her eyelids became more active. One eyelid opened and revealed a dark brown iris. "Levi?"

Her voice came out like a croak.

"Jacque?"

"We're here, Rach." Levi leaned past the nurse to touch Rachel's cheek. "Jacque and I are here for a few minutes. We both needed to see you."

Rachel opened her other eye. Her lips compressed and then opened.

The nurse helped her with another sip.

"Thank you."

Rachel's voice had improved.

"Jacque—your car."

Chloe leaned over the right-side bed railing and placed a hand over the gauze cap covering Rachel's hair. "Don't worry about my car. Insurance will take care of it. Right now, you need to focus on healing." She choked on the words and ran her gaze over

Rachel's beautiful, pale complexion. She wanted to say so much more, but now wasn't the time.

Yet, the entire situation brought clarity. Very soon, she'd share her story with Rachel and Levi. She should have confided in Rachel months ago. Should have told her about the flower delivery and the message on the note. Confided about finding her father's name on the campaign contribution list.

Her chest tightened. Rachel might have been forewarned and not have risked driving Chloe's car. Chloe gripped the bed railing and fought a gray wave threatening to take her down.

"You need to sit." The nurse touched her arm and guided her to an orange vinyl upholstered chair.

Chloe sank into the chair and closed her eyes.

The nurse cupped the back of her neck and brought her face closer to her knees. "Take a few breaths and take your time sitting up."

Chloe had no choice but to comply. She gripped her knees and gazed at the toes of her cream-colored pumps. Her vision began to clear. She sat straight and gazed toward the hospital bed.

Levi leaned over the bed railing, with his right hand resting on Rachel's head. He murmured in a soft tone about her surgery and how Doc believed she'd completely recover.

Chloe leaned into the chair and recalled the earnest sincerity in Carson Haynes' bright-blue eyes. An investigation was underway, but he didn't have all the pieces. Despite Paul's adamant warning, she had to protect her new friends.

Levi straightened, caught her gaze, and tilted his head.

The mannerism reminded her of Scotty when she said something he didn't understand. *Scotty.* She needed to go home and check on her boy. She pushed from the chair and moved toward the door.

"Jacque?"

Rachel's ragged whisper stopped her. "Yes, Rachel?" Chloe returned to the bedside. "I'm here. You should rest, dear." Her voice caught.

Rachel licked her lips. "Your car."

Her mind foggy from the anesthesia, Rachel mumbled the words, but her distress came through loud and clear. Chloe traced her fingers along the elastic edge of the surgical cap covering Rachel's dark hair. "Rachel, my car can be replaced. I can't replace my friend and protégée." She cleared the emotion from her throat.

Rachel moved her head from side to side. "No, you don't understand. He hit your car."

"Yes, I know. Officer Haynes explained what the witnesses saw. I'm so sorry you were hurt."

"He. Meant. To. Hit. Your. Car." Rachel's words came out in a staccato rhythm. She paused and swallowed—closed her eyes, and opened them. "He aimed for your car."

The declaration came out in full force. Chloe grabbed the bed railing. "Rachel, we don't have all the facts, but Officer Haynes will find the answers." The grayness returned and threatened to send her to her knees. Chloe measured her breaths. Never in her life had she fainted, but what happened to Rachel might push her over the top.

Levi rounded the bed and slipped a hand along the small of her back. "Rach, please don't worry about

Jacque. I'll make sure she's safe. I'll drive her home, and until you're back in the studio, I'll check on her every day."

Rachel lifted and lowered her chin. "Yes, watch over Jacque." She closed her eyes and sank farther into the stack of pillows.

The friendly and capable nurse checked the IV port in Rachel's left arm and pressed her fingertips to Rachel's wrist for a pulse check. "She's fine…just needs her rest."

Chloe allowed Levi to guide her toward the open doorway, but she paused one more time to glance at Rachel.

The nurse smiled. "Go home and get some rest. I'm sure she'll want to see you both in the morning."

"Thank you." Levi kept his hand on her back. "Our parents are on their way from Missoula, and they plan to visit Rachel early in the morning."

The nurse pulled the sheets under Rachel's chin. "Barring any unforeseen complications, they can visit at eight a.m."

Levi's smile didn't reach his eyes, but he nodded and guided Chloe from the room.

In the hallway, she straightened her shoulders and lifted her chin. Good heavens, she needed to get a grip. Rachel was the victim of this atrocity—not her. She gently disengaged from Levi's firm hold and hurried toward the bank of elevators.

He matched her pace into the elevator, his brows drawn. "What's your hurry? We're only a few minutes from your apartment."

The doors closed, and the lift lowered them three floors and bumped to a stop. The doors slid open.

"I'm anxious to see Scotty." Chloe rushed down the hall and through the electric doors. The moment she stepped into the night air, she drew a deep breath.

"Hey, slow down and watch your step." Levi touched her arm.

"I'm fine." Chloe glanced at her three-inch heels and continued across the dimly lit parking lot. How could he care so much after she placed Rachel in danger?

Tall streetlights cast shadows over the dark pavement. Chloe blinked to moisten her tired eyes and spotted Levi's large, dark blue pickup several rows away. She stepped over a curb and continued toward it. Something caught her right foot. "Ah!" In a blur, she pitched toward the pavement. Her left knee touched the asphalt, and strong hands caught her shoulders. Pain riveted through her right ankle.

"Jacque!" Levi lifted her to her feet. "Are you okay?"

Her head spun. She reached behind to grasp his forearms and tried to balance on her left foot. "Yes. No, My right ankle. I think I twisted it." She glanced at her foot and cringed. "So much for the heel on that shoe. What happened?"

"You charged out here like there were no obstacles and tripped over a curb separating the rows. Here, let's get into the pickup and look at your ankle.

"I'm so sorry." A sob escaped her throat. "It's already late, and you have to drive an hour to reach home." Okay, so when had she turned into a blubbering fool? Oh yeah, when she got the call that her new friend had been struck while driving her car.

Levi swept her into his arms and carried her to the

passenger side of his pickup. "My fault for not having you wait in the lobby while I moved the truck closer." He managed to support her and open the door, then set her on the leather upholstered bench seat. "Might be best to slide backward toward the driver's side and rest your ankle on the seat." He removed her broken shoe and tossed it on the floorboard before he ran his long fingers over her tender ankle. He gently pressed against the bone above and the meaty indentation below.

"Ugh." Chloe flinched, then moaned.

Levi stepped away and started to close the door. "I'll drive around to the ER entrance."

"What?" Chloe glanced toward the building she'd just exited. "No, please, I'll be fine. I'll ice it when I get home."

He leaned against the end of the seat.

Chloe suddenly didn't want him to leave. While she'd mindlessly flailed across the parking lot, predators could be observing. Levi's broad shoulders and muscled body provided a barrier between her and them.

"You'll be fine, after a doctor confirms the extent of your injury and treats it." He closed the door and rounded the hood of the truck to slide behind the steering wheel.

With her back toward him, and her right leg stretched over the length of the seat, Chloe had rarely felt this ridiculous. "I'm so sorry."

"Why do you keep apologizing?" He shifted the transmission into Reverse.

Chloe twisted to glance over her shoulder and caught his gaze. How did he interpret her need to apologize? Maybe as guilt for exposing his sister to danger? She blew a breath through inflated cheeks and shifted to look through the passenger window. "I'm sorry for everything that's happened."

Levi continued to back from the parking space and turned toward the main lane leading to the ER. "In the rodeo world, you learn to expect the unexpected. Sprains and breaks are a normal occurrence. Nothing to be sorry for."

An hour later, a nurse pushed the wheelchair Doc had insisted Chloe use to reach Levi's truck.

Levi walked by the chair and opened the passenger door of his truck.

Chloe clutched the bag, holding bottles with a pain medication and an anti-inflammatory. X-rays had confirmed she had a sprain, but it would still take days, maybe weeks, to heal.

If only the sprain could mask the pain in her heart. She couldn't get the alarm and fear in Rachel's dark eyes out of her head.

Levi remained silent as he drove to her building and parked in front. "Inside stairs or outside?"

"Huh? Oh, the outside stairs, please." As they entered the fenced yard, she touched the wrought iron gate. Tears of exhaustion pricked her eyes. With each step on the metal-grated stairs, Levi supported her weight. Keying in her access code, she heard the lock beep and click.

"New locks?" Levi opened the door and helped her inside.

Chloe wobbled to a dining chair and sank to the cushioned seat. Weariness washed over her. "Yes, new locks." She lifted her aching and bandaged right foot and rested it on another chair. "Last week, I realized I should have changed them before I moved in."

Levi didn't comment. Instead, he opened the door and urged Scotty to go outside. Then, without another word, he refilled the dog's water and food dishes and opened the door to call Scotty back inside.

Chloe wasn't someone who could sit by and be waited on, but when she placed her injured foot on the wood floor, pain zinged up her leg. Okay, so she'd accept the help.

Scotty munched on his kibble.

Levi crouched to pat his head. "Good boy." He rose and turned, his hands on his lean hips. "Need anything before I leave?" He shrugged his broad shoulders. "Like help to another part of the apartment, or maybe a cup of herbed tea?"

"You know how to make tea?" She blinked. Other than being Rachel's brother, she barely knew this man. She'd chatted with him every Friday since Rachel joined the studio. He'd drop by to say hello or to take Rachel out for dinner. Still…

He quirked his lips into a smile. "What? You're surprised a simple rancher can brew a pot of tea?"

"A pot of tea?" She raised a brow. "Not a teabag and a cup of hot water?"

"Yeah, a proper pot of tea."

A chuckle eased her tight chest. "I guess I did typecast you. Not the simple part, though." She waved a hand. "Thank you for the offer and your help with Scotty, but I'll manage. Please, don't let me keep you from heading home." She recognized the struggle in his expression with the sort of stretch and purse of his lips.

"Think I'll stay at Rachel's cottage tonight. That way I'm in town early in the morning to meet with my parents."

"Will they also stay at Rachel's?"

"No, I made their reservation at the resort." He clamped a hand on the back of his neck and yawned. "Ah, sorry. I guess I'm done for the day."

"I'm sure you are." She glanced at Scotty, who had planted himself next to her chair. "We'll be fine, won't we, Scotty?" She patted his head and smiled into his dark, gleaming eyes. She'd waited her entire life to have a sweet dog like Scotty.

"He's a great companion, isn't he? Don't know what I'll do when I lose Duke."

"How old is Duke?" She lifted her gaze to meet his.

"Seven, but he's a large dog breed. Anatolian Shepherd. They don't live as long as Scotty will."

"Wow, he'd probably devour Scotty."

"Not at all." Levi shifted his stance and cocked his right knee. "Duke's a lamb. Protective of everyone on the ranch. Even my cat, Oscar. He'd protect Scotty, too."

Chatting with Levi about their pets eased the stress that had gripped her body since the call from Officer Haynes. Her attention strayed to his wash-worn jeans and how they hugged his long legs and narrow hips. Equally worn, the chambray shirt molded over his broad shoulders. A hardworking man, a man's man, but she imagined plenty of women in Kootenai County and beyond, admired Levi Banks and would jump at the chance to date him. After his Friday afternoon visits to the studio, he normally had dinner plans at the resort. Did he meet someone?

Using the back of the dining chair as leverage, she

pushed to her uninjured foot. Okay, it wouldn't be easy to perform everyday tasks for a while, but she refused to ask for more help.

"If you're sure you don't need anything, I'll say goodnight." Levi moved toward the door.

Chloe tightened her grip on the chair back. "Thanks so much for your help. I hope you're able to get some sleep."

"Keep your foot elevated and take those meds. They'll help you sleep and to heal faster." He settled the brown cowboy hat on his dark, thick hair but hesitated another moment, then slipped from the apartment. The lock clicked in place behind him.

Chloe stood still while his booted steps rang out against the metal treads of the outside stairs. Through the silent night, she heard him slam the truck door, then the engine came to life. She hopped toward the dining room window overlooking the street and peered through the paned glass in time to see the truck's taillights glow red, and the pickup pull away from the front of her building. She gripped the windowsill and watched until he turned left at the intersection.

Scotty pressed his furry body against her left leg and whimpered.

Chloe returned to the table and sank into the nearest chair. "Oh, Scotty. Remember the bad people I told you about? They could have killed Rachel."

Chapter Seven

Chloe moaned and pushed from the wooden seat of the dining chair. Until morning, when she'd call a medical supply store, she needed something to lean on. Reaching the broom closet, she grabbed the yellow-handled broom and leaned against it. The nylon bristles caved under her weight. "Uh-oh, Scotty. This won't work. Maybe the mop." Awkward, but it sufficed as a make-shift crutch.

Now, to get ready for bed. She thought about Levi reaching Rachel's cottage and how lonely it must seem without his sister.

Chloe leaned against the mop handle feeling like her life had spiraled out of control. Again. She hobbled to the small desk in the alcove between the kitchen and living room and sank into the small office chair in front of an equally small desk. The right size for her laptop.

Paul answered her call after two rings. "Chloe, what's up?"

"Paul, Rachel Banks is in intensive care."

"What? What happened?"

Chloe related the events of the evening since the call from Officer Haynes.

"Chloe, what happened to Rachel could be a combination of bad timing and an under-the-influence driver."

"I'd believe that theory if not for the flowers and

the ominous note. What if Bruce, or Drew King, sent a thug to silence me? Right after I found the note, I should have called Bruce. The *Sacramento Times* article on Sunday probably sent him into a panic."

"Chloe, that doesn't explain how he found you. Besides, you've claimed you don't think Bruce is the violent one. Look, I'm doing the best I can, but my chief is watching me like a hawk." He huffed. "There is some good news—Hallie's cell phone mysteriously reappeared in the evidence room."

"What?" She gasped and tightened her hold on the phone. "Her phone went missing. Who had it?"

"That, we don't know, but my team's working to break the passcode. Once we're in, we'll review all voice messages and the call log."

She struggled to breathe around the tightness in her chest. "Paul, there's a mole in your department. Someone is supplying Drew King with information." She didn't mean to shout, but her voice rose with each word.

"Chloe, I'm aware there's a leak in the department. My partner is solid, and he's helping me keep this thing under cover. I made it known to the entire department, I won't tolerate any tampering of evidence."

She sputtered. "Too late for Rachel. She was caught in the middle of their deadly game. As for the messages, I left one for Hallie."

"Chloe, I've put my career on the line to keep you safe. Don't throw me under the bus." Paul's tone went hard.

She pressed a palm to her chest and drew a deep breath. "Paul, please don't misinterpret my lack of patience as a lack of confidence. You're doing all you can, but Hallie lost her life because of the file, and today, Rachel could have died. Have you contacted Bay City Investigations about the flowers?"

"Not yet," he stammered. "The chief has me chasing a drug ring who just dropped a load of fentanyl on the city. I'll make time to call Bay City, tomorrow."

"Please, call me after you've spoken to the PI office." Chloe gripped the edge of the small desk. If she heard another excuse, she'd completely lose her cool. She thanked him and disconnected.

The clock in the lower left of her computer screen read nine p.m. Gina and Diane should still be awake. She sent a video chat invitation to each of her friends.

Gina appeared first and immediately arched her dark brows. "Okay, what happened?"

"One moment." Chloe held up her index finger.

Diane joined the call, and her dark gaze darted between Gina and Chloe. "What's up?"

Chloe slumped against the desk. "I need to vent." The precarious dam holding back her emotions broke. Between sobs, she unpacked the timeline since Rachel left the studio driving Chloe's luxury sedan.

Gina opened and closed her mouth. "Paul doesn't believe the collision is connected with you-know-who?"

"Paul is like a brother, but he's distracted by his corrupt chief of police. I called him on Wednesday about the flowers, but he still hasn't contacted the PI who ordered them." She drew a breath, then blew her nose into a lotion-finished tissue. "Maybe I need to become more involved. Do a little sleuthing of my own. Paul admits there's a leak in his department, but who found me and how?" She moaned. "Now, Rachel's injured and facing a long road of physical therapy."

Gina rested her chin on her right palm. "Chloe, I feel your frustration, but don't expose yourself to even more danger. I'll talk to Paul. He needs to step up the investigation."

Chloe fiddled with the beach-themed, soapstone coaster next to her mouse pad. "Bruce won the primaries, and he's high in the polls for the general election. He must be nervous about any loose ends. I'm a loose end."

"It's all my fault!" Diane burst into tears.

Chloe blinked and exchanged a glance with Gina. "Diane, what are you talking about?"

She grabbed a tissue and blew her nose. "I've been so worried about you. You're so far away without a soul you can turn to. I mean, in person."

"Diane, where is this leading?" Gina raised a dark brow.

She dabbed her eyes with a fresh tissue and blinked several times. "I probably said too much to Melissa Parker." She compressed her lips, and the corners of her mouth turned down. "Two weeks ago, Melissa called to chat and catch up. Our fun conversation sort of lulled me into dropping my defenses." She paused, and her full, bow-shaped lips puckered even more. "I sort of broke down. I confessed how concerned I am about my good friend from Walters Design." She nibbled on her bottom lip. "I mentioned that said friend moved to Coeur d'Alene."

"Oh, Diane." Chloe tugged at her hair. "Melissa Parker must suspect Jacque Taylor is your friend. I'm the newest designer in town. She can connect the dots."

"I'm so sorry." Diane grabbed a third tissue. "I

didn't think it through."

Gina growled against her palm. "Paul and Keith were very clear. We weren't to say *anything* about Chloe's location to *anyone*." She shook her head, her dark eyes intense. "Melissa likely shared the information with Mike. Now, the timing of the *Sacramento Times* op-ed on Sunday makes sense."

"Does it?" Chloe blinked. "The article is about Hallie's unsolved death. How could Mike connect me with Hallie?"

"Most sharp journalists have at least one contact in the police department." Gina sighed. "Mike's a sharp journalist."

"Okay, even if you're right and Mike has a contact who shared Chloe's file, the op-ed didn't mention her part in Hallie's final day." Diane again blew her nose.

"Oh, Diane, you meant well." Chloe couldn't bear to see her friend cry. "Now, we need to figure out exactly what the Parkers know, how they learned it, and what action Mike intends to take. If he has access to my police file, he knows I drove Hallie to town that day." She raked her fingers over her hair and removed the clip to shake out her curls.

"Let me think." Diane rolled her lips and, for a moment, gazed away. "Since they're my friends, I can send out feelers and see what they know. Then, I'll ask Melissa those questions. I'll beg her to keep you out of Mike's investigation."

"If they're true friends, that might work." Chloe's stomach churned.

Gina narrowed her dark eyes. "Okay, Diane, that's your assignment for tomorrow morning. Call Melissa, and report back to us. In the meantime, Chloe Austin, you haven't shared everything. What else happened today?"

"What do you mean?" Chloe had a slim hold on her emotions. "I've told you everything."

Gina tightened her full lips. "I've known you long enough to know that's not true. Every time you move, you cringe."

"Oh, that." Chloe sighed. "I'm too embarrassed to mention my stupidity." She pressed her fingertips to her eyes. "Okay, so I tripped over a curb and sprained my ankle." She scoffed. "As if I didn't have enough to deal with."

"Oh, no!" Gina touched her screen. "You poor thing! I don't care what Paul says, you need my help. Tomorrow, I'll catch a flight into Spokane." She glanced at Diane. "We should cancel the winery tour to Napa. We can both visit Chloe."

Chloe held up a hand and shook her head. "No. An absolute no. Paul will go ballistic. Especially so soon after the collision."

"You're right. I don't like it, but you're right." Gina blew a breath.

Chloe planted her elbows on the desk and gripped her head. "Earlier, something occurred to me. We didn't take my photo off the Walters Design website. Mike and Melissa might have accessed it and matched me with Chloe Austin. I changed my name, but I didn't have plastic surgery."

"Coeur d'Alene isn't exactly a small town." Diane bobbed her head from side to side, and her shoulder-length hair brushed the fabric of her silk, hot-pink pajamas. "What are the odds of them seeing you close enough to recognize you as Chloe Austin?"

"This isn't a small town, but people tend to move in certain circles." Chloe rubbed her eyes, something she never did. "With the bits of information you shared, that they've connected the new designer in town with your friend from Walters makes sense." She shrugged. "Because of the floral delivery, someone else knows I'm here. Gina, you're right. I can't do this alone. Tomorrow, when I'm not so mentally trashed, I'll call Officer Haynes, and share everything. He seems trustworthy."

"Do you think it's wise?" Gina opened her mouth. "What if Officer Haynes contacts Paul's department?"

"Yeah, it wouldn't be ideal for him to alert Paul's police chief." Chloe nibbled on her bottom lip. "Still, Paul needs to buck the politics and cronyism. Lives depend on stopping whoever's behind Hallie's death and the threats to my life. I'll put Haynes directly in touch with Paul."

Silence, then Gina commented. "Okay, if you're sure. In the meantime, I'll ask Paul who has access to your file."

Diane had looked away and fiddled with something near her monitor. "And I'll call Melissa first thing in the morning. She is a good friend. I can't picture her, or Mike, being careless with information that could endanger someone."

Chloe shifted on the chair. Pain zapped through her ankle and up her calf. She closed her eyes. "Thank you, both. I can't imagine not calling or video chatting."

"Did you see a doctor?" Gina virtually touched Chloe's cheek.

"Yes, Levi insisted, and after all he'd been through with Rachel's collision, I didn't argue. Poor guy. He must be asleep by now. He's staying at Rachel's cottage."

"Ah yes, Rachel's brother," Gina said. "Doesn't he live quite a distance from town?"

"An hour's drive." Chloe nodded. "As we speak, his parents are driving from Missoula, Montana." She drew a deep breath. "This situation isn't all about me, anymore. The Banks family has been plunged into a nightmare not of their making." Weariness washed over her. "I have to make this right and trust Officer Haynes."

They reviewed their plans for tomorrow morning and ended the call. After the computer screen went dark, Chloe pushed from the chair and, with the aid of her mop handle, reached the outside door to let Scotty out one more time for the night.

The Clarks' porch light still glowed. She glanced at her watch. Ten thirty. It seemed so much later. So much had happened since Rachel left the studio for her appointment with Janelle Meeker. Chloe pressed a palm to her heart. Rachel had been so excited about the home consult, and about driving Chloe's car.

Scotty trotted up the metal-grated stairs and brushed past her to make a beeline for her bedroom, where she kept his bed.

Chloe locked the door and double-checked to ensure the keyless lock system had engaged. She switched off the kitchen light and hobbled toward the short hallway. She started to pass the small desk in the alcove, but her laptop beckoned. Maybe, she'd take another look at the Bay City Investigations website. As she opened the website and read each page, the backlit monitor glowed into the dark room.

Located in Oakland, and owned and operated by brothers, David and Gary Sims. Why wouldn't Bruce use a PI in Sacramento? She pursed her lips. Campaign donors resided throughout the state. After all, her father lived in San Jose, and he'd contributed to Bruce's campaign.

The magnitude of everything coming down hit her stomach with a curl of nausea. She pressed a palm to her midsection—time to stop running down the rabbit trail and go to bed. At least, she had clarity—clarity she shouldn't have left Sacramento.

****

Chloe roused from the deep sleep she'd achieved sometime in the early morning hours. Daylight filtered through the shades, but she snuggled deeper into the pillow and tugged on the down comforter she'd splurged on with her first design commission in Coeur d'Alene.

No matter how bright the sun shone, she couldn't face the day yet. She rolled to her back, and pain shot through her right ankle. "Ouch." She grimaced and threw back the comforter. "Time for a pain pill."

Her phone vibrated against the nightstand. "Who would be calling this early on a Saturday morning?" She frowned and shifted across the pillow-top mattress to retrieve her phone. Through sand-filled eyes, she squinted at the screen. An out-of-area number. Not unusual these days for people to move and retain their cell phone numbers.

She cleared her throat and touched the green button. "Good morning, this is Jacque Taylor."

"Ms. Taylor, I'm so sorry to call this early. This is Janelle Meeker, Rachel's client on Riverview Drive.

99

Rachel had scheduled an appointment for yesterday afternoon, but she didn't arrive or answer her phone."

Chloe stifled a groan. The collision. Rachel lying in a hospital bed hooked to monitors and an IV. A lead weight settled on her chest. She took a deep breath and pushed to a sitting position. The pain medication had turned her mouth to cotton, but thank goodness, her headache was gone. She ran her tongue over the inside of her mouth and explained the events of the previous afternoon.

"Oh dear, how terrible! I'm so sorry!" Janelle said. "Our project wouldn't be so urgent, but next month, my husband and I are traveling to China. We hoped to have the work on autopilot before we leave."

Chloe opened and closed her mouth. *Autopilot? When did that happen in design work?* She swallowed and wished she'd put a glass of water on her nightstand last night. "Mrs. Meeker, until Rachel recovers, I fully intend to cover her accounts. Are you available for a home consult later this morning? About eleven thirty?"

"Would you? I'm grateful for your help. I'll send you text with my address."

Chloe pulled the comforter to her bare shoulders. "Thank you for your understanding. I look forward to meeting you at eleven thirty." Still holding her phone, she dropped her hand to her side.

Scotty planted his paws on the edge of the bed and gazed at her with soulful eyes.

Chloe stretched to pat his head. "Okay, no time to waste." She threw the covers aside, swung her legs over the edge of the bed, and set her feet on the bedside rug. A throb of pain hit her ankle. Not that she'd accomplish anything with her usual speed. "No whining," she mumbled to herself. "Not you, Scotty, I'm referring to me not being allowed to whine. I did this to myself. She grabbed at the nightstand for balance and pushed off the bed.

Balancing on one foot, she let her shoulders drop. Levi's parents would have arrived close to midnight. Levi had stayed at Rachel's cottage in town, and he'd meet his parents at the hospital. Anguish coursed through her.

Leaning against her mop handle, she hobbled to the kitchen. On her way to the door to let Scotty outside, she activated the coffeemaker she'd set up before she went to bed. She'd need the entire pot before she left at ten thirty. She unlocked and opened the door.

Scotty trotted down the metal-grated stairs and into his grassy yard.

Despite the intense blue of the sky and the bright rays of sunshine peeking over the eastern mountains, the air held the nip of a late spring morning. Did it ever get warm in north Idaho? She rubbed her arms and wished she'd pulled a sweater over her nightgown.

She stepped back inside and closed the door. Time to take a pain pill and the anti-inflammatory prescribed by the ER doctor.

Back at the paned window overlooking the side-yard, she watched Scotty trot along the inside of the wrought-iron fence, then glanced across the street. Had Jim, or Pam, discovered the discarded flowers among their sheetrock and carpet scraps? Hopefully, the garbage truck had emptied the dumpster.

The faint hum of morning traffic carried from the boulevard three blocks to the south. The world moved on, as downtown merchants prepared for Saturday morning shoppers.

Scotty's nails tapped against the metal stair treads.

Chloe opened the door. "Okay, buddy. Time for breakfast, then we'll get ready to leave for Rachel's home consultation." *Ugh.* A drive from town and up Riverview Drive.

Setting a large white mug filled with steaming, dark coffee on the table, Chloe sank into a chair and gingerly unwrapped her ankle. Without the elastic bandage, it seemed to double in size. She applied a moldable ice pack and rewrapped it. Now, to soothe her swirling stomach. She peeled a banana and took a bite. She rarely ate this early, but she needed something to dilute her medication.

At nine, she called the nearby medical supply store and ordered the delivery of a cane, more icepacks, and stretchy bandages. Next, she called her insurance company and received approval for a rental car. They'd cover up to two weeks. By then, the fate of her car would be decided.

Refilling her coffee mug, she searched online for local car rental outlets and found a dealership on Highway 95. The salesman agreed to deliver the large sports utility vehicle, and by ten, he'd parked it along the curb in front of her building, and he even installed Scotty's new bed and the seatbelt modifier she'd ordered from a local pet supply store. She had no desire to retrieve those items from her damaged sedan. She might never want to see it again.

By eleven, weariness washed over her, but she pushed on. Rachel needed her help. She looped Scotty's leash over her left wrist and secured the straps of her purse over her right shoulder. The cane helped, but navigating the trip downstairs was dicey.

She stopped at the gate and gazed at the large SUV. Okay, so maybe she'd overreacted by ordering such a large vehicle, but after what happened yesterday, she'd drive a tank if it meant surviving another attack. She drew a deep breath and juggled Scotty's leash and her cane as she opened and closed the gate. At the driver's door, she loaded her computer case, purse, and Scotty. Once behind the wheel, she took the time to sync her phone to the vehicle's navigation system and tap in Janelle Meeker's address. Time to venture out of town and out of her comfort zone. Why did Rachel's clients have to live on a winding, mountain road?

She took her usual route when visiting the marina and avoided the intersection where the collision had happened. Why had Rachel gone the other way?

Chloe blinked and merged into the traffic. How could the driver of that pickup have known she'd arrive at the intersection at preciously the time Rachel had? She cringed. The only possible answer was that he'd followed her car from the studio. But still, strategy had been needed to meet her at the intersection.

Chloe squared her shoulders and focused on navigating the unfamiliar vehicle through the midmorning Saturday traffic on Northwest Boulevard. Beyond the marina, with its blue awnings and beautiful lake and mountain views, where she occasionally parked to think, she entered unknown territory.

She experienced a sense of unease as the highway wound through the mountainous countryside. A few dark clouds met the mountaintops and threatened to cover the sun. At least, with the above-freezing temperatures, snow wouldn't fall.

A text pinged through the SUV's connection. She glanced at the display. Diane. Chloe slowed the SUV and pulled onto a turnout. Instead of *calling*, like Chloe would have preferred, Diane had sent a very wordy, voice-generated text.

—*Melissa admitted she discussed my friend's situation with Mike. They referenced the Walters website and recognized you as someone they'd seen around town. I know, I'm an idiot, and I didn't think before I shared so much information. Mike even called Walters, and someone—maybe Mindy—said you're staying with a sick relative—*

Chloe moaned. She couldn't blame Diane. They'd all failed to remove her photo and profile from the website. Exactly why Paul had objected to her staying in the Portland office.

Another text from Diane.

—*Mike confessed to having a contact at the Sacramento PD. He read your file. How is this even possible? How could a reporter gain access to a confidential police file?—*

Chloe thumbed a quick response.

—*Thank you for the update. I'll be in touch—*

She blew a breath through tight lips. Surely, Mike wouldn't use Hallie's death, or Chloe's close calls, to advance his career. She flipped her blinker and reentered the southbound traffic flow. The male voice on the maps app directed her to continue one hundred feet and turn right onto Riverview Drive. She entered the right-hand turn lane, and a line of motorists sped past. Thankfully, no one followed her onto the mountain road.

A big raindrop splatted on the windshield.

Chloe leaned over the steering wheel and craned her neck to see the sky through the upper section of tinted glass. Another splat of rain landed, and several more followed. She touched the automated wiper control, and the blades cleared her vision. The drops gained speed.

Her phone rang through the SUV's system.

She touched the phone icon on the steering wheel. "Hello, this is Jacque Taylor."

"Jacque, it's Levi Banks. Sounds like you're in the rainstorm that's headed my way."

She blinked at the media screen. Levi? The number didn't match the cell he'd shared last night. "Where are you calling from? Is Rachel okay?"

"Rachel's fine. I checked on her about thirty minutes ago. Sorry, last night I didn't think to share the landline number at the ranch. Our cell service can be sketchy at times. How's your ankle this morning?"

Her tired mind scrambled to respond. "I-uh-I'm fine. I guess."

"Sounds like you're driving?"

"Rachel's new client, Janelle Meeker, called early this morning, concerned because Rachel didn't keep their appointment yesterday. I just turned onto Riverview Drive."

Silence, then. "Yesterday was hard on all of us."

His deep, soft tone filled the SUV. She huffed a breath and visualized Levi standing in the ER, his amber eyes shadowed with fear for his sister. Chloe blinked against sudden tears.

"Jacque?"

She shook off the threatening emotions. "I'm here. We might lose cell service ahead."

"I'll make it quick. I plan to visit Rachel at four this afternoon. Can I give you a ride to the hospital? Your ankle will need a break by then, and Rachel will want to see you."

"Um. Yes, sounds nice. This appointment should only take a couple of hours." A sense of comfort filled her. Someone would know where she'd gone and when she should return. The threats to her life had taken a toll, and she no longer enjoyed living alone.

"It's a plan, then," Levi said.

His statement jerked her from her self-analysis. "The plan to visit Rachel?"

"That, too. Look, you need to concentrate on driving. I'll let you go."

"Wait, did your parents make it to Coeur d'Alene last night?"

"They did. Thanks for asking. We met at the hospital this morning. The nurses are great about early access to the ICU. Rachel should be transferred to a regular room before we visit later today."

"Your mom and dad must be exhausted." She navigated a series of three curves, keeping the large SUV on the yellow center line, a rock cut on her right.

"They're pretty tired, but they'll never admit it. Dad insisted they check out of the hotel and commute to the ranch tonight."

She smiled. "The luxury mattress and bedding aren't his cup of tea?"

His chuckle rumbled through the speakers. "Hey, the beds at the ranch are top quality."

At the mention of the beds at the ranch, Chloe went unreasonably warm all over. The sound of his voice, and his touch of humor, made her want to tell him everything.

"Before we hang up," Levi said. "I made a reservation at Beverly's for six p.m. Had planned to take Rachel last night. Care to join me?"

His invitation threw her off balance. Her vision glazed on the narrow road. "We have a poor connection—did you just invite me out for dinner?"

"I did—if it's convenient for you. Hey, you need to keep up your strength, so your ankle heals faster. You're taking on Rachel's workload."

Chloe cleared her throat and searched for a response. The more time she spent with Levi, the greater the likelihood she'd say too much. She tightened her grip on the leather-wrapped steering wheel. "Can I respond later, after I see how my ankle feels, by the end of the day?"

"Sure. Hey, while I was at the hospital last night, the first vacation guest arrived. Odd guy, though. He'd left by the time I got home this morning. Didn't even eat breakfast with the cowboys."

Chloe glanced at the display screen to note the Meekers' driveway should be over the next rise. "Gone as in checked out after one night? Rachel mentioned a mandatory two-night minimum stay."

"According to the lodging app, he hasn't checked out. Just struck out early."

She slowed to watch for the driveway. "Rachel mentioned your hesitancy about strangers staying on the ranch. Do you vet the prospective guests?" Before the events of past few days, Chloe might not have thought about vetting guests.

"Yeah, it's been a big concern of mine, but Rachel convinced me it'll all work out. We collect their home addresses and dates of birth. Want to avoid the young college crowd."

"Since you're so far from town, you probably don't need to worry about party-goers. Where are this weekend's guests from?"

"The guy who checked in last night is from Oakland, California. He—"

The phone connection crackled and cut off.

Her chest suddenly tight, Chloe gripped the wheel.

Chapter Eight

Chloe touched the callback button on the steering wheel, but it didn't reconnect with Levi. She shivered and turned up the heater. Last night, a guy from Oakland had checked into one of the vacation cottages on the ranch. Had he just arrived, or had he been there since early Friday? She caught sight of a black, wrought-iron bracket holding a wooden sign with *Meeker* burned into the wood. The subject of the Oakland guest would have to wait.

She guided the SUV onto the winding, tree-lined drive and approached the two-story, New England, shore-style house. Dark stained, cedar siding contrasted with white framed windows. She took in the usual details of a subject home, but for once, the anticipation of diving into a new design couldn't distract her from Levi's announcement.

Chloe parked next to a black, luxury SUV, and cut the engine. Rain splattered on the windshield, gathering until her view of the covered porch blurred. She'd done so well to line out the car rental, the medical supplies, and to get her, and Scotty, here on time, but she'd forgotten her rain jacket. She drew a breath and opened the door. "Scotty, you have to stay here while I work. I'll try not to take too long, okay?"

Scotty had slipped from his restraint and propped his front feet on the console between the front seats. He gazed at her with querying dark eyes, with his rawhide chew trapped between his front paws.

"Hey, you. How did you get out of that seatbelt? Well, we're here so you have the run of the car." She touched his head and smiled before she slid from the leather upholstered seat. Laptop case and tote in one hand, she gripped the handle of the cane with the other and hobbled toward the covered porch. Raindrops dampened her blouse, and the damp, pine-infused scented air carried her back to that day in January when she'd hurried to reach the entrance of another large home in the mountains.

"Jacque, so happy you made it." As she opened the door and motioned for Chloe to enter, Janelle Meeker's smile curved her full lips. "Oh dear, you got caught in this rain we didn't expect."

A very attractive woman, Janelle appeared to be in her mid-fifties. Silver strands streaked her shoulder-length blonde hair, and the cream-colored, loose-knit sweater softened her tanned complexion. A tall woman, she moved with a polished grace and carried off the khaki knit equestrian-style slacks with panache. Chloe had seen the components of Janelle's outfit in one of her favorite online shopping sources—tasteful and expensive.

"You poor thing." Janelle unburdened Chloe of the computer case and her purse. "You didn't mention you'd injured your ankle. Here, slip this on and warm up." Janelle helped her into an eggshell-colored, Aran cable-knit sweater.

The soft knit carried a light fragrance of what must be Janelle's signature perfume. Too chilled to object to the hospitality, Chloe pulled the sweater around her.

Any similarity between her home consult with the Billings, and this one, had ended the moment Janelle opened the door.

Chloe stopped just inside the great room and ran her gaze over the configuration of styles, colors, and lighting. Opulent coziness prevailed with high-beamed ceilings and plaster-troweled walls. "Your home is beautiful."

A man, also in his mid-to-late fifties, joined them.

"You must be Jacque." He held out a hand. "I'm Cain Meeker. We're so grateful you're willing to stand in for Rachel while she recovers. We're devastated over everything she's been through." He glanced at Chloe's bandaged foot. "Looks like you're dealing with an injury, too. Were you in the accident?"

A couple of inches taller than Janelle, Cain sported a dark mustache and wore dark brown cords and a beige cardigan over a white shirt.

"Oh no, I'm a silly woman who tries to hurry in three-inch heels," Chloe said. "Now, please point me to wherever you'd like for me to set up, and I'll get to work."

"Janelle will take care of you. Just don't forget to call me when the cookies come out." As he retraced his steps toward the room off the great room, he waved.

Janelle shook her head. "You can dress them up…"

Chloe giggled and covered her mouth. "Sorry, but your comment reminded me of something my mom would say."

Janelle smiled and motioned toward a wide archway. "Before you start work, I made a pot of Earl Grey. Please have a cup and warm up." She glanced at Chloe's bandaged ankle and shook her head. "Dealing

111

with your injury must be exhausting."

"Earl Grey sounds wonderful." Following Janelle into the expansive kitchen, Chloe wondered why they'd want to change a thing about this lovely home. "Rachel's notes show the work will start in the great room and move into the bathrooms and kitchen."

Janelle's classic aquiline nose crinkled, and her mouth curved. "Probably the usual, huh? Kitchens and bathrooms go out of style—what—every ten years?" She filled two large, white mugs with tea and set them on the wide, granite-topped island dividing the kitchen from the window-lined eating area. "Please set up your workstation wherever it's convenient. There's plenty of room and lots of light. Cain might pop in and out. He's excited to see the plans and of course, the cookies."

For the first time in days, Chloe began to relax. She organized her laptop and notebook on the island and tried to sip the hot tea, but it burned her lips.

"Oh dear, I'm so sorry. How about we tour the house while it cools?" Janelle motioned for Chloe to accompany her from the kitchen.

Leaning on her cane, Chloe juggled a pencil and sketch pad and followed her client through the great room, to a bank of French doors, leading onto a covered, cedar-planked deck, running the back length of the house.

Janelle opened one of the glass-paned doors and motioned for Chloe to step outside. "When we first toured this house, this view is what cinched the deal."

Light rain dripped from the eaves, but Chloe still enjoyed the view and the scent of the tall pines dotting the hillside. Far below, the river wound from Lake Coeur d'Alene and became the Spokane River. She caught a glimpse of the bright-blue marina awnings. Chloe began her usual list of questions. "How much time do you plan to spend in this home? Only summers, or are you a winter enthusiast? Do you have deck furniture?"

Janelle's answers led to more questions, and they finished the tour and moved back to the kitchen, where the tea had cooled to a drinkable temperature.

Chloe opened her design software and began the basic layout.

Sometime later, Janelle set a cobalt-blue platter, filled with chocolate chip cookies, on the countertop near Chloe's laptop. "Please help yourself to the cookies and have more tea. I enjoy having you work here."

Chloe smiled and lifted her chin toward the platter. "I see why Cain's interested in the cookies, and the platter is beautiful. Is cobalt a favorite?"

The answer inspired the color scheme for the kitchen remodel. In her software, Chloe replaced the dark-oak cabinets with tall, white Shaker-style cabinets and dark knobs. The white countertops would be replaced with charcoal-gray granite. She'd search for slabs of granite with light-grey veins running through it. The focal point of the room would be the new shelves in the largest window, to display Janelle's cobalt-blue glass collection.

Cain drifted into the kitchen and claimed the stool at the island next to Chloe's.

Her creative juices flowed like they hadn't in days, and even Cain's presence didn't distract her from working out the placement of the new windows and shelving.

Janelle refilled her mug and spoke softly to her husband.

Chloe glanced at the time. "Wow, I've been here for almost two hours. My dog, Scotty, is in the car."

"No problem." Cain finished his coffee and slid off the stool. "Will he let me take him for a walk?"

"Oh, I didn't mean for you to take care of him. I should wrap this up and get out of your way." Chloe saved her file and, for the first time, noticed how she'd spread her supplies around her laptop.

"Nonsense." Janelle placed her manicured hands over the edge of the countertop. "Cain will take Scotty for a walk. Is he wearing a jacket? It's chilly out there."

Chloe caught her bottom lip between her teeth. "I forgot his rain jacket and mine. I should be finished soon."

"No hurry." Cain backed toward the archway. "Is your vehicle unlocked?"

Chloe glanced from Janelle to Cain.

Janelle chuckled. "Cain's having withdrawals from leaving our poodles with the house sitter in Portland. Will Scotty be receptive to another dog lover?"

Chloe relaxed and nodded. "I think so. If he's at all aggressive, please don't worry about walking him. I can wrap up in about fifteen minutes."

Cain left to walk Scotty.

Janelle issued Chloe a packet containing a key to the front door, the business card for a local property management company, and her business card with phone numbers and email. "Until mid-July, we'll be between here and Portland. On July sixteenth, we're flying to Beijing for six weeks. Cain's taking a sabbatical from Portland State University, and I'm tagging along."

Chloe nodded. "Sounds like a wonderful vacation."

Janelle chuckled. "That was the idea, but for years, Cain's dreamed of studying the Mandarin culture. I'm sure he'll spend some of that time in a classroom."

"Like when I travel and study architecture and interior design." Chloe stashed the key packet into her tote and sipped from her second mug of tea.

Cain returned, his hair damp from the continuing rain. "Scotty's very receptive and seemed happy to get out of the car for a few minutes."

"That's wonderful. Thank you, Cain." The final bit of tension riding her since she woke that morning dissipated. Chloe continued to add the finishing touches to the new kitchen plan. She reviewed them with both Janelle and Cain. They were the perfect clients, and she couldn't wait for Rachel to meet them.

Ready, but reluctant, to leave, Chloe gathered her art supplies and organized them in her laptop bag. No stray file folders on this trip!

Cain insisted on helping her to her car. "The rain's letting up now, and there's blue sky toward the west."

"Good news," Chloe said. "Thank you both. The moment Rachel's doctors clear her to take on light duty, she'll become involved with the redesign."

"We're eager to meet her." Janelle slipped two cookies into a small, waxed bag and stashed it in the large pocket of the sweater she'd insisted Chloe wear home. "A treat for Rachel, when you see her this afternoon."

Chloe smiled. "She'll be touched, I'm sure. I'll return your sweater on my next home visit."

Cain loaded her computer bag into the backseat

and stood by.

She started the large SUV and backed away from the house. Chloe's heart overflowed with gratitude for whoever had connected Rachel with these lovely people. She reached the blacktopped Riverview Drive and paused while a car headed downhill. As she retraced the route toward the highway, she had the road to herself.

The time at the Meekers' had relaxed her, and she began to enjoy the beauty of the steep mountains and the thick stands of pine. Granite outcroppings and the papery bark of birch trees added color and texture to the scenery. The clouds were clearing out, leaving a perfectly sunny afternoon.

Hyperaware of the deep ravine plunging from the right side of the road, she hugged the painted centerline and kept her right tire within the edge of the blacktop. On her left, the road cut into the mountainside, and in several spots, large wire grates prevented rocks from falling on the road.

"Scotty, when we reach the highway, I'll call Rachel and fill her in. She'll love working with the Meekers. Were you a good boy for Cain?" Sharing her thoughts with Scotty made her feel less lonely, less homesick, and less nervous about the drive back to town. For a few hours, she'd existed in a bubble of security and peace. Now, she needed to tackle the unanswered questions.

The pain medication had worn off, and her right ankle began to throb. She readjusted the seat to ease the pressure. If she'd had to sprain an ankle, why hadn't she twisted the left one? Once she reached the highway, she'd use cruise control.

In the meantime, she'd creep down the winding mountain road and navigate the series of three hairpin curves. Chloe tightened her grip on the steering wheel and maintained her position between the center yellow line and the edge of the blacktop. She guided the SUV into the first curve. A flash of sunshine off chrome made her blink. How had a vehicle caught up without her notice?

She glanced in the review mirror. A large silver pickup rode her bumper. Chloe's blood ran cold, and she split her focus between the truck and the road ahead. "Does he have to follow so close?" The calm she'd found with Janelle and Cain, wavered, and her shoulders trembled with an encompassing shiver.

Into the first curve, the large pickup moved closer to her bumper.

So close—she no longer saw the grill in her rearview mirror. She drew a long breath. "Okay, Chloe. It's silver, not black." But it could be the same driver. Her palms went damp, and her chest tightened. Earlier, she'd been happy to have the road to herself; now, she wished another car would appear.

Carson Haynes had mentioned the black truck had Washington state license plates, but with Coeur d'Alene so close to the state line, seeing Washington plates was a common occurrence.

Somehow, she needed to gain ground and read the front plate. She navigated the second curve and aimed for the third, and final, curve in the series. "Just focus." She spared a glance toward the large side mirror and gasped.

The pickup had moved over the center line.

She slowed the SUV and placed her right front tire

on the edge of the blacktop. If he planned to pass, then she'd give him the room.

He didn't pass.

She began to navigate the third curve.

The pickup moved toward her left rear panel and gained speed.

What in the heck? If an oncoming car appeared, she'd have to slam on her brakes to avoid becoming part of the collision. She slowed the SUV to a crawl.

The driver of the silver pickup slowed to match her speed.

Something squeezed her heart. Would this be the way her life ended—on a winding mountain road in Idaho—with no one at her studio or the apartment, anticipating her return? Eventually, someone would find her car over the embankment, crushed beyond recognition, with her and Scotty inside. She swallowed hard and slowed even more.

The pickup moved alongside and matched her crawling pace.

Her mind spinning, Chloe clutched the steering wheel. She couldn't see a way out. "Please don't force me off the road." She peered over the right fender. No guardrails would prevent her from plunging into the deep ravine below.

Scotty had again escaped his seatbelt. He leaped onto the console and growled and barked at the pickup.

"Scotty, please settle down. I need to focus." Her voice broke.

The pickup began to creep past. Their side mirrors almost touched.

She spared a glance at the dark, tinted window. If only she could identify the driver, but his window reflected her own.

He matched her speed around the final hairpin curve.

The road ahead straightened.

Chloe tensed for what might come next.

The other driver accelerated, and the silver pickup roared ahead, swerving in front of her.

She slammed on the brakes, and a wave of dizziness washed over her. "Please keep going." What if he stopped and blocked the road? She shifted on the leather upholstery and schooled her breathing, her gaze centering on the license plate. Red numbers and letters with *Washington* emblazoned across the top of the plate. "Okay, Scotty. We've got it. Remember, the string begins with a *C*." She blinked to moisten her eyes. "I wish I could see the rest!" She gripped the wheel and willed her racing heart to calm.

The silver truck continued toward the highway and drove out of sight.

Scotty settled on the passenger seat, his nose up, and his gaze on her.

"We're okay, Scotty. We're okay." She rested her forehead against the steering wheel and began to shake all over. This situation couldn't be a coincidence. Just yesterday, according to eyewitnesses, a man intentionally slammed into her car. What had prevented the silver truck driver from forcing her off the road? Nausea curled in her gut. She and Scotty wouldn't have survived.

She drew several deep breaths, and her head began to clear. The tightness in her chest eased. She shifted the transmission into Drive and applied pressure to the gas pedal. Pain shot through her ankle. She gasped and leaned into the steering wheel, waiting for the pain to settle down. She needed to reach home. "Levi," she breathed the name. Levi knew where she'd gone, and he planned to pick her up at four—to take her to visit Rachel. Someone would be expecting her. If the worst had happened, and she'd been forced from the road, Levi would have known where to search.

A realization hit home. The time had come to trust someone in Coeur d'Alene with her story. Levi Banks seemed the perfect choice.

Chapter Nine

Levi shared a final critique with the team roping class of the day. "The header needs to pick up speed and turn the steer, so the heeler has better access to the steer's hind legs. Make sense?"

Nineteen students nodded, but one, a kid from New Mexico, raised his gloved hand and asked for elaboration on the technique.

Levi adjusted his cowboy hat against the late afternoon sun. He'd stay around and provide a deeper explanation of the angles for successful team roping.

"Okay, Boss. We've got it from here." Riley made a shooing motion with both hands.

Levi grinned and waved. "Thanks. See you in the morning." He turned toward the house and slapped his hat against his thigh. A cloud of corral dust puffed around him, and a sense of having done this before hit him. A cascade of chills scattered over his shoulders. If he made it to the shower and into clean clothes, without the phone ringing with a message of bad news, he would've broken the cycle.

He paused to glance toward the vacation cabins. The renter of Cabin One still hadn't returned.

Yesterday, Gary Sims had called before noon to let Levi know he'd check in later that day. Before he arrived, Levi raced to the hospital and stayed at Rachel's in town. Before he returned the next morning,

Gary had gone somewhere.

"Hmph." Levi shook his head. Why stay an hour from town if he didn't spend time here? He entered the fragrant kitchen through the exterior entrance to find Janice in full dinner prep mode, moving between the granite-topped island and the large commercial range. Levi eyed a lone fresh cinnamon roll on a small plate and smiled. "Hey, Janice, is this for me?" He didn't wait for an answer— he knew she'd set it out for him to have with his afternoon coffee. Levi filled his favorite brown mug and took a sip. "Hear anything from our renters?"

Janice met his gaze, a stainless-steel spoon in one hand and a look of irritation in her bright-blue eyes. As usual, she'd swept her blonde hair into a twist and secured it with a clip that resembled a smaller version of the grapple on his tractor. "Hey, Boss. About an hour ago, the Portland family checked into Cabin Two. They're already having a great time and plan to have dinner in the dining hall with the cowboys. That guy in Cabin One still hasn't called, or messaged, since he left early this morning."

Levi finished eating the gooey roll in four bites and washed his hands before he touched the coffee mug. "I guess to each their own. It's his dime. I'm off to shower, then to town to visit Rachel. Since I missed dinner at Beverly's last night, I'll eat there. Mom and Dad will be here by six." He didn't elaborate on how he'd invited Jacque to join him.

Janice nodded and gave the contents a vigorous stir. "Don't worry about your folks. There's plenty of roast and all the trimmings."

Levi rinsed the coffee mug under the kitchen faucet

and set it upside down on the drainboard. "Thanks, Janice. I'll tell Rachel *hi* for you."

She twisted at the waist to meet his glance. "Poor girl. I sure hope they catch that pickup driver and fast." She wagged an index finger. "The man needs to be thrown in jail. Oh, before you leave, could you grab one of those pink bakery boxes from the pantry? I'd like to send Rachel a fresh cinnamon roll."

"Sure thing. She'll love it." Levi retrieved a box and set it on the island before he headed for his bedroom suite.

An hour later, with the bakery box resting on the bench seat next to him, he backed his three-quarter-ton pickup from the machine shed and shifted into drive. One more glance toward the cabins confirmed the minivan with the Oregon plates sat in front of Cabin Two. The pickup, he understood Gary Sims had rented, was still nowhere to be seen.

He rolled his lips and eased the truck out of the ranch yard. What in the heck was Sims up to? Maybe property shopping? Many visitors turned their vacations into a marathon home search. Reaching the highway, he turned left and accelerated. He'd resisted calling Carson Haynes, but he needed an update on the black pickup. He huffed a breath. Janice was right. The driver who slammed into Rachel needed jail time for the hit-and-run, and soon.

At four p.m., he parked his pickup in front of Jacque Taylor Designs. The two-story brick-and-stucco building served Jacque well. Somehow fit her personality. According to Rachel, the building hadn't been occupied for years and had served as an attorney's office. At the studio door, he noticed a new keyless entry system. Just like the one on the apartment door. Huh—what had prompted her to change them out? He tried the door and found it locked. He knocked.

"One moment!"

Levi imagined Jacque sitting in the consultation area with her foot elevated. While he waited for her to unlock the door, he glanced up and down her street.

The door opened and set off a small bell attached to the doorframe.

Scotty yipped and ran to greet him, his nails clicking on the polished hardwood floor.

"It's already four?" Jacque stepped aside and motioned for him to enter. She leaned heavily on a cane.

As he entered the studio, he noted the set of her shoulders and the shadows under her jewel-green eyes. Even considering her unusual, less-than-perfect appearance, his stomach fluttered from standing this close. His awareness of Rachel's employer had grown over the past two months, and he wasn't sure what he planned to do about it.

She closed the door behind him, and the lock engaged.

"Are you okay?" He cleared his throat. "How's the ankle?"

"Truthfully, I'm not okay. Do you mind waiting while I freshen up? Then, if you don't mind, I'd like to talk before we visit Rachel." She motioned toward the more comfortable chairs against the brick wall.

Several times, Levi had used the seating area to wait while Rachel finished a project before he took her out for lunch or dinner. He glanced around. "Think I'll stand. Something happen to shake you up?"

Jacque lifted the hand not clutching the cane and patted her hair. Gold bangles around her wrist tinkled together. "No, I just-uh-got rained on, and I didn't bother with my hair when I returned from the consult. Please help yourself to a cup of coffee."

He glanced at the beverage cabinet that separated the seating area from the desks and sample boards. A single-cup brewer sat next to an electric water kettle. "Sure. My parents are probably still with Rachel."

"Thank you, I won't be long." She turned toward the interior stairs.

"May I make you a cup?" Something seemed way off, and they both might need the warmth of a mug in their hands.

"Uh, I avoid caffeine later in the day, or I won't sleep tonight. Herb tea is my afternoon beverage of choice." She passed the foot of the stairs and disappeared through the bathroom doorway on the far wall.

Levi fit a pod into the brewer. On impulse, he flipped on the electric kettle. A white ceramic teapot with tiny, hand-painted, lavender flowers sat on a lower shelf. Next to it sat a clear glass jar holding dried lavender buds and a darker herb he couldn't identify. Jacque must have a thing for lavender.

He lifted the teapot to the countertop, and his hands stilled. He hadn't touched a teapot since Lucy died. She'd loved tea, and she'd taught him the proper way to brew a pot. In a cabinet drawer, he found a stainless-steel tea ball, filled it with the dried flower buds, and hooked it to the mouth of the pot. The coffee dripped into his cup, and the water boiled.

Jacque still hadn't returned.

He poured hot water over the tea ball and fitted the lid to the pot. A plastic honey bear sat on one side of the sugar bowl. He read the label. *Made in Oregon.* Probably didn't compare to the honey he harvested on the ranch.

Jacque exited the small bathroom.

Within the short time she'd been gone, she'd brushed her curly hair and wound it into a bun on the back of her head. Somehow, she'd recovered her usual well-groomed sophistication. She'd applied a fresh coat of coral lipstick, and she'd brushed soft color over her cheeks, but no amount of cosmetics could erase the shadows in her green eyes. His stomach clenched. Something had happened.

She glanced at the steam rising from the teapot and raised a dark auburn brow. "You made tea?"

"Yeah, you said you prefer tea in the afternoon."

"Yes, but…" She hobbled closer to the beverage bar and touched the delicate, matching cup and saucer. "I'm impressed. You're the first man I've met who knows how to brew tea."

He chuckled. "An avid tea drinker trained me. Here, I'll pour. Sit and elevate your foot. You're using a cane." He stated the obvious, but he wanted her to relax and share the details from her appointment with Rachel's clients. He set the cup and saucer on a small table at Jacque's elbow.

She twisted to pick up the cup, breathed the fragrant lavender tea, and sipped. "This is heavenly. Thank you."

He retrieved his mug, sank to the loveseat, and sipped the black coffee. "You have a right to be exhausted after dealing with your sprain, but I have a feeling something more happened. Is it something with Rachel's clients?"

Jacque glanced away. "The Meekers are wonderful clients. Rachel will enjoy working with them." She rested the cup and saucer on her lap.

He ran his gaze over the tan slacks hugging her long, slender legs. A creamy silk blouse accentuated her narrow shoulders and slim waist. Her light, reddish-blonde hair framed her peaches-and-cream complexion. Her manicured hands were tipped with coral polish, and the low-heeled sandals that accommodated her bandaged ankle showed off her coral-polished toenails.

Her shoulders lifted with a ragged breath.

He shifted on the loveseat, and his knees bumped into the coffee table. "So, what happened?"

"There's no simple, or short, answer to your question." She paused and clamped her white teeth on her bottom lip. "The time has come to confide in someone, and other than Rachel, you're the only person that I trust."

"So, Rachel knows what you're about to share?" Levi's chest tightened. He uncrossed his legs and shifted to the edge of the loveseat.

"No." Her blouse lifted on a deep breath. "I want to tell her, but now, I'll wait until she's recovered." She sipped her tea and ran her tongue under her lips. "Before I begin, please understand, I was sworn to secrecy by a police detective I've known and respected for years."

Levi's mind threatened to freeze. "Okay, go on."

Jacque unfolded a story he'd never dreamed could happen to anyone in his world, especially not to the woman who'd snuck past his emotional defenses and sparked a flame too deep to ignore. A part of himself he'd thought long dead.

"On Wednesday, a floral arrangement arrived with a note I shouldn't have ignored. I mean, it hit me hard. They found me. I notified Paul—Detective DeMers— and he needed time to assess the situation and possibly move me to a different location." She sighed. "I didn't want to leave Coeur d'Alene. Leave this…" She swept a hand over the studio.

His mind spinning, he clutched the cooling coffee mug. "So, you chose not to tell Rachel the truth. Even if the over-possessive ex-boyfriend in San Diego story had been true, she deserved to be warned. She works with you. Heck, she worships you!"

She opened and closed her mouth. "I never suspected Rachel would be caught in the middle."

Levi's heart pounded against his chest. "Or, more likely, used as leverage? We don't know if the driver knew she was driving your car." He set down the coffee mug and scrubbed his face with open palms. "Had she known everything, she might not have been so excited to borrow your car. You knew what they were capable of."

Jacque slowly shook her head. "Believe me, since Officer Haynes called yesterday about the collision…I haven't thought of much else." She ran a flat palm over her reddish-blonde hair and sniffed. "They've gone too far. I can't sit by until Paul figures out what to do, and I refuse to run again."

He exhaled through inflated cheeks. Wow, he hadn't seen this coming. He'd become more than attracted to a woman he'd thought he knew—could trust. He braced his forearms on his thighs and gazed directly into her jewel-green eyes. "You've lied to my sister and me, and now, she's in the hospital because she didn't know the risk in borrowing your car. You can't blame me if I'm angry—resentful."

Jacque lowered her injured foot to the wool rug and rested her forearms on her thighs.

Scotty moved closer to her feet.

"I'm so sorry, Levi. So sorry Rachel's taken the brunt of an attack meant for me." She fingered the curly fur on Scotty's head and swayed when she shook her head. "Rachel's become so much more than a protégée. She's a good friend and almost like a younger sister." Her voice caught.

Levi pushed a breath from deep in his diaphragm. "The feelings are mutual, and for Rachel's sake, I need to make sure you've shared everything."

Jacque nodded, and her delicate throat flexed with a hard swallow.

Even through the righteous indignation on behalf of Rachel and his personal feeling of betrayal, he wanted to forgive her.

"There is one more thing." She paused. "Jacque Taylor is an alias invented and documented by Detective DeMers." She folded and unfolded her hands, then caught the tear escaping her right eye. "I-I hated lying about my name. Especially to Rachel."

He blinked. "You're not Jacque Taylor?" The further deception hit him hard.

She shook her head. "My real name is Chloe Austin."

"Chloe." He repeated the name, and it flowed through his lips like a sigh. He cleared his throat. "I need a minute." He scraped a hand over his face. A minute? Ha! He might need weeks, or years, to recover from learning Jacque wasn't even Jacque. He drummed his fingertips on his knees. "Considering everything you've told me and the weaponized pickups, it's time local law enforcement knows what they're dealing with. Carson Haynes needs to know everything."

She lifted her injured ankle to rest it on the footstool. "The moment I returned to the studio, I called Detective DeMers in Sacramento. He ordered me to sit tight and to maintain my alias." She rested her head against the bright upholstery of the armless, high-backed, chair.

"I disagree with your detective friend." A twang hit him square in the heart. Rachel had trusted this woman. He'd trusted her. He'd come close to confessing he wanted to date her. "The threat is no longer contained in Sacramento. By not telling Officer Haynes your story, you're risking other innocent bystanders." He left the loveseat and touched the sides of the teapot. Cold, just like the feeling in his gut. She'd lied, but he didn't want her to leave.

Chloe pushed from the chair and wobbled on her uninjured foot. "How do you know Officer Haynes is trustworthy? Before January, I thought I could trust the Sacramento PD."

"I've lived in the county for over four years, and I pay attention. So do many other residents." He rolled and smacked his lips. "As far as Haynes goes, he's as trustworthy as they get. Corruption wouldn't hide for long," He paused. "If you don't call him, then I will." He'd protect Rachel from Chloe's story as long as possible, but she needed to know—once she'd gained strength.

"No, I'll call him." She hobbled toward her desk, gripping the handle of her cane so tight her fingers went white. "It's time to place trust in the right people." She picked up her cell phone and tapped in the number from Haynes' business card.

Levi pinched the bridge of his nose. His head spun as if he'd been thrown from the back of a rank bull. His goal this afternoon to begin a relationship with Jacque Taylor had taken an unexpected turn. Wow—she wasn't even Jacque Taylor.

Chloe ended her conversation with Officer Haynes. She swayed and gripped the edge of her desk. "He agreed to meet in my apartment tonight at eight."

"Did you mention, I'll be here?" Lost in his thoughts, he hadn't followed her conversation. He settled his hands on his hips.

She blinked several times. "No, but since you have a personal stake in my situation…"

"You darn right I do." He flinched. That came out too harsh. He turned toward the seating arrangement. "Are we finished here? Rachel's expecting me before five."

She sniffed. "Yes, I've told you everything."

He drew a sharp breath and faced her. Dang, but her shocking revelations hadn't dimmed his attraction to her—hadn't made him disillusioned enough to never want to speak to her again. "I promised Rachel, I'd keep an eye on you. While we wait for the meeting with Haynes, you should still have dinner with me."

"Still?" She twitched her lips and glanced at Scotty, then back to meet his gaze. "I don't recall agreeing to your dinner plans. I do want to see Rachel." She turned to stuff her phone into her large purse.

"First, Scotty should go outside for a minute."

His gut wrenched with conflicting feelings. How could a woman who loved her dog so much be untrustworthy? "How about I let Scotty out? On my way, I'll carry the teapot and cups to the kitchen."

She shot him a glance and raised a brow. "You're very kind, but you don't need to take care of me."

"My mama brought me up to help those in distress." The tension eased a notch. He found a tray inside the beverage cabinet and loaded the dishes. Besides, he needed to keep his hands, and his mind, busy.

During his weekly visits to the studio, Scotty had grown used to him, so when Levi called the terrier to follow up the stairs and out the apartment door, Scotty didn't object. "Go for it, buddy." Levi waited on the landing while Scotty sniffed the perimeter of the fence and did his business.

The green dumpster across the street caught his attention. He pictured Jacque—Chloe—lugging what sounded like a heavy vase across the street. She'd lifted the lid and dumped the whole thing into the garbage receptacle. He gripped the metal railing. She'd panicked with the knowledge that the bad guys had found her. He ran a hand over his mouth. Over the years, he'd learned about forgiveness. To forgive himself for allowing Lucy to leave that snowy night. Now, he needed to forgive Chloe for lying to Rachel and to him. She'd followed her detective friend's order to maintain her alias. Her life had been, and still was, in danger.

He called Scotty and opened the door. The terrier trotted into the kitchen. As the lock whirred and engaged, he thought of his renter. Gary Sims was from Oakland, California. Levi smacked his lips and drew a deep breath. So were many other visitors to the Panhandle. Rachel would scold him for casting suspicions on a guest. He'd wait to mention Sims until after they spoke with Officer Haynes.

Chapter Ten

Chloe caved to Levi's insistence that she should ride with him. She allowed his help onto the front passenger seat, but unlike last night, she refused to sit with her back to him. Instead, she placed her right foot against the wheel well. Hopefully, the painkiller would soon kick in.

"Comfortable?"

"I'm fine." She pretended interest in the buildings as they drove to the medical center. *Ugh,* she should have stayed home.

"Hey, go easy on yourself. You've been through a lot. I appreciate your willingness to visit Rachel." He reached to touch her left arm.

His large fingers warmed her arm, but didn't prevent the regret from washing through her. How would she get through the visit with Rachel? As for dinner, she might still refuse his invitation.

"Hey," he said. "We'll get through this."

"Yes." *We.* She couldn't deny loving the idea of not facing the evening alone. She sighed. "Like my mom would say, "this too shall pass." At least, I hope it does."

He guided the large pickup into the hospital parking lot and parked near the back entrance. "Stay put and I'll help you inside."

"Really, I have the cane and—"

He slammed his door and rounded the hood.

"Okay, so I'll gracefully accept his help," she murmured before he opened the door.

He reached to help her to the blacktop.

She forced a smile. "Thank you." Even through her frustration over being a semi-invalid, his touch sent warmth and tingles over her neck and shoulders. As they moved toward the hospital entrance, he kept his muscled arm around her back. An urge to turn in his arms, and press her lips to his corded throat, almost overwhelmed her.

Reaching Rachel's room, they found her sitting up in the hospital bed, her dark, silky hair brushed to a sheen and lying over her left shoulder. Her right shoulder and arm were swathed in bandages and bound around her middle.

"Jacque, I'm so happy to see you." She puckered her lips and smiled at Levi. "You, too, Brother." She tilted her head, offering her check for Levi's kiss, and extended her left hand toward Chloe.

Chloe leaned past Levi and over the bedrail to squeeze Rachel's hand. "Oh, Rachel, you look so much better this evening. Scotty and I already miss you. The studio isn't the same." Her voice caught. Everything she'd built at the design business included Rachel. Emotion welled, and she started to withdraw from the bedside.

Rachel kept a firm hold on her hand. "Levi told me about your fall in the parking lot last night. My gosh, are you sure you should be walking around?"

Chloe swayed under the weight of guilt. "A sprained ankle is nothing compared to what you've been through. I wanted to call this afternoon, but I didn't want to interrupt the time with your parents." She gave Rachel's hand another squeeze before she withdrew. Her dear friend resembled a delicate, and beautiful, bird with a broken wing.

Rachel closed and opened her dark eyes. "No worries. My parents were here all day. Poor things, they're exhausted after the late-night drive from Missoula and from spending all day in this dreary hospital room."

Chloe hadn't expected this visit to be easy but— "I met with Janelle and Cain Meeker this morning. They're so sorry about your accident." She stumbled over the word *accident* when her brain yelled, attack! She cleared her throat. "They've agreed for me to handle the redesign." She held up a hand. "Just until you're able to take over. They're hoping you'll gradually work into overseeing the project. I'll do the heavy lifting."

Rachel harrumphed. "In your present state, you can't do any heavy lifting, but I get what you mean." She pressed her left palm to her forehead. "I completely forgot to call Janelle when I woke up this morning."

"Sis." Levi leaned over the bed railing. "Don't be hard on yourself. You're still feeling the effects of the anesthesia."

"Levi's right." Fighting a sudden wave of dizziness, Chloe grabbed at the railing. She didn't deserve any slack, but how long could she casually talk with Rachel without spewing the entire story? Months of lying hung like a dark cloud. As difficult as it was to maintain the ruse, Levi knowing the truth made it twice as hard. She glanced at the IV needle connected to Rachel's left hand and followed the tube to the clear bag suspended from the chrome stand.

Rachel caught her gaze. "Antibiotics for another couple of days. Once I finish the strong course, I should be able to go home."

Levi patted Rachel's uninjured shoulder. "I talked with Doc this afternoon. He recommends you move to a physical therapy facility for about a week. Give yourself a chance to gain some equilibrium and learn how to manage with one arm while your injuries heal. You'll need to be careful with your cracked ribs, too."

Rachel frowned. "Sounds like you and Doc have it all figured out. With all your arranging, have you learned anything new about the collision?" She pinned her brother with her dark gaze.

Chloe cringed at the emotions passing over Levi's face. They'd agreed to give Rachel time to gain strength before they told her Chloe's story. But Rachel was sharp and very perceptive. She might see through their plan.

Levi remained silent.

Chloe gripped the bed rail. "There's nothing new yet, but the police department, and the sheriff's office, have issued an All-Points Bulletin for the black truck." She tightened her grip on the railing. The investigation might crack open her web of lies. Her chest tightened. Rachel might not forgive her.

Levi patted Rachel's hand. "Right now, just focus on healing. After the physical therapy center, you could move to the ranch for a week, or however long you need. I'll hire in-home care."

Rachel smiled, and her dark eyes twinkled. "Speaking of the ranch, how are the vacationers doing?"

Levi shifted from one booted foot to the other. "Both parties have checked in." He glanced at Chloe and back at his sister. "The kids from Portland are excited to attend the mini-rodeo tomorrow night."

Rachel raised a dark brow. "So, you're over your uneasiness about having strangers on the ranch. What about the guy from California? Is he fitting in?"

Chloe flinched. Between the scare on Riverview Drive, and confessing all to Levi, she'd forgotten to resume the cut-off conversation about his guest from Oakland.

Levi tightened and released his lips. "He hasn't tried to fit in. Hasn't spent more than a few hours overnight at the ranch." He turned toward the tray table and grabbed the pink bakery box he'd carried in from the pickup. "By the way, Janice sent you a fresh cinnamon roll."

Rachel quirked her mouth into a smile so like her brother's. "Yum. Maybe I should start dinner with dessert. Please thank her for me. Hospital food doesn't compare with Janice's cooking." She glanced at Levi. "Speaking of dinner. I'm sure your usual Friday night dinner at Beverly's didn't happen last night. Are you going after you leave here?"

Levi slowly nodded. "I made reservations for six. Plenty of time to visit without wearing you out."

Rachel raised a brow. "Well, I hope you invited Jacque to join you. She's injured and probably not eating right."

Chloe chuckled and raised a hand. "Hey, I'm standing right here. Levi invited me, but I should go home and elevate my foot." She glanced down at her throbbing ankle that had swelled against the stretchy bandage.

Rachel shoved her mouth to one side. "Nice try, but I don't like the idea of you spending so much time alone. We still don't know why that man slammed into your car."

Chloe exchanged a glance with Levi.

He tightened his lips and shifted on his shiny cowboy boots.

She cringed. Oh, how she hated forcing him to lie to his sister. "Okay, Rachel, I'll have dinner with Levi, but only if you promise not to dwell on the collision. Officer Haynes will find the guy." And she intended to help him.

"Good to know. Gosh, I'm suddenly very tired." Rachel used the bed controls to lower her head a few inches and closed her eyes.

"No worries. Rest now, and we'll see you tomorrow." Chloe ran her fingertips over Rachel's dark hairline.

Levi leaned to press a kiss to his sister's forehead and tilted his head toward the doorway.

Careful not to bump into the tray table, Chloe hobbled toward the hallway. She stopped just outside the room and closed her eyes. Lying to Rachel had become doubly difficult.

As Levi drove to the resort, their conversation remained stilted.

Chloe gazed out the passenger window and tried not to cry.

When Levi pulled the truck in front of the hotel, he stopped under the portico and opened his window to greet the valet.

"Good evening, Mr. Banks. Having dinner

tonight?"

"Evening, Sean. Yes, dinner at Beverly's." He slid from the truck and rounded the hood to open Chloe's door.

Chloe raised a brow and pursed her lips. She'd known he frequently ate at the resort, but she hadn't expected him to use valet parking and to be on a first-name basis with the employees. So much she didn't know about Levi Banks.

He helped her from the high pickup seat and escorted her into the resort hotel and convention facility that towered over every other building in town.

After arriving in Coeur d'Alene, she'd stayed at the resort for three weeks and became familiar with the layout. Just inside the tall, brass-framed glass doors, she paused to turn west and catch the first brush of dusk over downtown. Shades of violet and gold hues touched the manicured landscaping surrounding the resort. In four months, she hadn't become immune to the beauty of the area.

Chloe gripped the cane handle and straightened her shoulders. Now, to get through the evening with Levi and later through her meeting with Officer Haynes. She hummed a sigh. Levi deserved an animated dinner companion. She'd already put him through the wringer.

Reaching the seventh-floor five-star restaurant, Chloe inhaled the mouthwatering aroma of grilled steaks and baked potatoes. Thank goodness, the soft background music covered the rumble of her stomach.

A hostess seated them at a table large enough for four but set for two.

Chloe settled into the upholstered chair facing the entrance and dragged her attention from the door to gaze through the bank of windows overlooking the stunning view of the lake, and the mountains. The bright-blue awning at the resort marina sat below.

As the attractive hostess handed them menus, and described the dinner specials, she lingered and tittered over Levi.

Chloe smirked and raised a brow. She couldn't blame the young woman for giving Levi Banks celebrity status. He looked stunning in his white dress shirt and black Western-cut slacks. Specifically—the way he filled out the clothing—more than one woman had looked twice. She pretended interest in the menu. First, her life was a mess, and second, she'd soon be leaving Idaho. Now wasn't the time to fall for a man who lived a completely different life.

****

Settling across the table from Chloe, Levi struggled to focus on the menu and not the frazzled, but beautiful, woman who'd reluctantly agreed to join him for dinner. Something about her drew him, and even her shocking story of murder and intrigue didn't dampen his growing feelings. Instead, her tenderness with Rachel, and the way she was willing to work all hours to help Rachel retain her clients, intensified his desire to hold her—yeah—and kiss her. For now, he needed to support Rachel's recovery, and protect Chloe. Wouldn't be easy to keep the truth from his perceptive sister.

He fiddled with the silverware lying on the dark-blue linen napkin. He also needed to protect his freshly healed heart. He didn't know everything about Chloe Austin, and should prepare himself for more shocks.

Right now, Chloe seemed lost in her thoughts. She gazed through the double-paned windows toward the lake and mountain views he never tired of seeing. Her full lips curved into a soft smile. Yeah, he needed to use caution when around this woman. Spending time with her could lead to heartache.

A server arrived with his usual wine choice.

Jacque-uh-Chloe agreed to have a glass and tasted the Washington State vintage.

Levi studied the glisten of red wine on her lips and awkwardly ordered the calamari appetizer.

Conversation became silted. The calamari arrived, and he used his salad fork to spear a piece of the lightly browned seafood. "Did you eat here often while you stayed in the hotel?"

Chloe hooked a calamari ring. "Once or twice, but I usually ate downstairs at The Dockside. Eating alone isn't as much fun." She bit into the crispy calamari and slowly chewed.

Levi exhaled through his lips. Her every movement and expression fascinated him. "After hearing your story, I'm curious about why you entered into a building lease when you plan to return to Sacramento?"

She set down her fork. "No matter how nice it was, after two weeks of living in the hotel, I had to do something, and Paul wouldn't okay my return." She shrugged. "I needed to be busy and creative."

"I get it." He sipped from his glass of wine and gathered his thoughts. "Every morning, I look forward to spending another day on the ranch. Watching the sun rise over the mountains and the river."

She lifted her glass and raised a brow. "Sounds lovely. Funny, but I pictured you as a beer drinker." She took a sip, then smiled.

"Are you typecasting me?" He chuckled and the

tension in his chest eased.

She laughed, and her teeth flashed white against her deep coral lipstick. "Guilty. Or maybe a preconception of a rancher, and former bull rider." She nodded. "Yes, Rachel has talked about your career." Setting the glass down, she waved a hand toward the windows.

Night had begun to fall, and the double-paned window turned into a mirror. Levi glanced from her to the window and back.

"This is all so new to me." Her tone lowered. "I was born and raised in a big city in the California desert. For a few years, I lived in San Diego near the ocean. I never dreamed of living in a smaller town, and never in the mountains of the Northwest." She shrugged and wiggled her narrow shoulders. "The beauty is awe-inspiring."

"Sometime soon, I'd like to hear more about your life." He tightened his lips, then released them and drank a gulp of wine. *Easy, boy*. He caught her gaze and sank into her jewel-green eyes, noticing how the candlelight caught the richness in her reddish-blonde hair.

She touched her hair, and her chest rose on a breath. "In a nutshell, my father left my mom and me on my eleventh birthday. Mom had to work two jobs and had little time for me. I know it tortured her, but she did what she had to." She shrugged a shoulder.

A fist-sized knot settled in Levi's chest. He couldn't imagine a man leaving his family. He ran his tongue over his teeth and searched for an appropriate response. "Your dad didn't support you and your mom?"

"No, but let's talk about you. What were your early rodeo days like?" She straightened her silverware.

He caught the way her hand trembled and respected her need to change the subject. "Early days in the rodeo are a struggle. Waiting for a rank bull and a bigger purse. Sleeping in my truck and driving all night to the next rodeo. Eating cheap food. Lucky for me, the right bulls came along and I had the determination to win."

"I doubt luck was involved." She fingered the stem of her wineglass. "I've only known you for a few months, but your current success didn't just happen." She smiled and raised a palm. "First of all, I can't imagine driving all over the country and sleeping in my vehicle." She leaned into the edge of the table and raised a hand to the side of her mouth. "Only my close friends know this, but before I drove to the Billings home in the Sierras, I'd never driven past the city limits."

"Really?" Levi couldn't keep his eyes from widening. He shook his head. "Wow, how did you get back to Sacramento after high school? How did you visit your parents?"

She pursed her lips. "I caught commuter flights. Driving to Coeur d'Alene—especially alone—gave me a sense of victory, although I'm still not comfortable with leaving town."

"Which explains why you haven't visited the Riverbanks Ranch." He fingered his napkin and resisted the urge to leave his chair to pull her into his arms— chase away her fears. Her mouth formed something between a grimace and a smile.

"Now we're talking about me again." She took a

gulp of wine. "Let's change the subject."

Entranced with the vision of Chloe Austin in the candlelight, Levi started when their dinners arrived— delivered by none other than, Chef Rianna Dakyn.

The tall white chef's hat sat at an angle on Rianna's dark hair, and the white jacket, buttoned from hem to collar, outlined her gentle curves.

With her long, dark hair and wide, dark eyes, Rianna reminded him of a well-known Welsh actor. Beautiful and somewhat exotic, her native Welsh accent blended with the Bostonian influence from her teen years. "Wow, what service." He smiled at the woman he'd met almost two years ago, right after she moved to Coeur d'Alene and visited the Riverbanks Ranch. She asked to rent one of his saddle horses, and he'd matched her with his sorrel mare, Daisy. She continued to ride on the ranch every week.

With practiced ease, Rianna placed Chloe's plate in front of her, then set Levi's larger platter, holding a sizzling steak, in front of him.

Levi inhaled the aroma of grilled meat and melting garlic butter and grinned. "Perfect. I've looked forward to this for days."

"Glad to hear." Rianna smiled. "When the server ordered a very rare rib eye, I knew it had to be for Levi Banks." Her smile disappeared. "Last night, you were caught up in Rachel's car accident. I'm so sorry. How is she tonight?"

The thought of what might have happened turned his stomach. "Thank you for asking. She's doing well, considering the force of the impact. It threw her against the center console of the car and broke her arm in three places. Broke some ribs, too. An orthopedic surgeon happened to be on duty at the hospital, and he immediately took her into surgery. It's a miracle she's doing so well."

Rianna raised a dark, perfectly arched brow. "And the other driver? Have they found him?" Her lips compressed. "I read this morning's front-page article describing the collision. There were photos, too. Thank goodness, Rachel drove a high-quality car."

Levi shook his head. "No sign of the other driver. He left the scene before the police arrived. Yeah, turned out to be a blessing that Rachel borrowed Jacque's car." He met Chloe's gaze. The only flaw lingering between them—she could have warned Rachel there might be danger.

"Oh!" Rianna angled toward Chloe. "I agree—Rachel's small economy car wouldn't have fared well". She held out a hand. "By the way, I'm Rianna Dakyn."

Chloe accepted the chef's gesture and smiled. "Jacque Taylor. Rachel works at my design studio." Her smile faded, and her green eyes watered.

Levi's breath caught. Dang, the situation couldn't be more complex or heartbreaking.

Rianna extended her other hand to cover Chloe's. "Oh, you must be in shock, too. We have a friend in common—Tracie Woodward. She raves about your talent." She glanced between Levi and Chloe. "Here I am keeping you from eating. Please, enjoy your dinner. Levi, I'll see you tomorrow night. I assume you'll still hold the rodeo?"

He picked up the steak knife. "The rodeo will go on. Rachel's doing well, and the students deserve to perform in front of an audience. Thanks to Riley, everything's on track."

"Like me, you have a great crew you can depend on." Rianna smiled. "Now, please enjoy and let us know if you need anything."

Levi cut into the juicy steak. The cinnamon roll he'd wolfed down before he left the ranch was long gone. "Sounds good. Thanks, Chef."

Chloe sliced into a large scallop and glanced toward the kitchen door and back. "Rianna's very nice."

Levi dipped the healthy bite into the meat juice escaping onto the white platter. "She's become a good friend and a regular at the ranch. Right after she moved from San Diego, we arranged a long-term lease on my mare, Daisy."

Chloe slowly chewed the scallop and caught his gaze. "Does anyone else rent a horse at the Riverbanks?"

"So far, just Rianna. Rachel's probably mentioned I'm not a fan of having strangers on the ranch." He caught her questioning look. "The rodeo is the exception. It's contained to the arena, and afterward, to the dining hall for refreshments."

"Did something happen to make you feel nervous?" She dipped a bite of scallop into the dish of melted butter.

Unaccustomed to sharing his motivations and deep thoughts, he paused and cut another bite of steak. "Nothing's happened yet, and I mean to keep it that way."

She continued to eat. "I gather the rodeo marks the end of a school session."

Levi set down his fork and took a sip of the Cabernet. "Yes, and it gives the students a chance to show off what they'd learned over the three-week-long session."

Chloe made the appropriate responses to his descriptions of the rodeo school. Surprised by how much he'd shared, he blinked at his plate, realizing he'd eaten every last bite of the steak.

Chloe set her fork crosswise on her plate. She'd eaten everything but a few bites of wild rice. She picked up her wine glass. "Caring about your students has helped build a successful business."

Levi patted his mouth with the blue napkin. "Have you ever attended a rodeo? If you're up to the drive and sitting on a hard bleacher, you're welcome to join us tomorrow night. We put on a decent show for a small venue." After learning her story, her reluctance to visit the ranch made more sense.

"My adopted dad loves horses, so he introduced me to riding. My best friend, Gina, has a family farm near Sacramento, and we ride English at least once a month. Rodeo has never been on my radar." She patted her mouth with her napkin and glanced toward the restaurant entrance.

Levi twisted and followed her glance. What was going through that beautiful head? He slowly straightened and gazed into her eyes. Had she visualized the horse farm, or some thug breaking into her home? His chest tightened. Yeah, she'd lied about her identity and her history, but he recognized a caring and honest person when he met one. She'd maintained the ruse to protect her friends. The collision had come out of nowhere. He captured his bottom lip between his teeth. Why did he have to fall for someone in a witness protection program? Lucy's life had been an open book.

Chloe tilted her head and gazed at him. "We have

another hour before our meeting with Carson."

Once again, the candlelight caught the jewel-like facets in her emerald eyes. Her direct gaze made him shift on the upholstered chair. Until he met Chloe Austin, he'd never encountered a woman so beautiful and intense. Levi cleared his throat and glanced at his watch. "How about coffee and dessert?" Several hours would pass before he reached the ranch.

Chapter Eleven

After the lovely candlelight dinner at Beverly's with Levi, Chloe entered her apartment like an injured Cinderella, hobbling back to her hearth. Her ankle, her head, and her heart ached.

Levi urged her to sit in the living room with her foot elevated while he let Scotty outside and refilled the dog's water and food dishes.

For once, she didn't object to the help. In less than an hour, they'd meet with Carson Haynes. She needed to push through. Levi's presence took the edge off her fears and helped her to relax.

The outer door closed.

Scotty trotted to her chair to gaze at her.

She reached down to pat his head. "You're such a good boy." Levi could be heard in the kitchen, but she couldn't bring herself to ask what he was doing.

"Hope you don't mind, I started the coffeemaker." He'd stepped into the living room. "Your apartment is nice." He ran his gaze over her furniture and wall art. "More armless chairs?"

Chloe sputtered a laugh. "Yes, they work great in small spaces."

He frowned and tilted his head.

She restrained another giggle. He reminded her of Scotty, when he tried to figure out what she meant. "With no chair arms, they don't obstruct the view of the room."

He slowly nodded. "Makes sense."

The coffeemaker made a final sound, and Chloe shifted to push from the chair. "I'll help. Do you take anything in your coffee?" She couldn't remember from the restaurant.

"Stay there. I've got it." Levi disappeared through the archway and returned, carrying a white mug and a red teacup with a saucer. He set the teacup on the small round table at her elbow.

"Wow, thank you." Chloe leaned toward the table to catch the scent of lavender. "You found my favorite tea."

Levi claimed the matching armless chair on the other end of the coffee table. "You mentioned avoiding caffeine late in the day, and I didn't see decaf coffee in the cupboard."

Chloe lifted the cup and saucer and took a sip. The relaxing scent of lavender filled her nostrils. "This is perfect."

"Shouldn't you ice your ankle?" He shifted to the edge of his chair.

She glanced at her bandaged ankle. "Probably, but I'd like to wait until Carson leaves."

Levi pushed into the chair and his black slacks stretched over his knees to accommodate his long, muscled thighs.

Chloe snapped her attention back to her teacup. "Seeing Rachel in the hospital bed, bandaged and hooked to monitors, made me want to run home and hide." Her chest tightened. They'd come so close to losing Rachel. "If I were you, I'd leave right now and never speak with me again."

Levi crossed a leg and rested his ankle on his knee. "No, you wouldn't. You care too much to abandon your friends. You've sacrificed a lot to protect them."

"When I carelessly took that file, I set off a deadly chain of events." She bobbed her head. "Now, Rachel's been caught in the middle." She drew a breath and shifted to set her cup and saucer on the table. With Levi, the words seemed to flow. If she wasn't careful, something more could develop between them, and that couldn't happen. When she learned of Drew King's arrest, she'd return to Sacramento

She repositioned her foot on the hassock. Pain shot through her ankle. OMG—what a bother! In the middle of a near tragedy, she'd stupidly injured herself.

Levi pushed from his chair. "Time for the ice pack."

She opened her mouth to object, then changed her mind.

After the sound of the freezer door opening and closing and water running, he returned with the ice pack and a glass of water. Levi leaned to place the water glass on the table.

Her senses hyperaware, Chloe caught the way his dark, late-evening whiskers dotted his firm jaw. Her fingertips tingled. Were his whiskers soft or bristly? She cleared her throat. "Thank you, but you really don't need to wait on me."

He crouched next to the hassock and gently unwrapped the stretchy bandage. "Yikes, looks painful." He lifted one corner of his mouth. "Should have brought my horse liniment."

"Ah, that might do the trick." She chuckled. "You're well practiced with injuries, both with man and beast."

"I've treated my share of sprains." He shrugged. "For the breaks, I normally call Doc Princeton."

The doorbell rang.

Levi stood and left the living room in four strides.

Uh-huh. She wouldn't blame him if he walked away. If she could, Chloe would avoid what she knew she had to do. Tell Carson everything.

Levi greeted Carson Haynes and provided him with coffee.

Chloe stayed seated, fighting the anxiety building in her chest. Would Carson understand the situation or blow her cover? She was about to take a huge chance.

The men entered the living room.

Chloe immediately noticed the wrinkles in Carson's khaki uniform and the red lines in his blue eyes. Both testified to a long day. His short, dark-blond hair retained the impression of his hatband.

"Sorry, I ran a bit late." He leaned in to shake her hand. "The fishing derby's in full swing. Brings a lot of new people to town." His gaze moved to Chloe's elevated ankle. "Ms. Taylor, looks like you had an accident."

She cringed from the use of her alias. Now that Levi knew the truth, she wanted to shout it from the rooftops. She'd have to be content with telling Carson. "A hasty misstep in three-inch heels. Please have a seat. I appreciate your willingness to meet tonight."

Carson lowered his tall frame to the short couch. "Do you have more information about the collision?"

She drew a deep breath and slowly released it. "Possibly." Fifteen minutes later, another person in Coeur d'Alene knew her full story and her real name.

Carson leaned into the couch and cocked a dark-blond eyebrow. "No wonder you were skittish last night at the hospital."

She ran a hand over her hair and discovered several strands had worked loose from the French knot, but for once, she didn't care about her appearance. "Last night, I couldn't think beyond how Rachel had been injured in an attack meant for me. After I discovered the flowers and read the note, I should have heeded the warning. Ordered Rachel to stay away until I'd figured things out. Detective DeMers disagreed, and he ordered me to maintain my alias." She retrieved her teacup and drank the cooling tea.

Officer Hayes cleared his throat. "Ms. Austin, in hindsight you must realize the safe house in Sacramento would have been the best solution."

She shifted to place her injured foot on the floor and set her cup and saucer on the coffee table. "Maybe it would have been simpler but not the best solution for me. In Coeur d'Alene, I've had a life. The Sacramento City police chief continues to block Paul's efforts to flush out the people who killed Hallie."

Carson frowned. "Detective DeMers shared the challenging politics in his office?"

She rested clenched hands on her lap. Her stomach roiled, and she wished she could successfully refill her teacup. "He's an old friend from college, and he understands how much I need to return to Sacramento."

Carson glanced over the living room. "I'll be right back." He left the apartment.

Chloe shifted to the edge of her chair. "Is he calling his precinct?"

"Breathe, Chloe. He'll be right back." Levi left the

room.

The front door opened and closed.

Chloe's heart raced. What if Carson was crooked?

Carson returned, carrying a small black suitcase. He set it on the coffee table and unlatched the lid. "Had I known your situation before we spoke, I would have first swept the building for listening devices." From the case, he withdrew a black plastic wand that resembled a cell phone on a selfie stick.

Chloe pushed from the chair and balanced on her uninjured foot. "Who could have had an opportunity to plant a bug in my building? Only Rachel—and an occasional client— have been inside, and then, only in the studio."

He maintained a steady gaze. "Whoever ordered the flowers knows where you live. We need to determine how they found you. If you don't mind, I'll start downstairs."

"No, um, yes, please, of course." Chloe grabbed her cane and hobbled into the kitchen. Her raw nerves twanged, and she relived the violation of discovering her apartment had been destroyed. Hearing footsteps running down the metal-grated fire escape. Finding her bedroom window open, the curtains fluttering in the evening breeze. She shivered and crossed her left hand to clutch her right shoulder. She couldn't go through that again.

Carson followed Levi and Scotty downstairs to the studio.

Chloe sat on a dining chair and clutched a fresh cup of hot tea Levi had provided. From the open stairwell door, she heard the murmur of voices.

Boot treads on the stairs, and Carson appeared first.

He lifted his chin toward the hallway. "Mind if I sweep your other rooms?"

"No, of course not." She cringed. Had she put her nightgown under her pillow? Well, too late to worry about the state of her bedroom, Levi and Carson were already there.

Scotty bounded from the hallway and gazed at her, tail wagging.

The knot in her chest eased. "Yes, boy. I see you're helping."

Carson and Levi emerged from the hallway.

"Well?" She pushed from the chair and wobbled between her good foot and the cane.

"Good news," Carson said. "No listening devices. Which means they found you another way."

Relieved her building hadn't been compromised, she slowly exhaled. "Levi, would you mind retrieving the emerald-green file from the bottom, left desk drawer in the studio?"

"Are you saying, you made a copy of the campaign file?" Carson's brows drew.

"I needed insurance, in case Bruce or someone accused me of leaving Hallie on the interstate." She tightened her hold on the cane and blinked against sudden tears. "Now, with Rachel in the hospital." She choked back a sob. "I'm sorry, I need to sit down."

Carson's expression cleared, and he took hold of her left arm to help her back into the living room. "I get it. I can't imagine being in your position."

Chloe sank into the turquoise upholstery and lifted both feet to the ottoman. She had to get a grip, or she'd start crying.

Levi returned with the file in hand. "Should I hand

this to Carson, or would you rather show him?"

She waved a hand. "Please, just give it to him."

Carson accepted the file folder, flipped it open and scanned the list of names. He glanced at her, his blue eyes intense. "I even recognize a few names from the national news." He released his lips with a smack. "My contact with the Sacramento County Sheriff's Department will help with the investigation."

Chloe gasped. "No! You can't bring anyone into this!"

"Trust me." He held her gaze. "He's an old friend, and he has no use for politics mixing with law enforcement. He'll be our asset in Sacramento County."

"But he's way too close to Drew King and Bruce Billings." She pressed a palm against her palpitating heart.

"The situation is too big for just me and DeMers." He lifted the file. "Speaking of which, I'll contact Detective DeMers tonight. Let him know I'm working this end of the case."

"Oh boy." She clutched at her scalp. "When he learns I've shared everything, Paul will blow a gasket." He'd probably call her immediately.

"I'll take photos of this." Carson laid the open file on the coffee table. "I might need to refer to other names."

"Uh—" She lurched off her chair. "Just the first page. That's all you'll need. The following pages contain very small contributions."

"Chloe, this is a shadow file." He raised a brow. "No matter how little the dollar amounts fall over the legal level, they're illegal." He raised a hand. "I'll stop with the first two pages." He snapped two photos and closed the folder. "I can't post an officer outside your building, but the chief will agree to an hourly patrol." He moved toward the archway and paused. "Until I find the weaponized pickups, I'd like you to stay somewhere else for a few days."

Chloe's ankle throbbed. She clutched the back of the armless chair. "Leave my home again?"

Carson raised his right palm. "You were forced to leave your apartment in Sacramento, but this move is only temporary."

"I've heard those words before." Unable to get warm, she hugged her body.

Carson glanced at Levi. "It's likely Rachel wasn't the intended victim of the crash and when they learn Chloe wasn't driving the car, they'll strike again."

Chloe rubbed her shoulders. *Time to trust*. Levi's words echoed through her mind. "Carson, before you leave, there's something more in the file I should share."

"Okay." Carson crossed his arms over the wrinkled front of his khaki uniform shirt.

She bit her lower lip and flipped the file open to page three. "Before the flowers arrived, I hadn't looked beyond page one. On this page is a man named William Mathers. He's owner and CEO of Mathers Engineering."

"I'm not familiar with that name." Carson slowly shook his head.

She drew a breath. "William Mathers is my biological father's name."

Carson's gaze didn't waver.

"You didn't mention that earlier." Levi lifted his dark brows. "That he's on the list."

Carson shifted his stance and planted his hands at his waist. "Does he normally back a candidate?"

She averted her gaze to the impressionist artwork she'd hung on the wall over the couch. A reprint of the famous water lilies painting and one of the few things she'd hauled from Sacramento. The rest of her belongings were stored in Gina's garage. "William Mathers left my mother and me on my eleventh birthday. I haven't heard from him since." She met Levi's steady gaze. Now, what did he think of her? She'd withheld important information.

"Thank you for sharing," Carson said. "Just because he's on the list doesn't mean he's part of the threat or knows about it. Is there somewhere you can stay for a few nights—where you're not alone?"

"No place other than the hotel, but they might not allow pets. I won't leave Scotty." Hollowed by fear and distrust, she'd bared her soul and risked her safety by letting two more people into the circle of trust—as Paul had called it. She decided not to mention the email she'd sent to her father.

Levi leaned against the framed archway, with one leg cocked. His amber gaze settled on her. "No one expects you to leave Scotty."

"If I'm gone, someone might break in." She moaned. "They would destroy everything. I've been down that road before."

Carson harrumphed. "If someone breaks in while you're here, then they won't stop at damaging your apartment. There's a safe house a few blocks from here. Please pack a bag, and I'll drive you and Scotty. Leave your rental in the garage."

She pushed away from the chair. "A safe house in

Coeur d'Alene?" The very kind of place she'd moved to Coeur d'Alene to avoid.

Levi lifted a hand. "Hey, why not follow me to the ranch tonight? You've never been there, but the house is large. You'll have privacy and the use of my office. I have the best high-speed Internet in the area. Scotty can have the run of the place."

She blinked hard. "Stay an hour from town?"

One corner of his mouth lifted. "We won't be alone. My housekeeper, Janice, lives in the house, and my parents will be there for a few more days. You won't compromise your reputation."

"Ha," she said. "I'm hardly worried about my virtue. It's just—I don't like being so far from my apartment—my studio. If someone broke in, I wouldn't know about it until I returned to a disaster." Her voice caught on a sob. Chloe didn't know how much longer she could keep her eyes open and her act together.

Carson cleared his throat. "I understand your concerns. At least once a day, the patrols will check the entrances and the windows. If something seems out of place, they'll call for backup."

Her breath caught. Once again, her life seemed to spin out of control. She pressed a palm to her chest. King, or at least his thugs, had closed in. Staying alone didn't thrill her, still… "Okay, I'll follow Levi to the ranch. But Monday morning, if nothing new has happened, I'll return to my home and my business."

Carson set his empty mug on the kitchen counter. "Good. That'll give me a couple of days to investigate, without worrying about your safety. I'll keep you updated, and please, if you learn anything, no matter how insignificant it seems, call me."

Levi cracked a smile that didn't reach his amber eyes. "If there is a threat, then we have plenty of armed men at the ranch. Not to mention, Janice and my mom are pretty tough ladies."

Chloe hobbled to the counter and the coffeemaker. "Carson, there's another cup of coffee, if you'd like it to go."

"Thanks, but barring the unexpected, I'm off duty for the night." Carson grabbed his hat off the hook next to the door. "So, are you good with following Levi to the ranch?"

Gripping the carafe handle, Chloe released a tension-filled sigh. "Yes, if it helps you with the investigation. I don't want to burden the police department or endanger an officer."

"Good," Carson said. "Call me if you hear from anyone, including from Sacramento."

"I will." She gripped the edge of the counter and turned to glance between the two men who'd listened to her story and hadn't seemed to judge her. "I appreciate you both."

Carson's mouth softened. "Right now, we don't know which piece of the puzzle will crack the case, so every bit of information matters."

"I'm sorry I didn't sound the alarm sooner." She met his blue gaze. "Rachel might not have been driving my car." She exhaled. "I promise to watch and listen."

"Speaking of Rachel." He placed a hand on the door handle. "Even though she wasn't the target, I'll alert the hospital administrator to a possible intruder." He raised a palm. "Just out of caution."

Chloe drew a sharp breath. "Last week, a virus hit my office computer. Rachel saved my files and helped tech support with an update. Could the malware have been planted by whoever found me?"

Carson lifted a broad shoulder. "We'll add it to the list. Since the threat has moved to my town, my department will spend the resources to find the perpetrators."

"Okay." Chloe grasped the handle of the rented cane. "I'll try to make your job easier."

Carson gave a quick nod. "You folks have a safe drive to the ranch. Lots of deer out this time of night." He left, and the apartment went silent.

Chloe's brain threatened to stop working. She fumbled with the coffeemaker.

Levi moved closer and filled a travel mug. "I'll accept that offer for a cup to go, unless you need it for the drive?"

She shook her head and breathed in his spicy scent. "No, I'll take a cup of tea."

"Do you need help packing for a couple of days?" Levi added cream to his coffee and closed the refrigerator.

Her strength fled. "If you could take Scotty's supplies to the rental car." The prospect of driving through the dark countryside, late at night, filled her with apprehension, but she had to deal with it.

Levi nodded. "Show me what Scotty needs, and once you're packed, I'll carry down your bags."

She pointed out Scotty's dishes and the cupboard where she kept his kibble. "His bed is in my room." She moved toward the hallway. "Wait. My neighbors, the Clarks. I should call them so they're aware I'm leaving for a few days." She returned to the dining room window and glanced across the street. "Their lights are still on."

"Not a bad idea. I take it you've socialized with them?" Levi set Scotty's dog food bag near the door.

"Casually, but they've been very nice since the day I moved here. Both Jim and Pam said to let them know if I ever need anything." She retrieved her phone from her pocket.

"Depending on their view of a police presence, you might want to tell them Haynes ordered a patrol." Levi opened the cupboard over the coffeemaker and took down another travel mug. "Do you want honey in your tea?"

She dialed the Clark's landline. "No sweetener, please."

Jim Clark answered and, without interruption, listened to her explanation for leaving her building. She shared about the close call on Riverview Drive and the collision that hospitalized Rachel.

"We're so sorry for your troubles." Pam Clark joined the conversation. "If we see anything suspicious, we'll call the police, then you."

Chloe ended the conversation and hobbled to her room to pack a few clothes and toiletries.

Levi tapped on her open bedroom door. "Hey, I'm ready to take your bags to the car."

She straightened from closing the carry-on-sized suitcase. "Thanks, Levi. If you weren't here, then I'd crawl into bed and probably sleep through a break-in."

"I doubt that, but I get it. Sometimes, a person feels like covering their head and closing out the world." He smiled softly and lifted her bags.

Struck by his perceptiveness, she tilted her head. "You sound like you've experienced times like this."

"Can't get out of this life without a few of those moments." He gave a quick nod and moved toward the door, her suitcase in hand. "Do you want to take the laptop on that small desk?"

"Oh!" She snapped out of analyzing him and turned off the bedroom light. "Yes, the laptop, my design files, and the shadow file."

"By the way..." Levi set her suitcase in the kitchen and returned to help pack her computer case. "I think you rented the largest vehicle on the lot."

She bobbed her head side to side. "Can you blame me? After what happened this afternoon, I'm glad I did." Her voice broke. "At least, I had the illusion of safety."

Levi's mouth went tight. "I'm glad you did, too."

Chloe blinked through tears of exhaustion and filled her computer bag. At least, she could pass the time working on the Meeker and Wakely files. Design work had always balanced her.

Chapter Twelve

Morning sunshine filtered through the blinds and into her temporary bedroom at the Riverbanks Ranch. Chloe stretched, and pain shot through her ankle—time to take her prescriptions. Grabbing her cell phone from the nightstand, she peered at the screen and blinked. Eight o'clock? *Wow*, she'd slept for a solid eight hours.

Scotty planted his paws on the edge of the fluffy white comforter and stared.

"Good morning, Scotty. We slept in, didn't we?"

She laid a hand on his head and, for a moment, closed her eyes. Last night, she'd followed the red taillights on Levi's truck like a storybook character following a trail of breadcrumbs. Driving to the ranch through the dark countryside had taken her completely out of her comfort zone—but she survived. The buildings, on either side of the large, graveled area, were shrouded in shadows cast by the tall yard light, but she'd been impressed with the sheer size of the barn and the ranch-style house.

Levi carried her belongings into the house without comment or question and showed her to this bedroom.

She swung her feet over the edge of the queen-sized sleigh bed and gingerly planted her injured foot on the bright-colored, wool runner rug. For a moment, she admired how the rug selection complemented the dark-stained, hickory plank floor. Whoever had decorated the home had known what they were doing. Rachel?

She wiggled her toes and moaned. The sprain hadn't miraculously healed overnight.

Scotty backed to the door and continued to stare.

She grabbed her cane from where she'd leaned it against the nightstand and pushed off the bed. Slipping into the same camel-colored cashmere slacks and coral silk blouse she'd worn yesterday, she glanced in the mirror. "Huh, probably too dressy for the ranch." She glanced at Scotty and nodded. "I agree. I'll wear the black T-shirt I packed."

Fully dressed, with her feet in a pair of slides to accommodate the stretchy bandage on her right ankle, she slipped from the bedroom and followed Scotty through the great room to the bank of French doors facing the backyard. This house didn't fit her picture of a ranch house. At a sprawling forty-five hundred square feet, Levi had spared no expense in the quality of the materials and furnishings.

Stepping outside into the chill of the morning, she closed the door and allowed Scotty to extend his leash to the max.

He reached the sprawling maple tree and sniffed the base of the trunk. Did he catch Duke's scent?

Duke, Levi's dog, had met them in the foyer last night. The white, Anatolian Shepherd and Great Pyrenees mix had appeared mellow from his wagging tail to his large brown eyes. He'd sniffed Scotty but in no way acted aggressive. After all her worry about having the large dog around Scotty, her boy turned out to be the aggressor.

He'd jumped and snarled at Duke, who blinked,

backed off, and ambled away.

Levi had assured her Scotty would adjust; he was being protective of his mistress.

Scotty gave a single bark and tugged on the leash.

"Hey, buddy. How about we take a walk after I find coffee?" She drew a breath of fresh-mown, grass-scented air and gazed over the lawn that sloped to the riverbank. She couldn't see the river from here, but a set of red Adirondack chairs near the bank caught her attention. How cool. Maybe later, she'd amble across the wide lawn and relax in one of those chairs.

Despite the fully exposed sun perched on the mountaintop, a chilly breeze moved over the river and sent goose bumps over her bare arms. She shivered. She'd forgotten to wear her cardigan. Even in May, with the afternoon temperatures reaching the mid-seventies, the mornings still held a chill.

Scotty continued to explore the length of the house and pulled her along.

Chloe grimaced. Her choice of footwear didn't help her navigate the cushiony surface of the short, thick grass.

They passed a smaller bank of windows, and Chloe tugged on the leash to glance inside. A large dining table and chairs dominated a room she had yet to see. Moving on, she passed a cross-buck style door with a multi-paned window. "Okay, Scotty, that's far enough."

Scotty had other ideas. He continued to the end of the house and stood at attention.

Chloe sighed. "Scotty, come. Let's go inside." She might be strict about drinking herbal tea in the afternoons, but in the mornings, she needed coffee.

He persisted with whatever had alerted him.

"Okay, I'll follow." Chloe reached the corner of the house, and there they were—the cottages. "Ah, Rachel's creations." Since they met, Rachel had urged her to visit the ranch, if for no other reason but to see the vacation guest cottages Levi had agreed to have built. Rachel had designed and overseen the building and furnishings. The cottages would give vacationing town, or city dwellers, the opportunity to experience a real working ranch.

A van sat in front of Cottage Two, but nothing was parked in front of Cottage One. She rested her shoulder against the cedar siding of the house. That's odd. Yesterday, when Levi called during her drive to the Meeker home, he'd mentioned the first renter had arrived the night before. Then, the renter came from Oakland. That was when the connection ended along with her calm.

With the memory, her stomach fluttered. That's right—his guest came from Oakland. So much had happened, she'd forgotten to ask for details. Did the guest drive a silver pickup? Had he been sent to deal with her? A chill went deeper than the morning temperature. Last night, she'd only seen a large, shadow-enshrouded vehicle. Okay, logically, why would someone sent to silence her stay an hour from town?

She tugged on Scotty's leash and retracted the length to a few feet. Time to go inside. Entering through the cross-buck pattern door, she closed the door and took in the long, narrow room. Cabinets stretched to her left, and to her right, open shelves held glass jars of dried beans and baking ingredients. A washer and dryer combo sat at the far end. Through the open doorway ahead, the soft hum of a woman's voice, and the aroma of fresh coffee, drew her. She'd never met Levi's housekeeper, Janice, but Rachel mentioned her often and always in glowing terms.

"There you are." Janice paused in front of the commercial-sized, stainless range and wiped her hands on the bright floral-patterned apron protecting her jeans and blue T-shirt.

With her tall, slender form and youthful appearance, she defied Chloe's image of a ranch cook.

Janice's pretty face broke out into a warm smile. "You must be Jacque. How'd you sleep?"

Chloe smiled. She'd done it again and had typecast Janice, just like she had with Levi. "I am Jacque, and I slept well, thank you. Where is everyone?"

Using a large wooden spoon, Janice gave the contents of a large bowl a quick beating action and chuckled. "Everyone's been up since daylight. Levi's parents left about an hour ago to visit Rachel. Levi's outside, doing his usual day of rodeo chores. How about a cup of coffee and breakfast?"

Chloe drew a breath of mixed aromas, and her stomach growled. "I don't usually eat this early, but the coffee smells heavenly." She motioned to Scotty, who sat near her feet. "If this guy hadn't awakened me, who knows how long I'd have slept."

Janice nodded. "You were exhausted. Please, help yourself to coffee. There's a clean mug near the coffeemaker and fresh cream in the fridge door."

Chloe grabbed the large white mug and filled it with the fragrant brew. She took a sip and sighed. "Ah, this is great."

Janice chuckled and continued with her food

preparations. "Roasted at one of those fancy coffee roasters in town. How about eggs and bacon?"

"Uh, maybe just toast?" Chloe wrapped her fingers around the mug and hobbled toward the large, pine table with eight chairs.

"I just took blueberry muffins from the oven. How does that sound?"

Chloe's stomach growled again. "Sounds heavenly. Point me in the right direction and I'll wait on myself."

"No need for that. You've got your hands full just walking around." Janice transferred a large muffin to a saucer and placed the plate and a dish of creamy butter on the pine table. "Levi told us about your injury. How's your ankle feeling this morning?"

Us? Janice was a force to be reckoned with, and Chloe immediately liked her. She assumed she meant he'd told his parents, too. She sank to a chair and lifted her right foot to the under-table support. "A sound night's sleep helped, but the swelling persists. I should grab the medications from my room." She sipped her coffee and peeled the paper cup from the muffin. With her first bite, fresh blueberries exploded against her taste buds. "Ah, the muffin is amazing."

Janice topped off her mug. "Good to get something on your stomach before you take medication."

Chloe smiled her thanks and ate every bite of the muffin. "Janice, that was delicious." She wiped her fingers on a gingham-checked napkin. "You're an amazing baker, and your kitchen is spectacular. You must enjoy working here."

Janice spooned cookie dough onto the large baking sheet. "Between you and me, Levi was a mess when Rachel insisted, he hire me and Riley. I had my misgivings, but turns out, there's no better place to work or a better boss."

Chloe bit at the inside of her lower lip. A mess? Levi Banks remained a complex man.

"Levi probably mentioned the rodeo tonight?" Janice slipped the baking sheet into the oven.

"He did." Chloe half nodded.

"Well, most of the students will leave right after the rodeo, but a few stragglers will spend another night. Have you met Fiona Carmichael? She's the sous chef at Beverly's, and she's building a catering business. Levi insisted on hiring her to help with the rodeo food prep. He's convinced I'm working too hard."

Chloe pushed from the chair and hobbled to the sink. She rinsed her cup and set it on the drainboard. "I haven't met Fiona, but Levi's probably right. You have a lot on your plate with your regular schedule. He mentioned at least fifty people will attend tonight."

Janice straightened from setting the oven timer and wiped her hands on a white dish towel. "Won't be long, and he'll have to either cap the invitations or build another set of bleachers." She set the towel on the granite countertop and propped her hands on her waist. "Levi said you were almost forced off Riverview Drive yesterday. Sounds like you've had a scary time."

Chloe swallowed hard, clutched the handle of her cane, and gripped the edge of the countertop with her free hand. Okay… "What else did he say?"

"Enough to let us know you're in danger." One dark-blonde brow lifted. "He had to say something, because Levi Banks doesn't bring women home, let alone, late at night." Her mouth tightened. "He also said the driver might have been the same one who slammed into Rachel." She shook her head. "The police need to find that man, and soon."

"I agree, they do." Chloe's mind spun. She glanced at the coffee cup she'd set on the counter. Oh yeah, her pills. "May I have a glass of water?"

"Of course." Janice took a tall glass from the cupboard. "How about I watch Scotty while you go take your medications?"

"Thank you." A measure of tension escaped her tight chest. "Scotty, I'll be right back." She secured the handle of his leash under a chair leg.

"In case you're worried about him hurting anything— don't. He can be off the leash in the house, and even outside." Janice returned to her baking.

Chloe paused in the archway that opened into the front foyer, where last night, she'd entered the house. The kitchen seemed to have been added onto the main house. Had Levi done that, or some previous owner? She continued through the great room and down the hallway to her door. After swallowing an antibiotic, an anti-inflammatory, and a pain pill, she returned to the kitchen and retrieved Scotty's leash. "Thanks so much, Janice. Do you know where I might find Levi?"

"Maybe in the large barn—beyond the dining hall—or the arena. Mornings are busy on the ranch, especially on rodeo day." Janice washed her baking dishes in the farm-style sink. "He'll be happy to see you, that is, if you want to wander out there."

Chloe glanced at Scotty, who had found a bone. "Scotty has made himself at home."

"He's just fine, and Rachel will be, too. She's an amazing young woman." Janice dried her hands on a blue towel and turned to motion toward Chloe's feet.

"And you, young lady. Take it easy on that ankle."

Janice radiated comfort and warmth. Chloe debated whether to find Levi or hang out in the cozy kitchen with Janice. "Did Levi tell you I tripped over a curb?"

Janice puckered her lips. "Don't be so hard on yourself. You've had a lot on your mind. Now, why don't you leave Scotty with me while you find Levi? He's welcome to some of Duke's wet food."

"Oh, my gosh. I went to my room and forgot to grab his kibble."

"No worries. He'll enjoy a change."

"Well, thank you." Chloe conceded and turned toward the door facing the front yard.

"Wait, you should slip on one of my flannel shirts." Janice grabbed a green plaid flannel shirt from the row of hooks. "Doesn't exactly match your outfit, but it'll keep you warm."

Chloe slipped on the worn, cozy flannel. "Thank you. You're so kind." She glanced back at Scotty, who didn't seem concerned with her movements, and opened the door. Sunshine flooded the graveled ranch yard that separated the house from the large building Rachel had turned into a dining hall. A patio ran the length of the house, with first the main entrance, then another door toward the far end of the house. She angled the rubber tip of her cane against the natural slate tiles and stepped onto the gravel surface.

A breeze traveled around the end of the kitchen, and Chloe snugged the flannel shirt closer.

Later, after Chloe asked Levi about the renter from Oakland, she'd like to tour Rachel's creation. Following the sounds of cheers and groans, she passed the dining hall and reached a fenced area with a cross-buck pattern gate. Beyond the gate stood a multi-row set of bleachers. To her right stood the arena.

Cowboys on foot lined the outside of a split-rail fence. Jean-covered-backsides, work shirts, in either blue chambray or khaki, covered broad shoulders. Western hats were pushed to the backs of their heads to open the view of the action in the arena. Most rested one booted foot on the bottom fence rail and arms stretched across the top rail.

A particular cowboy stood out in the crowd.

She drew a breath, gripped her cane handle, and took another step. A twinge of pain reminded her to take it slow. She paused for the pain to ease and continued toward Levi's broad shoulders, tapered waist, and narrow hips. His wash-worn jeans stretched across his, uh, rather perfectly shaped, backside. A few feet away, she cleared her throat.

But right then, a cowboy riding a bucking, twisting horse shot from the corral to the right of the arena. He gripped the reins with one hand and the saddle horn with the other. Somehow, probably by pure determination, he stayed on board.

The cowboys along the fence cheered and waved their hats, which seemed to increase the horse's ire. Others whistled and yelled encouragement.

Crazy! "You're not in downtown Sacramento anymore." She murmured the comment, but she could have yelled, and no one would have heard her.

A loud buzzer sounded.

Chloe jumped and grimaced. Not a smart move!

Another cowboy rode horseback into the arena and grabbed the bucking horse's bridle, while the rider slid off in a poof of dust and scrambled out of range of the flying hooves.

She glanced at Levi, and her breath hitched. When had she become so hyperaware of this man? Oh, yeah, since about a month ago, when he stopped to visit Rachel at the studio, and something sort of clicked between them. She'd attributed the reaction to homesickness for Sacramento and her friends, but she had to admit a chemistry existed between them. For now, she had specific questions and needed answers.

Another cowboy standing next to Levi lifted his chin and smiled.

Chloe returned the smile. Was he one of the ranch hands or a student?

The cowboy tapped Levi's shoulder.

Levi pivoted away from the fence and planted his other boot on the dusty ground, his gaze centering on her.

She sucked in a breath, and her throat filled with brown dust. She coughed. *Ugh*. After this adventure, she'd need a shower.

Levi left the fence.

The backdrop of cowboys mastering the beasts faded into the background. Like she'd become part of an old Western movie, where the heroine finally works up the courage to approach the hero. She cleared the dust and emotion from her throat. Gina would love this place, but Chloe felt completely out of her element.

Levi closed the distance and took hold of her left arm. "I'm surprised you're willing to tangle with the corral dust. "Let's step into the dining hall where we can hear each other."

Without comment, Chloe allowed him to guide her from the arena and through the back-facing double doors into Rachel's dining hall. The cacophony of cheering cowboys dimmed. She turned to face him. "Remember yesterday when you mentioned your renter, and then, we were cut off? Levi, what kind of vehicle does he drive?" She clasped his arm and held his amber-brown gaze.

He rolled his lips. "Keep in mind, until last night, I hadn't been here when he was. We haven't met in person." He paused. "According to Riley, he rented a silver, half-ton pickup."

Chloe released her hold on his arm and took a step backward. She opened and closed her mouth. "Your renter from Oakland is driving a silver pickup?" She struggled to draw a breath. "Since he rented it at the airport, I assume the truck has Washington plates."

"Yeah, most likely. Like I said, I haven't met him or seen the truck." He planted his hands on his hips.

"What is his name?" Chloe's chest tightened with anticipation.

"Gary Sims." Levi tapped his hat back with one knuckle.

"Gary Sims?" The plank floor seemed to buckle under her feet.

He frowned and clasped her elbow. "Do you recognize the name?"

Chloe tugged from his grasp and swayed. She tightened her grip on the cane handle. "With blood-chilling clarity. Gary Sims and his brother, David, own Bay City Investigations in Oakland, California. His company ordered the flowers and the message. Oh. My. Gosh. Last night, I slept next door to him." Her mind raced. "This morning, he would have seen my rental car. Is that why he left so early? He recognized the car and left to—what? Search my apartment?"

Levi cupped her elbows with both hands. "Hold on and stop jumping to conclusions."

"Jumping to conclusions?" Her vision blurred. "They destroyed my home in Sacramento! They killed Hallie, and they could have killed Rachel!"

"Breathe, Chloe. Right after I met with Riley this morning, I called Carson with the description of the pickup. He alerted city and county law enforcement." He paused. "Wish I'd known the PI's name last night. I would've pounded on the cabin door and demanded answers."

"I thought I mentioned his name." She moaned. The walls of the dining hall seemed to close in. "He might have been in the area since Wednesday."

Levi removed his hat and tapped it against the side of his leg. "Maybe, or he ordered the flowers before he made the trip. He reserved the cabin on Monday." He clamped a hand on the back of his neck. "Look, I'll call Carson with the update."

Chloe grabbed the back of a chair and fought dizziness. They could be so close to finding the thugs who tried to silence her.

Chapter Thirteen

Chloe sank to the hard surface of the ladder-back chair and grabbed her leg just above her knee to lift her injured foot from the plank floor.

"Carson, Levi Banks calling." He held her gaze. "We have vital new information. The PI who ordered the flowers is Gary Sims. Gary Sims is the ranch guest in Cabin One." A pause. "I agree. Too much to be a coincidence."

Chloe's mind raced. At least, she wasn't alone in her apartment—running to the window every time someone drove by. Levi and Carson would help find the thugs. If only she'd responded to the floral delivery. If only she'd confronted Bruce Billings—forced him to confess to Hallie's death—confess to harassing her. She ran her palms over her hair. Maybe Rachel wouldn't have been in the collision.

Levi ended the call and closed his flip phone. "I need coffee. How about we stop in the kitchen on our way to my office?"

Chloe pushed off the chair. "Do your guests download an app to check in and out?"

He nodded. "We'll review the reservation software in case he checked out after he left."

"My thought exactly." She blinked and forced air through her tight chest.

Levi again cupped her elbow and guided her

toward the front-facing doors.

She felt like a bubble-headed invalid, but she'd accept all the help she could get. Inside the kitchen, the cozy, domestic scene eased her tension just a hair.

"Ready for coffee and a cinnamon roll?" Up to her elbows making bread, Janice glanced up with raised brows.

"Coffee, for sure." Levi headed for the coffee maker. "Cinnamon rolls won't hurt, either. Coffee, Jacque? Or tea?"

"Coffee, please." She sank to a kitchen chair and elevated her foot.

Levi set a white mug holding steaming coffee in front of her and carried his cup to a small desk next to the kitchen doorway to the pantry. He opened a laptop. "Janice, I suspect Sims checked out a day early."

"Nothing would surprise me about that man." Janice washed her hands and then dished out two cinnamon rolls. "He didn't eat one meal at the ranch. Why even stay here?"

"That's part of what we need to figure out." Levi's fingers flew over the keyboard. "Yep, he checked out about an hour ago. What time do you estimate he left?"

"No estimating needed. Startled me when I heard his truck engine start at five o'clock." She carried a jar of cream to the table and added a generous dollop to Chloe's cup.

Levi opened his flip phone. "I'll call Carson again, then we'll use my office to research Mr. Sims."

Chloe's thoughts ran wild. "Levi." She leaned against the table. "Please tell Carson, someone needs to check my apartment. Gary might have broken in."

The phone still pressed against his ear, Levi lifted a

brow. "Carson, hold on. Uh, Jacque's worried about her building." He touched the speaker button.

"Jacque, don't even think about going home today." Carson's response came through loud and clear. "A patrol drove by at five and again at seven. No sign of disturbance was reported, but I'll check your windows and doors."

"I brought the file to the ranch." The coffee churned in her stomach.

"Carson, while you check on Jacque's building, we'll search the cabin Sims occupied. He might have been careless and left something."

"Good idea," Carson said. "Keep me posted, and I'll do the same. Jacque, could you text me your key code? You can change it later." Carson disconnected.

She patted the side pocket of her slacks. "I left my phone in the bedroom. Levi, could you please text Carson, nine-one-one-nine?"

Scotty nudged her leg.

Chloe glanced at her dog and found her breath. Since adopting Scotty, she'd gained a better understanding of people who had service dogs. His presence and simple appreciation for life helped calm her. Even during the harrowing event on Riverview Drive that could have killed them both. She leaned down to pat his back. "You're such a good boy." She still couldn't believe his aggression toward Duke last night.

"He can go outside with us. He and Duke have worked things out." Levi left the desk and stood in the doorway. "Janice, while we're in Cabin One, we'll grab the linens and trash."

"Thank you." Janice transferred their coffees and

cinnamon rolls to a tray. "When you return, I'll reheat your coffee in the microwave."

"Thank you." Chloe's heartstrings tugged at her thoughtfulness. She pushed from the chair and hobbled toward Levi. She sincerely hoped this situation didn't stop his willingness to rent the tiny guest homes.

Levi patted his leg to get Scotty's attention. "We won't need the leash—he'll stay with us."

Chloe pursed her lips and stifled an objection. She followed Levi out the back door and over the route she and Scotty had taken a short time ago. Gosh—it seemed like hours ago when she took her dog outside. At the steps to the small front porch, she gripped the railing and maneuvered to the top. They needed to find something to connect Gary Sims with the flowers and anything else he'd done while in the area.

Levi opened the front door and waited for her to precede him.

She entered, then paused to take in the artfully furnished living space and how a bar separated the living room from the kitchen, yet allowed a spacious impression. The plans and photos hadn't done the cottage justice. "This is adorable!" She continued toward the bar and placed her hand on the cool, smooth granite countertop.

The hint of a smile touched Levi's lips. "Rachel did an awesome job."

Chloe read the conflict in the set of his mouth and the pain in his eyes. He didn't want to disappoint his sister by closing the vacation rental business.

"I'll check the bedroom and bathroom and grab the linens. Could you look around in here?" He disappeared into a room off the short hall.

"Sure." She ignored the discomfort in her right ankle and moved the short couch and coordinating chair from the walls. Nothing under or behind them. She opened the narrow door to a small coat closet. Empty. Next, to search the kitchen cabinets. She rounded the granite-topped bar and reached over the sink.

Levi returned and dropped the armful of sheets and towels on the polished wood floor near the back door. "Did you check the trash baskets? There's one under the bar and a rubber kitchen trash container under the sink."

She started with the kitchen garbage. The lavender scent of the trash liner barely masked the smells of the discarded coffee grounds and fast-food wrappers. In a drawer, she found a flat box of new dishwashing gloves. She slipped them on and pawed through the garbage. "Well, there's nothing unusual in here. I'll pull the bag so we can take it out."

"I'll add it to the bathroom trash." He took the bag and tied the top.

Chloe moved to the bar and the woven basket trash receptacle. "He used this basket for crumpled papers." Her heart seemed to skip a beat. She removed the rubber gloves and laid them on the counter. Smoothing a piece of white, glossy thermal paper on the bar, she gasped. "Car rental paperwork! Levi, the dates show he rented the truck on Wednesday."

Levi moved closer to look over her shoulder. "He lied about his arrival date."

"I'm not surprised. The man's here on false pretenses." She wove on her uninjured foot. "This means he arrived shortly after the flowers were delivered."

"And before the black truck hit Rachel."

Levi's voice rumbled from over her right shoulder. Chloe turned and met his gaze. He stood so close, she had to steel herself not to step into his arms and bury her face against his broad shoulder. "We've confirmed his arrival date and the color of his pickup. Could he have rented a second truck? A black one?"

Levi's chest rose and fell, lifting the dusty chambray of his shirt. "The man has a lot to answer for. Let's look at the yellow paper."

She unfolded and smoothed it against the countertop. Handwritten notes leaped off the page. Her head went light. "He wrote my real name and my alias." She gasped. "He added—*turn up the heat*. Wait, what's this at the bottom? *Call Joss*." She gripped the edge of the counter. "Who's Joss?" She traced the name with the tip of her coral-polished fingernail.

Levi clicked his tongue. "Another mystery to solve, but for now, we know when Gary arrived in Spokane and that he rented a silver truck." He pointed at the make and model on the paperwork. "Does this description match the truck on Riverview?"

"I didn't notice the brand. It was about the size of my SUV and had Washington state plates. Why didn't he knock on my door and simply ask me to call Bruce? Cut the drama? We should update Carson."

Levi accessed his flip phone and found Carson's recent call. He touched her arm. "Are you okay?"

She pivoted on her uninjured foot. "We've confirmed Sims is our man, but truthfully, I'm even more freaked out."

Levi called Carson and updated him on their finds. "Yeah, I'll look into that." He disconnected and caught her gaze. "Carson's at your building. He'll text after he finishes a walk-through."

"We might be close to solving everything." Her body seemed to deflate.

Levi touched her arm. "Let's head to my office and research car dealership sites. You might see a model that matches the pickup on Riverview." He pointed at the car rental agreement. "Carson asked that we seal these in a plastic food storage bag. Preserve the fingerprints." He reached to open an upper cabinet and retrieved a blue box of gallon-sized bags. Using his thumb and forefinger, he slipped both papers into the clear bag. "While we're online, we'll search for men named Joss."

Chloe clutched her cane. "I'll carry the trash bags if you grab the linens."

Levi nodded and gathered the used linens. He opened the narrow set of French doors and stepped onto the back deck.

Chloe followed and paused to take one more glance at the darling cottage. "Later, I hope to tour when I'm not so distracted."

"You bet." Levi smiled softly.

She navigated the two steps and hobbled to the back kitchen door.

Inside the pantry slash utility room, Levi deposited the linens into a tall laundry container and the trash bag she'd carried into a large rubber garbage can in the corner. "Let's grab the coffee tray on our way to my office."

Janice paused from slicing onions and dabbed her tearing eyes with the hem of her apron. "Okay, what did you find?"

Levi stuck their coffee mugs in the microwave and set the time.

Chloe took the lead. "For one, Gary's car rental paperwork. He arrived on Wednesday, not Friday." She shook her head. "Besides ordering a floral arrangement with a threatening note to be delivered to my doorstep, we don't know his motivation." She swallowed hard. "We'll research truck models online in hope of jarring my memory of the truck on Riverview Drive."

Janice touched her throat. "Yikes. To think our cabin guest meant to hurt you."

The microwave beeped.

"We don't know that for sure." Levi removed the mugs and set them on the tray with the small plates holding cinnamon rolls. "Could be a long shot, but if Jacque recognizes the make and model of the truck, we'll confirm or eliminate Gary as the driver." He lifted the tray and headed toward the archway. "Thanks, Janice. We'll keep you posted."

Chloe took a step to follow, and pain radiated through her ankle. "Uh, Levi, I'll be right there. Janice, do you have an ice pack I can use? I forgot to stick mine in the freezer."

"You bet." Janice hurried into the pantry. "Have a seat while I grab one."

Levi paused. "When you're ready, the office is at the end of the hall."

Scotty glanced between them, then followed Levi.

Chloe raised a brow. So, her dog now included Levi in his every move.

Janice returned with a moldable ice pack and handed it to Chloe. "Hasn't the pain medication kicked in?"

"It helped, but the ice will do the trick. Thank you." Chloe blew a breath of frustration. She didn't like asking for help. She left the kitchen and hobbled through the great room to the hallway. She'd never seen a house with so many doors and outside entrances. Later, she'd explore, but for now, she needed to catch up with Levi. She detoured into her bedroom and grabbed her laptop case.

Scotty had made himself at home in the office and stretched out on a Native American-patterned rug, in front of the gas fireplace. A small blue flame flickered just enough to take the chill off the morning air.

Levi stood behind a long, walnut-stained desk, transferring paperwork from the slightly distressed desktop to one end of a matching credenza. He'd set their coffee break tray on the other end. "Make yourself at home. Rachel uses that space when she's here." He pointed toward a smaller office chair pulled into the opposite end of the desk.

Chloe set her laptop in the designated space and gave the rest of the room a scan from her designer's perspective. Cozy, with a very masculine flavor.

Facing the fireplace sat two nutmeg-brown, leather upholstered chairs that bracketed a short, walnut-finished cabinet. A coffee table, made from a two-inch-thick piece of hickory, rested on a black, wrought-iron frame. Rustic yet modern with the high-gloss epoxy surface.

She sank to the office chair and twisted to study the painting on the wall above the credenza. Framed in weathered barnwood, the Western setting included towering Saguaro cactus, which placed it somewhere in the Sonoran Desert of Arizona. A herd of horses raced across the canvas. She turned back to her laptop.

Levi had taken his chair and glanced at her before he typed on the white, wireless keyboard, paired with the freestanding computer screen. "Comfortable?" He moved the mouse and clicked on a site.

"Very. Your home is beautiful." Chloe drew a breath and powered up her laptop. She wasn't here to admire the ranch or this appealing and complex man. "What's your Wi-Fi log on?"

"Dukesdomain, all smalls with no spaces." His attention remained fixed to the screen.

She smiled. "Cute. What are you looking at?"

"Gary's photo on the investigation business site. Just to be certain, I'll ask Janice to come take a look. Remember, I didn't meet him in person." Levi reached for the receiver of the black plastic landline phone on his desk.

Chloe gazed at his strong profile. "You don't need to keep reminding me, I believe you. But speaking of Janice—she mentioned you told her and your folks about Riverview Drive. How much more did you share?"

He met her gaze. "That a powerful businessman in Sacramento sent thugs to intimidate you." His lips tightened. "Rachel got caught in the middle." His broad chest rose and fell. "Shouldn't be long, and you'll be able to share everything."

Her stomach dropped with the prospect of meeting his parents. Under different circumstances, she'd love to meet them, just not after they'd spent the day, heck, the past two days, at their daughter's hospital bedside. Not to mention, the grueling, four-hour drive from Missoula. She nodded. "I understand, you had to say something." She huffed a laugh. "Janice made it clear—Levi Banks doesn't bring women to the ranch."

He harrumphed and picked up the receiver. "Janice, do you have time to look at something on my computer? Great, thanks." He set the receiver on the cradle.

Chloe smiled. "An intercom system?"

His mouth tilted. "A real, live landline. The cell reception can be sketchy, and we use it to communicate between buildings on the ranch."

"A sure thing, right?" She chuckled, grateful for the levity. "It's quite the collector piece." She woke her laptop and opened a browser. "While we wait for Janice to ID Gary, I'll search for Joss." Her search turned up a short list of men named, *Joss.* She filtered the search by adding, *Bay Area.* "Cool, here's Joss Whedon, the movie producer."

Levi rolled his chair toward hers and leaned close to read the screen. He blinked twice and opened the top desk drawer to grab a pair of readers.

His fresh, spicy, masculine scent, mixed with horse and dust, drew her. She angled her laptop to better share her screen.

"Oh, yeah." He chuckled. "*Firefly.* Last winter, Rachel and I binge-watched all the seasons."

Chloe raised her brows. The tough cowboy wore cheaters and liked fantasy sci-fi movies. In some way, it made him even more appealing. In contrast with the short fur of whiskers on his jawline, the light-gray plastic frames perched on the bridge of his very masculine nose gave him a studious look. *Huh.* He hadn't shaved that morning.

She drew a sharp breath and wished she hadn't

when another whiff of his oh-so-appealing scent raided her senses. *Back off, Austin. This isn't the time or place for romance.* She averted her gaze from the potently handsome man and noticed a tall curio cabinet just inside the hallway door. The wood-framed glass doors showed off a collection of belt buckles, pairs of shiny spurs, and various trophies.

She left the desk and hobbled to the cabinet. "Are these your awards? Rachel mentioned you had a very successful rodeo career." She glanced over her shoulder and caught a tight smile overlaid with humility and pride.

"Yeah, just a few to show the students if they work hard and stay focused, they can go far. At least earn a trophy or two."

"Or ten or twenty." She read the plaque on the statue of a cowboy riding a bucking, twisting, bull. "Impressive. Did you choose to retire while you were at the top of your game?" She turned to catch his amber gaze.

For a moment, he remained silent. "Reality hit when a rank bull threw a close friend against the fence. My friend ended up in a wheelchair. Disability didn't mesh with my plans to own a ranch. Open a rodeo school. Raise a bit of rough stock and teach others how to avoid injury." He shrugged. "As a rodeo cowboy, you can't completely avoid injury, but learning the right techniques is crucial."

She took in the way his chambray shirt fit his broad shoulders. How he always rolled the long sleeves to just below his elbows, exposing tanned forearms. She cleared her throat and hobbled back to the desk. "Well, you have a right to be proud of your accomplishments."

He tapped the tip of his index finger on the desktop next to his keyboard. "So do you. In two months, you've made a name for yourself in Coeur d'Alene. Rachel praises your work and your business sense."

"A name for Jacque Taylor." She grimaced and woke up her laptop. "Rachel is very generous with her praise, but I have to credit my client, Tracie Woodward. By happenstance, we met at the coffee shop and immediately clicked. She's a California transplant with ambition and money. She hired me to help with her primary residence remodel, and now, I'm redesigning her new investment." She moaned. "Had I known so many of the residents of Coeur d'Alene moved from California, I might not have chosen this area to lay low." She huffed a breath. "Wednesday, Tracie announced she'd shared my name with an acquaintance from the Bay Area."

"Maybe Coeur d'Alene chose you." Levi raised a corner of his mouth. "At least a newcomer doesn't stick out." He lifted his mug and drained the contents. "Hey, you haven't touched your coffee or cinnamon roll."

"I had two cups before I went outside to find you." She fingered the handle on her heavy, white mug. "I also ate a fresh muffin."

"So, it's teatime?" He grinned.

Janice sailed into the room, her apron still tied snugly around her trim waist. "What's up, Boss?"

Levi jiggled the mouse and woke his computer. "Hoping you got a good look at Gary Sims. Is this him?" He pointed at the computer screen.

Janice angled for a better look at the webpage. "That's him, all right. Dressed differently, of course. He didn't spend much time here, but he dressed the part.

What a phony-baloney!"

Chloe compressed her lips to keep from chuckling over Janice's colorful disgust with their odd guest.

"Thank you for being observant. You probably didn't see much of him, either." Levi leaned into his chair and crossed his arms over his chest.

"I notice everyone on this ranch." Janice propped her hands at her waist. "Just got a call from Jen, the pork farmer. She apologized for calling on a Sunday, and for bothering me on rodeo day, but her butcher needs freezer space, so she has to pick up an entire hog today. Needs me to pick our order up early."

"Hey, we'll get it all done." Levi shrugged. "Do you need my help?"

"Jen will help load it, but I could use your help unloading. A two-hundred-fifty-pound hog turns into a lot of packages."

"No problem." He generated a print of the Bay City Investigations homepage. "I'll watch for your return."

"Thanks, Boss." Janice swept from the office.

Chloe returned to her Bay Area search. "Janice is amazing."

"We're lucky to have her." He handed her the Sims' printout. "While I grab fresh coffee, could you start a file? Feel free to print anything you find." Levi grabbed the tray and left the room.

Scotty roused from his nap to glance toward the doorway, then to her.

"It's okay, boy. He'll be right back." She ran her fingertips from her chin to her collarbone. Her dog had taken quite a liking to Levi Banks. She could relate. "Back to work, Scotty."

Scotty sighed and closed his eyes.

Chloe opened the business page of a Bay Area law office and scanned the header. *Joss Hoffman, Attorney-at-Law*. "*Specializes in counsel for political candidates and corporate law.*" She hit the print screen button. "Just what I was looking for."

She glanced toward the doorway and smiled. If he returned in the middle of a conversation with Scotty, Levi might question her sanity. She hobbled the few steps to the printer and grabbed the printout on the Bay City Investigations page. Depending on how long Levi took, she might accomplish a bit on the Meeker design. Relocating the dining room, and Cain's office, would take strategy.

Levi returned, carrying the restocked tray complete with a full tea service.

She blinked and pushed to her foot. "Wow, Janice went all-out."

"Janice left for the pork." He set the tray on the credenza and lifted the blue ceramic teapot to pour dark tea into a matching cup. "Would you like honey?"

"Uh—occasionally—sure." She chuckled. "I thought you went for coffee."

"Remember yesterday, when I made tea in your studio?" He set the delicate blue cup and saucer on the desk next to her laptop, then added a small jar of honey and a tiny spoon.

"Wow, I'm impressed." She leaned over the cup and breathed in one of her favorite tea scents. "Ahh, Earl Grey. The perfect late morning choice, while I can safely consume caffeine without losing sleep tonight."

"I reheated the rolls." Levi set the plate holding cinnamon rolls between their computers.

"Okay, I'll humor you and have a few bites." Chloe moaned and pressed a hand to her stomach.

"Ask my dad when you meet him. He brags about Janice's cinnamon rolls. Says, they're the best in two states." He cut into a flaky roll. "Any luck with finding a Joss who fits our profile?"

"Yes, here's the printout of the business page belonging to Joss Hoffman, an attorney in San Jose. Get this—he specializes in representing political campaigns."

"Good work." Levi slowly chewed as he read the page.

The words of praise made her go warm all over. She hastily sipped Earl Grey, and the scent of Bergamot filled her senses.

"Now, let's analyze Drew King's page." His fingers flew over the keyboard. "We might have missed something."

Chloe took a bite of the gooey roll. The blend of butter, cinnamon, and sugar sent her taste buds into a tizzy. "These are amazing."

"I found something." Levi's attention remained squarely on his computer screen.

She lifted her cup to wash down the roll. "Not surprising, the man is a giant in the tech world." For the first time, she noticed a few thin white scars on Levi's long, tanned fingers. No doubt, souvenirs from handling hemp ropes. She pictured him being so intent on calming a startled horse or capturing a steer, he'd forge on and forget to put on gloves. *What in the heck?* She edged closer to his chair and focused on the screen. *Stop ogling Levi Banks.* "What did you find?"

"According to a recent article in the *Sacramento*

Times, he's fighting San Jose officials over the rights to a parcel next to his main software facility. Native American land. The guy is bucking the *Department of the Interior*."

"I'm not surprised after the note in the shadow file." She grabbed the blue gingham napkin he'd supplied and wiped her fingers.

"Interesting." He took an audible breath and traced his fingertip over the screen. "This link takes us to an update in the case. He won. Huh, appears he didn't need Billings in office after all."

"Or he bribed someone in the Department of the Interior." She shifted closer to read the fine text and bumped against his arm.

"I'll print the page." He touched the prompt and swiveled his chair. "Billings might already influence the three-letter agencies."

"Something must have changed." Chloe tapped a fingernail against her front teeth and gazed at the monitor.

"How are you doing on the truck model investigation?" Levi returned to add the new printout to the growing stack of papers.

"I didn't get back to it. Call me a chicken. Instead, I worked on Rachel's new design." She leaned into the chair. Time to *buck up*, as Levi would say.

Chapter Fourteen

"We'll look at them now." Levi reclaimed his chair and typed into the search bar.

Chloe pressed a hand to her fluttering stomach. A sugary dessert, working closely with this handsome man, and pursuing the people who wanted to silence her, rolled into an overwhelming combination.

"Here are two dealerships that specialize in Chevrolet pickups."

Chloe rolled her chair closer to his just as the hum of a vehicle sounded from the yard. She touched his arm. "Someone's here."

"Probably Janice." He stood and moved to the screen door. "Yeah, she's back with the meat. While I help unload the boxes, go ahead and study the trucks on those sites."

"Sure." She nodded and pushed his chair aside to make room for hers. She took a deep breath. Matching a truck style to Gary's rental meant confirming or disproving that he was the thug who tried to run her off the road. She glanced at Scotty. "Maybe I need fresh air." She stood and took a step toward the screen door. "Yikes! My ankle stiffened up." She grimaced and took another step. Movement might be good, but it wasn't easy.

Janice had backed the van close to the kitchen entrance and opened the cargo doors.

Levi carried a box into the house, his shoulders flexing under the weight.

Chloe moaned. *Okay, stop with admiring him as a man and keep your relationship in perspective.* Alone, she allowed the words to leave her lips. "He's Rachel's brother, and he's helping me solve the evil plot that put Rachel in the hospital." She leaned against the doorjamb and breathed in the fresh spring air. "That's all there can be." Still…she stayed by the door.

Levi made several more trips between the van and the house.

Janice closed the cargo doors and drove the van into the car barn-style building where the other ranch vehicles were parked.

Chloe hurried to her chair. Before Levi returned, she needed to make progress.

Poor guy—he'd spent the morning working on *her* situation when fifty rodeo attendees would arrive this evening. He had duties that didn't include babysitting her.

She glanced at the tea tray and pursed her lips. Another cup might help clear her head. Behind the tray, a framed photo caught her eye. How hadn't she noticed it before? She rolled closer and lifted the silver frame for a better look at the three people, posing near the river. A younger Rachel, her dark hair in a long braid over one shoulder. A woman Chloe didn't recognize stood between Rachel and Levi. Couldn't be their mother—she seemed too young—and she didn't resemble the brother and sister.

She tilted her head and gazed into the woman's blue eyes. Would she meet her before she left Coeur d'Alene? Her stomach fluttered. Was she who Levi typically met at Beverly's for dinner? Rachel hadn't mentioned him having a woman in his life. Janice said he didn't bring women to the ranch. Yet, in this photo, the three stood near the place where she'd seen the red Adirondack chairs.

She sighed and set the photo where she'd found it. Time to stop stalling and look at the pickups. She returned to Levi's computer.

"How's it going?"

Chloe started and bumped the keyboard. "Oh shoot—I accidentally closed a window."

"No problem. Windows can be reopened." He leaned over his chair and pulled up the dealership. "Sorry, that took so long. After I unloaded the meat, I got sidetracked strategizing a cattle roundup with Clay." He placed his hands on his hips. "You haven't met them yet, but Clay and Travis are my full-time ranch hands."

"I'm sorry to take up so much of your day. Do you need to help them?"

"They have it under control. It's a common occurrence for a few strays to cross the river." He tightened and released his lips. "Let's get the pickup description out of the way so we can update Carson." Levi folded into the chair and changed the descriptions to silver and half ton. "What do you think? Does this look like the pickup on Riverview?"

"No, it's not quite right." Chloe gazed over the photo. "Can you enlarge a different truck? Maybe show the tailgate?"

"Sure." He rotated the images.

"Yes!" She ran her fingernail below the description of the truck. "That's it. Like your truck."

"Except mine's dark-blue and several years older." He tapped the screen. "Are you sure this matches the truck on Riverview Drive? If it does, Gary Sims isn't the culprit. His rental paperwork confirms a different brand. Time to call Carson."

Chloe leaned into her chair. "Darn. Confirming it had been Gary Sims would make things easier."

"Humph." Levi lifted the landline receiver. "Why didn't Sims stay in town? Why did he need to distance himself?" He forked his fingers through his thick, curly hair. "You wouldn't have recognized him."

"You talk to Carson, and I'll find this truck on my laptop and save it to the file."

"Carson, Levi Banks, here. Yeah, calling from my landline. Say, we found some useful information online. Chloe's preparing a hard copy of the web pages we've printed, plus, she'll email an electronic file. Joss, from the yellow legal pad, is Joss Hoffman, an attorney in San Jose. Chloe also identified the pickup from Riverview Drive. It doesn't match the make and model of Sims' rental."

Chloe tuned into the conversation and emailed the desktop folder to Carson's department email address.

Levi finished his conversation and set the receiver in the cradle. "Back to Joss Hoffman?"

"He might have access to my police file." She reopened the attorney's page and nibbled on her bottom lip. "I've been concerned about Mike Parker sharing information from my file, but Joss could have a contact at the Sacramento PD."

"Witness protection files should be sealed." Levi humphed.

"You know this, how?" She raised a brow.

"Hey, when I'm not training cowboys or chasing cows, I've been known to kick back with a good mystery." He half smiled. "When I find something I'm not familiar with, I research the subject." He typed *witness protection* into his search bar. "The U.S. Marshals Service site states *their office provides twenty-four-hour protection to all witnesses.*" He ran a hand over his whiskered jaw, his calloused fingers making a scraping noise. "*While the witness is in a high-threat environment, including trials and court appearances.*"

"Really? Well, Paul is my only contact." She didn't like the doubts creeping into her mind. She cleared her throat. "I've come down hard on Paul, but I still believe he has my best interests at heart."

"Humph." The sound came from deep in Levi's chest. "Before I rent the cabins again, I'll contact a company that pulls credit for property managers and checks social media and web pages."

"I'm so sorry, Levi." Chloe touched the sleeve of his blue chambray shirt. "Don't let my situation sour you on Rachel's dream. The Portland family is excited about the rodeo and has spent most of their time at the ranch."

"How about we make a deal?" He folded his arms over his chest. "I'll quit beating myself up over renting to Sims if you stop blaming yourself for Rachel's collision."

"That's a tall request." She fingered the pen on the desk next to her laptop. It wouldn't be easy to stop blaming herself for not acting when the flowers arrived.

From under the desk, Scotty nudged her leg.

She pushed her chair back and peeked at her dog.

"Hey, Scotty. Do you need to go outside?" She grabbed her cane. "Mind if I take him to the backyard?"

"Not at all. You could let him run off the leash. He won't get hurt out there."

"I'm not in the right emotional state to take the risk." She stopped at the screen door and gazed through the mesh toward the ranch yard. "Where's Duke?"

"Outside somewhere. Probably hot on the scent of a coyote. Heck, he might be sacked out in the sunshine." He continued to read his screen.

"Aren't you worried when he's out of your sight?" She forked her fingers through her hair and loosened the clip enough to ease the tightness in her scalp.

"The ranch is Duke's home." Levi removed his readers and angled his head to meet her gaze. "He learned at very young age what to avoid."

The intensity in his amber-brown eyes sent warmth coursing through her. She sighed through parted lips. His eyes were such a unique color of brown that she wondered who he'd inherited them from. Soon, she'd meet his parents and find out. Aside from his good looks, Levi had a caring heart and strong ethics. She'd witnessed those attributes since they met in March.

She glanced at the photo on the credenza. He smiled so tenderly at the woman beside him. Just who was she, and where was she now? Chloe bent to attach the leash to Scotty's collar and opened the screen door. Time to get her head on straight. Coming to Idaho had been about refuge, not romance.

"Uh, wait."

Levi's tone made her release the screen door and let it softly close. "What is it?" She leaned against the doorjamb.

He tapped his forefinger against the computer monitor. "Drew King has an office in Spokane. Under the name, Software Solutions."

Chloe wobbled on her feet. Her cane handle slipped from her hold and crashed to the hardwood floor. "What?"

Scotty yipped.

"Uh, I'll be right back." She retrieved her cane and opened the door while her mind raced with the implications. Drew King had an office close to Coeur d'Alene.

Scotty pulled her around the corner of the house, and the vista of riverbank and mountains opened.

Duke lay stretched out in the cool, green grass.

Chloe hesitated, then let the leash extend.

Scotty circled the big dog.

"Good boy. Be nice to Duke."

Scotty sniffed Duke's head.

Come on, Scotty." Chloe recoiled the leash. "Leave Duke alone and do your business. Levi just dropped a bomb."

Seeming unconcerned, Duke pushed to his feet and wandered around the end of the house.

She waited while Scotty lifted a leg toward the lilac bush, then reeled him in. For a moment, she gazed across the lawn at the red Adirondack chairs facing the riverbank. Ahh, she'd love to forget the political intrigue and threats to her safety and sink into one of those chairs. Listen to the whisper of the river passing by, the bird songs, and the occasional frog. She paused to drink in the wide, green expanse and the mountains beyond. She hoped with Sims' departure, that nothing threatened this peaceful place.

Urging Scotty back to the office entrance, she encountered Duke at the closed screen door. "Look who we found." She opened the door and the gentle giant ambled into the office.

"Hey, Duke." Levi smiled and patted his dog's large head. He glanced at Chloe. "Come look at this page."

She rounded her end of the long desk and sank to her chair. "I looked at King's business page. How could I have missed the Spokane office address?" She rolled her chair closer to his and peeked at the computer screen.

"No wonder you missed it." He touched the tiny links at the bottom of the page. "I confirmed the office is located near downtown—meaning, his satellite office is maybe forty-five minutes from your studio."

She fought to draw a breath. "Why didn't Paul catch this? He was so worried I might stay in Portland, he must have performed due diligence about my location."

Scotty nudged her leg.

"Oh. Sorry, boy! I forgot to unhook your leash." She must be losing it. She disconnected the hook from his collar.

"Sounds like Paul has a lot on his plate." Levi swiveled his chair in order to face her. "Even more reason to work with Carson." His mouth tightened. "Carson's right. A safe house in Sacramento might have been the best choice."

She stared into the warmth of his eyes. Hard to imagine never meeting him or Rachel. "I'm sorry to have dragged your family into my mess." She blinked. "I wonder if Mike Parker is aware of Software

Solutions and that it's one of Drew King's satellite offices?"

"Possibly—but why would a local journalist care?"

"The Parkers are the reason my friend, Diane, recommended I come here." She drew a breath. "I've avoided him and his wife, Melissa, for months. Unfortunately, Diane shared enough information to pique any journalist's interest." She pressed her fingertips to her lips. "Maybe I'm looking at this all wrong. Mike could use his investigative skills to help crack open Drew King's corruption."

Levi lifted an index finger. "First, we'll discuss this with Carson. He's aware of the key people in his town."

Chloe ran her gaze over Levi's face and rested on his strong neck and broad shoulders. *Hum*—did he ever work without his shirt? She warmed with an image of tanned, defined pecs. Imagined him planting a fence post or gentling a green-broke horse. The flex of his biceps and deltoids. She drew a sharp breath. "Mike still writes for the *Sacramento Times*. He likely has a contact at the Sacramento PD." She waved a hand. "I mean, Carson has a contact at the Sacramento Sheriff's Department. What are the odds?"

Levi narrowed one eye. "The wild card in this idea is what Mike might do with your information."

Her head began to ache. She pressed her fingertips to her temples. "Besides the U.S. Marshal's office, I need to know who has access to my police file."

"DeMers needs to buck the system and protect you." Levi slipped the readers on and turned back to the screen.

"Paul's been a good friend since college, and Gina's friend since high school." She nibbled on her bottom lip. "However, I've experienced those very same frustrations. Is he working to solve Hallie's murder and the threats to me, or is he too focused on his career?"

Levi nodded. "One of the many answers we need to find."

She picked up the blue teacup, sipped the cool tea and shivered—or was it from their recent discovery? "Levi, I should leave the ranch before they realize I'm here."

"No." He pushed to his feet and retrieved the borrowed flannel shirt from where she'd laid over the back of a curved leather chair. "No way am I letting you leave until tomorrow and then only when Carson deems it's safe."

"I just hope Sims is on a flight for San Jose." Chloe accepted the flannel shirt and slipped her arms into its warmth.

"Carson might have a way of confirming Sims boarded a plane and if he returned the rental pickup." Levi glanced at his pocket watch. "How's your ankle doing? Do you need to take a pain pill?"

"I'm fine." She ignored her throbbing ankle and woke her laptop. "I need a clear head."

"Fine, but it's noon. You should eat something substantial."

Chloe barked a laugh. "A few bites of Janice's cinnamon roll are substantial, but a salad sounds great."

"In that case, I'll be right back." He disappeared down the hallway.

Chloe gazed toward the doorway for a moment, then pushed from the office chair. The comfy leather chairs and the low flame in the fireplace beckoned. She sank into the buttery leather upholstery and closed her eyes. Exhaustion, from the discovery of King's proximity, and just how many were involved in the plot to silence her, sucked her under.

The soft clinking of glassware dragged Chloe from a deep sleep. She opened her eyes, blinked, and ran her tongue inside her mouth to chase away the cotton.

Levi sat in the matching curved chair with a coffee mug in one hand.

On the small cabinet between them sat a fresh cup of Earl Grey and a clear glass bowl holding a tossed salad with chunks of chicken. "Is that a drizzle of Balsamic vinaigrette on that salad?" She met Levi's amber gaze.

One corner of his mouth lifted. "Yes. I didn't ask, but you seem like the vinaigrette type."

"Hum, and exactly what does that mean?"

He shrugged. "Prefer things light and tangy. Give it a try. If you don't like it, Janice makes a killer blue cheese dressing."

She straightened in the chair and cringed at the twinge of stiffness in her neck. "Wow, I can't believe I fell asleep." She yawned and reached for the teacup, then the salad bowl. One bite and energy coursed through her. "Very good. Thank you for going to all this trouble."

"My pleasure." Levi continued to watch her. "What about contacting your biological father again? Call him, instead of waiting for an answer to your email."

Chloe paused, a fork filled with salad halfway to her mouth. "Today is Sunday, and I only have his office number."

"Bet he has an answering service." He set his mug

on the table and leaned forward to clasp his hands between his knees. "Chloe, there are things parents don't want their children to know—even adult children. Some of your childhood assumptions could be incorrect. You might be pleasantly surprised by communicating with him."

She sipped tea, and the hot liquid soothed her throat. "After my father left, my mother worked hard to make a living and wasn't always there for me." She sighed. "I mean, she tried to be, but she had to keep a roof over our heads. At night, I felt so uneasy. I missed my father. When I questioned Mom about why Dad wouldn't help financially, I'd get shut down. Still to this day, I don't know why he didn't at least attempt to visit me." She rubbed her upper arms. "Now, I'm afraid to learn how involved he is in the plot to silence me."

Chapter Fifteen

Levi gave a silent whistle. "I'm so sorry you had to go through that." His heart hurt for her, and he couldn't imagine his parents separating or deserting their child.

"It's been so long ago, it shouldn't still hurt like it does." She sniffled. "Finding Will Mathers brought it all back." She gazed toward the fire, then glanced at him. "Look, you have work to do, and I should hop on the Wakely design file. Right now, there's nothing more we can do."

Levi glanced at his pocket watch. "Dinner's at five. The rodeo begins at seven."

She pushed from the chair and hobbled toward the desk. Reddish-blonde curls had escaped the large tortoiseshell clip, and they trailed along her creamy, graceful throat to rest on her shoulder. His fingers itched to free the mass of curls from captivity. He cleared his throat. "We can organize the printouts for Carson."

Chloe sank to her office chair and lifted the new file folder. "Done. I sent the electronic file, too. I should send one to Paul." She gazed at the cream-colored file folder. "I wonder if I'll ever be able to look at an ordinary folder without having a flashback to Bruce Billings' file." She sighed. "The oversight changed my life."

Levi raked a hand over his mouth and moved to his

office chair. The dejected expression in her jewel-green eyes, and the slump of her delicate shoulders, made him want to take her into his arms. *Cripes, Banks, focus.* He settled for touching her arm. "Maybe, you were meant to be here."

Her shoulders, under the borrowed flannel shirt, rose and fell. "You and Rachel both believe things are meant to be. But I can't accept that Hallie's death was meant to form my destiny." She placed her fingertips to her keyboard. "Okay, what link are we missing?"

Maybe later, they'd discuss destiny and his take on coincidence. Right now— "Who hired Joss Hoffman, and did he hire Sims?" Levi pulled his gaze from her profile. Early in their acquaintance, he'd recognized her strong work ethic. Now, he had a hunch her childhood trauma might have driven her to succeed. He opened the new file. "Let's review."

"Joss hired Gary to confirm my location and deliver the note." She shivered. "Meaning, Bruce hired Hoffman. Sims probably followed me for days. Oh, and I have a photo of the floral note on my phone. I'll print it for the file."

Levi couldn't stop turning to gaze at Chloe. Her intensity fascinated him. Her sharp mind impressed him. She'd trusted him with the most vulnerable times in her life, and he meant to protect her. Did she share his awareness? Recognize the chemistry between them? He cleared his throat. "To preserve our own records, I'll take photos of the pickup rental agreement and the yellow paper. Let's feed the printouts through the copier."

"Good idea." Chloe nodded. "When is Carson going to call with a report on my building?"

Levi ran the copies of the web pages and started a new file. "If we don't hear soon, then I'll call him."

"It appears we're dealing with two factions." Chloe held up a finger. "One that ordered the search—the destruction—of my apartment, the attempted abduction at Luigi's, the collision, and the intimidation on Riverview Drive. All violent acts." She held up a second finger. "The other faction is passive-aggressive. Likely Bruce instructed his attorney to hire a PI to observe my life in Coeur d'Alene. Deliver a subtle message. Opposite methods of communication."

Levi caved to his need to touch the silky, corkscrew curl trailing over the green plaid flannel.

She widened her eyes and parted her lips, but she didn't pull away.

Something like a lightning bolt shot through him. *Whoa.* "Chloe." His voice came out hoarse. "When this is over, and you're reclaiming your life, please don't forget about Idaho. People here care about you."

His phone rang.

Levi released the silky curl and snapped his cell phone off the desk. "Carson, what's new? Is Chloe's building secure?"

"Yeah, I'm involved with another case in town, but please tell Chloe her building is fine. With the new case, I'll need to wait to pick up the evidence you've gathered."

"Sure. Makes sense." He glanced at Chloe. "If you don't mind, I'll put you on speaker. Chloe and I are at my desk."

"No problem."

Levi touched the speaker button. "Carson, what do you have on Sims?"

"Sims boarded a flight for Oakland about two hours ago. With the information you've gathered, I'll call Joss Hoffman. Chloe, please send the information to Paul."

"I will, thank you, Carson." She opened her email account.

"Uh, Carson, there's something new." Levi glanced at Chloe. "Drew King has an office in Spokane. Software Solutions."

Carson's whistle carried through the phone. "Explains a lot about access to local thugs and the Washington plates. You two are quite the team. I'll see you both tonight at the rodeo. Until then, please keep me updated, and I'll do the same."

"Thanks, Carson." Levi closed his phone and set it on the desk.

Chloe opened her father's web page and scanned her green gaze over the screen like summer lightning dancing on the lake.

Levi rolled his chair closer. "What's on your mind?"

"You were right. It's time to call him." She pursed her lips, then grabbed her cell phone. Tension emanated from her body, and while she waited for a response, she blinked several times. "It's ringing." She cleared her throat. "Hello, this is Chloe Austin. I realize it's Sunday afternoon, but I must speak with Mr. Mathers." She left her number and disconnected. Her body seemed to deflate.

Levi's hands itched to touch her, stroke her back, and offer comfort. He couldn't imagine not having Dad in his life. "Your adopted dad must have had a solid influence."

Her mouth softened. "Zach Austin saved my mom's life—and mine—from a difficult four years of bad neighborhoods, long work hours for my mom, and long, lonely hours for me."

Her vulnerability threw him off base. Levi rotated his neck and flexed his shoulders. "If he's any kind of a man, Will Mathers will return your call."

Chloe fingered the gold hoop in her left ear. "Maybe I shouldn't have called him. What if he calls my mom and upsets her?"

Levi got it, but— "He's on a list of over-limit campaign contributors. Even though his name is on page three, the list is about to become public. Wouldn't it be better to prepare your mom?"

She shook her head. "I refuse to call her about it until the danger is over." She paused. "Deep inside, I'm still that little girl who couldn't understand why her dad didn't visit." Her delicate throat flexed with a hard swallow, and she blinked against the moisture pooling in her eyes. "Levi, you've gone above and beyond. Please, don't let this consume what's left of your day."

He studied her amazing eyes. Yeah, he normally met with Riley before the rodeos, but his foreman had everything under control. Chloe didn't. "You're stuck with me." He tapped his knuckles against the desktop. "Okay, let's review. Carson confirmed Sims has left the state. We now have Drew King's Spokane address, and we know who hired Sims. We also know Sims wasn't the driver on Riverview."

She ran the pads of her fingers under her eyes. "We still don't know who drove either of the pickups." She cleared her throat and squared her shoulders. "Time to work on the Wakely file. No." She held up a forefinger.

"First, I should work on the Meeker file. Create an initial bid for Rachel."

Had she sent a cue to leave her alone? Levi stood and moved to the door. "Guess I'll check in with Riley." He unhooked his hat. "Oh, one more thing."

Chloe sputtered a laugh. "Now, you sound like an old episode of a detective series."

He grinned—happy she'd rediscovered her humor. "I know the one. Another favorite on cold winter nights. Now, about Mike Parker and your earlier thoughts. Maybe we should use his connection with the *Sacramento Times*. Use the power of the pen to expose the Sacramento police chief and crack open the corruption."

She stilled with her fingertips on the keyboard. "He certainly has the talent and the need for recognition. If he does have access to my file, what's to stop him from including my role in Hallie's final day?"

"Professional integrity? He'll be more interested in solving a crime than winning an award." Levi fingered the screen door handle.

"Well, I need assurance he won't hang me out to dry." She propped her elbows on the edge of the desk and clutched her head with both hands. "Everyone seems to have selfish motives."

Levi shoved his hat on his head. "Not everyone. Don't let a few bad people taint your view of life and the good people in it. As for Mike—the steer is out of the chute, so to speak. Time to rope him and take the points." He spotted the hint of a smile on her lips.

"Whatever that means." She leaned into her chair and laughed. "Rachel's taught me some ranch lingo, but that's a new one."

"After the rodeo tonight, you'll know all kinds of lingo." He appreciated how she'd ended their conversation on a light note. "Hey, Duke, want to go outside?"

Duke pushed off the rug and ambled toward him.

Scotty stretched and closed his eyes.

Levi smiled. Deep into the investigation, Chloe had eased her control over the dog. Scotty appeared to be completely at home.

The lure of sunshine and fresh air won over Levi's reluctance to leave. He let the screen door close behind him. Instead of heading directly to the barn and arena, he rounded the end of the house and made for the red Adirondack chairs. After Lucy's death, he'd continued her seasonal routine of bringing them out in the spring and back into the barn in the fall.

He sank to *his* chair and gazed over the river. His memory flashed to that final fall with Lucy and how they'd sat here one evening wrapped in blankets and sipping cocoa. He remembered her laugh and the scent of autumn leaves.

A weight settled on his chest. Lucy was gone. He grabbed the flat, wooden chair arms. Would she be okay if he fell in love again? He'd never stop loving her. He exhaled, and an image of Chloe Austin filled his mind. He could picture her sitting out here next to him.

From his shirt pocket, his phone rang, and the moment splintered. He fumbled to pull it out. "Hello."

"Levi, Carson Haynes. Just spoke with Joss Hoffman."

"What did he say?" Levi pushed out of the chair and moved toward the sprawling maple tree. He leaned against the rough bark.

"After I asked him about Gary Sims, he clammed up. Gary's liable to get an earful when he steps off the plane in Oakland."

"Did you inform Hoffman that Sims could be implicated in the local threats?" Levi strolled toward the cabins.

"Yeah, right after he danced around client confidentiality. He finally confessed; he hired Sims on behalf of a client who has an interest in Coeur d'Alene. That's it. My contact at the Sacramento Sheriff's Department will get a subpoena. Hoffman will have to talk."

Levi paused near the first cabin. "Hoffman must realize the trail leads to him, and he'll be dragged into a police investigation."

"Exactly. I'll bet my next bonus—he's already on the phone with Billings or maybe King."

"Chloe will be thrilled to hear this. She's inside working on a design file, but she's wound tight." Levi continued past the cabins and aimed toward the ranch yard. The sound of tires against gravel alerted him to an arrival. "Carson, I have to go. Company just pulled in. See you this evening."

Dad parked the ten-year-old, half-ton pickup next to the machine shed and slid from behind the wheel. In their early sixties, his parents were vibrant and energetic, but Rachel's accident had taken a lot out of them. He sighed and moved to greet them.

****

As it passed the office door, the hum of a car engine startled Chloe. She hobbled toward the screen door, her entire body aching from sitting so long. The ice pack Janice provided had thawed, and her ankle had doubled in size.

Levi stood near the tailgate of a pickup, hugging a woman whose height might reach his shoulder.

The driver, a man about Levi's height, rounded the truck to slap Levi on the back.

Even from this distance, Chloe knew the newcomers were Ray and Katie Banks. A knot formed in the pit of her stomach. The time had come to face Rachel's parents.

Levi slid an arm around his mom's back and walked toward the kitchen door.

Chloe angled to continue her appraisal of the couple. Time to get the meeting over with. Another vehicle, this time a large SUV, coasted into the yard and parked close to the kitchen door.

Levi reappeared to greet the driver.

A young woman, tall and slender, with blonde hair caught in a clip at her crown, lifted a hand and said "hello."

Willowy came to Chloe's mind.

Levi helped unload stainless-steel chafing pans and carried them to the dining hall.

Ah, must be Fiona Carmichael, the caterer, and Rianna's sous chef, arriving to help with rodeo day cooking. Chloe patted her thigh. "Hey, Scotty, coming with me?"

He raised his head and gazed at her with sparkling, dark eyes.

"You've had quite a nap, buddy. Ready to meet Rachel's parents?"

His ears perked at the mention of Rachel.

Her heart sank. Scotty loved Rachel, and so did

she. Her exhale emerged on a groan. Reaching the front foyer, she caught snippets of conversations from the kitchen. Maybe she should give everyone a chance to settle in before she joined them.

"Glad you're here." Levi appeared in the kitchen archway. "My parents and Fiona have arrived."

"I heard the cars and looked outside." She pressed the flat of a hand against her stomach. "Maybe I should wait to introduce myself."

"If you're afraid my parents blame you for Rachel's collision, don't be." He touched her arm and smiled. "Come on, you'll see."

His touch and reassurance sent a flutter through her midsection. At some point, he'd moved from simply being Rachel's big brother to the handsome and very appealing man who fascinated her more each day. She touched his bicep, and a thrill ran through her core. Inner strength and honed muscles radiated from beneath the wash-worn, blue chambray of his shirt. Suddenly, she didn't want to remove her hand.

He cleared his throat. "Before we join the others, there's something that might come up in conversation. I'd like to tell you first."

"O-k-a-y." She blinked. Did he plan to let her down easy? A perceptive man, Levi might have noticed her growing attraction. She drew a breath, then followed him through the front door and onto the slate patio. She weaved against her cane. "Something's not wrong with Rachel, is it?"

He gently squeezed her arm. "Rachel's fine. Sorry, I didn't mean to worry you. I just…there's something that might come up in conversation with my parents. I don't want it to be awkward." His broad chest expanded on a deep inhale.

A tingling of apprehension rolled through her, and she sank to one of the cushioned patio chairs.

Scotty plopped down at her feet.

She absently scratched his neck. "Oh, I forgot his leash."

"He won't leave your side." Levi's mouth flexed. His gaze scanned the gravel-topped area. "I don't recall—if I mentioned Lucy in connection with the ranch house remodel." He raised his dark brows. "Did I?"

"I-I don't think so. Please, go on." She studied his amber-brown eyes and recognized sorrow and deep pain. She braced herself for hearing the unknown.

"Lucy was my wife."

Chloe flinched. She hadn't seen that coming. "You were married." She voiced the obvious. "The photo in the office, the woman who stood between you and Rachel—is she Lucy?"

His shoulders stiffened.

Chloe's stomach clenched.

"Yeah, a neighbor took that photo the fall before Lucy died in a car accident. It happened four years ago last January."

"Oh, Levi." She pressed a hand to her collarbone. "The collision on Friday—it must have brought back every horrible memory."

"Full force." He brushed a hand over his dark hair. "Along with the old guilt of how I could have persuaded Lucy to wait and leave the next morning." He waved a hand. "She taught English at the University of Montana in Missoula. After I retired from the rodeo circuit, I bought the ranch, and every weekend, she commuted between here and Missoula. The rodeo years had kept us apart far too much." He raked both hands through his hair. "I should have nixed the rodeo and stayed home. Became a rancher like my dad and Lucy's. Instead, I chased my dreams of riding bulls." His Adam's apple bobbed, and he planted his hands at his hips. "A heavy snowstorm hit Lookout Pass that night. Snowplows couldn't keep up. A semi-truck jackknifed and forced Lucy's SUV off the road and into a deep ravine. They figured she died on impact."

Her heart splintered. Chloe pushed from the chair and clutched his right forearm. "Oh, Levi. I'm so sorry. Sorry for your loss and for being instrumental in bringing back the memories and pain. Your family—oh, my gosh. The collision." She couldn't breathe right.

He tilted his head, and his amber gaze met hers. "Yeah, Rachel's collision scared us all. We'd been there before. At the hospital, the memories and fear for Rachel rolled into one ball of anger. I kind of lost it when Carson mentioned the other driver intentionally hit your car." He dragged a hand over his face.

Tears threatened and Chloe swallowed hard. She tightened her hold on his arm. "I don't blame you for being angry. You were frightened for your sister. Oh, Levi, your poor parents." She released her hold and pressed a hand to her forehead. "I should go home."

He bracketed her shoulders with both hands. "No, you shouldn't. We don't know who's still out there, waiting and watching your building. You need to stay put, at least until morning."

She moved her gaze to his tanned throat. "I wonder why Rachel never mentioned Lucy. Were they close?"

"Very. Lucy and I grew up on neighboring ranches.

Before we even dated, Rachel considered Lucy her big sister." He barked a laugh. "After dating for several years, Lucy proposed to me. No way did I believe an English professor would be happy with a rodeo cowboy." His chest rose and fell.

Chloe's vision blurred. She knew the sharp pain of loss from when her father left and from the shock of her mom's cancer diagnosis. *How did one measure grief?* The collision had not only threatened Rachel's life, but had thrown Levi back four years when he lost his soul mate. "Levi, I'm so sorry"

He dipped his chin and locked his gaze with hers. "Have you ever been in love?"

She slowly shook her head. "Not in the sense of falling in love. No one's tempted me to give up my independence." She flashed a tight smile. "Hitch my wagon to his." This time, humor didn't ease the tightness in her chest. She squeezed his arm. "Now, your anger at the hospital makes more sense."

Levi lowered his tall frame to one of the patio chairs and gripped the metal armrests. "I stepped over the line. You didn't deserve my anger. You were helping Rachel keep a client appointment." He clamped a hand on the back of his neck. "Do yourself a favor. Don't carry the burden. You couldn't control Hallie's actions, and you had nothing to do with Rachel's collision. Guilt won't change anything. It only tears you apart."

"I'll work on it." She fished inside her slacks pocket for a tissue.

For a few moments, they remained silent.

Levi finally pushed from the chair and slid his fingers into the front pockets of his faded jeans. "I've observed how much Rachel likes and respects you. I'm surprised she didn't mention Lucy." He paused. "Like you, Lucy mentored her."

Chloe's thoughts scrambled. Levi might not blame her for thinking she'd protected Rachel by keeping her in the dark. She still blamed herself. Rachel had months of recovery, and Levi had been forced to relive the pain of losing his wife.

"Ready to meet my parents?" He extended his right arm.

"I don't know how I can face them." Chloe slowly shook her head. Rachel's car crash hadn't been their first family tragedy. They'd all lost Lucy.

"Chloe, my parents are thankful for all you've done for Rachel."

Palms damp, she took hold of Levi's bicep and allowed him to guide her toward the kitchen. They entered a flurry of activity.

Janice and Fiona commanded the space between the granite-topped island and the six-burner, stainless-steel commercial range. Janice wielded a long carving knife and sliced a huge beef roast.

Fiona bent to remove a large baking sheet of shortbread cookies from the oven.

Ray and Katie Banks sat at the large, pine table with two coffee mugs and a plate of cinnamon rolls between them. Cutting into a cinnamon roll, Ray glanced toward her.

Chloe froze. She'd love nothing more than to exit through the back door and hobble to the red Adirondack chairs. Postpone this meeting. But what would that help?

Chapter Sixteen

"Jacque!" Katie rounded the table and grasped Chloe's hand. "We're so happy to finally meet you." She turned toward her husband.

Ray hadn't budged or set down his forkful of cinnamon roll.

"Aren't we, Ray?" She enveloped Chloe in a very motherly hug. "Now, you need to sit and elevate that foot."

"Uh, thank you." Chloe cleared her throat. "I'm so happy to meet you both." Up close, she noticed more about Levi's parents. Both had dark brown hair, but Katie's eyes were amber, and Ray's eyes were very dark brown—like Rachel's. A dramatic silver streak ran from Katie's right temple to where her hair length ended just below her shoulders. Silver strands lightly frosted Ray's hair.

At his wife's glance, Ray stood and reached across the coffee mugs and cinnamon rolls to shake Chloe's hand. "Good to finally meet. Rachel speaks very highly of you."

Chloe's breath hitched. Up close, Ray's bone structure and build could be a predictor of Levi in his sixties. Still muscled and lean, fine lines fanned from the corners of his dark eyes, but he carried the vibrancy of a much younger man.

Katie rested her hand on Chloe's shoulder. "In case

you're wondering, Levi told us about your sprain." She audibly sighed. "Just what you needed, along with the car accident and worry for Rachel. I understand your family is in California."

"They are." The weight of lying to her parents settled on her shoulders. They didn't know she'd fled California. "Everything has become very complicated. I should have driven Rachel to her appointment."

"Then, you'd both be in the hospital." Ray sat and folded his hands on the table next to his empty coffee mug. "Rachel said you'd blame yourself, but she doesn't blame you, and neither do we. You loaned her the car out of trust and friendship. Period. Sometimes, we're in the wrong place at the wrong time." He lifted his right palm. "Regardless of the police report saying the driver aimed for your car, we don't know the entire story. Might be a case of time and chance."

Tears pricked Chloe's eyes, and she pressed her fingertips to her lower lids. "Mr. Banks, there's more to the story and you deserve to know it."

Levi had yet to sit down. He touched her other shoulder. "Are you sure?"

"Your parents deserve to know more." She captured a corner of her bottom lip between her teeth. "Last Wednesday, a local floral shop delivered an outrageously large arrangement to the landing of my apartment." She propped her elbows on the table's edge and clasped her hands. "The message on the card simply read *it's time to talk*. I knew who sent the message, but I didn't respond. I deeply regret not calling and demanding he leave me alone."

"Rachel said you moved here to escape an ex-boyfriend who wouldn't accept the breakup." Katie reclaimed her chair across the table.

Chloe cringed. "I used that excuse so I wouldn't have to mention the real danger. I was wrong." She glanced between Rachel's parents. "Soon, I'll disclose my entire story, but for now, I'm in witness protection."

"Oh, dear." Katie pursed her lips. "The incident yesterday—is it connected to Rachel's collision?"

"Yes, we believe so." She moaned. "Rachel's so worried about my car—I need you to know—the car means nothing compared to Rachel's life." She glanced at Levi and recalled the pain when he suspected the car was her concern. Hopefully, they'd moved far beyond that point.

"Jacque, would you like a cup of coffee?" Ray stood.

"Uh, maybe." Her headache had intensified, and she had difficulty tracking the conversation.

Levi left his chair and moved toward the kitchen's workspace. "Jacque prefers tea in the afternoon. I'll make a pot. Dad, I'll top off your coffee."

"I can do that, son." Katie smiled softly and rose.

"I'm good, Mom. How about you pour the coffee?"

"I'm so glad you're making tea again." She puckered her full lips and, for a moment, closed her eyes, and with a smile, she opened them.

Suddenly, Levi's tea-making expertise made sense, and so did the subtext between mother and son. Lucy had loved tea.

Levi moved to the far wall and, just inside the pantry, opened the wood frame glass doors of a curio cabinet.

How had she missed it on her way through the back door this morning? The cabinet contained an extensive collection of teapots, cups and saucers, cream pitchers, and sugar bowls. A lump formed in her throat. How did a family survive such a loss?

Levi selected a white teapot with tiny lavender flowers and set it on the counter next to the coffee maker. He started the electric kettle and prepared a tea ball with dried lavender buds.

Katie filled a white, thermal carafe and carried it to the table to refill Ray's mug, then hers. "Coffee, Levi?"

"Sure. Thanks, Mom." Levi hooked the tea ball to the mouth of the teapot, then returned to the curio cabinet for a matching cup and saucer.

"Since Rachel's doing so well, Dad and I have decided to head home in the morning. We don't have a foreman like Riley to run the ranch." Katie sank to her chair.

"I understand and so will Rachel." Levi poured boiling water into the ceramic pot. "I'm blessed to have a good crew."

The comforting fragrance of lavender floated over the aroma of roast beef and buttery shortbreads. Chloe breathed in the scent and sighed. Levi kept lavender.

"Jacque."

Chloe cringed at Katie's use of her alias and physically felt sick.

"Rachel said you've generously offered to cover her clients' needs for however long she needs help. If juggling her clients alongside your own becomes too much, please let us know. Ray and I are happy to help Rachel with expenses."

"I'm happy to help. Rachel's current account is well on its way to completion, and yesterday, I met with her new clients."

Levi arrived with the tray, outfitted with the tea service and small honey jar. "Your tea, Madam."

"Why thank you, Sir." She choked on a laugh.

He winked and sat beside her.

She sputtered. A wink? She touched the delicate porcelain cup handle. "I'm impressed." She filled the cup and took a sip. "Just what I needed."

"Jacque, have a cinnamon roll. Best pastry in two states." Ray pointed his fork at the roll he'd been eating when they entered the kitchen.

She stifled a laugh. Exactly what Levi expected his dad would say. "I agree and will increase that estimate to three states." She patted her stomach. "But I ate an entire cinnamon roll and a blueberry muffin this morning, so I'd better pass."

"Plus a green salad." Levi helped himself to a cinnamon roll.

"Exactly. I'll survive until dinner." Another mystery Chloe aimed to solve. How did Janice maintain such a slender form when she baked delicious sweets and worked with food all day?

The kitchen occupants became distracted with a discussion about ranch operations. Chloe leaned into the chair and sipped her favorite tea. She examined the small jar of honey with the red-and-white-plaid metal lid. "Is this brand available in the stores?"

"Nope." Janice responded. "Comes from the hives on the ranch. Levi and Riley suit up and harvest honey each year. Wait until you taste it."

She angled to gaze at Levi. "You keep honeybees, too?" She shook her head. "What doesn't the Riverbanks Ranch provide?"

He smiled. "Pork, for one thing. We buy it from a

local farmer, and our flour comes from a mill near the Canadian border."

"Well, I'm impressed. My honey comes in a plastic bear."

"I noticed." Levi chuckled.

Janice and Fiona immersed themselves in preparing dinner for nine and refreshments for at least fifty-nine.

Levi's gaze followed Janice and Fiona. He propped his elbows on the edge of the table and ran a hand over his mouth. "Ladies, I know you're busy, but could I have your attention for a few minutes?"

"Of course, Boss." Janice wiped her hands on the front of her apron.

"Yes." Fiona nodded.

"For your security, I'm about to share some information, but you mustn't share it with anyone." Levi paused. "Our renter, Gary Sims, is a private investigator who came to spy on Jacque."

"I knew the man was dodgy." Janice's mouth tightened. "But a spy?"

"A private investigator," Levi repeated. "Hired by the attorney representing the man who's been searching for Jacque. Officer Haynes of the Coeur d'Alene Police Department has been assigned to find the drivers of the pickups used as weapons over the past few days."

Chloe exhaled. Levi had maintained his promise to protect her alias. Still, she despised forcing him to lie to his family.

Katie glanced between Levi and Chloe, and her amber-brown eyes filled with compassion.

Ray nodded, and his lips tightened like Chloe had witnessed Levi doing when calculating information.

She tightened her hold on the teacup and resisted telling all.

No one questioned Levi's request, and they agreed to use situational awareness.

"Officer Haynes has confirmed Gary Sims caught a flight back to California." Chloe plunged into the conversation. "He's gone, but we don't know who else is involved."

Levi finished his coffee before continuing. "Fifty people have RSVP'd for the rodeo. A few will bring guests. A perfect opportunity for an uninvited character to slip in." He glanced at her. "At all times, please stay close to my parents, Carson, or me. Once I finish the opening ceremonies, I'll join you."

"I promise." Chloe's stomach churned. She'd brought trouble to the Riverbanks Ranch.

"What if we see someone we don't recognize?" Janice responded first.

Levi lifted the thermal carafe and refilled his mug. "Find me, Dad, or Carson."

"Security on the Riverbanks Ranch." Janice shook her head. "Never thought I'd see the day."

Chloe moaned under her breath.

Fiona's eyes were wide. "Wow, Jacque. This must be scary. I'm so glad you're not alone in town."

"I'll return to town tomorrow morning." Chloe glanced at Levi. "Levi's sacrificed enough to protect me. Besides, it's Monday, and I need to open the studio."

"We'll see what happens in the meantime." Levi held her gaze.

Chloe lifted her chin and a brow, but she didn't challenge his comment. He had enough on his plate without her adding to it. Ultimately, his sister had been injured in the collision meant for her. Still…he didn't use that against her.

Ray snagged another cinnamon roll from the platter.

Katie swatted the back of his hand."Ray, dinner isn't that far off."

Chloe suppressed a chuckle. If she began to laugh, she wouldn't stop until she cried. She fingered the gooseneck handle on the silver spoon Levi had set next to the honey jar.

"I believe Lucy found that spoon in a Missoula antique store." Katie rested her folded hands on the table.

"It's beautiful." The absent Lucy, who still had a special place in this family and would never be forgotten. She gazed at the unique design for a moment longer, then used it to stir homegrown honey into her tea.

"Jacque, can you tell us about your parents?" Katie took a sip of coffee." Where do they live? Have they visited since you moved?"

Chloe studied Katie and realized she bore a striking resemblance to a former presidential candidate. Even in her mannerisms and soft tone. "My parents live in San Diego. I haven't been cleared to even tell them I left Sacramento. Besides, my mom just finished her final round of chemo, and I don't want to worry her and Dad."

"Oh, I'm so sorry." Katie's dark brows met. "I hope the treatments were successful, and she soon regains her strength."

Sitting in the warmth of the kitchen at the

Riverbanks Ranch, Chloe's heart squeezed with gratitude and more than a touch of regret. She straightened her shoulders and lifted her chin. "Thank you, Katie. As usual, I call them every week. Two Fridays ago, my mom's doctor declared she's in full remission."

"Oh—I didn't know. Glad she's on the mend." Levi left the table, rinsed his coffee mug in the farm-style sink, and set it on the drainboard.

"Thank you." Chloe averted her attention to her teacup and added more honey. Levi's simple, everyday actions filled her with something complicated. From the way he moved to the measure of his smooth, low voice and the compassion in his amber eyes. He'd awakened something new and powerful deep inside. Somehow, she needed to end this meeting, return to the office, and take a breath.

"It's wrong that you can't share your location with your parents." Katie stood and gathered their dishes.

Her emotions overflowing, Chloe set her empty teacup next to the pot on the tray. "I agree, but my contact in the Sacramento Police Department is adamant that I do not tell them."

Levi returned to carry the tray to the drainboard. "C-Jacque, are you heading back to the computer? Would you like a fresh pot of tea?"

Chloe's heart skipped a beat. He'd almost used her real name. "No thank you." She pushed from the chair and tested her right foot. "I'd better grab a fresh ice pack, though." She gripped the chair back. "Katie and Ray, it's so nice to finally meet you."

Katie smiled and glanced between Chloe and Levi. "You two are quite the detective team."

229

Levi disappeared into the pantry and returned with an ice pack. "The Internet makes researching everything easy. Good and bad—we just followed the leads."

"Well." Ray retrieved his Western hat off the hook by the door. "Officer Haynes is fortunate to have you both on the team. Jacque, I hope to see you at dinner."

Chloe exchanged a glance with Levi and nodded. "Thank you for your understanding about…the situation." A weight settled in the pit of her stomach. Would they be so forgiving when they heard her entire story? She hobbled from the kitchen and through the great room. As she reached the hallway, her phone chirped. Juggling the ice pack and her cane, she managed to open the app.

—Diane and I will leave Napa mid-afternoon. Missed you!—

Chloe sighed. She'd missed the annual girls' trip to the wineries. The date on her calendar had come and gone—without her. She thumbed a quick response.

—I'll video chat tonight, after the rodeo—

Stuffing her phone into her slacks pocket, she continued to the office and sank to her chair. Spending time with Levi's parents, hearing them not only forgive her, but not blame her in the first place, filled a space in her heart. She missed her parents even more.

She opened her father's website and gazed at the photo of the man that helped create her but left in her formative years. Tomorrow, a new week began. Maybe he'd return her call. Her stomach clenched. If he did, what should she ask? Are you involved with the threat against me? Do you ever regret severing ties with me? So many questions. She propped her elbows on the desktop and rested her head in her hands. If she were the type to run and hide…well, she wasn't. She'd stay and face the uncertainty.

With a sniff, she opened the Meeker file in her design software and removed the wall separating Cain's office from the guest bedroom to form a much larger workspace and a long, narrow closet. She tried to focus on the plans, but the framed photo behind her begged another look. She swiveled the chair and met Lucy's blue gaze. They were such different people.

She blinked and turned back to her laptop. Why did that matter?

Chapter Seventeen

Levi joined Riley in the elevated announcer's booth.

Guests were filing through the gate and choosing their positions on the planks of the bleachers.

From the booth, he had a birds-eye view, and so far, he recognized everyone. With the possibility a thug could show up, he'd updated Riley on "Jacque's" situation. He could count on Riley to keep the information confidential, even from Rachel, until the danger had passed.

He'd seated Chloe with his parents, but once he'd conducted the opening ceremonies, he'd hand the mic to Riley and join her.

At dinner, she'd been skittish as a new foal, and he suspected something had hatched in that beautiful head of hers. He half smiled. She'd thrown him off when she stepped into the dining room, dressed in blue jeans, a blue-green, long-sleeved blouse, and wearing tooled leather cowboy boots. A matching leather belt emphasized her slender waist, with a belt buckle that read, *Design*. Custom made, or something from an interior designer site?

As if she enjoyed throwing him for a loop, she'd grinned but didn't pursue the subject. She'd directed his attention to her boots, claiming they supported her ankle better than the stretchy bandages. The new outfit bridged the gap between her usual city fashions and ranch wear.

Like a cornered bull, he blew a breath and repositioned his hat. *Focus, Banks*. His students, and the fifty-plus guests, depended on a good show. Tonight marked the third anniversary of the end-of-session mini-rodeos, and he needed to keep his mind on the students and off the beautiful woman in the bleachers. At least until Riley took over the program.

Weaving through a line of guests, Carson moved toward the announcer's booth.

Levi waved and climbed down the ladder to meet him under the booth. "Carson, thanks for coming tonight."

"No problem. I look forward to watching the rodeo." Carson's gaze scanned the arena and bleachers. "I see Chloe's sitting with your parents. How's she doing?"

Levi ran his knuckles over his fresh-shaven jaw. "She's wound tight."

"Can't be easy to live with half-truths. Any response from her father?"

"No, and I can tell his silence frustrates her."

"I can't blame her." Carson repositioned his after-work-hours ball cap. "Until her father proves otherwise, he could be part of the threat."

Levi glanced toward the line of guests and caught sight of the grain store owner from Mica Flats, Washington. "Excuse me, Carson, there's someone I need to greet." As he passed, he clamped a hand on Carson's shoulder. "Thanks for being here." He approached the rotund store owner and his petite wife. "Clarence, thanks for making the drive." Levi shook his hand and smiled at the missus.

"Your rodeos are worth every mile." Clarence smiled and shook Levi's hand. "And so are Janice's baked goods after the rodeo." He patted the front of his brown plaid shirt. "Do you remember my wife, Anne?"

"Yes, of course. Thank you both for attending. I'll find you after the rodeo." Honored by the growing number of folks willing to make the effort to attend the rodeos, Levi moved toward another group of arrivals. Several drove from over two hours away. He might need to build another set of bleachers. So far, the guests were all familiar.

He tugged his hat brim to block the glare of the sinking sun and noticed Rianna had just arrived with her three friends. He tightened his mouth. On Wednesdays, Rianna visited to ride Daisy. Maybe he'd ask her to postpone this week. Huh—guess he'd play it by ear.

She raised a hand in greeting and passed through the gate, a jacket over her arm and a picnic basket in hand.

Levi lifted his hat and raked his fingers through his hair. He didn't like having to worry about ranch security. Next weekend they'd planned to celebrate Janice's birthday. Rachel would insist the party go on, even if she was still in the physical therapy center Doc had scheduled for her to move to this Wednesday.

"Levi." Chloe tugged on his white shirtsleeve. "Mike and Melissa Parker are here."

He followed her gaze toward the bleachers and a couple dressed in brand-new Western-wear. "I wonder who invited them?" He grasped her arm and guided her toward his parents. "Sit tight. I promise, we'll find them afterward." He'd prefer to talk with them away from the rodeo crowd.

"Mike's an award-winning writer. Maybe, he learned I'm on the ranch and plans to use me for another *exposé* about Hallie. Look, he's carrying a camera." She hesitated and touched his arm.

"Maybe, you're reading too much into this." Levi pulled her arm through his crooked arm and patted her hand. He settled her next to his mom, then climbed two more steps to where Carson sat. "The Parkers are here." He tipped his head toward the other end of the bleachers. "Please try to keep Chloe in her seat. I'll be back after the opening ceremony."

Carson gazed toward the couple. "Is this the first time they've attended?"

"Yeah, not sure who invited them."

Carson gave a quick nod. "I'll watch them and Chloe."

Levi hurried back to the raised announcer's booth, his mind on far more than kicking off the rodeo.

"Okay, Boss." Riley handed him the mic. "Everything's ready to roll. Hey, I spoke with Rachel while you were away. She wished us good luck this evening. Sounded much better than she did yesterday."

Levi clasped the muted microphone and clamped his other hand on Riley's shoulder. "Knowing Rachel, she'll be chomping at the bit to reclaim her life. If I haven't said this before…thank you. I couldn't have gotten through the past two days without your help."

"Happy to do it, Boss." Riley lifted his chin toward the bleachers. "You've got your hands full."

Levi gave Riley's shoulder another squeeze and ran his gaze over the arena. Time to activate the mic and give these folks the show they'd traveled miles to see.

Cowboys on foot lined the inside of the arena, hats in hand. Others on horseback rode into the arena and lined their mounts side by side to face the unfurled flag backlit by the setting sun.

The repeat guests knew the routine and stood to face the flag.

Levi took a breath and soaked in the moment.

Mom slipped an arm around Chloe's waist and waved at him.

His parents were always there for him. He blew a breath and nodded toward his dad.

Ray removed his felt cowboy hat, held the wireless mic to his mouth, and led the Pledge of Allegiance, followed by an opening prayer.

The crowd murmured, "Amen."

Riley touched the sound system and a recorded version of "The Star-Spangled Banner" filled the evening air.

Riding horseback, Clay and Travis led the procession of students around the inside of the arena. Some on foot, others on horseback, each cowboy carried their state flag.

The crowd cheered and clapped.

Levi's blood sang. A huge part of his dreams had come true. If only Lucy could be here. She would've loved the traditional ceremony. He drew a breath, and his gaze found Chloe. He still had a chance to share all of this—with someone.

The final student joined the procession, and the anthem ended.

Levi lifted the microphone and with a silent prayer for strength on his lips, he smiled and welcomed his guests.

****

Tears dampening her cheeks, Chloe enjoyed the old-fashioned pageantry of the opening ceremony. She especially liked watching Levi.

He'd welcomed the rodeo guests, and soon, he turned the mic over to Riley.

Riley introduced the first bronc rider from Wyoming.

According to Levi, skill and agility, and the seconds spent on the back of an animal, determined the score of each rider.

The rider clung to the bucking horse, one hand gripped the braided, single rein and the other one held high in the air. She noticed the saddle didn't have a horn, and the stirrups hung free. She cringed. She supposed a saddle horn could be hazardous.

Dust rose over the arena, and the buzzer rang at an ear-shattering volume.

Chloe gripped the edges of the smooth plank on either side of her thighs.

Another rider entered the arena to grab the bucking animal's bridle and lead him until he calmed.

The bronc rider slid from the saddle and stepped out of the way of the flying hooves.

The crowd cheered, yelled, and clapped.

Through a cloud of dust, the rider raised his hat to more cheers.

The decibels of the event, between the cheering crowd, Riley's announcements, and the buzzer, rivaled any rock concert Chloe had attended. She swiped at damp cheeks and chuckled. Since when did she cry over any event, let alone a rodeo? Somehow, the energy in this microcosm of Kootenai County caused her emotions to overflow.

Levi arrived in front of the bleachers.

Her heart performed an odd flip-flop. She blinked and touched her stomach. Okay, so he looked devastatingly handsome, dressed in black Western-cut dress pants and a white shirt. His polished, black, tooled leather boots were covered with dust, and a high-wattage grin showed his white teeth and laugh lines. The man did odd things to her insides.

He sank to the plank beside her and playfully bumped his shoulder into hers. "What do you think, so far?"

His lips brushed her ear and sent thrills—like the effervescence of a newly opened bottle of sparkling wine—over her shoulders. "It's loud!" she yelled over the buzzer.

His amber gaze danced. "That it is, but two riders have made the buzzer!"

Chloe's brain quit functioning. Okay, what just happened? Between his nearness and his spicy scent, she couldn't breathe properly. Must be the corral dust kicking up allergies.

The buzzer sounded, signaling another rider had finished his ride.

The crowd cheered.

Gina would love this, but soon, Coeur d'Alene would be in Chloe's rearview mirror. She shifted toward Katie and exhaled.

Katie patted her back and leaned to speak near her ear. "You'll get used to the noise and fast pace!"

"I'm not sure about that." She laughed.

A camera flashed from the other end of the

bleachers.

Chloe straightened and glanced at Mike and Melissa Parker.

Mike held a camera with a very long lens toward the arena and produced a series of flashes. His smile widened, and not once did he look her way.

Hmm. Maybe she'd misjudged Mike Parker. He could be here to write an article about the Riverbanks Ranch. Her paranoia had her expecting a threat around every corner.

Levi leaned his shoulder against hers.

She turned to meet his gaze.

"Been crying?" He raised his brows.

"My allergies." She sniffed and pulled a tissue from her jacket pocket.

The crowd gasped.

A snorting, twisting, snot-blowing bull erupted from the chute.

The bull seesawed to the center of the arena, and a cowboy clung to his back. Suddenly, the rider flew over the bull's head and hit the dusty ground.

The buzzer sounded.

The crowed groaned.

"That's what you did for a living?" Chloe grabbed Levi's right arm and tried to imagine him on the back of an angry bull.

Levi nodded slowly, his attention on the arena.

The cowboy came to his feet and hurried toward the fence.

The angry bull continued to buck and toss its massive head.

A rodeo clown distracted the animal by performing comedic moves.

The rider climbed to the top fence rail and turned to wave at the crowd.

Chloe pressed a hand against her pounding heart and swallowed hard. How many times had Levi hit the dirt to earn the money to buy this ranch and to open the rodeo school? The trophies in his office attested to his success. Now, he used his experience to train new riders and provide jobs to four full-time employees. Not to mention, how he watched over his younger sister.

Through it all, he'd lost his wife. Chloe swiped at a stray tear. Lucy had been the queen of this ranch, and she still held prominence with the Banks family. She could imagine Lucy sitting here between Levi and Katie, clapping and cheering with the crowd.

The buzzer signaled the end of the time and the crowd roared.

Chloe blinked. Her daydreaming had made her miss the next bull rider.

Levi leaned closer.

His breath feathered her ear.

"Enjoying the show?"

She shivered with awareness. Good criminy, how could watching a rodeo turn into romantic awareness? Okay, she'd read far more than he intended—right? They had to be close to be heard over the cacophony. She cleared her throat and brought her lips close to his right ear. "Now, I understand why people are so fascinated with rodeos." She paused. "And the cowboys." His spicy cologne flowed through her senses.

The buzzer ended the ride.

Chloe pulled away from Levi's solid and oh-so-masculine frame.

The spectators roared, and a heavy cloud of brown dust descended on the bleachers.

Chloe coughed and patted her throat. "What happened?"

Levi spared her a glance, and lifted one corner of his mouth. "A rank bull I bought in Great Falls, Montana, happened."

"Oh, my gosh! He hit the ground so hard! Is he okay?" She squirmed to the hard edge of the plank, her heart in her throat.

"He'll be sore for a day or two, but look at his grin." Levi slowly nodded.

"How interesting." Chloe blinked hard. "He looks like he won the lottery."

"In a way, he has. He's holding the highest score so far."

She shifted on the hard seat and flexed her injured ankle. The Western boots had helped, but sitting so long in one position had stiffened her ankle.

"Are you okay?" Levi slipped a hand over the small of her back.

Her nerve endings began to dance. He exuded a magnetism that sent her body into hyperawareness. She turned her head to study his almost square jaw.

Levi turned and caught her gaze.

For a moment, the air caught in her lungs, then escaped on a sigh. Thank goodness, he couldn't hear her over the racket surrounding them.

He continued to touch her back and held her gaze with his amber-brown eyes.

Whoa. Chloe forced her lungs to expand. Suddenly, she wanted the rodeo to go on for hours.

Levi removed his touch and leaned forward to rest

his forearms on his thighs.

A wave of disappointment hit her. What the heck? How had this man become so important in such a short time? Okay, so maybe she'd noticed him from day one—when he visited the studio open house. She swallowed hard. *Back off, Austin. Focus on the upcoming meeting with the Parkers and helping Levi reclaim his life.*

The buzzer intruded on her thoughts, and she snapped her attention to another cowboy, jumping free of yet another angry bull.

She sighed. Somehow, returning to Sacramento didn't hold the same excitement it had since she arrived in Coeur d'Alene. Her temporary life had turned into something solid. She no longer minded the vast countryside or the corral dust settling over her. She loved the ranch and Idaho.

She side-glanced at Levi. Earlier, when he'd stepped outside, she'd researched the origins of the rodeo—a sport that sprang from the everyday, hard work of ranch life. The processes of roping and branding—breaking a mustang—evolved into publicly attended events where—so claimed a website—in 1888, Prescott, Arizona, held the first rodeo to charge admission and award trophies. She'd searched Levi's name and found a stings of references, including video clips and photos of the champion bull rider.

The arena lights flashed on.

Chloe blinked against the harsh brightness and brought her attention back to the event.

The cowboys paraded into the arena, much like they had in the beginning.

Levi sat straight and grinned. "You're a trouper.

Covered in dust and still smiling."

"I surprised myself. I had fun." She pursed her lips but broke into a smile.

He grasped her left hand and helped her stand. "Are you aware, there are rodeos in Sacramento?"

"There are?" Chloe's jaw dropped. "I had no idea."

His grin widened. "I rode there at least once a year."

More tingles. She scrunched her neck. To think, they'd been so close and never met. "Admit it, even you were concerned about the last bull rider."

His lips flattened. "If they hit the ground, there's a moment when things could go sideways."

"Well, even to my untrained eye, it's obvious they've worked with a champion. Amid the mind-blowing speed, they knew what to do." She'd studied the inscriptions on the trophies and belt buckles in the curio cabinet. *All Around Cowboy, National Finals Rodeo, Las Vegas. Champion Bull Rider, Calgary, Alberta.* Levi had reached the top in this profession.

"Be careful or you'll inflate my ego." The brim of his cowboy hat shadowed his eyes, but his white grin flashed. "Are you ready to climb down?"

She clamped her bottom lip between her teeth. "I still can't feel my behind."

"I won't let you fall." He stepped down a level and grasped her left arm.

Chloe glanced around for Katie and Ray and found them in the line of spectators making their way to the gate. Chloe hobbled on her stiff and painful ankle. She had no choice but to allow Levi to support at least half her weight.

Levi shortened his stride to match hers. As they

emerged through the gated area, he gazed over the crowd.

"Can you see the Parkers?" At five-eight, she still couldn't see over half the people in the crowd.

"No. When they exited the gate, I lost sight of them." He angled and helped her pass several attendees.

A pain stabbed her ankle and traveled up her calf. Chloe moaned. "Go ahead and catch them, and I'll follow."

He shook his head. "I'm not leaving you without support. If we miss them, we'll figure out a Plan B."

They reached the gate and stepped into the parking area. At least thirty cars remained parked between the house and the dining hall.

"Maybe they're inside." Simultaneously, she both dreaded and looked forward to meeting the Parkers. Kind of like facing a nemesis head-on.

Carson stepped from the wide-open doorway of the dining hall. With a paper coffee cup in one hand and a cookie in the other, he joined them. "If you're looking for the Parkers, they just drove away." He lifted his chin toward the driveway. "I'll stop by the newspaper office tomorrow. They've lived here for two years, and Mike's a reputable journalist. Once he's fully informed, he might be willing to work with us."

"Fully informed?" Chloe tensed. "How much do you plan to tell him?" She glanced at Levi for support.

His dark brows furrowed. "Don't expose her to Parker until we know what he's up to."

A group of passing rodeo attendees called out to Levi.

He smiled and raised a hand.

Chloe edged closer to his side and searched the

face of each guest. Were they all legit rodeo attendees, or had Drew King sent someone?

Levi pulled her close to his side.

The contact defused her unease. "Carson, Mike needs to agree not to use my name or location. Have you communicated with Paul about the discoveries we've made?"

Carson swallowed his last bite of cookie and chased it with coffee. He nodded and brushed the crumbs from his mouth. "Earlier today, Hallie's phone mysteriously reappeared in the evidence room. Paul has tech support working to break the password. Once they access the records, they'll confirm Billings' multiple calls. I hope he left at least one voice message."

"I left Hallie a message." She pressed her fingertips against her collarbone "I asked her to call me." Her voice broke. "Turned out, she had already been struck down."

"The timestamp on your message, along with the footage from the Crazy Bean, completely clears you of leaving Hallie on the Interstate." Carson adjusted his ball cap.

"I so regret not taking her home." She drew a sharp breath.

Carson ran his gaze ran over the parking area and back to meet hers. "Hallie made choices that took her to that ditch. You're not responsible for those choices." He crushed the paper cup in one hand. "Are you still determined to return to town tomorrow?"

"Yes." Chloe refused to argue the point. She needed to regain her life.

A rotund man and his slender wife stopped next to them. The man shook hands with Levi. "Levi, your rodeos get better every month."

"Thanks, Clarence. I always appreciate seeing you and Anne." Levi retained his hold on the man's hand for a moment.

Anne nodded. "Please ask Janice to email me her blueberry cobbler recipe. It's the best."

"I'll be happy to pass on your request." Levi touched the woman's arm. "If you're up for another trip to the ranch soon, this Saturday at four, I'm hosting a surprise birthday party for Janice."

"Sounds good." Clarence nodded.

"A party, so soon after your sister's accident?" Anne frowned. "Isn't she still in the hospital?"

"Knowing my sister, she'll insist the party go on. Wednesday, she's scheduled to move to physical therapy facility. After that, she might move to the ranch for a few days."

"Such a generous and understanding young woman." Anne nodded. "We'll let you know by Wednesday."

Levi continued to watch the couple until they disappeared into the dining hall. "I expect more questions about hosting the party next weekend."

"It'll all work out." Chloe clasped his forearm and shifted her weight to ease the growing discomfort in her ankle. "I'm sorry to bow out, but I have to elevate my ankle."

Carson touched his hat bill and crooked an elbow. "I'll be happy to escort you to the house. Levi, go ahead and join your guests. We'll resume this conversation after I speak with Mike Parker."

Levi glanced between her and Carson. "Thanks. Chloe, I'll check in on you soon."

"No problem. Please enjoy your guests." Chloe slipped a hand over Carson's proffered arm and hobbled toward the house. "Let's use the kitchen entrance." She couldn't shake the uneasiness of potentially encountering a thug, and the residual concern over confronting Mike Parker. "Carson, if Mike pledges to crack open the corruption, then I'll work with him, but we need a firm agreement."

Carson matched his step to hers. "I'll make our agreement very clear." He opened the kitchen door. "Before I take off, do you need help with the ice, or anything?"

"Thank you, but I'll manage." She knocked the bulk of dust from her boots. "How did life become so complicated?"

"Has a way of doing that." He cocked a tight smile. "Please keep me informed."

Entering the warm, dimly lit kitchen, still fragrant from the day's cooking and baking, Chloe paused to soak in the alone time—the space to let down her guard and think. To strategize on how to handle her growing feelings for Levi.

Several ice packs lay in the deep freezer, but first, she'd turn on the electric kettle. She didn't want to track dust all over the house, but if she removed her new Western boots, she wouldn't have ankle support.

Reaching her room, she slipped into a heavy Aran knit sweater and portioned one of each prescription. Back in the kitchen, she filled a glass with water and swallowed the capsules. Weariness washed over her. Okay, she'd love a proper pot of tea to drink while she called her friends, but no way could she carry everything to the office. She settled for a mug and a teabag and put an ice pack in a plastic grocery bag with a handle. She hobbled to the other end of the house office and sank into one of the curved-back leather chairs facing the fireplace. "Ahh, this is heaven."

Scotty moved to sit next to her feet.

"Hey, buddy. You've been alone for a long time, haven't you? I'm here now, and I'm going to call Gina and Diane. They should be home from the girls' trip."

Scotty's tail thumped against the thick wool rug.

She smiled at Duke, who stretched out in front of the fire, and took her phone from her pocket. Ugh. First, she'd remove her boots and ice her ankle.

Chloe pulled off one boot, then the other, and wiggled her toes. Her injured ankle expanded against the stretchy bandage. She unwrapped it and applied the ice pack. Ah, immediate relief.

Okay, now she could focus on the call. She sent Gina and Diane links to video chat and leaned into the chair. Should she tell them about the Parkers attending the rodeo? No, Diane would freak out and blame herself. Chloe's chest tightened. What if Mike had taken pictures of her? He could plaster her photo all over social media, or worse, the *Sacramento Times*.

Chapter Eighteen

"This is Gina."

"Gina, it's me, calling as planned." Chloe frowned. Gina seemed to have answered on her phone, instead of her laptop, and she had the phone to her cheek. "Remember, we're scheduled to video chat? Are you okay? You sound odd."

"Uh, I'm fine, but I'm not home yet. I'm driving."

"Then, why aren't you using the hands-free? I hear music playing in the background." She scooted to the edge of the chair and planted her injured bare foot on the thick wool rug. "Is Diane with you?" *What the heck?* Gina sounded like a robot. Chloe gripped the chair arm. Her expressive and colorful friend didn't do monotone.

"Diane's home. I'm fine." The word fine ended with a squeak.

"Okay, where are you, and why do you sound strange? Did you and Diane quarrel?"

"I'm fine." As if hypnotized, Gina repeated the words.

"I'm not convinced. Exactly, where are you?"

"Uh, on a street. Please call Pizza Depot. Order a regular crust loaded with sausage."

"Gina, is someone else in the car?" Chloe's breath caught in her chest.

"Please. Meet me at home with the pizza."

Chloe froze. Gina didn't do gluten or pork. Pizza Depot didn't exist in Sacramento, and Gina knew darned well Chloe wasn't in town. Could she be referring to Paul's college nickname? Chloe pressed a hand to her sternum. "Should I invite Paul to join us?"

"The more, the merrier." Gina's voice quavered.

"Got it. Stay on the line and I'll order right now." She pushed from the chair and hobbled to the desk to use Levi's landline. She fumbled with her cell to avoid disconnecting from Gina while searching for Paul's contact. "Hang on, Gina. I'm searching for the number for Pizza Depot. Please be sure your phone isn't on speaker." She punched Paul's number into the vintage phone and pressed the large plastic receiver to her left ear. She tapped the speaker icon on her cell. "Paul!" She shouted the moment the connected. "Gina's on my cell phone. She's in trouble."

"Chloe? Exactly where are you calling from?" He moaned. "Never mind, why do you believe Gina's in trouble?"

"Paul, just listen. Gina's on my speaker function. She sounds stilted, like someone else is in the car. Someone other than Diane. She asked me to order pizza from Pizza Depot."

"Slow down, Chloe. Disconnect with Gina, and I'll call her. Stay on whatever phone you're using, and I'll put her on speaker."

"Please hurry!" The room around her went gray. "Gina, Pizza Depot will call to confirm the order." Her voice shook. "I'll disconnect for now."

"O-k-a-y," Gina said.

Chloe hated to disconnect, but Paul would call her back. She clung to the plastic receiver and counted the seconds ticking by. Her ankle weakened, and she sank to Levi's office chair. "Come on, Paul. Why haven't you reached her?"

"Patience, Chloe. It won't help to freak out." Paul's voice came through loud and clear. "Gina, this is Pizza Depot. Can you pick up your order? Our delivery people are swamped tonight."

Chloe opened her mouth. Had Paul just asked Gina to help herself and find a precinct?

"I'm not sure." Gina's response came through Paul's speaker, but faint. "I don't have control over where I'm driving."

The connection ended.

"Paul!" Chloe didn't pretend to be calm. "You lost Gina!"

"Yes, I'm aware."

"Well, call her back!" She clutched the edge of the desk.

"Chloe, I'll handle this. While I find Gina, call Diane, and confirm her location. Later, I want to know where you are."

"Just find Gina." Her vision blurred, and she had to squeeze her eyelids shut twice to see her contact screen. The call went directly to voice mail. "Diane, it's Chloe. Gina's in trouble. Please call right away!" She shifted the chair to better reach the landline, and pain zinged through her ankle. *Ugh.* She'd left the ice pack next to the curve-backed chair. She pressed fingertips against the twang of pain in her temples and dialed Paul. "Diane didn't answer. Maybe she's with Gina!" Silence. "Paul? Did you hear me?"

"Yes, Chloe. I'm in the middle of ordering an all-points bulletin on Gina's car. I'll swing by Diane's and call you back." He disconnected.

Chloe set the receiver on the black base and clutched her cell phone to her chest. "Oh, Scotty. Gina's been abducted." Heart breaking, she hiccupped on a sob and pushed from Levi's chair to retrieve her ice pack. Sinking into the leather upholstery, she conformed the flexible bag to her ankle.

How could this be happening? She'd left Sacramento to protect her friends, and now, a hired thug had a gun to Gina's head—forcing her to drive—somewhere! She rested her head on the chair-back and gazed at the natural-finished pine, tongue-and-groove ceiling. In hindsight, she should have stayed put and prodded Paul daily to find Hallie's killer. Her fear had driven her to follow Paul's orders and leave. She'd been wrong to adapt to this pseudo existence and form a new life, a new business, and new friendships.

Still clutched in her cold right hand, her cell phone rang. "Paul? Did you find Gina and Diane?

"Diane's safe. I'm at her house. After Gina dropped her off—over an hour ago—Diane turned off her phone and went to bed."

"That's odd. We always stay up until everyone's confirmed they're home."

"Well, you'll have to discuss that later. Have you heard from Gina?"

"No, but Paul, Gina helped me escape the thug in front of Luigi's. What if he has her?"

"Until we find her, we'll consider all possibilities. All law enforcement in the area is on high alert. Now, where are you?"

Chloe clutched her phone like a lifeline. "I'm at Rachel's brother's home. The Riverbanks Ranch. With everything that's happened over the past few days, Officer Carson Haynes advised me not to stay alone at my apartment."

"Good advice. Well, stay put, and I'll keep you in the loop on the search for Gina. I'll also connect with Officer Haynes. I'm glad there's a local officer to keep you safe." He disconnected.

As his contact photo faded, Chloe blinked. He'd probably expected her to argue about staying at the ranch. She'd cooperate tonight, but tomorrow, she'd return to town. She repositioned the ice pack and rested her forehead on her knees. Despair washed over her. Being hundreds of miles away hadn't protected her friends.

Scotty stretched and groaned, then resettled at her feet.

Chloe straightened and accessed Carson's contact, but maybe she should give Paul time to call Carson.

The outside office door opened, and Levi entered on a wave of chilly night air.

Chloe shivered and rubbed her arms.

His gaze found hers. "What happened? I figured you'd be in bed." In two strides, he reached her chair and sank to one knee. "You look like you've had a shock."

Chloe opened her mouth to respond. She struggled to form the needed words. "My friend, Gina, is missing."

"What?" He placed his hand over hers where it clutched the chair arm. "When? What happened?"

"We'd planned to video chat tonight, but Gina answered on her phone and Diane didn't respond. Gina sounded odd—very strained and almost robotic." Her voice broke. "Using a code from college, she asked me to contact Paul DeMers." The words ended on a sob. "He's called in all available law enforcement." She began to shake.

Levi caressed her hand for a moment, then moved to sit in the matching chair, with a small table between them. "Okay, DeMers is on the job. He'll find her." He quirked a dark brow. "We should inform Carson."

"Paul contacted him, but I agree. We might need law enforcement help." She dragged her hands over her hair. Her phone rang against her lap and illuminated with Paul's photo. Chloe hit the speaker button. "Paul, did you find her?"

"Not yet, but I want to make sure you're staying at the ranch. I know you, Chloe, and I don't want you to get some harebrained ideas about helping to find Gina."

"Paul, I won't do anything to hamper the search." Clutching the leather-covered chair arm, she pushed from the chair. "Oh, Paul. After the flowers arrived, I should have called Bruce. I might have prevented Rachel's accident, and now"—she stifled a sob— "Gina's driving somewhere with a gun to her head."

"Whatever you do, do not call Bruce Billings." Paul's voice barreled through the speaker. "We don't know the part he played in Hallie's death and in the threats against you."

"Bruce is a philanderer, but Drew King is ruthless." She cringed. "Did you speak with Carson Haynes? He'll fill you in on the details, but we discovered King has a satellite office in Spokane—right over the state line."

"Uh-huh, could explain how he found you. My other phone's ringing—gotta go. I promise to keep you updated."

Chloe's mind raced. She lowered the phone and blew a breath through dry lips.

"Is everything okay?" Katie Banks entered the office from the hallway.

Ray followed. "We heard a lot of conversation in here and wondered if you'd learned something from Rachel."

Both of Levi's parents were dressed in their robes and slippers.

Chloe sighed. They didn't need another thing to worry about.

"Rachel's fine." Levi raised a hand and pushed from the chair. He reached his parents and hugged his mom. "There's another situation. Jacque's best friend, Gina Russo has been abducted."

"What!" Katie raised a hand to her mouth. "How terrible! Jacque, is there something we can do?"

"Nothing any of us can do, except remain at the ranch until Gina's rescued." Chloe slowly shook her head.

"Jacque's friend, Officer Paul DeMers, is heading the search." Levi nodded. "There could be a connection between the threats to Jacque and Gina's situation. I don't expect trouble here at the ranch, but I'll update Riley, Clay, and Travis to be aware."

Katie and Ray looked at each other, then at Chloe.

"I'm so sorry to bring you all into this." Chloe ran her hands over her eyes—something she never did. *Could the situation get worse? Yes,* a small voice spoke in her head. *It just did.*

Levi clasped his mom's hand. "You both should turn in. With the drive home tomorrow, you'll have a long day."

Ray scoffed. "Turn in? If a hired thug is out there, I can't rest. I'll grab my ought-six from the truck." He disappeared down the hallway.

"Oh, Jacque…I'm so sorry about your friend. I'm sure the police will soon rescue her." Katie moved toward Chloe and crouched next to her chair.

Chloe choked back tears. Katie reminded her how much she missed her mom. "Thank you. Detective DeMers and Gina were childhood friends. He'll exhaust all resources to find her."

"I'm sure he will." Katie rose and turned toward Levi. "Please build up the fire in the living room. I'll make tea and coffee." She left without a response.

"Oh." Chloe scooted to the edge of the chair. Levi's parents were "salt of the earth" people, and they'd trusted her to have Rachel's best interests at heart. She moaned. She'd kept Rachel in the dark and exposed her to danger.

"Come on." Levi caught her gaze. "Let's move to the living room. You're shaking."

Heartbroken, she tried to smile. "Your parents are amazing. A cup of tea with your mom sounds heavenly." She pushed to balance on one foot.

"Here, let me help." He moved closer and crooked an arm.

Scotty stood and stretched.

"Hey, buddy." Chloe gazed into Scotty's sparkling eyes. "If you want, you can stay with Duke." Funny how secure she felt at the ranch. To the point of leaving Scotty in another room.

Pausing in the hallway, she angled toward Levi to speak her mind. "I realize it's late, but your parents deserve to know my story. Would you mind if I share a thumbnail sketch?"

"How about we elevate your ankle." He pulled an ottoman to face her chair.

"Thank you so much." Chloe sank into the buttery leather and rested her aching ankle on the ottoman. "Have all of your guests gone home?" With Gina missing, she'd lost track of everything else.

"Everyone's gone, and the ranch hands are helping Janice and Fiona clean up." Levi leaned an elbow against the beefy, carved timber mantel. "Before I came inside, I saw most of the students off. A couple are staying overnight."

A deep cold still in her bones, Chloe pulled the folded afghan from the chair arm, and laid it over her lap.

Katie returned, carrying a large tray she set on the coffee table. "Coffee for you men and hot chamomile tea for us ladies." She filled two delicate blue cups with the golden brew. "Levi, could you please hand this to Jacque?"

"I don't get how you can drink this stuff." Levi complied, but crinkled his nose.

Katie half scowled, half smiled. "Yes, I'm aware you don't like chamomile, but it's very therapeutic and helps calm the nerves."

"Hey, Dad, how about a dram of Scotch with our coffee?"

Chloe chuckled at the lighthearted family interchange and sipped from the delicate cup. An herby-sweetness flowed over her taste buds. "Thank you, Katie."

"Sounds good, Son." Ray nodded at Levi. "How

about the Tennessee whiskey you keep?"

"You got it." Levi moved to a wooden trolley standing against the back wall and lifted a heavy glass bottle half-filled with amber liquid. "I'm grateful you and Mom are here."

Chloe finished the cup of sweet tea and set it on the matching saucer. "Katie and Ray, if you're not too tired, I'd like to share something." The decision felt right. Time to start setting the record straight.

"I'm all ears." Ray accepted a glass of whiskey from Levi and sank to the edge of the couch.

"Yes, please feel free to share." Katie sat next to her husband. "Don't be concerned about the hour."

Chloe swallowed hard and began by telling them about Hallie and the awkward scene at the Billingses' house. She ended by revealing her real name.

"I don't know what to say." Katie had scooted to the edge of the couch and clutched her hands in her lap.

"I do." Ray's dark brows drew over his equally dark eyes. "Corrupt politics rules far too much of our country, especially in the big city. Exactly why I live on a ranch."

Chloe exhaled on a sigh. She hadn't expected such understanding and gratitude. They had a right to be angry and to blame her for Rachel's collision. "If Detective DeMers rescues Gina, he'll restore my faith in him." She twisted her hands in her lap. "Officer Haynes seems to be an upstanding office of the law." She glanced at Levi, then shifted back toward his parents. "Do you have any questions?"

"My mind is spinning." Katie brought her dark hair over one shoulder, the silver streak prominent. "I can't imagine how terrified you must have been. You had to leave your home, your friends, and your career." She lifted a dark brow. "How much of this does Rachel know?"

"Very little." Chloe puckered her mouth. "I should have told her before she drove my car." She swiped at fresh tears and sniffed. "This morning during a call to check in with her, I told her about being at the ranch and the episode on Riverview Drive." She cleared her throat. "I stopped there. The entire story needs to be told in person."

"I agree." Katie crossed the space to touch Chloe's shoulder. "Thank you for trusting us with your story. We can't possibly blame you for following the orders of law enforcement, and maintaining your alias."

"You mentioned your biological father. I hope you can work out things with him." Ray stood and stretched his lower back. "He made some bad choices, but time can heal all wounds. It's not too late for forgiveness." He shrugged. "Maybe your dad doesn't know what happened."

"Maybe." Chloe folded her arms over her stomach. "Maybe his answering service won't deliver a personal message over the weekend."

"Humph," Ray said. "Let's hope Will Mathers' biggest offense was to leave you and your mom."

"I agree." Chloe swiped at the tears she couldn't seem to stop. "Even though he abandoned me, I need to hear he had nothing to do with Drew King's schemes." Maybe tomorrow, he'd return her call.

****

Levi set another large piece of tamarack on the half-burned stack of wood and replaced the metal screen. He brushed his hands together and glanced at his parents. Their understanding and sympathy to Chloe's story didn't surprise him. They'd always been supportive.

"Well, Chloe Austin, think we'll turn in." Dad set his empty whiskey glass on the tray. "Let us know if you need us."

Chloe snuggled under the afghan Mom had crocheted years ago. She tilted her lips into a soft smile. "I can't thank you enough for your understanding."

"Thank you for trusting us."

Mom's amber-brown eyes seemed to transmit a warm hug.

"Chloe, Rachel considers you her mentor, and a dear friend. Don't wait too long to share your story." Mom looped her arm through Dad's, and tugged him toward the hallway. "Ray's right—wake us if you need anything."

The moment they disappeared down the hallway, Levi faced Chloe. "Could be a long night. How about I change out that stinky tea for a pot of lavender and honey bush blend?"

"You have lavender *and* honey bush?" She raised a dark auburn brow. "I'm impressed. But seriously, Levi, you don't need to wait on me. Please feel free to go to bed. You must be exhausted."

"I can't sleep while you sit here waiting for Gina to call." He gathered the cups and set them on the tray. "I'll be right back." As he left the room, he released a trapped breath. He should retreat to his bedroom and lock the door. Keep away from the temptation to take Chloe into his arms.

Janice and Fiona were still in the kitchen, finishing up for the night.

"Great job, you two." He unloaded the tray and turned on the water kettle. "Fiona, are you going home tonight? You're welcome to use a guest room."

"Thank you, Levi, but I have a five a.m. date with the kitchen at Beverly's." Fiona lifted a forearm to brush back a stray, blonde curl that had escaped her wide headband. "I'm fine with driving to town tonight."

Levi slowly nodded and as he poured hot water into the teapot. Thugs had abducted Gina in Sacramento, but with King's satellite office less than two hours away, would he increase pressure on Chloe? They could be watching Chloe's building—know she'd left and possibly where she'd gone. Gary Sims might have reported seeing her rental SUV parked in the yard.

He set the cap onto the pot and reached to touch Fiona's arm. "When you get home, please give us a call."

"Will do, but please don't worry." Fiona smiled and stuck the last of the dessert plates into the dishwasher.

Levi picked up the tray. He'd return to brief Janice before she turned in. Everyone on the ranch needed to be prepared for trouble.

Chapter Nineteen

Chloe waited for Levi to return before she called Paul.

He set the tray on the coffee table and poured a cup before handing it to her.

"Ah." She closed her eyes and sighed. "Chamomile is medicinal, but the scent of lavender is heavenly." She drew another deep breath.

"No comparison." He chuckled and poured himself a cup.

"What? You aren't having coffee?" She half smiled.

"Think I've had enough for tonight." He carried it to the chair matching hers.

"I'll call Paul, now." She touched the contact and the speaker button.

"Chloe, what's up?" Paul's voice sounded gravelly.

"What's up?" Chloe blinked rapidly. "Don't you have an update on Gina?"

"Nothing yet. Look, every on-duty officer in the county and the city is out there. Just sit tight, and I'll find Gina."

"Have you forgotten—I've been sitting tight for four months?" She caught Levi's raised brow. Was he surprised over her repartee with Paul?

"Of course, I haven't," Paul huffed. "None of this should have happened. Wait, another call's coming in.

I'll be in touch." The connection ended.

She watched his photo fade.

"Breathe, Chloe." Levi repositioned his chair to better face her. "Paul seems determined and capable of finding Gina. Maybe Carson has an update." He retrieved the flip phone from his shirt pocket. "Huh, looks like he sent a text and I missed it."

"What did he say?" Chloe shifted to the edge of her chair and rested her bare feet on the wool rug. She should hobble to her room for a pair of socks, but the heat from the fireplace has begun to ease the chill.

"That Sacramento officials are on high alert. Interesting. He then added this thing could go down tonight." Levi glanced at her. "I'll call him."

"Please put the call on speaker. I don't want to miss anything."

Carson answered after one ring. "Levi, I take it you saw my text."

"Yeah, and Chloe's listening. What do you mean about things going down?"

Chloe clung to Levi's amber gaze. She couldn't imagine this night without him.

"Sorry about the cryptic message." Carson's voice carried through the small speaker. "With Gina's disappearance, DeMers has stepped up the pressure on his chief. He believes Gina's disappearance is directly linked to Hallie Smith's death." He paused and cleared his throat. "The countywide APB brought in the sheriff's department, and the sheriff doesn't care whose toes he steps on. He demands that justice be served"

"It's about time." Levi raked calloused fingers over fresh whiskers. "Wasn't Hallie found in the county? The sheriff should be handling the case."

"Not sure how that all played out. Big money can grease a lot of palms."

"Chloe's on the verge of calling Bruce Billings to demand his help." Levi met her gaze.

"Uh, Chloe," Carson said. "I get your frustration, but stand by and let DeMers handle Billings."

Chloe lifted her chin and straightened her shoulders. "Carson, my life has been uprooted. My friends have been placed in danger. I'm finished with patiently waiting for Paul and his department to act." She snapped up her phone and scrolled through her contacts. "Gina's out there somewhere and needs help. Time to get to the core of the matter." She found Juanita's contact, but nothing for Bruce."

"Carson, if trouble strikes at the ranch, we're prepared." Levi clamped a hand on the back of his neck.

Chloe pressed a hand to her stomach. The idea Levi's ranch could be the scene of a crime made her nauseous. Surely, King wouldn't send thugs here. She couldn't let that happen! She swallowed hard and ran her gaze over Levi's broad shoulders, his muscled arms, and the way he propped a hand on his narrow hip. He radiated strong masculinity. A sensation she'd never experienced traveled through her. Uh—time to focus on finding Gina and reclaiming her own life. She forced her attention back to the contact list.

Levi ended his call and closed the flip phone.

"I expect backlash from Carson and Paul, but I'm calling Juanita for Bruce's number. They might even be together." Chloe tapped the contact.

"They should be at this time of night. It's ten thirty." Levi sank to the chair and crossed an ankle over a knee.

Her stomach clenched. After four months of silence—after disappearing without a word—what would Juanita say about her call? Chloe pushed from the chair. "I'm a little too warm. Think I'll move away from the fire." She leaned heavily on her cane and hobbled to the couch, sinking into the buttery leather upholstery.

"Chloe, wait. You've been under an extreme amount of pressure. Is now the right time to call after four months of silence?" Levi followed and sat at her side. He rested a hand on her knee.

"Yes, for Gina's sake, it's the right time." She pressed the contact. The ringing filled the quiet living room. She quickly turned down the volume.

"Who is calling this late?"

"Juanita." She swallowed hard. "It's Chloe Austin."

"Chloe? Why isn't your contact showing on my phone? Where have you been? Even after Keith assigned a different designer, for weeks I tried to reach you. The other girl didn't have your vision or efficiency. We barely completed the work before the first primary election party."

Chloe leaned into the couch, lifted her right foot to the edge of the coffee table, and allowed Juanita to vent. "I'm sorry I left without a word. Believe me, I didn't want to abandon your redesign, but—something happened. Uh, is Bruce there?" Her heart pounded against her chest. Pandora's box was about to open. "Could I speak with him?"

Silence, then—

"Bruce is still at the office." Juanita cleared her

throat. "At least, that's what he claimed at eight o'clock. He called to say he wouldn't be home for dinner."

"Uh, I really need to talk to him." Chloe captured her bottom lip between her teeth. "There's a situation—only Bruce can help."

"What? What does Bruce have to do with your situation?" The uncertainty in Juanita's tone tripled.

"Juanita, my best friend is missing. I can't share more now, but Bruce might be able to help."

"I-oh-Chloe. Does this have anything to do with Hallie's death?"

"In a way." She held her breath.

"The morning we met—I couldn't bring myself to mention her name. You must have thought me completely insensitive." Juanita's voice quavered.

Chloe angled to meet Levi's amber-brown gaze, and her breathing eased. Her courage returned. "Juanita, I try not to pass judgment, but your lack of comment shocked me." She drew a breath. "I'd like to catch up, but right now, I need to speak to Bruce."

"Okay." Juanita sniffed. "When I hang up, I'll text his number, but later I need to know what's happening." She cleared her throat. "You could have found the office number on our website, but I appreciate your call."

"I didn't expect he'd still be working at this hour." Her heart ached for the woman. "Juanita, I promise I'll be in touch soon." Ending the call, Chloe gazed at the screen until the text appeared. She hovered her finger over the two numbers underlined with hyperlinks and touched the office number. She'd see if Bruce had been truthful about working late.

"Mind putting the call on speaker?" Levi patted her right knee.

"Of course not." Her chest tight, she activated the speaker function.

"Bruce Billings." The male voice boomed into the living room.

Chloe lowered the volume more. "Bruce, it's Chloe Austin."

A long pause, then—

"Chloe? Uh, why are you calling?"

"Mr. Billings." She reverted to the formal address. "I thought you wanted me to call." She straightened her back and scooted to the edge of the couch. "Well, here I am. You have my full attention."

"Ms. Austin, I have no idea what you're referring to, other than you left our design job without a word. Juanita had to work with an unvetted designer. She was not happy."

"You can stall with reprimands, but I think you know why I'm calling so late on a Sunday night. My friend, Gina Russo, is missing, and you're possibly the man who can find her." Her voice shook, and her vision grayed. She forced her breathing to regulate.

No response.

"O-k-a-y, Mr. Billings, let me enlighten you. About nine this evening, I called Gina. She was driving and—well—she spoke in code. Someone is controlling her, and they might have a gun to her head." Oh. My. Gosh. A sob rolled through her core. Uttering the words made this all too real. "Mr. Billings, call off your goons. Order your thug to release her!" Her voice broke.

Levi slid a hand over her shoulder.

She leaned into his touch, and a dam of emotions

released.

"Now, wait a minute." Bruce blustered. "Are you referring to the HR Director at Walters Design? Who would take her hostage and why?"

"Why indeed?" Chloe forced her back to remain straight and resisted the draw into Levi's strong arms. She pictured Bruce in his office, behind an ostentatious desk with his chin raised in defiance. How she'd love to connect her fist with that arrogant jaw. "Bruce, Gina had nothing to do with the file. I accidentally took it, but I gave it to Keith Walters. Keith tried to reach you and arrange the secure return of the file. Even then, someone destroyed my apartment. Later, someone attempted to abduct me."

"Chloe." He cleared his throat. "I had nothing to do with either of those events. Until this call, I didn't know Gina Russo was in danger." He paused. "I take partial responsibility for Hallie becoming a suspect in the disappearance of the file. We argued, and I believed she took it out of spite. When I received no response to my calls, I had to warn my largest donors." Again, he cleared his throat. "I did not condone his methods."

"His? I think you're referring to Drew King. Call him off, Bruce." She switched her phone to her left hand, and with her right hand, she reached toward Levi.

His large warm hand encased hers.

"Bruce, tell Drew King the Sacramento County Sheriff and the city police force are searching for Gina. Tell him the police file with the details of the vandalism to my apartment contains both of your names."

"Wait, I have no power over Drew King! When I received the file from Keith, I begged King to back off." Bruce's tone turned pleading. "My campaign is important, but not worth the cost of lives."

Chloe worked her jaw back and forth. The gall of the man to claim innocence! She glanced sideways toward Levi, and his steady gaze settled her. "Bruce, this has gone too far. Call Drew King, now. If he doesn't immediately release Gina, then I'll share a copy of the file with the press."

"You can't do that!" Bruce bellowed. "Your friend's situation might have nothing to do with the file."

Levi squeezed her trembling hand.

"Maybe, but right now, it's my best tool. Call King." The culmination of almost losing Rachel, and what Gina must be going through tonight, settled in her bones and strengthened her resolve to do whatever she could to rescue her friend.

Levi slipped the phone from her trembling left hand and massaged her ice-cold fingers. "You're doing great." He mouthed the message.

A log shifted in the fireplace, and flames curled over the fresh wood. While Chloe waited for Bruce's response, she heard the wall clock over the mantel tick away the seconds.

From eight hundred-plus miles away, Bruce's exhale carried through the connection.

A distance that had kept Chloe safe—until the flowers arrived.

"Chloe." Bruce's voice roughened. "This is all a misunderstanding. A panic-driven reaction. I didn't intend for anyone to be hurt."

"A reaction?" She blinked and opened and closed her mouth. "To brutally strike down a young woman and leave her in a ditch?" She pressed a hand to her breast. "Don't try to sanitize Hallie's death or the crimes that followed. Do the right thing and confront King. Demand he order Gina's release and return to safety."

A pause—her heart raced.

"I will contact him," Bruce finally said. "But for the record—Joss Hoffman is my attorney. He hired the PI who found you in Idaho. I had nothing to do with any other actions. I only wanted to talk."

The image of her father's business photo swept through her mind. "What other contributors did you alert?" She had to know…

"Only the top few names on the list. After I learned about Hallie's death, I realized I should have called you before I alerted King."

Chloe gazed at the fireplace and found comfort in the blue and orange flames. She still clasped Levi's hand.

"Chloe, you must believe—I'd do anything to rewind the past four months and save Hallie's life. Prevent the terrible things that happened to you and now, to your friend."

"Sadly, we can't go back." Her anger eased a notch. Fallible and egotistical Bruce might be, but she knew all too well how humans made rash judgments they wished they could rewind. "But Bruce—tonight, Gina needs your help." A sob broke through. "I'll give you ten minutes to have her released unharmed into the care of a police precinct, or I will call a reporter."

Bruce uttered a singeing swear word. "Ten minutes isn't enough time. You can't do that."

The wrap of knuckles on wood echoed through the phone connection.

Chloe glanced toward the foyer.

"It's on his end." Levi squeezed her hand.

"Bruce, what's happening?" Chloe leaned closer to where Levi held the phone.

"Someone's at my office door." His breathing accelerated. "Who is it?" he shouted.

More rapping, then muffled male voices ordered Bruce to unlock the door. Chair casters scraped against the hardwood floor.

"Why are you here?" Bruce's voice tremored. "How did you access the building?"

Her stomach churning, Chloe gazed at the phone screen.

"Mr. King wants to see you. Now," a deep male voice demanded.

Chloe met Levi's gaze. She'd needed justice but...

Levi lifted a finger. "Hold on, he forgot you're on the line."

"This is ridiculous." Bruce's tone turned cajoling. "I was about to call King."

"Mr. King wants to see you in person, now."

Something crashed to the floor. A chair? The connection ended. Chloe collapsed into the couch. "King sent his thugs to get Bruce."

"Call DeMers." Levi placed her phone in her right hand. "He needs to know what happened."

"And Juanita." Her concentration wavered, and she fumbled her phone. She managed to access Paul's recent call.

Levi pushed from the couch. "While you update Paul, I'll call Carson." He stepped into the front foyer.

"Chloe, have you heard from Gina?" Paul answered on the second ring.

"I wish. No, it's something else." She shared the crux of her conversation with Bruce and her decision to contact Mike Parker. "I'm sure you're angry, but Gina's life is on the line."

"I'm not angry, but you might have just lit a firestorm. Chloe, you can't be serious about confiding in Mike Parker. Hey, he's an excellent journalist—I met him through Diane—but if an *exposé* about Hallie hit the newsstands, you'd guarantee retribution from King. We don't have Gina back yet."

"If we don't very soon hear from Gina, then I'll give Mike an interview. Please post an officer at the Billingses' residence in town. Juanita could also be in danger."

Levi passed through the living room and disappeared down the hallway.

Chloe frowned. Where had he gone? What had Carson said? "Paul, I have to go. Carson Haynes knows about Bruce and our conversation, so we're raising the alert."

"Good, because you might need added protection. Sit tight until I get back to you." He ended the call.

Levi returned, his mouth flat, and his shoulders back. "I alerted my dad to possible trouble, and my ought-six is by the office door."

Her stomach clenched. "Does Carson believe King would send thugs to the ranch?" Her hot mess might force Levi and his dad to shoot someone.

"We have to be ready." Levi clamped a hand on the back of his neck. "Sims might have local connections. He might know you're at the ranch."

"Yes, my car was parked in the open." Chloe pushed from the couch and hobbled toward the hearth to sink onto the warm, slate ledge. "Isn't it amazing how an open fire offers such comfort?" She shrugged. "I've never had a wood-burning fireplace.

"How are you holding up?" Levi touched her shoulder.

She sputtered a tension-filled laugh. "Part of me feels victorious for telling off Bruce, but I fear for his life. I won't rest until Gina's safe and I know Juanita's safe, too."

Levi planted a booted foot on the ledge and rested a forearm against the mantel. "When Bruce chose politics over human decency, he dug his own hole."

"Well, if Paul doesn't confirm Gina's location in ten minutes, then I will call Mike Parker." She lifted her chin to meet his gaze. Wait—she scrolled through her contacts and frowned. "I don't have Mike or Melissa's number." She tipped her head to gaze toward the tongue-and-groove pine ceiling and laughed. "After months of warning Diane not to discuss my case with the Parkers, I have to call her for their number."

"Welcome to the human race." Levi chuckled under his breath.

This time, Diane answered immediately. "Chloe, have you heard from Gina?"

"Not a word." Chloe pushed from the hearth and reclaimed the winged-back chair she'd occupied earlier. She gave Diane a brief description of her conversation with Bruce. "I promise to let Paul know after I speak with Mike, but Gina's in trouble."

"Are you kidding? You intend to call Mike and share your story?" Diane gasped. "They're my friends, and I trust them, but Paul's working on this."

Chloe glanced at her wristwatch. "I spoke to Paul

ten minutes ago and Bruce before that. It's closing in on midnight. Time to take action."

"Well, okay. I want to find Gina, too. I'll text their contact."

Chloe's phone tinged. "Thanks, Diane. Please keep me posted, and I'll do the same."

"But Paul's career—his position at the department! A front-page article could get him fired."

Chloe frowned. "Diane, right now, Paul's career is the farthest thing from my mind. Please call if you hear anything."

Chapter Twenty

Chloe rubbed her arms and fought to keep her teeth from chattering. Nerves. She tapped the number Diana sent and noticed her coral fingernail polish had chipped. Huh, it'd been hours since she'd given her appearance a thought. She probably looked like a train wreck. The call went directly to voice mail. She left a brief message and disconnected.

Her phone immediately rang. "Melissa?"

"No, it's Mike. Is this Jacque?"

Chloe hesitated and gazed into the fire. "Chloe Austin. I'm calling for help, Mike. Help with finding my best friend, Gina Russo, and with bringing justice to Hallie Smith's murder."

A pause. "Okay, well, Melissa's talking to Diane, so I had a briefing before you called."

"Oh." She drew a sharp breath. "So, you know our friend is in danger."

"Yes, and so are you." Mike cleared his throat. "Don't blame Diane. She has your best interests at heart. After you opened the studio, I did some digging. Your photo is still posted on the Walters Design site."

"I recently remembered we didn't take it down. Still, how did you connect me with Jacque Taylor?"

"Not many interior designers arrive in the dead of winter. When Diane mentioned her friend and coworker had relocated to Coeur d'Alene, and how worried she was about you being alone, I connected the dots. Speaking of which, Melissa and Diane are still talking, so I'll move to my office."

Chloe waited until Mike spoke again.

"Okay, I'm at my desk. Now, what do you have in mind?"

Chloe inflated her cheeks with a puff of indecision. So, she'd called Mike, and she'd opened Pandora's Box. Once she initiated the press release, it couldn't be undone. She plunged into sharing her theory about Hallie's death and the close calls since. "Paul is taking too long. He should have solved Hallie's murder and who broke into my apartment."

"Back to Drew King," Mike said. "You believe he's behind the violence, but do you have proof?"

"He's the top contributor to Bruce's campaign. Other than Bruce, he has the most to lose. Tonight, Bruce's chickens came home to roost, and I'm even more convinced King is behind the violence."

"Uh-huh." The music of a laptop opening carried through the connection. "One moment—okay, I've pulled up a list of King's known interests. Software tech giant, with offices in several locations. Including Spokane, Washington. What's your angle, Jacque?"

Chloe exhaled. "Mike, you have my permission to dispense with the alias and call me, Chloe. I'm so tired of lying to my new friends and associates in the area." She lifted her throbbing ankle to the ottoman. "I'm curious why you left the rodeo so fast. I intended to introduce myself."

"As Jacque Taylor or Chloe Austin? Honestly, I feared a heated discussion, and I wanted to avoid disturbing Levi's guests." He drawled the words.

"Heated? Well, I guess I could have lost it. I've become paranoid about someone exposing my location. Full disclosure, I'm still at the ranch, and my phone is on speaker. Levi's helping with my security and to find Gina."

"Hey, Levi. Sorry about Rachel's accident. Chloe, I don't have access to the local police files, but I have a contact in the Sacramento PD. The recent opinion editorials in the *Times* about Hallie Smith are mine. My goal is to create public outrage over the apathy of the city government regarding many cases, but especially, their lack of action in the Hallie Smith murder case." He paused. "During my investigation, I encountered your file."

Chloe's stomach dropped. "I had a feeling you'd seen it."

Mike scoffed. "Don't lump the local police with your distrust for law enforcement. Carson Haynes is a stand-up officer, and so is his chief. I only know what happened with Rachel because of the PD's report in the paper."

"Well, that's a relief." She shared her theory on who had driven the black truck.

"Uh-huh. With his satellite office so close, it makes sense that King hired local thugs. So far, they've only frightened you, but it seems King is turning up the heat. You're right about Billings. He's an ego-centric, want-to-be politician, but he draws the line at killing."

Chloe set her phone on her lap and folded her cold hands. "Who knows what pressure King is putting on Bruce? Juanita could also be in danger."

Levi returned from the direction of the kitchen and set a fresh cup of steaming lavender tea within reach.

Chloe smiled and lifted the honey-sweetened brew to her lips. Over the rim of her cup, she locked her gaze with his. Completely unexpected, this handsome, and so compassionate and kind man had worked his way into her heart. Leaving Idaho suddenly didn't seem so attractive.

Chloe lifted her shoulders and scrunched her neck, recalling the touch of his large hand on her shoulder. She tingled and blinked against growing moisture in her tired eyes. He'd helped her through the past two days.

"Chloe?"

She swiped at her eyes and stared at the smeared mascara on the back of her hand. Great! "Sorry, Mike. My brain shut down for a moment."

"I'm not surprised—it's after midnight. Rest assured, your alias is safe with Melissa and me."

She took a breath. "Thank you, Mike. I wish I'd confided in you sooner. Maybe Gina wouldn't be fighting for her life." Her voice cracked, and an image of Gina with a gun to her head flashed through her mind. No—too unbearable.

"Chloe, don't blame yourself," Mike said. "You followed legal instructions and maintained your alias. From here, we highlight the situation through an updated exposé. Hit the stands in the morning with a new slant on the Hallie Smith case, adding a layer of big business involvement."

"Can you connect the proximity of King's Spokane office to Rachel's collision, or should we stay focused on Sacramento first?" She shivered with the idea more thugs could be let loose in Coeur d'Alene.

"We focus on Sacramento." Mike tapped on his keyboard. "Later in the week, we write an exposé on crime crossing state lines."

"Good. Let's do it." She caught Levi's gaze. "We—Levi and I—have investigated but can't go further. We need help."

"There will be fallout," Mike said.

"Do you plan to name me in the *exposé?* Billings and King already know my location." She set her cup on the table, tangled her fingers in the French braid she'd worn that evening to look more ranchy for the rodeo, and massaged her tight scalp. The rodeo seemed like eons ago.

"They know right where you are, but the exposé could be insurance to prevent them from threatening you again. Are you up for a late-night review and editing session?"

"I'm ready." She moaned under her breath. She couldn't change the past decisions, but now, she'd work with Mike.

"Hey, according to Diane," Mike said. "You left Sacramento to protect your friends. Says a lot about your character. Now, let's bring justice to Hallie's memory. I'll send a draft to your inbox within the hour."

Chloe glanced at her watch. Twelve thirty. "Thank you, Mike." She ended the call, and an uncontrollable shiver grabbed her. She wrapped her arms across her middle.

Levi sank to the hearth and folded his hands between his knees. "You're exhausted."

She sent him a soft smile. "Please don't feel like you need to stay up until the draft arrives. Morning comes early on the ranch." She shifted her gaze to the blue and orange flames in the fireplace, hyperaware of the intimacy of the quiet night, with only the crackling of the fresh log he'd set on the fire.

Chloe flexed her shoulders and heat like a hot coal centered under her shoulder blades. *Ugh*, her entire body ached with fatigue, but her heart ached more for Gina.

"Nope, I won't turn in until you and Mike finish the exposé." He tilted his head and gazed into her eyes.

"Thank you," Chloe slowly nodded. "I can't tell you how much I appreciate your support." She pushed from the chair and hobbled to the couch. Reclaiming the corner, she let loose with a giant yawn and closed her eyes. "Just a few minutes…"

Through the fog of sleep, the sound of rattling dishware came from somewhere nearby.

Chloe forced open her eyelids and rolled her head to look toward the coffee table.

Levi leaned over the table, gathering their used cups and saucers. He met her gaze. "Sorry. Didn't mean to disturb you." He straightened. "Please go back to sleep. I promise to wake you in thirty minutes."

"Thank you." She slurred the words and closed her eyes, but an image of Gina in distress flared through her mind. She stifled a sob. How could she sleep, or even relax, with Gina out there somewhere?

****

"Chloe."

Levi's voice and gentle touch on her shoulder broke through the layers of deep sleep. "Yes." She pushed to sit straight. Oh, my gosh—she'd fallen asleep again. Her throat dry, she ran her tongue over her mouth. "What time is it?"

"Just after one thirty. Time to check for Mike's

email."

She rotated her neck and stretched her shoulders. A glass of water and the three prescription bottles sat on the coffee table. "You got my medications."

"Yeah, wasn't sure which one you need right now, but maybe the pain pill?" He ran a hand over his mouth and turned his head. "Would you like to move to the office or—I can bring your laptop to the couch?"

She yawned again. *Wow.* Exhaustion had sucked her into a deep, dreamless sleep. She ran her hands over her face. "Let's work in the office." Gripping the cane handle, she pushed from the buttery leather upholstery. Pain gripped her ankle, but she suppressed a moan. "I'll take the anti-inflammatory." She swallowed the pill and chased it with cool, well water. "Thanks, I'm ready, now." Following Levi down the hall, she stepped into the office. The glow of the desk lamp cast shadows over the rest of the room, broken only by the blue glow of the gas flame in the fireplace. "Where's Scotty?"

The terrier appeared at her feet, stretching and yawning.

"There you are, buddy. Did you think I forgot about you?" She balanced to pat his head. "I could never forget you."

"Scotty's fine." Levi set her water glass beside her laptop. "He and Duke went outside about half an hour ago."

"Without a leash?" She blinked.

"It's okay." He held up a palm. "I stayed close, and so did he. No way will I put your dog in danger."

Her shoulders caved, and she swallowed against the emotion building in her throat. "Sorry to snap. I know you wouldn't risk Scotty's safety."

She sat in the smaller office chair and opened her laptop. "Paul must have an update by now. Why isn't he calling?" She accessed her email account. Mike's email sat at the top. "It's here."

"Mind if I read it?" Levi rolled his chair closer and put on his glasses.

"Please do." She glanced at him. "You and Rachel deserve to know everything."

He touched her cheek with the backs of his fingers. "You deserve justice and peace." His shoulders lifted and fell. "I just don't look forward to seeing the taillights on your car."

She dragged her gaze from the amplified view of his amber eyes and fingered the condensation on her water glass. Had he just asked her to stay? She again met his gaze. "You know I won't leave until Rachel's ready to take over the business."

"As in completely take over or run the studio while you're away? "He lifted a brow.

"If Rachel's agreeable to the idea, I'd like to keep the studio but of course, I'll split my time between here and Sacramento." She gulped. Where had that come from? Could she work both locations?

"I like the idea." Levi slowly nodded. "Means you'll maintain a connection to Coeur d'Alene."

Chloe tore her gaze from his and back to the laptop screen. Time to focus on exposing evil and freeing Gina. Later, she'd remember how it felt to sit so close, how dark whiskers peppered his strong jawline, and dark curls dipped over his forehead. She scanned the document. "This is far from a draft."

"I agree."

Levi's voice came close to her ear and sent a

scattering of tingles over her shoulders. She shifted in her chair.

"While you work on any edits," he said. "I'll text Carson. He might have an update from DeMers."

"Yes, thank you. Please ask him to call with details." Chloe typed her approval to Mike and hit Send.

Levi rolled his chair toward his workspace and thumbed in the message.

She missed his nearness and her attention darted between him and the exposé. He still wore the black, Western-cut slacks and white shirt he'd worn to the rodeo, and as usual, his shirtsleeves were rolled to just below his elbows, exposing his tanned forearms. The overall image of potent masculinity took her breath away, but Levi surpassed merely handsome. His deep level of care for his family and ranch hands demonstrated his character. Since Friday, he'd stood beside her, even after she confessed her story, and how Rachel's collision had been meant for her.

He finished texting and met her gaze. "Finished with the edits?"

"Yes, there wasn't much to edit." Her voice came out in a whisper. His gaze sent more tingles over her body.

"Cold?" He raised a brow.

"Far from cold." Chloe cleared her throat and closed her laptop. "The *exposé* is perfect. Mike enlarged on the Sunday op-ed and captured the Hallie situation without naming me. He laid the responsibility on the corruption of big tech and the incompetence in city government."

"I agree, it's a great exposé." He picked up his

phone. "Feel like checking your new email account and see if Will Mathers responded?"

A small sound escaped Chloe's throat. "I'll check, but I almost hope he hasn't. I'm not sure I can handle it tonight." She logged onto the Loy Mathers account. "Nothing, other than the usual random advertisements. I'll check my account on the off chance he found it on the Walters site. Ahh, Diane sent a link for the vineyard they visited in Napa." Emotion choked her. "What if Gina's really gone?"

Levi rolled his chair closer. "Don't go there. Being your friend, I'm sure Gina's resilient." His cell phone vibrated against the desktop. "Hey, Carson—wasn't sure you'd still be awake."

Chloe pointed at his phone, then her ear.

He lifted an index finger and left the room.

She frowned. What the heck? Carson must have news about Gina. She pushed away from the desk, and pain immediately spiraled up her calf. Okay, time for bed. Maybe she wouldn't sleep, but she needed to get prone. She pressed a hand against the angst in her midsection. Gina could be tied up in some cold, damp basement—frightened and feeling hopeless. Chloe patted her cheeks. Scratch that. Gina didn't do hopelessness.

Levi returned. "Are you okay?"

"What did Carson say?" She hobbled from behind the desk.

He scrubbed at his face with both hands. "Sorry, I left the room in case he had bad news I needed to frame before I shared it."

"Don't try to shield me, Levi." Her heart fluttered. "What did he say?"

He leaned against the desk and raised a palm. "Gina's still missing, but the FBI is involved. He wanted to give you a heads-up. An agent might call."

"Who notified the FBI?" She gripped the edge of the desk, willing the inflammation in her ankle to calm.

"The Coeur d'Alene police chief. Carson was right about his boss. He doesn't play games. Carson also shared that DeMers has gathered a group of clean cops in the Sacramento PD. They're willing to stand for the truth, no matter what." He scratched at the shadow of whiskers peppering his jaw. "I took the liberty of updating Carson about your conversation with Billings and Parker. He needs to know about anything that could cause a retaliation."

She held his gaze, and the air left her lungs. "Bruce could be dead before the *exposé* hits the stands. Gina might still be missing." She couldn't use the word *dead* about her dear friend.

Levi tapped his fingertip against the desktop. "The chickens have come to roost for Billings. When he contacted King about the file, he started this mess." He waved a hand. "He admitted as much."

She tightened her lips. "Not that it can ever be enough, but maybe he's learned a valuable lesson. He bet his soul on winning that senate seat." She closed her eyes. "I doubt I can sleep, but I need to stretch out in bed."

"I get it, but we're not helping by staying awake." He cleared his throat. "We've done everything possible from this end. Now, we wait."

She opened her eyes and clung to his amber gaze. She must be exhausted because she loved how he wanted to take care of her. Independent Chloe Austin had met her match—or was he her complement?

He tipped his head toward the hallway. "If someone calls me, then I promise to wake you."

"You're exhausted, too." She glanced at his long, tanned fingers, the tiny white scars the evidence of a tough, hardworking man. "You've gone above and beyond and for a person you hardly know. Even after I told you the truth, you believed in me."

"The alias protected you to a point, but it didn't change who you are. Rachel will see that." He slowly shook his head. "I'll walk you to your door."

Her body and mind beyond weary, Chloe accepted his extended hand. The thought of leaving Idaho, and Levi, caused a pain in her heart that rivaled the roaring inflammation in her sprained ankle.

As she hobbled toward her bedroom, she leaned heavily on her cane. Once inside, she sank to the edge of her bed.

Levi leaned over the nightstand and fit the power block for her phone into the outlet.

In the process, he presented a very appealing backside clad in pants that could have been tailor-made for his long, lean frame.

"There, you're all set." He turned and caught her gaze.

Lost in his amber-brown gaze, Chloe ached to be held. All night would be marvelous. She cleared her throat. "Thank you."

Her phone vibrated against the dark-stained wood of the maple nightstand. Chloe squinted at the screen. "Paul." She fumbled to answer. "Paul, tell me you have good news."

"Gina's safe and at a precinct." His voice carried

through the speaker.

Levi clasped her shoulder with a gentle squeeze.

"How is she?" Chloe folded forward and rested an elbow against a thigh. She pressed a hand to her eyes.

"Shaken, and still frantic over the ordeal, but not injured."

Chloe reached next to her knee and clutched the cotton comforter. Her head swam with relief. "Did she say what happened?"

"She shared the bare bones. After she left Diane's house, she drove directly home, but her garage door malfunctioned. She left the car to manually open it, and a thug grabbed her. At gunpoint, he forced her back into the car and ordered her to keep driving."

The image made Chloe's stomach roil. "Did they go anywhere in particular? See anyone else, like Drew King?" She fought the building nausea.

"No, he didn't order her to stop until after he received a brief phone call. Gina has no idea who called, but they had the authority to order the thug to leave the car. She'd driven for over four hours and nearly ran out of fuel."

"Poor Gina!" Tears filled her eyes. "Where is she now?"

"She drove straight to a police precinct on the east side of Sacramento. I arrived a few minutes ago. The moment she finishes her statement, I'll drive her home. Oh, one more thing—as the thug left the car, he warned her— she either testifies against you, or he'll be back, and this time for more than a Sunday drive."

Chloe glanced at Levi. "Testify against me? About what? Did she recognize him? Was he the thug from Luigi's?"

"She's still looking at mug shots, but no, she didn't recognize him. Thanks to the digging you and Levi did, there's no doubt King is behind this. Likely, he plans to pin Hallie's death on you."

"Wait until King reads the morning paper." She chuckled with dark humor. "He's about to be exposed for the corrupt, evil man he is. Oh, Paul, I'm so relieved Gina's safe, and that you're with her."

"Well, I hope you know what you're doing. As for Gina, I won't leave her side until an officer's available to park outside her house. We made a breakthrough, Chloe. I now have the cooperation of the department to protect Gina and Diane. Oh, and Gina's filing endangerment charges against Billings and King."

Chloe sputtered a laugh through tears of relief. "Sounds like Gina! Please, ask her to call me so I can hear her voice. We'll leave the disturbing details for tomorrow."

"Oh, I'm sure she'll call to ease your mind."

"Wait, has Bruce Billings turned up?" She shouldn't care, since he started this string of nightmares, but she did.

"Not yet. Two deputies are en route to his home in the Sierras."

"I know that place well." She shivered from the memory of the day that ended with Hallie's death. She drew a deep breath. "Goodnight, Paul." She hung up and sought Levi's warm, gaze. Her body warmed.

Scotty whined and bumped her leg.

"I'm okay, buddy. Everything's okay, now." Her voice broke. Through the blur of tears, she noted a change in Levi's expression.

He sank to the edge of the bed and pulled her into

his arms.

Chloe pressed her face against the soft cotton of his shirt and released the tears and bottled angst from the past four months. She'd maintained a stiff upper lip to keep from racing back to Sacramento.

Sometime later—maybe only moments—she pulled from his broad shoulder and attempted to smooth the damp, wrinkled cotton-blend shirt. "I got mascara on your shirt." She dabbed her fingertips below her eyelids.

Levi ran a thumb under her right eye, then her left. "As usual, Chloe, you're beautiful. You weathered enough to break most people, but you stayed strong and cared more about others. Now, it's time to let down."

Chloe inhaled his spicy scent and slid her hands over the defined pecs under his shirt, bringing her hands to rest on his broad shoulders. "I can't believe it's over. Tomorrow morning, the exposé will hit the newsstands and the doorways of every subscriber in Sacramento. The truth will flush out the corruption." She drew another deep breath and, for a moment, discarded all the reasons why she shouldn't lean against him and did just that. She pressed a cheek to his shirt front.

His arms came around her shoulders. "We should turn in."

Goose bumps scattered down her neck and over her body. Oh, the image his words evoked—of spending the night in his arms. Every night. She pulled back and lifted her gaze to meet his.

He ran his hands over her back. "Gina might not be up to calling tonight."

She nodded and used all her inner strength to put distance between them. "I'm so glad Paul's staying with her." She fingered the white buttons on the placard of his shirt.

"Sleep well, Chloe Austin. Tomorrow is a new day." Levi covered her hand with his and pressed a kiss to her forehead.

The door closed behind him.

Scotty remained near her feet.

"Oh, Scotty, how will I find the strength to leave?" She pushed to her uninjured foot and hobbled to the chair where that morning she'd draped her nightgown. Knuckles tapped on her door. "Yes?"

The door opened just enough for Levi to stick his face in the space. "Sorry to bother you, but there's something I need to ask."

"Oh?" She hugged her nightgown.

His gaze settled on her nightgown, then moved back to her face. "When things settle down, will you go out with me? On a real date?"

She blinked at the last thing she'd expected him to say and scrambled for a response. "Uh, sure." Dating would complicate her departure, but well, they'd face those consequences later. "Yes, I'd like that."

"Okay, good. Rest well." He smiled softly and closed the door.

Her hands trembled, and she ran them over the silky fabric of her nightgown. Levi had just asked her out on a real date.

Her phone chirped with a text.

Chloe hobbled to the nightstand. *Carson*. She touched the contact. "I'm too tired to text. What's up?"

"Thought you'd be interested to know—Paul's team discovered a tap on Gina's cell phone." He paused. "Someone has been monitoring her conversations."

Chloe sank to the edge of the bed. "All this time—we spoke at least once a week. I shared everything. But how? Can a phone be tapped without touching it?"

"I'm no tech expert, but Paul will share the details. The tap has been disabled. While he focuses on Gina's security for the remainder of the night, Paul asked me to share the info."

"Did Gina identify the thug from the mug shots?"

"No, but there is more."

"Okay." Chloe shifted on the edge of the bed and elevated her throbbing ankle.

"The Sacramento city attorney ordered the mayor to step down. The police chief has been placed on extended leave, and Paul was appointed interim chief until a new mayor is appointed and selects a new chief."

Chloe lay back on the down comforter and stared at the tongue-and-groove ceiling. The corruption in Sacramento had begun to crumble—even before the *exposé* hit the stands. Soon, they'd see justice for Hallie—and Chloe could go home.

She slid a hand over her face. "Amazing. I've waited for months to hear this, and now, I'm struggling to believe it could really be over. Carson, I can't thank you enough for the call and for all you've done. I hope you can get some sleep now."

"My pleasure. Yeah, my shift's over. I'm heading home. There could be a few ripples—even locally. Call if you hear or see anything suspicious."

Her thoughts raced with Carson's final words. Call if I hear something? Wouldn't she be safe on the ranch, and at home with Drew King under scrutiny? She pushed from the bed and hobbled to the window facing the large maple tree. She cracked it open just enough to catch the scents of lilacs—the earthy scents from the river. She sighed and decided to leave it open.

Half-hopping back to the bed, she changed into her nightgown. In a few short days, her reality had changed drastically. She'd worked with Mike Parker. Gina had been kidnapped and returned. The exposé would open the flood gates of truth.

Chapter Twenty-One

The tambourine-like sound of maple leaves fluttering on the chilled morning breeze roused Chloe from a deep sleep. She snuggled under the comforter. From somewhere on the ranch, a rooster crowed. The very distinct impression of being stared at forced her to open her gritty eyes. "Yes, Scotty, I see you. Do you have to go outside?"

His lower body wagged, and his eyes twinkled.

"Okay." She hadn't slept until after Gina called about three. Through tears and exhaustion, they'd shared the events of the evening. This morning, her mouth felt dry as cotton, and her head ached.

She carefully swung her legs over the edge of the bed and gingerly planted her feet on the wool area rug. Pain zinged her right ankle. *Ugh*, she couldn't wait to be fully healed. Never again would she take her mobility for granted. "Brrr, Scotty, it's cold in here." She'd left the window open, and the gas fireplace set on low. Hobbling to the window, she closed the window and pulled on the jeans she'd worn to the rodeo, but instead of wearing the teal shirt, she opted for a long-sleeved, olive-green T-shirt. Topping it with her Aran knit sweater, she eyed her cowboy boots. "We're just stepping out back, right? Think I'll wear the slides."

Leaning heavily on her cane, she reached the French doors in the great room and slipped outside onto the patio without making too much noise. The leash clipped to Scotty's collar, she allowed him to extend the cord to the max.

He reached the maple tree and lifted his leg.

Morning sunlight topped the mountain across the river and washed the side of the house in a golden glow. Because of the proximity of the mountains, the river still lay in shadows.

She rubbed her arms and, staying close to the house, gazed toward the red Adirondack chairs situated close to the riverbank. Maybe before she left this morning...

Scotty tugged on the leash and growled.

She blinked to moisten her eyes. Scotty had pulled on the leash until he reached past the kitchen backdoor. What caught his attention? She followed, recoiling the length of leash until she'd reached the kitchen door. Lights glowed through the lattice-patterned window on the crossbuck door. Janice must be up preparing breakfast. "Scotty, come!" She kept her voice low, but firm.

He ignored her command and stiffened into a picture-perfect alert stance.

Levi had mentioned Duke kept the bears and cougars away from the immediate area. Where was Duke now?

Like the leader of a dog sled pack, Scotty continued to pull against the leash.

She fumbled to lock the plastic handle, but the mechanism had jammed. "Okay, Scotty, enough. I need coffee and my prescriptions. We can come out later." Cajoling didn't work.

Scotty fixated on whatever had raised his hackles.

Chloe wobbled away from the house and toward the graveled surface in front of Cottage One.

Scotty bounded up the steps to the small, railed front porch. His back straightened, and his nose pointed toward the door.

Chills passed over her shoulders. Someone must be in the cottage.

The rays of the rising sun angled through the back French doors and illuminated the small kitchen and living area. A large form emerged from the short hallway.

She tightened her grip on the leash handle and worked to retract the cord. Who would be in the cottage this early? Almost paralyzed with fear, she tugged on the leash. "Come on, Scotty." Had Gary Sims returned to destroy the evidence she and Levi had already recovered?

Scotty growled.

He'd never act this way if Levi was inside the cabin.

Maybe one of the remaining cowboys had decided to check out the unoccupied cabin before he left.

Chloe backed toward the end of the ranch house. If she could reach the window over the kitchen sink, she could signal Janice.

The cottage door opened, and the man, dressed in dark slacks, a blue button-down shirt, and navy sports jacket, stepped onto the porch.

His brows shot up, and his gaze locked with hers.

Not Gary Sims, at least judging by his business photo on the Bay City Investigations page.

Fear filled her throat, and she struggled to speak. "Who are you, and what are you doing?"

Barking and growling, Scotty leaped toward the stranger.

He ignored Scotty and descended the stairs. He wasn't a rodeo student checking out the cabin.

The hairs on the back of her neck pricked, and she pressed her back against the dark cedar siding of the main house.

"Ms. Austin, so nice of you to meet me. You're not easy to corner." He held up a palm. "Now, quietly come with me and nobody gets hurt." He moved fast and grabbed her right arm.

"Release me." Her cane fell from her hand. She pulled against his hold, but he held tight. "I need that cane. My ankle's sprained." She searched for a way to escape. Maybe she could use the cane like a club.

"Whatever." He released her right arm and grabbed her left arm in a punishing grip. "Pick up the cane and control that dog, or I'll silence him." The command came out on a snarl.

Chloe reeled against his grip. "I'm not going anywhere with you! Who are you?"

Barking, Scotty circled them, his leash tangling around their ankles.

"I said—control the dog." Using his left hand, he lifted the tail of his sports jacket and revealed the black handle of a gun shoved under the waistband of his slacks. "This time, you're not getting a warning."

Fear made her reel. *This time*?

He dragged her toward the graveled area.

She glanced over her right shoulder. If she shouted and Janice came running, then he might start shooting.

Scotty continued to bark and growl.

The stranger uttered a low profanity and kicked at

him. His boot connected with the dog's shoulder.

Scotty yelped but didn't back off.

"Shut that dog up—now."

"Don't. Hurt. My. Dog." She clenched her teeth. "You can tell Drew King it's over. He's about to be arrested." The house was so well insulated, maybe no one heard Scotty or their voices. She almost hoped they didn't because the thug radiated violence.

He stepped out of the tangled leash and twisted her arm to her back. "Shut up and walk. This isn't over."

Pain shot through her shoulder. Chloe flinched but righted her balance by planting the rubber tip of the cane into the gravel.

He tugged her again, this time toward the dining hall.

"You have no idea, do you?" Her voice tremored.

"What are you talking about?" He glared with dark eyes.

"You're on a working ranch, staffed with men who carry guns. They're early risers, and soon, they'll gather in that building for breakfast. You're outnumbered." She hoped the threat carried more strength than the sound of her voice.

He paused, pursed his mouth, and looked around.

The sun had risen fully—was Levi outside? Someone had to have heard the struggle.

Waves of chills scattered over her. To save lives, she should stop fighting and go with him. Later, she'd find a way to escape. She dropped the handle to Scotty's leash. "Go to the house, Scotty. You stay here."

Scotty quieted, perked his ears, and tilted his head side-to-side.

Tears blurred her vision. What would happen to him if the thug succeeded in abducting her?

Her plan to cooperate and go with the thug changed. Using the man's grip on her left arm, she gritted her teeth, tightened her abs, and swung the cane with all her fury and strength. The solid maple staff connected to the stranger's forehead with a crack.

He howled and stumbled backward, pulling her with him. He uttered a string of profanities.

Ignoring the pain shooting through her ankle, she followed his backward movement and dropped her cane to free her hand. Reaching under his jacket, she wrapped her fingers around the grip of his gun and jerked it from his waistband.

He growled and narrowed his eyes. "You don't know what to do with that." He dropped his hold and held out a hand. "Give me that."

Chloe wobbled and almost lost her balance but managed two backward steps. "I'm not going anywhere with you." She took two more steps away. If he got close, he'd overpower her and take the gun. Would she have the nerve to shoot a man at close range? "Help!" Her voice squeaked. She drew a deep breath and tried again. "Help me!"

Scotty raced toward the house, barking and yipping.

She wobbled backward toward the open dining hall door—the gun wavered, and she gripped it tighter.

The man bent and pulled another gun from the top of his ankle boot. "Shut up the dog and toss me that gun, or I'll shoot you both." He waved the barrel of the gun. "Doesn't matter if I kill you here or somewhere else."

Chloe gasped. "Scotty. Enough."

The man glared and waved the smaller handgun.

She wouldn't give him that chance. She aimed the barrel of the .09mm toward his gun hand, but her right ankle gave, and she wove onto her left foot.

In three long steps, the thug moved in and grabbed her right wrist in an iron grip. He ripped the gun from her hand and shook her like a rag doll. "Now, walk with me or you'll die here."

She glanced around. No sign of a car. How long did she have before the point of no return?

Behind the thug, a low growl rumbled from a much deeper and louder voice than Scotty's.

Chloe gasped. If Duke was here, Levi should be close. "No, Duke. I'll be okay."

The thug turned and aimed the handgun directly at the large Anatolian Shepherd.

Duke widened his shoulders and bared his teeth.

The blood left Chloe's head. "No! Don't hurt him. I can calm him. I'll go with you."

Duke's growl rolled into a ferocious snarl.

Chloe screamed and slammed her left shoulder into the stranger's right. "No, Duke. Run!"

The thug recoiled and swung to strike her.

She clamped her teeth and used all her strength to fight for the gun in his hand. This time, she wouldn't hesitate to shoot. Her hand over his, she twisted his wrist.

His finger on the trigger tightened.

A shot split the morning air and echoed between the house and the dining hall.

A streak of white fur sailed through the air and knocked the thug onto his back.

He took Chloe with him.

Duke pinned the man under one hundred twenty pounds of fury.

The man pulled his hand from hers and covered his face.

She scrambled to her knees and shuffled across gravel toward the gun—wrapped her shaking hand around the grip and aimed it at the thug.

He raised his hands and rolled side-to-side. "Get this dog off me!"

Duke's large front paws pressed against the man's shoulders, and he kept his bared teeth just above the stranger's face.

Chloe pushed to her feet, favoring the left one. She glanced around for her cane. Dang, she couldn't reach it. "Duke, good boy! Now back!"

"Duke! Release." Levi's command echoed between the buildings.

Duke took a step back but didn't release the man.

Levi appeared at Chloe's side and gently removed the gun from her shaking hands. "Duke, back."

Overwhelming relief swept through her. Chloe's left knee buckled, and she sank to the sharp gravel.

Scotty jumped against her and planted his paws on her shoulders to lick her face.

She pressed her face into his soft, black fur. "You're such a good boy." Deep tremors shook her.

Duke backed off the thug and sat next to Levi's booted feet.

Levi patted Duke's head and murmured praises.

Ray Banks strode into Chloe's narrow visual field with his rifle in hand. "Okay, whoever you are, get up. You're lucky this isn't a hundred years ago, or you'd receive some ranch justice."

The man pushed to his hands and knees, then to his feet.

"Do we have all of his weapons, son?" Ray maintained his aim and his gaze on the thug.

"I'll search him." Levi stepped closer and patted down the man. He located a pocketknife and tossed it toward his dad's booted feet. Then, he grabbed the front of the thug's shirt and gave him a shake. "Who are you, and why are you on my ranch?"

Chloe glanced around for Scotty's leash handle and her cane. She pushed to her feet, and realized, in the scuffle, she'd lost her shoes. The sharp gravel bit into her bare feet.

"Chloe, go inside until we have this under control." Ray lifted his chin toward the dining hall.

She nodded and gingerly took two steps to retrieve her cane, then her slides.

Levi and Ray continued to question the intruder.

Clay and Travis arrived with Riley right behind. All were carrying rifles.

"I called the sheriff!" Janice yelled from just outside the kitchen door.

Chloe debated on whether to take shelter in the dining hall or the kitchen. Her brain power fled, and the world around her blurred.

A strong hand gripped her upper arm. "I'll help you to the house."

Chloe glanced up to discover Clay owned the gentle voice. She'd met him last night at the rodeo. "Thank you."

He tipped his cowboy hat and one corner of his mouth tilted. "Glad you're okay, ma'am. You put up quite a fight. Sorry, we didn't get here sooner. We were all out back in the stock barn."

"I'm thankful you came when you did." The strength went out of her, and she leaned against his broad shoulder. She glanced toward the thug, now trussed up in a hemp rope like a steer about to be branded. Chloe gulped a sound of hysteria. One weekend on the ranch and she'd begun to think in ranch lingo. Gina would chuckle. She tightened her hold on Clay's arm and hobbled toward the kitchen door.

Janice met them and looped her arm around Chloe's waist. "When that gun fired, I swear my heart almost stopped. I'm so sorry. Scotty's barking should have tipped me off, but I prioritized breakfast prep."

"It's okay, Janice. It all happened so fast." How much time had elapsed since she left the house to take Scotty out for a simple morning chore? With Clay and Janice's help, Chloe reached a kitchen chair and sank to the wooden seat. "Thank you both."

Katie entered the kitchen, her long, dark hair flowing over her shoulders. "Ray? Where's Ray?"

"He's okay, Katie. Everyone is." Janice hurried to pour Chloe a mug of coffee. "Except the intruder, who's probably wishing he hadn't stepped foot on the ranch."

"Intruder? Did those men from Sacramento send someone?" Katie cinched the tie of her robe.

Chloe nodded, but she couldn't stop her teeth from chattering. "Duke. Someone needs to check over Duke. Ma-make sure he's okay." She choked back tears. "That man kicked Scotty."

Scotty glanced at her and blinked his dark eyes.

She leaned to run her hand over his fur.

Scotty wiggled against her hand.

"Thank goodness, he seems to be okay." Her voice broke.

Katie laid an arm over Chloe's shoulders. "You poor thing. You must have been so frightened. Levi will check on Duke. That dog means the world to him. I'm so glad you and Scotty aren't hurt." She sank to the chair next to Chloe's.

"Chloe?" Janice sat the cup of steaming coffee in front of her. She'd added fresh cream. "Okay, now everyone's calling you, Chloe. What did I miss?"

Chloe lifted the mug to her lips with shaking hands. The distinct whiff of whiskey hit her senses. She took a sip. "Ahh, thank you, Janice." She took another sip, and the whiskey soothed her throat and warmed her chest. "I intended to share more of my story this morning, but we were kind of interrupted."

Janice set a mug in front of Katie and lifted another one to her lips. "I had a feeling there was more to your story."

Chloe nodded. "My real name is Chloe Austin. I'm in Coeur d'Alene under witness protection. The tech mogul who's behind all the violence sent that man to abduct and silence me."

Janice shook her head and took another sip of coffee. "Lordy, there are times when nothing happens, then times when decades happen."

Two cups of coffee later—both laced with Irish Whiskey—Janice knew Chloe's story. As she shared the details, the tension began to release her shoulders. Only one burden remained—telling Rachel the truth.

Janice glanced at Katie. "Just when did you find out?"

"Last night." Katie sipped her coffee. "Chloe's friend, Gina, went missing. While we waited for word, she told Ray and me everything. Levi's known since Saturday."

"You've all been so good to me." Chloe stared at the dregs of coffee in the bottom of the white mug. Adrenaline and whiskey had masked the pain in her ankle, but now, it screamed for help. "Think I'd better grab an ice pack." She started to stand.

"You stay right there, and I'll get the ice pack." Katie pushed from the table and moved toward the pantry. "I don't imagine you took your medications before you went outside."

"I didn't plan to encounter a hired thug." The enormity of what had happened hit her. Chloe grabbed at the edge of the table.

You poor thing. Are your meds in your room?" Janice reached the doorway.

"Yes, on my nightstand." She leaned into the spindle-back chair and sighed. No sense in objecting to their help. Right now, her legs probably wouldn't work.

Janice returned with her meds.

Katie crouched at her feet and removed a slide to mold the ice pack over her ankle. "Let's hope that goon is the final threat."

Chloe opened the prescription bottles. "Me, too. I'm so sorry to have brought danger to the Riverbanks Ranch."

Janice set a tall glass of water in front of her and refilled Chloe's cup with straight coffee. "Well, it's good you were here and not alone in your apartment."

"I'm just grateful no one got hurt." She shivered.

Janice propped her hands on her narrow hips.

"Well, now for a hearty breakfast. I was just about to take the cowboys theirs."

The outside entrance opened, and Levi, Ray, Carson, and a man in uniform Chloe didn't know entered.

Duke followed.

Levi introduced the county sheriff, who took Chloe's statement and assured her the thug had been handcuffed and locked in the back of a patrol car. He'd never step foot in this county again. The sheriff politely declined Janice's offer of coffee and a cinnamon roll and left.

Scotty scooted closer to her feet.

She patted his head. "Levi, is Duke, okay?"

Levi ruffled the heavy fur on Duke's neck. "He's just fine. He looks proud of himself for defending you."

"He's a hero." Chloe sighed and glanced around the table. "You're all heroes."

Levi sank to the chair next to hers. "Well, I'm glad you were here and not alone in town."

"That's exactly what Janice and Katie said, but I'm still sorry the thug came to the ranch." She gripped her warm mug with both hands.

"Sure you're okay?" His strong throat flexed with a swallow.

"I will be." A rush of mixed sensations coursed through her. She nibbled on her bottom lip and rubbed her palms over her jean-covered thighs. Right now, she could have been in the back of a vehicle, fighting for her life. "My ankle took another hit, but Janice and your mom have taken excellent care of me."

Katie turned to her husband. "Ray, are you drinking spiked coffee? Don't forget we're leaving soon to visit Rachel, and then driving home."

"Don't get excited, Katie-girl. Just taking the edge off." Ray chuckled. "Besides, we'll have a big ranch breakfast before we leave. Janice, got any more of those cinnamon rolls?"

Chloe choked back a laugh. She already loved Levi's parents.

Under the table, Levi rested a hand over hers.

She tingled from head to foot.

"Carson, Chloe needs to hear about Marsh." Levi's voice scraped from his throat.

"Marsh?" Chloe twisted toward the end of the table where Carson sat.

"Steven Marsh." Carson's mouth tightened. "Once his rights were read, he spilled the beans about Drew King. Marsh was the driver of the black sedan who drove Hallie from town. King ordered him to retrieve the file." Carson ran a hand over his mouth. "His orders were to silence her by any means needed. Marsh claims he just tried to frighten her into keeping the entire situation to herself. He stopped and pushed Hallie from the car, then someone behind them hit her.

"He can plead for mercy all he wants, but he's responsible for Hallie's death, and he tried to abduct me." A lead weight had settled in her stomach.

Carson gave a quick nod. "He confessed to breaking into your Sacramento apartment, and he hired the thug to grab you at Luigi's."

"Wow." She blinked rapidly "You learned a lot in a short time. The threat is over." She allowed her shoulders to cave. "Wait, what about the black and silver pickups? Who drove those?"

Carson finished his coffee and set down the mug.

"Hired thugs who have likely left town. When Marsh is in the custody of the Sacramento officials, he'll continue to spill information.

Under the table, Chloe turned her hand and squeezed Levi's, then withdrew and gripped her mug.

Carson snagged a blueberry muffin from the platter Janice placed on the table. "Think I'll take this to go and track some gas thieves in Harrison."

"Isn't that in the county?" Ray lifted his mug.

"Yes, but they were in town last night." Carson shrugged.

Chloe fiddled with the mug handle. "Before you leave, I want to thank you all and offer an apology. I came to Idaho to lay low and to protect my friends. Everyone here accepted and welcomed me." She chuckled. "Except maybe Ted Finney. He's still not happy Rachel left him at Lake City and came to work with me." She tightened her lips. "I'm sorry that I put you all in danger."

"Friends stand by, no matter what." Katie reached across the table and patted Chloe's wrist. "You've done so much for Rachel."

Chloe smiled. "Rachel's become more than a protégée. She's like a sister." The moment the words left her mouth, she cringed. *Awkward*, with Levi sitting beside her, and last night, he'd asked her out on a date. Nobody seemed to notice the comment.

Carson gave a nod and took his hat from the hook by the door. "We're happy to have you in town. When you reach your building, send a text, and I'll swing by to check things out."

"Thank you, I will." She sat straighter and lifted her chin. "With Marsh in custody, it's time to reclaim my life."

Carson clamped a hand on the back of his neck. "Just remember, with Drew King's satellite office in Spokane, he has a local presence." He lifted a hand. "Just saying, don't completely let your guard down, and call if you see anything suspicious."

She drew a quick breath. "Oh, okay. Well, after the events of the past weekend, I'm behind on my design client files anyway. I'll remain in the building until we know more." She glanced between Levi and Carson. "Wait—Bruce Billings—has he been found?"

Carson settled his uniform-issue hat over his short, blond hair. "Forgot to mention—early this morning, sheriff deputies located him at his vacation home in the Sierras. The thugs left before the officers arrived. Billings was shook up but unharmed. Seems he's ready to talk."

"I'm relieved he wasn't killed." She rubbed her clavicle and imagined the large house where this epic journey had begun.

"Very generous of you." Janice refilled her coffee. "That man needs to face the music."

Chloe slowly nodded. "He does, but not with his life. There's been too much of that." She glanced at Levi. He'd remained quiet during the mention of returning to town. Did he still plan to follow?

He met her gaze. "Hey, Mike's exposé. Are you up to reading it?"

"More than ready." Chloe pushed from the table. "I forgot about it." She grabbed her cane. "Maybe the exposé caused the panic that sent Marsh to the ranch." She hobbled toward the archway. The flame in her ankle zinged up her calf. She pushed on and encountered aches and stiffness from Marsh's rough handling. She wobbled and grabbed for the doorframe.

"Hey, take your time." Levi appeared at her side and cupped her elbow.

Ugh, she couldn't wait to go home, where she didn't have to pretend to be strong.

Levi helped her to the office and settled her in the smaller office chair. He sank to his chair and swiveled to face her. "Riley will handle the ranch this morning, so I'll follow you home and help you settle in."

The earnestness in his amber-brown eyes touched her with an unsettling intensity. Early that morning, he'd held her and rubbed circles over her back. She cleared her throat.

Levi rolled his chair even closer.

Her hands trembling, she fumbled with her laptop. *You're on emotional overload, Austin. Stay on track.* "Levi, you've gone above and beyond." She struggled to speak through her constricted throat. "Please don't feel an obligation to protect me."

"Huh, I think we both know obligation isn't why I want to see you safely home." He lifted an escaped curl lying over her shoulder.

Chloe reached to re-gather her hair in the large clip. "Wow, I must look like I've been through a whirlwind."

"A very beautiful whirlwind."

His tone rolled over her like melted butter. "Okay, back to the exposé." From her favorites, she opened *Sacramento Times* and focused on the newspaper article that could work as the most effective tool against Drew King. She needed to suppress her feelings for Levi and return to reality. They lived in different worlds.

Chapter Twenty-Two

Four days had passed since Levi followed her home and secured her building. Four long days of waiting while the local and Sacramento officials rounded up the thugs and the powerful men who'd hired them. Paul and Carson advised she wait to tell her parents where she'd gone, and her entire situation over the past months.

Chloe refreshed Scotty's water and returned to the studio—without her cane—and without pain shooting through her ankle. The low-key days had forced her to follow the doctor's care instructions and to think about what came next—like breaking the truth to Rachel.

At her desk, she opened her laptop but remained standing. Maybe, she'd make a pot of Earl Grey, then read Mike's latest op-ed. He'd been busy submitting a series of op-eds, laying out details on the senate election campaign and the top contributors. So far, her biological father wasn't considered a top contributor.

By Wednesday, Bruce resigned from the senate race and agreed to testify against Drew King for the crimes he'd committed against Hallie and Chloe.

Carson had been right about Marsh. As a plea bargain, the thug continued to point the finger at King.

She turned on the electric kettle and prepared the teapot. While the stainless steel kettle crackled and popped with heat, Chloe gazed at the chair Levi had occupied while he patiently listened to her story. Janice was so right—nothing might happen for months, but a decade could happen in days.

She poured hot water over the tea ball and breathed in the comforting scent of bergamot. A lemon scone, fresh from Lindy's bakery, would be perfect with a cup of tea. Thank goodness, Lindy's delivered.

Scotty followed her every step and sat by her feet. He gazed up and licked his chops.

"You can have one of Lindy's doggie treats" She retrieved a bone-shaped treat and allowed him to take it from her fingers. "You're such a sweet boy, but we're okay now. The bad men are locked up. How about we take drive to the marina? You can play with the ducks."

Scotty danced from paw to paw and tilted his head one way, then the other.

Chloe laughed. "You know what I'm talking about, don't you?" *Hmm*…after a week spent indoors, she needed a change of scene.

Scotty settled on the area rug and munched on his biscuit.

Chloe sank to the armless chair and rested her left foot on the edge of the small, oval table. She really needed to review Tracie's newest remodel plans. Tracie's repeat business, and Cheryl Wakely's remodel, would keep her busy for weeks and in Coeur d'Alene.

She pushed her mouth to one side. The prospect of delaying her return to Sacramento no longer bothered her. She loved working with Rachel, and she enjoyed her clients.

She bit into the flakey pastry, and her mouth watered from the lemon zest. She swallowed and licked her lips. Rachel's reaction to Chloe's story would determine the future of the studio. If she accepted why Chloe had kept her in the dark, she might agree to take over the studio when Chloe returned to Walters Design.

She sipped tea and thought back to her Wednesday meeting with Tracie Woodward. Tracie had displayed disbelief, then acceptance. She'd understood Chloe's need to use the alias and insisted Chloe should make Coeur d'Alene her permanent home.

Chloe promised Tracie she'd think about it, but really, how could she juggle both areas? The idea made her head spin. Rachel held the key to her final decision.

She pushed from the chair and returned to her desk.

Next week, Rachel would be released from the physical therapy center she'd entered last Wednesday. Chloe had a few days to prepare her explanation.

Lowering to her office chair, she opened the Loy Mathers email account. Nothing new, other than random advertisements. She propped her elbows on the edge of the desk and gazed at the screen. She'd sent the email to her father five days ago. He had to have seen it. Wouldn't the missive, from the daughter he hadn't seen or spoken to in almost nineteen years, leap from the screen?

She pulled the French braid over her right shoulder. What was Levi doing this morning? She missed working by his side, exposing the players in the plot to silence her. Her stomach fluttered. This past week had been the off week from the three-week rodeo sessions, and every morning, he'd called to check in. Maybe she could call him to hear his voice. She fingered her cell phone. No, he'd be busy preparing for Janice's birthday party. She frowned. Had he formally invited her? She slapped a palm against the desktop. Dang it! She had a life in Sacramento. Keith had held her position at Walters. Time to find a new apartment and clear her belongings from Gina's garage. She sighed. Did Tracie's idea have merit? Could she juggle both studios—of course—with Rachel's help? If Rachel still spoke to her after she learned she'd been lied to.

The entrance door lock buzzed and clicked.

Chloe froze, and the blood left her head. Only Rachel and Carson knew the code, and Carson would call before he came.

Scotty barked and growled. His body stiff, he trotted toward the door.

The door swung open.

"Hello?" Backlit by the bright afternoon sun, Rachel eased through the doorway. "Jacque, are you down here?"

"Rachel?" Heart in her throat, Chloe pressed her fingertips against the desk and stood. "Oh, my gosh, you're here!" She waved her hands and hurried to greet her. "I want to hug you, but I don't want to hurt you."

"I am a bit sore." Rachel chuckled. "A half-hug would be welcome.

Avoiding the casted and bound arm, Chloe hugged Rachel's uninjured side. "I'm so happy to see you. I thought you were in the center until next week."

"They scheduled me to be discharged next Wednesday, but I went stir-crazy. Doc agreed to release me early if I have in-home care, and I keep up on the exercises." She ran her gaze over the studio. "Aww, I've missed this place." She moved toward her desk. "And, of course, I've missed you and Scotty. Working over the phone, and even on video chat, isn't the same."

"I agree." Chloe coughed a laugh. For the past four

313

months, she'd only had video visits with Gina and Diane. Technology would never replace meeting in person. "You should sit—I just made a pot of Earl Grey." She suddenly couldn't breathe. She couldn't carry the burden of truth weighing on her shoulders.

"I've missed our tea breaks." Rachel supported her casted arm and continued toward the conversation area seating. "I'll stay at my house tonight, but Levi insists I move to the ranch tomorrow and stay for a week. He made arrangements for in-home care." She sank to the loveseat. "Besides, tomorrow is Janice's party. I'm excited to see everyone, and we have a lot to celebrate."

Chloe set a cup of tea in front of Rachel, her hands trembling. "Uh, yes we do. How did you get here from Post Falls?

Rachel performed an awkward shrug. "I called a rideshare. Doc says not to even try driving for two months—or more—depending on how quickly I heal."

A lump settled in the pit of Chloe's stomach. Onto the subject of her car... "On Wednesday, I bought a new vehicle and I'll be happy to be your chauffeur." She swallowed hard. "The least I can do."

"Jacque, please stop feeling guilty. The collision wasn't your fault." Rachel shifted on the loveseat and cradled her arm. "Time and chance can befall us all. I chose to drive a new route that day, and I encountered a whacked-out driver. End of subject."

"You sound like your dad." Chloe puckered. "Which is a good trait. By the way, your parents are wonderful." She drew a breath. "I—" Her phone rang. "Oh, I'd better grab that."

"Of course." Rachel awkwardly lifted her teacup. "Friday is a workday."

"Be right back." She hurried to her desk and retrieved her cell phone. *Carson.* Her stomach churned. Rachel sat well within hearing distance.

The call rang again.

"Hello, Carson, how are you? Guess what? Rachel's here."

"Uh, hello—Rachel's there?" He paused. "Should I call back later?"

Chloe angled to glance beyond the beverage cabinet and to the top of Rachel's dark hair. The cabinet wouldn't mute the conversation. "Go ahead. I'll catch her up after we talk."

"Won't be easy. Want me to swing by?"

Chloe scribbled an abstract design on a notepad. "Thanks, but no. Is there something new?"

Rachel left the loveseat and came into full view, her dark eyes wide and her lips trembling. "Is it about the trucks?"

"One moment, Carson." Chloe's heart ached. The next few minutes would bring clarity, but maybe the end of their friendship. She lifted her free hand. "No worries, Rachel. I'll explain soon."

"O-k-a-y." Rachel returned to the loveseat.

"Carson, go ahead." Nothing like adding pressure.

"Just spoke with Detective DeMers. King's under arrest for his part in Hallie's death. He ordered Marsh to silence Hallie and anyone who had seen the file." He paused and cleared his throat. "He's lawyered up to the hilt, so we'll see how it turns out. Be prepared for him to buy his way out of this."

"Surely, he can't do that—he's a monster! What if I file a complaint with the Sacramento PD?"

"In a way, you already did when you reported your

break-in. The good news is, you're safe to leave your building. With his freedom on the line, King won't threaten you."

"Oh, that's good news." She released a long sigh. With Rachel still out of the loop, she wouldn't ask about returning to Sacramento. Knees weak, Chloe sank against her desk. Joy, relief, uneasiness about leaving Idaho—a slew of emotions rolled through her.

"Are you okay?" Carson asked.

"I will be. Thank you again—for everything."

"Happy to help. Is Rachel able to stay at her place?"

"She plans to stay here tonight, then tomorrow go to the ranch." She cleared her throat. "Are you attending Janice's party?"

"Yes, if nothing comes up in town. If you and Rachel are okay with fitting into the cab of my pickup, then I'm happy to provide transportation."

"Uh—thank you but I haven't decided if I'm going. I'll let you know, after Rachel and I have talked."

"Sure. Call if you need reinforcement."

"Thanks." Her fingers icy, she disconnected and set her phone on the desk.

"Jacque? Are you okay?"

Chloe drew a deep breath. Time to face the fallout. She returned to the seating area, sank into the armless chair, and picked up her cooling teacup.

Scotty followed, sat near her feet, and glanced between her and Rachel.

"Carson Haynes called with more updates." She met Rachel's dark gaze and swallowed hard. "Would you like a refill?" She started to stand.

"My tea is fine." Rachel held up her uninjured

hand and narrowed her eyes. "What was the update?"

Hand trembling, Chloe lifted her cup and took a gulp. "It's a long story—are you sure you're up to sitting here for another thirty minutes or so?" She pressed a hand to her fluttering middle.

"I'm fine." Rachel raised a dark brow. "Does the update include information on the pickup drivers?"

"It does, but I need to start at the beginning." Her chest tightened.

"Okay, I'm ready." Rachel held Chloe's gaze.

Chloe straightened and squared her shoulders. Nervous energy crackled through her like static electricity. "I didn't move here from San Diego, I came from Sacramento." She drew another breath. "Care for a fresh scone from Lindy's?"

Rachel twisted her mouth and arched a brow. "Sure. If it means you coming to the point." She reached for her teacup. "Are they lemon-ginger?"

"Yes, our favorite." Chloe busied herself with refreshing Rachel's tea and setting a scone on a saucer within Rachel's reach. She returned to her chair and continued to talk about her life in Sacramento, her job, and her friends. She moved to the appointment with the Billings and driving Hallie to town. Her voice caught as she told about the next morning, and the front page article about Hallie's death.

Rachel's dark eyes went wider. "How terrible! Did they find whoever left her alongside the highway?" She awkwardly scooted to the edge of her chair.

"Not until last Monday, when he attacked me at the ranch." Chloe filled in the details.

Rachel opened and closed her mouth. "Levi must have gone ballistic. He's been so reluctant to advertise the ranch stays."

Chloe clutched at the seat on either side of her legs. "Levi's awesome. He and your dad rescued me, and they locked Marsh in the tack room until the sheriff arrived."

Rachel blinked against tears. "I suspected there was more to your story than a troublesome ex-boyfriend." She swiped at her cheeks. "No wonder I couldn't find you online, you were in witness protection."

Chloe drew on inner strength she'd doubted she possessed. "Part of the protection program is taking a new name." She clamped and released her lips. "Not using my real name has been one of the most difficult aspects of the past four months."

Rachel stilled. "What's your real name?"

Chloe released a breath. "Chloe Austin." *Ah,* that felt good.

"Chloe Austin," Rachel repeated and raised a brow. "Okay, I still believe the collision was a matter of time and chance, and you need to let go of the burden. Even if you'd called Billings after the floral delivery, Drew King sent thugs to deal with you." She glanced around, her shoulders caving. "So, what now? Will you close the studio and return to Sacramento?" Her voice caught.

"I'm still working out the details," She took the leap. "My preference is for you to take over the studio."

"Me, take over your studio?" Rachel blinked and opened and closed her mouth. Her phone rang from inside her slacks pocket. She fumbled to retrieve it. "It's Levi—hi, Levi."

Chloe cringed at the catch in Rachel's voice and the shock in her dark gaze.

"I'm at the studio. I'll put you on speaker." She set the smart phone on her lap. "Okay, please continue."

"Glad you're visiting with—uh—" Levi hesitated.

"—Chloe." Rachel supplied the name. "I know everything, so no need to dance around it like you've been doing all week."

"Good, I'm glad you know. Maintaining the ruse has tortured Chloe. Are you sure you should be out of the physical therapy center?"

Rachel lifted a corner of her mouth. "Yes, I'm sure. Chloe's reclaiming her life, and we have big decisions to make about the studio." She caught Chloe's gaze. "It's a lot to take in. Hey, if Riley's coming to town this afternoon, I could catch a ride to the ranch."

Chloe's chest tightened. The truth had formed a gulf between them. Of course, Rachel would turn to her brother for support.

"Not that I know." Levi's voice carried from the phone speaker. "Can you ride out with Chloe tomorrow?"

Chloe stood to make a fresh pot of tea. "Levi, not to intrude on your conversation, but I don't remember being invited. Besides, I've been restricted to the building all week, so I haven't shopped for a gift." She chuckled. "I even bought my new car online."

"Hmph. Thought I invited you. Guess I assumed you knew you were included." He cleared his throat. "Chloe, would you like to attend Janice's party?"

Awkward didn't begin to describe having this conversation through Rachel's phone, with her intently watching Chloe's expressions. "I-I'd like to attend. Carson just freed me from house arrest, so I'll go shopping this afternoon."

"Good. Janice keeps asking about you." His voice deepened a touch.

Rachel set her phone on the coffee table and pushed to her feet. "Levi, I'll stay at my place tonight. I'm feeling a bit wiped out."

"How will you manage with dressing? Should I call in help?" A cow bellowed from somewhere in the background. "Look, Riley just brought in an injured cow. I'll text the number for the agency I hired to help here next week. They might be able to send a helper this afternoon."

"Don't stress about it. I'll manage and see you tomorrow." Rachel disconnected and slipped the phone into her pocket. She cradled her casted arm. "Mind if I grab the Meeker file?"

"Yes, of course." Chloe wrapped a tea towel around the hot ceramic pot. "You're welcome to use my guest room. Stay here, and tomorrow, I'll drive you to the ranch."

Rachel wobbled toward her desk. "Thank you, but I need to be alone and think."

"Of course, I understand." Shock was the expected response to her story. She just hoped… "I'll grab the file, and how about I send scones with you?" Chloe knotted her hands, then took the bright-pink folder from her desk drawer.

"Thank you, Jaq-Chloe." Rachel ran a hand over her hair. "Wow, it'll take a while to get used to calling you Chloe."

"I get it." Chloe fluttered her hands. "What time do we need to arrive for the party?"

"It starts at three, so maybe pick me up at two?" Rachel thumbed something into her phone.

Chloe took a cloth bag from the beverage cabinet and loaded it with a thermos of tea and a paper bag holding two scones. "If you work on Janelle's file today, please call with any questions."

"I'm sure your notes are well organized. I just ordered a rideshare, so I should step outside." She moved toward the door.

A sharp pain of loss hit Chloe, and she gripped the edge of her desk. "Oh, that must be your overnight bag by the door. I'll help you outside." She carried the bag of treats and Rachel's suitcase outside.

Scotty followed and sat just outside the door.

"It's okay, Scotty." Choked with the pain of losing Rachel's friendship, she drew a fresh breath. Somehow, she needed to work through this.

A black sedan pulled close to the curb.

Chloe was struck with the memory of the sedan at Luigi's, but a young, smiling driver emerged and erased her fear.

"Rachel?"

"Yes, and you're Mark?" Rachel referred to her phone screen.

"Yeah, that's me. Here, I'll load the suitcase, and I'll help you to your door when we arrive."

Chloe handed Mark the suitcase, then escorted Rachel to the back passenger door.

"You won't change your mind, will you?"

"About the party or the studio?" Chloe's voice caught.

"Both." Rachel puckered her mouth.

"Nope—see you at two o'clock on the dot." She backed from the car. Now, she hoped their friendship survived the night.

Chapter Twenty-Three

At two p.m. sharp, Chloe parked at the curb in front of Rachel's garden cottage. *Huh,* wasn't that Carson's pickup parked just ahead? She glanced toward Rachel's gate and gripped the wheel. Maybe she'd send her gift with Rachel and Carson. A clean break might be best. *So, why did I pack an overnight bag?*

"Nice ride." Carson appeared at her window and tapped on the glass.

Chloe rolled down her window. "I'm surprised to find you here. Did something change?" She took in his crisp blue jeans and blue plaid shirt. "Or is Levi afraid I'll drop Rachel off and flee?"

"Maybe." He straightened and adjusted his ball cap. "How's the ankle?"

"Almost back to normal. I brought my cane just in case it flares again." She opened her door.

"No need to get out." Carson tapped knuckles on the hood of the SUV. "You sit tight, I'll help Rachel." He moved toward the white picket gate.

Chloe shrugged. Okay, she'd let him do his thing. She closed her door and rolled down the passenger window.

Rachel appeared at the gate and glanced between Chloe's and Carson. "Has something happened?"

"Nothing's wrong." He tipped his ball cap. "Just thought it'd be nice to caravan." He opened the gate and took the suitcase from her good hand. "I'll stow this in Chloe's hatch."

Chloe studied Rachel's expressions through the open window, but her protégée successfully masked her thoughts.

Carson closed the back hatch and opened the passenger door.

Rachel angled and slid gingerly onto the leather seat. "I like your new car."

Scotty yipped and bounced onto the console between the seats.

"Scotty, so happy to see you." Rachel patted his head with her uninjured hand. "I didn't get to see enough of you yesterday."

"Scotty broke out of his new restraint." Chloe opened her door and accessed the back seat to secure Scotty in his new dog seat and belt. He'd always loved Rachel, so maybe his antics would help ease any lingering tension. She slid back behind the wheel and started the engine. "Thanks, Carson. I'll follow you."

"See you at the ranch." Carson waved.

Chloe raised Rachel's window and shifted into Drive.

"Is Carson telling the truth, or are you both trying to protect me?" Rachel waved her good hand.

Chloe lifted a palm from the wheel. "I swear I'll never again keep anything from you." She glanced in the side mirror and guided the mid-sized SUV onto the street. "It doesn't hurt my feelings to follow Carson." A breath caught in her sternum. She pressed a hand to her chest. A week ago, she'd followed Levi through the darkness.

"Are you still nervous about leaving town? You

drove to the ranch last weekend."

"Yes, and your brother led the way." She glanced at Rachel. "How did you manage on your own last night? You look beautiful, and you even wore accessories."

"I cheated and called the in-home agency Levi hired. An aide arrived early this morning."

"Ah, I wondered how you managed to braid your hair and put on jewelry." Chloe followed Carson's pickup as he entered the interstate. She stayed in the right lane as a large pickup towing a huge boat roared by in the passing lane.

Chloe tightened her hold on the steering wheel and blew a breath. She used her thumb to turn the radio on low.

Rachel chuckled. "How you commuted in the city is beyond me. I'd rather drive on this highway and the country roads."

"All in what you're used to, I suppose." Chloe shrugged and settled in for the rest of the drive.

The engine purred and the tires whirred against the cement sections of the Veterans Memorial Bridge. The landscape transitioned from the lake view to a tree-lined highway, then to open pastures.

After ten minutes of silence, she glanced toward Rachel to find her dozing. She probably didn't sleep well last night. Chloe tilted her head side-to-side to ease the tension in her neck.

"I didn't get to the Meeker file last night." Rachel broke the silence.

Chloe started and shook her head. "I don't doubt it. Hey, I'm happy to assist however I can." She motioned with her right hand. "Have you thought about what I said? About taking over the studio?"

"Part of why I couldn't sleep last night." Rachel's tone went stilted.

Chloe glanced toward her. "What do you mean?"

Rachel raised a dark brow. "First of all, I came to work at Taylor Designs to gain knowledge from you. Second, I'm not ready to own the business and build my portfolio."

"Oh." Tension coiled in Chloe's stomach. Owning her business had been a dream come true, even if it wasn't in Sacramento. She spared Rachel another glance. "What if I stayed involved as the owner, and you managed in my absence?"

Rachel met her glance. "So, you are leaving. When Levi called this morning, he let slip that you might."

Chloe focused on the highway and the tailgate on Carson's pickup. "I'll stay until you're healed enough to resume your full workload."

"Levi mentioned that you'd made that commitment. I appreciate it. He's also concerned that you might drop me off at the ranch and return to town. Are you uneasy about being there after what happened with Steven Marsh?

"Not at all." Her heart twinged. "Steven Marsh's attempt on my life can't diminish my appreciation for the ranch." She sighed. "After the chaos I brought to your lives, I'm surprised Levi wants me to return." She didn't want to dwell on the scene with Marsh, struggling for her life. She shivered. "I tarnished his beautiful world." She glanced at Rachel. "And yours. Forgiving myself won't come easily."

Rachel rested her uninjured hand on Chloe's arm. "Forgiveness is the key to happiness, Chloe. I've forgiven you for keeping the truth from me. Under the circumstances, you had no other choice."

"You're amazing, Rachel Banks." Chloe shook her head. "Speaking of which, between sleuthing out the bad guys and dodging a thug, I toured Cottage One." She'd leave out the part about searching the cottage for clues left by Gary Sims.

"Oh, good. I'm happy you finally saw them." She moaned. "I'm afraid Levi will close the vacation rental business. It took some talking for him to agree to allowing strangers on the ranch."

Chloe pushed her mouth to one side. "He didn't mention closing the business, but he did vow to dive deeper into vetting guests." She shifted in the seat, and a new thought struck—Gina would love staying on the ranch. Diane would tolerate roughing it. The thought of her friends in Idaho helped her shoulders relax. She smiled and began to enjoy the beauty of the tree-scattered pastures on both sides of the road. Then a new thought entered her mind. "Rachel, I'm curious why you never mentioned Lucy."

"Oh." Rachel clicked her tongue. "I take it Levi told you about her." Her chest rose and fell. "Levi's marital status never came up. She was amazing, and it's sometimes painful to think about how suddenly she left us."

"I'm so sorry." She reached out to pat Rachel's left arm. "Sounds like he struggled after her death."

"Oh boy, he was a mess. Sounds like he shared a lot about that time in his life—all of our lives."

"He said you left a great career opportunity to move closer and help out. You helped hire Riley and Janice."

"Yeah, well, he needed me, and I'd do anything for my big brother." She sniffed and lifted a corner of her mouth. "Besides, look how it worked out. I'm working for the famous Chloe Austin."

Chloe sputtered a laugh. "Or infamous, depending on how you look at it. Do you know who's on today's guest list?"

"Yes, Fiona emailed the list. Riley, Clay, Travis, and Carson. Wade Creighton—the general contractor who remodeled the ranch house and built the cottages. Wade would be a great referral partner for the studio." She cleared her throat, "If the studio stays open."

Chloe blinked and decided to let the subject rest for now.

Carson's turn indicator flashed, and he took the Rose Lake exit.

Chloe followed. "I'm sure I would have liked Lucy. She had wonderful taste in tea accessories. Levi even made several pots of tea."

"Levi loved her very much." Rachel sniffed. "But it's time he opened his heart to love again."

Chloe's stomach fluttered. "Has he dated anyone?" She flashed back to the lovely Rianna Dakyn. They were friends and shared a love for horses. Did they share something more?

The tires hit a rougher seal-coated road surface. Chloe gripped the wheel. "Yikes, when I followed Levi, we didn't take this route."

"Levi prefers the scenic route along the lake." Rachel chuckled.

Scotty appeared on the console again.

"Scotty, you're a naughty boy today." Chloe shook her head.

Rachel crooked her good arm to scratch his neck. "I think the road noise bothered him. But back to Levi, he hasn't dated but he is interested in someone."

"Oh."

The road smoothed, and the silence returned.

Chloe hesitated to ask who Levi might be interested in. She puckered her mouth. He deserved to be happy. Besides, she had a life to resume. She glanced at Rachel, and her heart twanged. With her right arm in a cast and bound to her body, she resembled a wounded bird.

"Chloe." Rachel caught her glance. "Please don't hurt my brother."

Chloe started and blinked. "What do you mean? Why would I?" She snapped her attention to the two-lane highway.

"Because you're the person he's interested in. Since the studio open house, he's become available. Haven't you noticed how he suddenly began to show up every Friday afternoon, dressed to the nines?

"What?" Chloe shot her a glance. "I had no idea."

"When I worked at Lake City Furniture, he never stopped by." Rachel half shrugged. "Something changed after he met you. I've considered matchmaking, but if you're leaving, then I don't want him to be hurt. Not when you're the first woman he's shown interest in."

"Wow." A weight settled on her shoulders. "I must have been too distracted with my situation to notice. *Whoa.* "Well, he's very handsome, charming, and has a long list of attributes. Our lives just don't mesh."

Up ahead, Carson slowed, turned on the blinker, and made a left onto Riverbanks Ranch Road.

A new kind of uncertainty filled her. After Rachel's epiphany, could she face Levi? Her heart rate kicked up.

"Hey," Rachel said. "Don't let my observations ruin your evening. I'm a mother hen when it comes to my brother."

Chloe slowed and followed Carson. "No worries. My life's far too complicated to think about romance." Her stomach clenched. What if Levi took one look at her new, Western-flavor outfit—right down to her boots—and thought she was trying to fit into his world?

Carson parked his pickup near the house.

Chloe guided the SUV into a row of vehicles closer to party central in the dining hall. She turned off the engine and gazed toward the wide-open barn doors. Burning indecision paralyzed her. She'd help Rachel inside, make her excuses, and leave. Plenty of daylight was left for her to reach town before darkness fell.

"Chloe, are you getting out?"

Chloe forced a smile. "Of course. Let's get you into the dining hall." She opened her door and stumbled to the back hatch. Sitting for an hour had stiffened her ankle.

"Hello, Ms. Austin." Riley appeared at Rachel's door. Dressed in a new, brown-plaid shirt and new jeans, he wore a big grin. "I'll help Rachel inside. How's your ankle?"

Chloe pressed the button to open the hatch. "Hi, Riley. Much improved, thank you, and thanks for helping Rachel. I'll take care of her suitcase." She leaned into the cargo area.

Scotty leaped over the back seat.

"You rascal. Wait while I get your leash." She set

Rachel's suitcase on the graveled surface and returned to the back door. "Okay, boy, settle down. Just a quick walk through the pasture." She clipped the leash to his collar. Was she staying or heading back to town?

Scotty trotted toward the pasture with his nose close to the ground.

Chloe allowed his leash to extend to the max. If Rachel correctly read Levi's interest in her, the situation could become complicated. She strolled after Scotty. Yes, Levi had been kind and attentive. He brought her to the ranch and over the past week, called her daily. But Levi had strong protective instincts. She moaned. He'd asked her out on a date. Wow, somehow, she'd pushed his parting words late Sunday night from her mind. He hadn't brought up the idea again.

Scotty tugged on the leash.

"Okay, mister. Let's go see Duke." She reeled in his leash and tugged him toward the office entrance. *Make an appearance at the party, then leave before darkness falls.*

"Chloe."

She started and whirled toward the sound of a deep, sexy voice. She met an amber-brown gaze, and goose bumps scattered over her shoulders. "Hello."

Levi braced a hand on is lean hip and with the other hand, scratched his jaw. "Thought I'd better come get you before you hightailed it back to town."

Late afternoon sunlight streamed over the peak of the towering barn-turned-dining-hall and backlit him in a golden glow.

She swallowed hard. "I-uh-no, of course not. I assume it's okay to put Scotty in the house?" Her awareness of him made her tongue-tied.

Wagging his tail, Scotty trotted toward Levi.

She knew how her dog felt.

Levi crouched to pet him.

Chloe noticed the way the white shirt stretched over his broad shoulders. How the black slacks perfectly fit his long legs and muscled thighs. Her stomach heated. *Wow.* Rachel had worried about Levi's heart, but what about hers? The phrase toe-sizzling handsome came to mind. A man she could fall in love with. Uh, where had that come from? She drew a sharp breath that didn't quite reach her lungs and wavered on her boot heels.

He straightened and moved to stand within reach. "Are you okay?" He touched her right elbow.

She glanced everywhere but into his eyes. "Uh, yes, I'm fine." His spicy, warm scent blended with the fresh outdoors flooded her senses. She glanced toward the dining hall and the spot where she'd struggled with Marsh. Odd, but with Levi close, the memory didn't paralyze her, but it reminded her of what she'd brought to the ranch. "Marsh could have killed you, your dad, and the ranch hands."

"Don't go there." He touched the end of her braid, then slid his hand to her right elbow. "You're not responsible for Marsh showing up. How about we join the party?"

She exhaled on a hum. "Sounds good, but first, I'll let Scotty inside." She half turned toward the door. "If that's okay?"

"Of course. Duke's in there napping." He stepped around her and opened the door.

Duke had been napping in front of the gas fireplace. Now, he lifted his head and blinked his large brown eyes.

The low, blue-and-orange gas flame gave off a comforting heat.

"Scotty, be nice to Duke." Chloe unclipped the leash and patted his head. "This is his home. I'll check on you later."

"Hey, last weekend they worked out their differences, and now they're buddies." Levi caught her gaze. "I think we're all getting along well."

She shifted. "I'll swing by my car and grab Janice's gift." She paused and placed a hand on his muscled forearm. "Thank you for inviting me. After everything that's happened, you had every right not to want me here."

"I want you here." He feathered a thumb over her elbow and cleared his throat. One corner of his mouth tilted. "There's a therapy practice called immersion. I highly recommend you spend a lot of time on the ranch and replace the memories of Marsh with peace and pleasure."

"Very good recommendation, Dr. Freud." She used humor to lighten the intense moment. "The prescription for happiness." Her emotions threatened to unravel, and she fumbled to open the screen door.

Levi followed. "Did you bring an overnight bag?"

She hesitated and glanced at him. "It's in the car—that is if you're okay with me spending the night?"

"More than okay." His mouth flexed and tilted.

Chloe drew a sharp breath and resisted the urge to step into his arms. Instead, she hurried outside and toward her car. "Hey, did you notice my new ride?"

"Nice vehicle." He caught up and cupped her right elbow. "Exactly how you described it. Since you're staying over, how about a horseback tour of the ranch in the morning?"

Chloe reached her SUV and paused, her hand on the door handle. "A tour on horseback?"

"Yeah, you mentioned riding on Gina's farm." He crossed his arms and leaned his hip against the white SUV.

"Uh, as long as Chocka is patient with a green rider." She opened the door and, with an unsteady hand, grabbed the gift bag, then faced him. "Are you sure you have time? The new rodeo students start arriving tomorrow."

He ran a gaze over her and a hand over his smooth-shaven jaw. "So, through all the chaos, you've kept track of my schedule." He grinned. "First of all, you and Chocka are a perfect match. Second, the students arrive later in the day."

She searched his gaze for any hesitancy. "I don't want to mess up your schedule again."

He laughed. "Oh, Chloe, you've gone beyond interfering with my life, but I like it."

"Uh, well." Chloe gulped. "If you're sure."

He closed her car door and pulled her arm through his. "How about we join the party?"

Background music filtered from inside, along with the murmurs of conversation. Judging by the number of cars in the parking area, most of the guests had arrived.

"Before we step inside, Rachel and I had a brief conversation." She drew a breath. "I mean, about when I leave and what will happen to the studio." She squared her shoulders. "She insists she's not ready to take over the business and wants to focus on her clients." She shrugged. "I appreciate her dedication.

We're nothing without our clients, so I plan to offer her a partnership."

"A partnership?" He quirked a brow. "Meaning you'll maintain a presence and visit often?"

"Yes," She half whispered. "I haven't worked out the details, but I've begun to feel at home in Coeur d'Alene." She released a breath through parted lips.

"Good." He cupped both of her shoulders. "Now, I can enjoy the party."

She raised her brows but resisted another comment. Levi needed to attend to his guests. Several of whom called out to him.

He shifted and grasped her right arm. "We'll talk more later." He guided her into the dining hall.

Chloe tingled from head to foot. So, he wanted her to stay—had already made plans to take her riding. Her mind raced as he led her into a cluster of guests.

Levi introduced her to Maggie Jones, a neighboring rancher and Janice's friend.

She met Wade Creighton, who took an interest in the design studio.

"The boots still helping your ankle?" Levi leaned closer.

She glanced at the tooled, brown leather boots and lifted her gaze to meet his. "Since they're new, they offer a lot of support." She gulped at the warmth in his eyes and forged on. "I might manage a dance or two."

He tugged his masculine lips into a smile. "By the way, I like this new Western look, and the classy designer still shows through."

"Why, thank you." She grabbed at her French braid. Not her first compliment from a handsome man, but somehow, Levi's admiration rocked her world.

Pausing at the buffet for drinks, Chloe turned to assess the transformation from dining hall to country club. "Someone did an amazing job with the decorations."

"Rachel and Fiona video-chatted several times last week, and the guys helped with hanging the lights and setting up tables and chairs." He handed her a stemmed glass of red wine. "Janice hasn't seen it, and let me tell you, keeping her out of here for two days became a challenge. You know how she takes charge of serving meals."

Chloe chuckled. "She'll love this." She waved a hand over the room.

He *clinked* his wine glass against hers. "Cheers to having you back on the ranch."

"Cheers." The crisp wine went down well and left subtle tones of blueberry on her tongue. The result brought the tension down a notch. She lifted her glass. "Exactly what I needed." But maybe not. The last thing she needed was to lower her defenses and further complicate her relationship with Levi.

Chapter Twenty-Four

Chloe mingled with the guests until her ankle reminded her it wasn't completely healed. "Mind if I sit while you continue to circulate?" She glanced around, but the only chairs were the ones scooted into the square, linen-draped tables set for four.

"Ankle bothering you? Here, let's seat you at the table we're sharing with Rachel and Riley."

Chloe nodded and balanced her wineglass as she wove through the groupings of five four-top tables. She sank to a chair and crossed her right leg akimbo over the left to elevate her ankle. "Ah. Thank you, but please go enjoy your guests."

"I'll be back after Janice arrives." Levi nodded and touched her shoulder.

Rachel and Riley approached the table.

Riley pulled out a chair for Rachel.

"You look comfortable." Her cheeks rosy, Rachel settled on the chair and smiled at Riley.

Chloe would have to be blind not to see that the two were a couple. Why hadn't Rachel shared the good news? "I'm giving my ankle a rest and people watching."

"Exactly what I plan to do." Rachel patted Riley's hand. "Please go enjoy yourself. I'll be here until the appetizers arrive."

Still standing, Riley tipped his cowboy hat. "I'll

check with the boss and see if he needs anything."

Aww. Chloe's heart tugged over the sweetness of the two. She almost felt jealous to see such a direct display of affection. Why couldn't her life be so simple? "Rachel, you and Fiona did a marvelous job with the décor." Chloe lifted her glass in a toast.

Rachel's smile widened. "Thank you. Hey, I know, I haven't told you about Riley and me. We haven't been dating long, and I guess I didn't want you to worry about me getting married and leaving the studio."

"Are you getting married?" She blinked. "If you are, I'm very happy for you, but why would you leave the studio?"

Rachel shrugged her good shoulder. "I wouldn't, but I thought you might worry about me leaving the business."

"I'd never question your dedication to the studio and your work." She lifted a palm. "I'm eager to talk about an agreement that works well for us both."

Rachel's shoulders relaxed. "Me, too. When Riley visited me in the hospital, our relationship sort of picked up speed."

"In that case." She lifted her wine glass. "Here's to a happy ending."

The tuning of instruments brought Chloe's attention to the three-piece band. "I had no idea Clay was a musician." She leaned into the table to speak closer to Rachel. "Honestly, I didn't expect live music."

"Don't tell me." Rachel laughed. "You pictured Levi setting up a boombox with CDs."

"Sort of." She shrugged, then laughed.

Rachel lifted a glass of water to her lips.

Happy to be off her own antibiotics and pain

killers, Chloe enjoyed having wine.

"My brother has his work cut out to convince you he has old-fashioned values and manners, but he's also modern." Rachel winked.

"Oh, I used his up-to-date Internet, and I get the feeling he's an efficient businessman." She smiled and tiled her head. "Somehow, I've come to enjoy the ranch. Tomorrow, Levi's taking me on a ranch tour." She lifted a brow. "On horseback."

"Just don't let him keep you in the saddle too long." Rachel chuckled.

More activity near the buffet pulled Chloe's attention from their conversation. "Ah, Fiona's setting up the appetizers. Looks like Rianna and two of her friends just arrived."

"Oh, good!" Rachel waved her left hand. "They're such a fun group. Rianna visited me in the hospital. She mentioned meeting you at Beverly's."

"Yes, she seems very nice." Chloe cringed. Rianna stood out in the crowd, both in height and her sense of style. Was Levi attracted to her?.

Rianna caught her gaze and moved toward them, a glass of champagne in hand. "So fun to see you both. Rachel, you look so much better than you did last Tuesday."

"I'm feeling better." Rachel raised her voice to be heard over the growing conversations around them. "Levi arranged for in-home help at the ranch, so I'm staying for a few days. Why don't you ladies join us until the guys show up?"

Rianna glanced around. "Thanks, but Marisa and Gracie have found our table." She smiled at Chloe. "Jacque, I'm still very interested in consulting on sprucing up my rental. Will one day next week work?"

Rachel sent Chloe a thumbs-up and a raised eyebrow. "Great idea. We should add renters to our advertising."

Chloe's heart lightened. Would Rachel agree to a partnership? "Yes, I'm sure I'm available one day next week. May I call you on Monday?"

"Excellent!" Rianna set her glass on the table and fished a small notebook from her shoulder purse. "Here's my number and address." She wrote on a page, tore it out, and handed it to Chloe. "I'd better get to my table. Maybe we'll have an opportunity to talk more tonight."

"I look forward to it." Chloe accepted the paper and raised a hand when Rianna turned to leave.

Rachel caught her gaze. "Rianna still thinks your, Jacque Taylor."

"I know." She cringed. "On one hand, I'm not looking forward to the explanations, but on the other, I can't wait until everyone knows. Tracie came to the studio to review plans, so I told her everything. At first, she was shocked, but she understood and sympathized with the situation."

The band cut them off with the rendition of a grand entrance tune.

Chloe and Rachel turned toward the doors.

"Oh, my!" Janice had entered the dining hall and stood just inside the double doors, her palms pressed to her cheeks. "Levi Banks, you're one sneaky man!"

Laughing, Levi joined her and crooked an arm to escort her into the party. "You deserve a celebration. Okay, everyone, time to sing."

Clay and the band led everyone with the classic

Happy Birthday song.

With the final note, Janice threw up her hands and laughed. "Glad I didn't show up in jeans and a T-shirt!"

Chloe's emotions bubbled. Her life had been turned upside-down, but out of the chaos, she'd met a community of wonderful people—especially the Banks' family.

Janice filled a small plate with appetizers and joined Maggie Jones, Carson, and another friend from farther north. More guests moved to the buffet for bacon-wrapped prawns, stuffed mushrooms, and pepper boats.

"I'm starving." Rachel started to rise. "Hospital food is so bland."

"Relax, I'll grab you a plate." Chloe held up a hand and stood. She'd barely pushed in her chair when Riley arrived with a heaped plate.

"Here you go, Rachel." He set it in front of her. "Would you like more sparkling water?"

Chloe gripped her chair back and watched Riley fuss over her protégée. They made an adorable couple. Her stomach rumbled. Time to grab her plate. She dished out a sampling of each item and returned to her table.

Rachel and Riley had their heads close, nibbling on bacon-wrapped prawns.

"Fiona did an amazing job, didn't she?"

Chloe blinked and glanced up to find Rianna carrying her plate and a flute of champagne. "She did, indeed. Why not join me until Levi shows?"

Rianna sank into the chair but didn't touch her food. "I don't mean to be a pain, but I overheard Levi referring to you as Chloe." She raised a dark brow.

"Did I miss something?"

"Uh, not at all." Chloe gulped the bubbly she'd switched to. "I planned to tell you next week, but in a nutshell, when I came to Coeur d'Alene, I was in witness protection."

Rianna widened her dark eyes. "Okay, so I guess it's a long story, but is Chloe your real name?"

"Chloe Austin." She pressed a hand to her chest. "Feels so good to be able to tell you. The reason I left Sacramento is no longer an issue, and I've been permitted to reclaim my life."

"Wow. Not what I expected. Well, whatever made you choose Coeur d'Alene, I'm glad you came here. I've heard you and Rachel make an excellent design team." She glanced at Rachel and smiled. "Not that she's hearing any of this. She and Riley are fully engrossed with each other."

"So, I've discovered." Chloe raised a brow. "By next week, I hope Rachel will accept a partnership in the studio. Right now, she needs to relax and enjoy herself."

"She's been through a lot, but so have you." Rianna slowly nodded. "Speaking from personal experience, don't hurry to leave Idaho. This area has a way of drawing you in and healing wounds."

"I agree." She ran her gaze over Rianna's jeans and spiced-pumpkin-colored peasant blouse. "You've also fit in well. I'm curious—what's the interesting symbol on your belt buckle?"

Rianna leaned back and pressed her short, unpolished fingertips to the silver buckle. "The design is called a Trident. You might not be familiar with the Navy SEALs, but my husband, Ben, served as a

Commander in the SEAL teams. He had this made before he left." Her voice went soft.

Chloe met Rianna's shadowed gaze. "Left?" The way she'd said the word sent a chill down her spine.

Rianna's lips tightened. "Two years ago, Ben was declared killed in action." She drained the champagne glass and set it next to the plate of untouched appetizers.

At the palpable grief in Rianna's eyes, Chloe pressed a hand to her breast. "Where were you living at the time?" A Naval submarine testing facility sat on the south end of Lake Pend Oreille, but no SEAL teams.

"Coronado Island. It's—"

"I'm very familiar with Coronado." She touched Rianna's arm. "When I was fifteen, my mom remarried, and we moved to Mission Bay. I'm so sorry for your loss. What brought you to Coeur d'Alene?"

"I followed Gracie's lead." She smiled and motioned toward Gracie, sitting several tables away. "She and Todd moved here for a new start, but that didn't work out. Gracie and I helped each other through a dark time." She gazed toward the empty dance floor.

"I look forward to visiting more." Chloe's heart ached for the deep sorrow in Rianna's dark eyes.

Levi approached with a plate of appetizers and a fresh bottle of beer. "Is everything okay? You two look way too serious."

"Just getting to know each other." Chloe smiled at Rianna.

Rianna stood and gathered her plate and glass. "I'm looking forward to our consultation."

The drummer tapped a short tune, and Clay announced dinner.

Levi half-turned toward Rianna. "You're welcome to ride Daisy again. I have a feeling Chloe filled you in on some of what's been going on." He glanced between her and Rianna.

Rianna nodded. "We touched on her story. So glad all is well, and thank you, I'll be out next week." She waved and wove through the tables to join Gracie and Marisa.

Wade Creighton had joined their table.

Levi sank to his chair and angled to face her. "I had a feeling you and Rianna would click. Her past is somewhat of a mystery, too."

"I'm relieved to start sharing my identity." She bit into a prawn, chewed thoughtfully, and swallowed. "Clay is a multitalented cowboy."

"Yep," Levi chuckled. "The ranch's employees are multitalented. "Ready for dinner?" Levi stood and gripped the back of her chair.

"I haven't even finished these." She gestured to the small plate.

"We'll box them up for later. Wait until you see the feast Fiona created."

Chloe followed Levi to the buffet and realized her ankle felt better.

The chafing pan filled with grilled salmon, drizzled with a huckleberry sauce—a local berry that grew wild in the mountains—woke her hunger. She grabbed a dinner plate and added a filet, scalloped potatoes, and a small serving of green salad.

Levi chose tri-tip steak and a twice-baked potato.

Returning to their table, they passed Janice's table. Chloe paused to wish her a happy birthday.

Janice grabbed Chloe's free hand. "I'm so happy

you're here. Have you met my friend, Maggie Jones?

Carson sat next to Maggie.

Interesting, "I did meet Maggie." The band began to play soft background music, so she smiled and waved. "See you later." At her table, Chloe took a bite of salmon and sighed. "Wow, Rianna has trained Fiona well."

"I agree." Levi slowly chewed a bite of steak and closed his eyes.

Chloe scooped a bite of the buttery, cheesy potatoes and focused on eating instead of competing with the band.

Levi reached for his beer bottle, and his sleeve brushed her bare arm.

Chloe swallowed another bite of potatoes and resisted the urge to touch the back of his hair-sprinkled, tanned hand. She'd been so torn over coming tonight, and maybe she'd had one or two too many glasses of wine, but everything suddenly seemed right.

Two high school students, working as bussers for the evening, arrived and filled their coffee cups.

Clay ran his bow over the fiddle. "Hope you folks saved room, because Fiona and Travis are here with the birthday cake." He sawed another grand entrance tune.

Guests nearest the buffet gasped.

Chloe stood to look.

The mobile cart Janice used to transport food to the dining hall now held a very large, white frosted, layer cake. Live flowers draped over the sides, and each layer held a few lit candles.

"Let's check it out." Levi pulled Chloe's chair out of her way.

Janice approached the cart, her face wreathed in a

smile.

The guests gathered around.

Janice blew out the tiny flames and laughed. "I think Fiona shorted me on candles."

Everyone clapped and cheered.

Fiona took over and sliced into the bottom layer. She plated a slice and handed it to Janice.

Janice gave Fiona a one-armed hug and returned to her table.

Other guests lined up for a piece of cake.

Chloe unconsciously slipped her hand onto Levi's right bicep, and heat coursed through her. She started to withdraw.

He covered her hand with his. "How's your ankle? After dessert, there'll be dancing."

"My ankle is fine." *Oh, yeah, but after tonight, my heart might be broken.* She cleared her throat and leaned against his shoulder. "As long as I don't overdo it." Yearning to be part of this community—part of this man's life—ripped through her. She wavered on her boot heels.

"You seem unsteady." He half turned to grasp both of her arms.

"I just…" What? *Realized I'm in love with you?* "Just lost my balance for a moment." She followed Levi to the cart and complimented Fiona on the entire evening. A small cake plate in hand, she returned to her table. Overwhelming emotions brought tears to her eyes. She swiped at them and blinked. No way, could she explain why she felt like crying. She forced her attention to the dark cake. "Yum, what kind is this?"

"Carrot." Levi spoke around a large bite. "I'm not crazy about eating the flowers, but Janice loves it." He gingerly removed an orange nasturtium and set it on the saucer.

Chloe sputtered a laugh. "I've heard of carrot cake but had never tasted one. Interesting how a few ingredients can turn a root vegetable into a dessert."

"You like pumpkin pie, don't you?" Levi chuckled.

She angled a smile. "I see where you're going with that." Despite the butterfly sensations, she managed to eat every bite.

The bussers removed their plates and refilled their coffee cups.

Stomach full and emotions high, she leaned into the cane-backed chair and enjoyed the opening notes of a country song.

"Ready to dance?" Levi stood and moved to pull out her chair.

"Uh, I think I'll have another flute of Rianna's champagne. Without looking back, she hurried toward the half-barrel filled with ice. Pouring from an open bottle, she filled a flute.

"You're acting skittish." Levi had followed. "Is something wrong?" He tilted his head and gazed into her eyes.

"Not at all. I just need a few minutes to think." She glanced around and landed her gaze on the doors. "I think I'll step out for a breath of fresh air. Be right back." She'd love to escape to the red Adirondack chairs on the riverbank—Lucy's spot—but she wouldn't unless Levi gave her permission. She sidestepped him and made for the exit.

"Chloe, take your time." His voice followed. "When you're ready for that dance, I'll be here."

His statement seemed to carry a layered meaning.

She gulped the bubbly. She might be heading for a meltdown. The music and lights faded behind her, and she stopped to gaze upward and witness the first twinkle of tonight's stars. In the western sky, the final glow of daylight turned to violet and apricot. Later, the night sky would be magnificent, but she was tired of stargazing alone. Standing on the upper landing of her building sipping lavender tea—while Scotty made one more run around his fenced yard—before she entered her quiet apartment to spend another evening alone.

She loved Scotty, and she loved her career and working with Rachel in their charming studio. Still…something was missing from her life. At night, when she was alone in her building, she longed to turn into strong arms and rest her head against a solid chest.

The music changed, and the band played a song about making choices.

Oh boy, what timing. She glanced toward the office. Maybe she'd slip away and visit Scotty and Duke. *Yeah*, and when Levi came looking for her, what would she say?

An approaching car motor snapped her from her turmoil. Headlights swept through the dusk and illuminated the other parked cars. She backed toward the dining hall doors. Who could be arriving at this point?

A dark sedan coasted into the graveled yard and stopped.

Chloe's legs went weak. *A dark sedan.* She gripped the wine glass. Could Drew King have ordered a new strike from behind bars?

The back passenger door opened, and someone got out.

347

Chloe squinted. The person appeared to be a woman.

The trunk popped open, and the driver removed several pieces of luggage.

Huh, whoever it was planned to stay for at least a week.

The woman instructed the driver to set the luggage near the front door of the house.

That voice—it couldn't be! Chloe moved forward.

The newcomer stepped into the light.

"Gina?" Realization hit her. "I can't believe you're here!"

"Hey there!" Gina enveloped her in a hug. "Did Levi spill the beans?"

Chloe held the wine glass away from Gina's turquoise blouse. "What do you mean? Levi knows you were coming?

Gina bracketed Chloe's shoulders with both hands and smiled. "He arranged my visit. Uh, in case you haven't noticed, he's crazy about you."

"I haven't. How did you two connect?" she slowly shook her head.

"Paul." Gina glanced around. "Hey, are my suitcases okay there for now? Judging by the music, the party's in full swing, and I'm starving."

She bobbed her head side-to-side. "Your luggage is fine, and there's plenty of food. I can't believe you're here! Where's Diane? Why didn't she come?"

Gina drew a breath. "Diane's wallowing in guilt."

"Why?" She frowned. "During our most recent video chat, I assured her all is well with the Parkers."

"There's more." Gina cleared her throat. "Paul and Diane are engaged."

"What?" She clutched Gina's arm and tipped her glass, spilling the final drops of wine over her hand.

Gina pulled a tissue from her pocket and dried Chloe's hand. "I was shocked, too, but I'm happy for them." She glanced toward the dining hall doors. "Right now, a cowboy's waiting at the doors, and based on my online research, he's Levi Banks."

Chloe turned, her breath caught, and a flame flared in her core. *Whoa.*

Levi leaned against the doorframe, his arms crossed over his broad chest, and one knee was cocked. The glow of the overhead sconce illuminated the direction of his gaze.

"Uh, he asked me to dance." She tore her gaze from his. "I've never danced to a country tune."

"Girlfriend, that man will teach you every step you need to know. He's a celebrity in the rodeo world, and he even posed for a calendar sponsored by the American Cattlemen's Association. The cover, no less."

"Really?" Chloe nibbled at her bottom lip. "I shouldn't be surprised; he's definitely cover material." The mother of all tingles gripped her, clear to her boot-covered toes.

"Listen to your heart, girl. This could be the time and the place."

Dangling the empty wine glass between two fingers, she pointed at Gina. "Tomorrow, I'm calling my parents to tell them everything."

Gina clasped her arm and guided her toward Levi. "I'm glad. Now, let's go inside."

Levi straightened and met them partway. "Hi, Gina. Hope you had a good trip."

"So good to meet you in person." Gina shook

hands with him and tilted her head toward the dining hall doors. "Now, I'm in search of dinner, and you two have a dance. We'll catch up later."

Levi cocked a grin. "Looking forward to it." He reached for Chloe's hand. "Ready for a few turns on the dance floor?"

Chloe hesitated for only a second, then accepted his hand. "I'm in shock. Thank you for arranging Gina's visit."

"You deserve happiness." He slipped an arm across her back and moved toward the light spilling through the open doorway.

She angled with a half-smile. "Should I be nervous about more surprises?"

"Nothing sinister. I only work for good, kind of like a masked ranger."

Chloe laughed and knocked her shoulder against his. "You're also a comedian." She placed her free hand on the front of his white shirt. "Warning—I'm a total rock and roll girl, so you'll need to teach me the steps."

He tugged her closer to his side. "No problem. I know the steps"

Clay's band transitioned into a slow song—about a man who's amazed by his woman.

Yikes. She moistened her lips and swallowed hard. Had to be a coincidence.

Several couples, including Rachel and Riley, swayed to the romantic tune.

Levi captured her other hand and moved into steps that perfectly aligned with the music.

She stumbled, then righted herself and matched his rhythm. Over his broad shoulder, she met Rachel's glance and wiggled her fingers.

Rachel smiled and lifted her chin, her mobile hand in Riley's large clasp.

Chloe couldn't wait to introduce her to Gina.

Levi pressed his lips against her hair.

Sensations she'd never experienced charged her nerve endings like lightning dancing over the lake. She slipped her right hand from his left and cupped his shoulder. Muscles hewn from hours of hard work on the ranch sharpened her awareness of this man.

His hand went to her waist.

After two more steps, she slid her hand to his white, starched collar and fingered his silky, dark curls.

His large, RBR belt buckle moved against her belly.

Whoa. She brought her face into the bend of his neck and inhaled his spicy, warm scent. Life didn't offer guarantees—but maybe she should think hard before she walked away.

The song changed, and Levi tugged her into a quick step.

"Whoa, Cowboy. I've never done this." Chloe stumbled and clung to his broad shoulders.

"Okay, here are the basics." He spoke close to her right ear. "Step forward with your right foot, then step with your left, then bring your right to your left. Then left and right. Just relax and go with it."

Relax? While this tall, strong man sent her feet and her senses into overdrive? She'd never imagined dancing in a hay barn with a former bull rider as her partner. Never imagined falling for a cowboy turned rancher.

He dipped her over his right arm.

She shrieked, then laughed. He steadied her until

she caught her balance. Trust and safety were two attributes that could build a relationship. Okay, so on her list of the ideal man, Levi checked the box for a successful businessman. He'd reached the top in the rodeo field, then made a success of the ranch and rodeo school.

She angled to gaze at his smooth-shaven jaw. He had to be the most handsome man she'd ever met. Even after a long day on the ranch, covered in dust and sweat, he looked amazing. Tonight, dressed in form-fitting black slacks and a white shirt, he took her breath away. *Check.*

Okay, so he exceeded her expectations of any man, but had he truly forgiven her for Rachel's collision? Had Rachel forgiven her? Distrust could extinguish a relationship.

"I expect we'll soon hear an announcement."

Levi's words feathered her ear.

He lifted his chin toward someone behind her.

Chloe glanced over her shoulder.

Rachel and Riley had continued to sway in tiny moves.

Levi dipped his chin and smiled directly into Chloe's eyes.

Her breath caught, and the wattage behind those amber eyes carried a ping like summer lightning. She swallowed hard. "Rachel's never mentioned her feelings for Riley, and until this afternoon, she hadn't mentioned Lucy."

"Yeah, we Banks are kind of like the dark and mysterious river you haven't had a chance to appreciate."

Chloe choked on a laugh. "Do you mean from the

red Adirondacks? Right before Gina arrived, I thought about slipping away to that very spot." She resisted the urge to rise to her tiptoes to press her lips to the smooth-shaven jawline. "Would you mind if I sat there?"

"Why would I?" He blinked.

"I just thought, maybe since you sat there with Lucy…" Her throat swelled with emotion.

He pulled her closer. "Lucy would want her special spot to be enjoyed. How about we have coffee there in the morning?"

Chloe's breath caught. "Assuming I stay overnight."

"Remember your horseback tour of the ranch? Gina has her heart set on it." He swung her in the other direction. "Did you pack the jeans you wore to the rodeo?" He lifted one corner of his mouth, and his eyes danced.

She gulped. He'd noticed her jeans. "I did include the jeans." If he kept this up, then she'd never want to leave Coeur d'Alene or the ranch. "Levi, I can't thank you enough for…everything."

He brought his face closer. "Every day this past week, I forced myself not to drive into town to make sure you were still there."

She slid a hand to his chest and rested her palm over his heart. "I promised I wouldn't leave until Rachel's able to take over." She cleared her throat. "I'd never leave without saying goodbye."

"I'm glad." His Adam's apple bobbed.

The song ended, and the guests applauded.

She didn't move from Levi's arms. "If Rachel accepts the partnership, I'll spend a lot of time in

Idaho."

He kept his hands at her waist.

Carson and Maggie walked by, still holding hands.

Chloe raised a brow and smiled. "Tonight is full of surprises."

"Yeah, funny how things can sneak up on us."

She moistened her lips. "I should check on Gina." She held his gaze for another moment, then turned toward the table groupings, her mind spinning.

Chapter Twenty-Five

Gina dabbed cream cheese frosting from her full lips and smiled. "I haven't eaten carrot cake since my grandmother made it." She glanced around Chloe. "Where's Levi?"

"He went for another piece of cake." Chloe sank to the chair next to Gina's.

Gina shifted closer. "You two looked very good on the dance floor. I don't think I've ever seen you glow like this." She winked and sipped from her coffee cup.

"He's a very special man, but there are lots to figure out." Chloe touched the French braid lying over her shoulder. So, why did she lean to one side and watch Levi eat his cake in three bites?

"All you need is a fan to hide behind." Gina grinned, then glanced toward Levi. "Opposites make life far more interesting."

"So, where is your opposite?"

Gina shrugged. "Haven't met him yet, but with your attachment to Coeur d'Alene, I have a whole new field to select from."

She laughed. "Here we are, speaking in puns like the old days."

"Don't be in a hurry to leave." Gina touched Chloe's left arm. "Give this a chance."

Chloe glanced at Levi, and her heart flip-flopped.

He'd moved to the buffet and chatted with Fiona.

His every expression and movement sparked something deep inside. She rose. "Think I'll go compliment Fiona on dinner. Be right back."

"I'll be here." Gina waggled her fingers.

She reached the buffet and smiled. "Fiona, dinner was delicious, and the cake is spectacular.

"Why, thank you." Fiona clasped Chloe's right arm. "I'm happy to see you here, safe and sound. How about another tiny piece of cake?"

"You might be able to persuade me." Chloe accepted the plate.

"Good, life's too short not to eat dessert." Fiona grinned.

"You're so right." A bite halfway to her lips, her chest tightened. If not for Levi, Carson, and Paul, she might not be standing here right now.

"Oh, excuse me, but I need to grab Travis." Fiona glanced between them. "Time to pack the leftovers to the house. The cake will stay until after the party. If someone leaves early, there are bakery boxes under the shelf. Feel free to send cake home with the guests."

"Good idea." Levi touched Fiona's arm. "There's enough for twenty more guests."

Gina joined them and set her dirty dishes into the black rubber bus tub. She cleaned her hands with her napkin before she tossed it into a trash can. "Levi, everything from the dinner to the wines, and the dancing is amazing." She swept a wave toward the ceiling. "Who knew a converted barn could become a nightclub?"

"Happy you're here and enjoying yourself." Levi slid a hand over the small of Chloe's back.

Chloe shivered with pleasure, and her body

warmed. "Rachel and Fiona did an amazing job. Wait until you see it back to its usual function as a dining hall."

"I look forward to spending time here." Gina smiled and nodded.

Clay and the group led off with a legendary tune and guests gathered to form a line dance.

"I doubt your ankle's up for kicking and spinning." Gina touched Chloe arm. "Mind if I join Rianna and her friends?"

Chloe smiled and waved toward the dancers. "Go ahead and enjoy yourselves."

"Ready for another dance?"

Levi's breath brushed her ear, and Chloe's senses went on overload. "I-uh-I'd better sit this one out."

"How about we dance to our own tempo?"

"Oh." She tingled from head to foot. "Well, okay." She accepted his large, proffered hand and followed him to the dimly lit dance area.

He stopped when they reached the far side of the jumping and gyrating dancers and pulled her into his arms.

She had no idea how they'd manage not to look ridiculous, dancing slow to this song, but when Levi pulled her closer and rocked them back and forth, she no longer cared. She cupped his broad shoulder with one hand and his large hand with the other. Emotions bubbled like hot lava, and she tipped her head back and laughed out loud.

Ray Banks was a wise man, but he had her situation all wrong. Timing and chance hadn't brought her here. No way. Everything that happened to push her to Coeur d'Alene had been destiny.

****

Still riding on an emotional high the following morning, Chloe rose early and dressed for the ranch tour. She and Gina managed to get two cups of coffee down when Levi announced the ranch hands had their horses saddled.

Two hours later, she shifted in the large Western saddle and groaned.

"Are you okay?" Gina slowed her mount, Shadow, and twisted to face her.

"Stop asking me that." She clung to the saddle horn and clutched the reins.

A magnificent image, Levi rode ahead on his gelding, Sundance, leading the way over cattle-dotted pastures, and through pine forests. For a while they followed the winding river. So far, no steep terrain, but Levi had warned them they'd encounter a small climb to a spot he wanted to share.

"Remember, when we climb to lean forward and hold onto the saddle horn," Gina instructed. "Squeeze Chocka with your legs." Gina held back Shadow and let Chloe pass her. "I'll ride behind, in case you have trouble.

"Oh good." She couldn't stop the sarcastic tone. "My rear is asleep, and my legs are like limp noodles. Not sure how well I can squeeze." She drew a breath and gazed over the changing terrain. Okay, so the pain was worth the experience of riding with Levi and Gina, and seeing more of the Riverbanks Ranch. She nudged Chocka and caught up to where Levi waited at the bottom of an upward trail.

"I hope you're not too uncomfortable." He grimaced. "After this, we'll head back."

"I'm fine." She shifted for the millionth time and forced a smile. "The ranch is beautiful."

"You're about to see the view that cinched my decision to buy the ranch. The climb is short and fairly easy, but—"

"—I'll remember to lean forward and clutch the saddle horn." Chloe nudged Chocka to follow Sundance. The trail wound through a thick stand of pine trees and became steep. Chloe followed the repeated instruction and held on with every aching muscle.

"You're doing great!" Gina shouted from behind.

"Almost there," Levi called over his shoulder as he and Sundance disappeared over the rise.

She resisted the urge to close her eyes. She could get knocked off by a branch.

Chocka bounded up the last of the trail.

"Oh, my gosh!" Chloe lurched and shrieked.

They crowned the hill, and the broad vista opened.

"Wow!" She blinked rapidly and pulled her phone from her jacket pocket. "I have to take pictures."

"Glad it was worth the ride." Levi smiled and maneuvered Sundance to allow room for Chocka and Shadow.

"Very much so." She snapped several panoramic shots and allowed her shoulders to relax. "It's so peaceful up here."

"Levi, this is amazing." Gina reined Shadow to stop by Chocka's other side. "Thanks so much for bringing us here.

"Sometime we'll come back with a picnic basket." Levi leaned over his saddle horn and pushed his hat back. "Never have taken the time, but I always thought about it." He straightened and smiled at Chloe. "Ready to head back?"

Chloe tipped her head. "Do we have to leave so soon?"

Levi chuckled. "Janice will have my hide if we don't get back for breakfast."

Reluctantly, Chloe turned Chocka to follow Sundance back down the trail.

"Brace your heels behind the stirrups." Gina instructed from behind. "Lean back in the saddle, grip the saddle horn with one hand, the reins with the other."

The mountain trail opened to the pasture, and they picked up pace to gallop toward the ranch yard.

Travis and Clay met them just outside the stables.

Travis grabbed Shadow's bridle and held her head while Gina dismounted.

Gina handed him the reins. "Thanks, Travis, but I'm happy to unsaddle and brush her down."

"Boss said you have a meeting in the kitchen, so I'll finish up here."

A meeting in the kitchen? Chloe raised a brow. Breakfast wasn't exactly a meeting.

Clay held Chocka's head while Chloe slid from the saddle.

"Oh, my gosh, my legs are tingling." For a moment, she clung to the saddle skirt.

"Need some help?" Levi handed Sundance over to Riley and rounded Chocka's rump. He crooked his right arm. "Here, hold onto me."

Chloe grasped his arm and lifted her chin. "Okay, Mr. Banks. What's this about a meeting in the kitchen?"

"I mentioned we were having breakfast." He slipped his arm from her hold and slid it behind her waist. "Gonna make it?" He lifted a brow.

"Who knew horseback riding could be so strenuous? I thought the horse did all the work." She leaned into his side and forced her legs to move.

"My friend, you are so out of your element." Gina caught up and sputtered a laugh. "If only your Sacramento clients could see you now."

"Thanks a lot, *my friend*." Blood rushed through her, and the pins and needles sensations eased. Trouble was—leaning into Levi's tall, muscled body caused all sorts of other sensations.

"Next time, we'll take it easier." Levi reached for the kitchen door handle.

She squinted against the mid-morning sun and met his amber gaze. "I sort of look forward to our next ride."

An approaching car engine grabbed her attention. Chloe pivoted toward the driveway. A black SUV coasted onto the graveled ranch yard. "Who's that?" She clutched Levi's left arm.

"No worries." Gina squeezed Chloe's shoulder. "We know who it is."

"*We*?" She angled to gaze at Levi. "Okay, what's going on?"

"Another surprise." Levi slipped his arm from her waist and turned her toward the black SUV.

The driver's door opened, and Zach Austin emerged. "Carrots!"

"Dad?" Chloe gasped, then squealed.

"We tracked you down, Carrots." He waved and grinned. "Come say *hi* to your mom."

Her limbs suddenly pain-free, she hurried toward the other side of the SUV.

The passenger door opened, and Mom stepped out. "Chloe Jean Austin, you had us so worried!"

Chloe enveloped her into a hug and was shocked by the lack of meat on her bones. The familiar sweet, floral scent brought tears to her eyes. "Oh, Mom, you're here! How did you—" Her mind raced. *Levi.* The other surprise. "Mom, should you have taken such a long trip?"

"Chloe, dear." Samantha Austin touched Chloe's cheek. "It's only a flight away." She smiled. "But kind of a long drive from the airport."

Chloe hugged her again and cringed. She seemed so fragile, but her soft brown eyes still held the usual strong character.

Dad patted her back. "Seeing you is the best medicine. After we're settled, your mom will have a good nap."

She pulled Zach close for a family hug. Over Mom's shoulder, she threw Gina a glance. "You sneak! You knew they were coming." But she couldn't stop smiling.

"We've all been worried about you." Mom brushed a curl from Chloe's forehead. "Look at you, beautiful as ever. Your cheeks are rosy." She ran her gaze over Chloe's dusty jeans and T-shirt. "Have you been horseback riding?"

Chloe laughed. "Yes, attempting to. I can barely walk, but I plan to ride again soon."

"My fault for trying to cover so much ground." Levi clasped her mom's hand. "Samantha, it's good to meet you in person."

"Levi, I can't thank you enough for arranging the trip." Color flooded Samantha's cheeks.

Chloe opened and closed her mouth. Had Mom just blushed? And what was this—Levi had arranged their trip? She pursed her lips. "You could have told me." She bobbed her head.

"Then it wouldn't have been a surprise." Levi winked.

Mom looped her arm through Chloe's. "Gina told us about your sprain. Should you be walking without help?"

"I'm healing just fine." She motioned toward the kitchen door. "Let's go inside for coffee." She didn't want her clumsy stunt to worry Mom.

Janice welcomed them inside and filled mugs with coffee.

They gathered around the completely set up kitchen table.

"You all knew my parents were coming!" Chloe grabbed the back of a chair and shook her head.

Dad lifted a mug. "Let it rest, Carrots. Just be happy, that's all your mom and I ever wanted."

Chloe pushed through a tiny bit of resentment over being left out of the plan and sank to a chair. "Okay, Dad."

Dad took a sip of coffee. "Uh-huh, just what I needed. Hey, it's an honor to meet the famous Levi Banks."

"Not so famous." Levi turned a bit red under his tan. He added cream to his coffee.

Chloe tried not to gape. "Dad, how do you know about Levi's rodeo career?"

"Carrots, for years I've watched bull riding on TV. You just didn't notice. Levi Banks is a legend."

"You're a rodeo fan?" Chloe tilted her head and

blinked. "I guess, I didn't know." She felt like she'd become part of a mind-bending movie.

"Chloe Jean Austin, why didn't you call before you left Sacramento?" Mom sighed. "You could have stayed with us in San Diego."

Chloe glanced between her parents. "Do you know about the file?"

"Gina told us a few days ago, but for months, I knew something wasn't right." Samantha tilted her head. "Even though you called every week, you sounded uneasy, and then your father called. Now, I understand you were trying to protect us."

"My father?" She pressed a hand to her chest and glanced at the man who'd adopted her on her sixteenth birthday.

Dad ran a hand over his mouth. "Will Mathers. He wanted your mom's permission before he answered your email. He explained about the political contributions and how the big donors panicked."

"Panicked?" She huffed a breath. "Hallie Smith was murdered, my apartment was broken into, and I was forced to flee under an alias. I might have to testify in court."

"Oh, Chloe!" Mom gasped. "Will didn't word it exactly like that. I'm so glad Paul's helping you."

"Paul took months before he had the courage to stand against his captain." Her head swam with the details. "Rachel, who is Levi's sister and my protégée, was caught in the middle when a thug slammed into my car." Her voice caught, and she raked a hand over her hair. "Her arm was broken in multiple places, and several ribs cracked."

"Oh, dear." Mom pressed a hand to her mouth. "Is

she going to be okay?"

"Rachel's here on the ranch and resting in her room." Levi cleared his throat. "She has a long road to complete recovery."

Chloe met his gaze. Had it been only nine days ago that they met at the hospital? They'd gone from acquaintances to—to what? Much more than friends—at least on her part.

Scotty trotted into the kitchen and sank next to her dusty boots.

"Hey, Boy." She pulled him to her lap. "Mom and Dad, meet my new buddy, Scotty."

"He's adorable!" Mom left her chair and rounded the table to pet Scotty. "You've always wanted a pet."

Scotty wagged his tail and stuck his tongue out.

"Oh, did you see that, Zach? He smiled at me." Mom kissed Scotty's head.

"Yes, he's cute." Dad smiled and lifted his mug. "Happy for you, Carrots. Now, since the threat's over, what's your plan? Gina told us about your studio. We're excited to see it."

Chloe glanced at Levi and back to Dad. "I'm working on a plan, but it depends on how involved Rachel wants to be. Uh, do you mind sharing what else Will Mathers said?" Discussing her bio-dad in front of everyone might not be comfortable for Mom, but after all that had happened, she needed to know if her father played a role in the plot to silence her.

Mom tore away a bite of the cinnamon roll from a platter in the center of the table and bit into it. "Oh my, this is good." She chased the pastry with more coffee and set down her mug. "Chloe, dear, I'd rather have this conversation later." Tears spilled over pale cheeks.

"Of course, Mom." Chloe's heart twinged. "I'm sorry to have brought it up." She glanced at Levi. What thoughts lurked behind those amber-brown eyes? For one, she read compassion. She dropped the subject and let her parents enjoy their coffee and cinnamon rolls.

They asked Levi about the ranch, and Dad voiced his enthusiasm about watching the new rodeo classes while they were there.

She frowned? "Are you planning to commute from town?"

Janice bustled around the table, setting large plates heaped with scrambled eggs, sausage, and bacon in front of them. She added a plate of buttered toast in the center.

Chloe's stomach rumbled.

"Levi's offered us lodging for three nights." Dad thanked Janice and glanced toward Chloe. "We'll move to the resort on Wednesday."

"Your cabin's ready, so you're welcome to rest after breakfast." Levi dove into the scrambled eggs.

Chloe blinked. *Okay.*

Mom rested her fork on her plate. "Janice, you're an amazing cook, I'm just suddenly exhausted."

Dad patted her shoulder. "I'll help you to the cabin."

"Dad, please enjoy your breakfast." Chloe left her half-empty plate and pushed to her feet. "I'll help Mom." Her stiff muscles cried out, but she couldn't pause, or Mom would notice. She guided her mom out the back kitchen door and toward the front cottage steps.

Entering through the French doors, Mom gasped. "Oh, my! I expected something rustic." She moved toward the island and leaned in to smell an arrangement of flowers. "Beautiful."

Chloe hesitated just inside the kitchen and gazed from the floral arrangement on the island, to the early pink roses in a clear glass vase on the coffee table. "Someone went to a lot of trouble." She moved to the bedroom and found yet another arrangement of lilacs and lady's slippers in a mason jar on the dresser. Back in the living area, Mom had sat on the loveseat and gazed toward the kitchen.

"Mom, you're exhausted. Let me help you into the bedroom."

"Chloe, I'm not an invalid, but I am tired." She pushed up from the bright-teal upholstered loveseat and patted Chloe's shoulder. "Your new friends are wonderful."

"Yes, they are." Chloe guided her into the bedroom and pulled back the fluffy white comforter. "I'll help you with your shoes." She crouched to unbuckle the sandals and set them aside. "Mom, maybe later after you've rested, you'll feel like sharing more about my father." She lifted her mom's legs and helped her slide under the comforter. Pressing a kiss to her smooth forehead, Chloe stood to leave.

"Wait, Chloe." Her mom touched her hand. "I need to say this much." She closed her eyes, and her lips quivered. "He didn't desert us. Yes, he had an affair, and I couldn't live with the betrayal, but he wanted to be part of your life. Afterward, he called every day, but I didn't answer. He finally came to the door when you were at school and tried to convince me to take his money. I refused. Will betrayed me, but he wasn't a deadbeat dad." Her soft brown eyes filled with moisture. "My pride pushed me to work two jobs, and I left you alone far too much." She squeezed Chloe's hand. "I'm so lucky nothing bad happened."

Washed in disbelief, Chloe reeled on her boot heels. She sank to the edge of the bed and clutched Mom's hands. "I assumed he didn't love me."

Mom moaned. "When he called a few days ago, we spoke for over thirty minutes. We agreed it's time to put the past behind us." She gazed into Chloe's eyes. "For your sake. Use your own judgment, but please give him the opportunity to explain. Forcing your father to stay away—I was so wrong."

Breath trapped in her chest, Chloe hugged her. "Thank you for sharing. I'm sure it's still painful. I mean, he cheated on you, so stop feeling guilty about reacting. You provided a loving home, sometimes in sketchy neighborhoods, but we made it, didn't we?"

Mom smiled softly and closed her eyes. This time, she dozed off.

Chloe smoothed her hair and listened to her rhythmic breathing. The moment settled her racing thoughts. Leaving the cottage, she stood on the back porch and gazed over the lawn toward the red Adirondack chairs. Levi had given her permission to use them last night, but then Gina arrived, and they went riding this morning. Then, shock of all shocks, her parents arrived.

She gripped the porch railing and breathed. He'd spoken more about Lucy. Was he really ready for a new relationship? Navigating the stairs on stiffening legs, she returned to the kitchen. A hot Epsom salts and lavender bath sounded heavenly.

Inside the kitchen, Chloe was greeted by savory

and aromatic smells from the late afternoon dinner preparation.

Everyone but Janice, Gina—and now Rachel—had left the kitchen.

Janice glanced up from working dough on a floured board. "Get her settled?"

"Yes, she's already sleeping."

Rachel and Gina glanced toward her, their coffee cups between them.

"Rachel, you look radiant and well-rested." She also looked natural in blue jeans and a large, blue-plaid cotton shirt with one sleeve hanging loose. Chloe touched the braid lying over Rachel's right shoulder. "You had help this morning."

"My in-home helper arrived early. I'm so bummed that I took so long to get ready and missed your parents' arrival." She motioned toward Gina. "We were just reviewing the party."

"Like, the number of times you danced with Riley?" Chloe teased. Ah, it felt good to think about Rachel and not where she'd go from here.

"Maybe." Rachel traced her fingertip over the floral-printed tablecloth. "Go ahead and ask why I haven't mentioned dating Riley."

"Later. Right now, I need a hot bath." Chloe glanced between her friends.

"I can't believe Levi kept you in the saddle for over two hours." Rachel shook her head. "He really wants to impress you."

"Well, he impressed me." She sank into a chair and cringed when her behind hit the wooden seat. "He's been so busy planning surprises, it's a wonder he had time for the ranch."

"He's a good man." Rachel smiled softly. "He hasn't looked twice at a woman for over four years."

Chloe's heart threatened to burst. She darted a glance at Gina.

Gina slowly nodded. "I just arrived, and I can see how he looks at you." She raised both palms. "Makes me believe in love at first sight."

Her throat swelled with emotion. "We'll see how things turn out." She rubbed her palms over the thighs of her dusty jeans. "Hey, I'm heading for the bath, but then let's head to town. I can't wait to show you my building."

"It's a special place." Rachel smiled.

Gina raised a brow. "What's your hurry? We have all week. Levi invited us to stay for dinner."

"I know, but…" Chloe returned her friend's gaze. For some reason, she suddenly felt shy about seeing him.

"No buts. A bath and a visit, then dinner. In that order." Janice set a tray holding a complete tea service on the table. "On your way, could you please deliver this to Levi's office? He's busy with student registration forms. The new group arrives later today."

"A tea tray for Levi?" Chloe raised a brow. "There are two cups. Is he meeting with someone?"

Janice grinned like a Cheshire cat. "I hoped you'd stick around for a cup."

Chloe pushed from the chair. Her calves seized. "I-I-ouch." She leaned to rub the knotted muscles. "Okay, I know what you're all up to."

"Good, then take the man his tea." Gina raised a hand and fluttered her fingers.

Chloe frowned. "Okay, but we'll discuss this

later." She lifted the tray and hobbled through the archway and into the living room. She'd leave the tray with Levi, then escape to the bathroom. Grimy with dust and sweat, and her muscles drawing into balls, romance was the last thing on her mind.

Reaching his office door, she paused and took a deep breath. She'd spent last weekend in that office, sleuthing out evidence and clues, so why the nerves now? Her hands trembled. Because something had changed, and he was no longer helping her unravel a plot. He was no longer just Rachel's brother.

Chapter Twenty-Six

Chloe stood outside the open doorway and glanced at her jeans and dusty boots. It would've been nice to bathe first—dress in something feminine—like the sleeveless cotton shift she'd impulsively packed for just in case.

"Well, hello."

She started, and the china teacups rattled on their saucers. "Oh! I-uh-you startled me."

"You didn't know I was here?" Levi removed the gray plastic-framed readers and tossed them on the polished desktop. He pushed from his chair and crossed the room to take the tray from her hands. "Looks like you plan to stay."

She shoved her trembling hands behind her back. *Huh*, she suddenly remembered how it felt to dance in his arms. Their difference in height and build—his broad shoulders and raw masculinity. "Janice set up the tray."

"Setup is a good way to put it." He chuckled and carried the tray to the credenza. "How are you feeling? Muscles ease up?"

She forced her stiff legs to move toward the credenza and accepted a cup. She sipped the fragrant bergamot tea, and her world began to center. "I'm on my way to soak in an Epsom salts bath." She sipped again, then chuckled. "I had the preconception you normally preferred coffee." He'd probably shared tea with Lucy, and last weekend, he'd had tea with her. Her stomach tightened, and she set her cup on the corner of the desk. "Uh, I should clean up."

He kept his gaze squarely on hers. "Can't believe you'd waste a good pot of tea."

"Normally, I wouldn't, but…" She suddenly wished she didn't share a passion for tea with his deceased wife. She nibbled on her lower lip, then reclaimed her cup.

"Mom's the one who got me started appreciating a cup now and again." Levi ran a hand over his jaw, then lifted the delicate, dark blue cup and sipped.

She retrieved her cup and willed for her pulse to settle down. He'd read her mind—her uncertainty. "Thank you for all you've done. You went to a lot of trouble bringing Gina and my parents to Idaho." She paused and took a breath. "So, I'm curious why." The intensity in his amber-brown eyes unsettled her, and not even the fragrance of bergamot could calm her jittery nerves. She set her cup on the edge of the desk and shoved her unsteady hands into her jeans pockets.

He drained his cup in two swallows. "Well, my actions have been entirely selfish." He gathered their cups and returned them to the tray.

"Oh? How so?" She watched his backside and braced herself for where this conversation might lead.

He turned and flashed a smile, then sobered. "My way of proving the world doesn't drop off at the California border. Your parents and friends can travel here, and you can go there whenever you want."

She pressed her fingers to her throat. Good heavens, she suddenly felt like a starstruck teen. The teenager, who years ago, attended a concert with Gina and scored backstage passes. *Hmm*—had to be the cattleman's calendar Gina had mentioned or Dad's raving about the famous Levi Banks. For months, she'd been aware of his good looks and charm, but today, something different crackled between them—something that sent tingling from her head to her feet.

As if about to step off a cliff, she ran damp, trembling palms over her dusty jeans. "When my client, Tracie, suggested I could keep the studio and maintain clients in Coeur d'Alene, I began to realize how much I wanted it to work." She swallowed hard. "I hope Rachel agrees to a partnership."

Silence. His gaze held hers.

"Uh, thank you for renting the cabin to my parents." Dang, what was he thinking? "Mom loved the flower arrangements."

"The cabin?" A grin split his face. "Not the cottage?"

Chloe covered her mouth. "I-uh-I guess I slipped." She laughed, then cringed at the hysterical tone. "The horseback ride jarred my brain." The afternoon sun filtered between the wide, wooden blinds and caught the twinkle in Levi's amber eyes.

He laughed. "Sorry, I couldn't resist. You and Rachel were adamant about calling them cottages." He propped his hands on his hips and winked. "I like how you're using ranch lingo."

Whoa. Chloe went warm all over. Suddenly, she wasn't in a hurry to leave the office, or the ranch. On stiffening legs, she lurched toward the credenza and clutched the warm porcelain teapot. She refilled her cup. "In the *cottage*, my mom shared more news about my bio-dad."

"I figured she'd open up once you were alone." He hooked his thumbs on the front pockets of his jeans and leaned against the desk.

She gulped the Earl Grey. "She confessed to not allowing him to visit me, and she wouldn't accept child support." She shook her head. "Considering he cheated, I understand her anger and resentment. But, later, when I became an adult, why didn't he contact me?"

"Maybe he researched and learned you'd become a very successful, well-adjusted young woman. He didn't want to mess with your life."

"Is that what you would have done?" She held his gaze. Somewhere over the past week, she'd become comfortable with sharing her innermost thoughts with this man. She'd rewritten her list of the ideal man and rolled the list into one drop-dead handsome package.

"I would have never cheated on my wife." He tilted his head and flexed his lips. "Having said that, there are always two perspectives to every situation. None of us is perfect, and life is too short to pass up the opportunity to forgive. Give him the chance to explain." He stepped closer and cupped her cheek with a calloused hand.

Yes, forgiveness." She blinked back tears. "I've had to grant myself some forgiveness." His spicy scent wrapped around her and excited her senses. The Sacramento Chloe might have been repelled by the undertones of horse and dust. She might have suggested he take a shower and they'd meet later. But the new Chloe stood there covered in dust and horse. She stifled a chuckle and stepped away to set her cup down.

Gripped by the urge to plunge into the unknown,

fear of rejection and heartbreak stopped her from stepping into his arms. She strode toward the front-facing window and parted the two-inch wooden blinds. Time to slow down this train. Take a few days to think about the impact of falling in love. "I need time to—uh—to revise my preconceptions of Will Mathers." And the assumptions about what she really wanted. She cleared the emotion from her throat. "This week will be busy. I'm covering for Rachel and spending time with Gina and my parents. Now, I'm feeling a bit overwhelmed."

"And not so anxious to leave Coeur d'Alene after all?" His voice went gravely.

Her breath caught in her diaphragm. She gazed at the board-and-batten-sided dining hall and gripped the edge of the wide, oak windowsill. Levi and Wade had covered every detail to convert this place into an upscale ranch—from the outbuildings to the house. Maybe she and Levi weren't so different… She ran a hand over her eyes and turned to face him. "Time to pack and return to town."

Levi closed the distance and fingered her braid. "Time to stop running, Chloe. Pause and take a breath. Enjoy a soak and later, Sunday dinner at the ranch." His brows creased. "I hope you'll forgive me for going to such an extent to keep you in Idaho."

She touched the front placard of his chambray shirt. "How do you manage those tiny buttons?"

"Do you realize, you're a master at changing the subject?" He quirked a dark brow and half smiled.

"Funny." She continued to finger his buttons. "That's what my friends say."

"Okay, now it's my turn." He ran a hand over her

hair and ended with the tip of her braid. "How do you manage to capture those wild curls into a braid?"

She sputtered a laugh. "A lot of patience and practice."

"Now that I've met your mom, I see where you inherited this hair color. Like blonde dipped in a sunset."

"Yes, from my mom." Her breath caught, and she exhaled on a sigh. "Mom did something with the photos of my dad, but when I researched his business page and saw his photo, I remembered I have his green eyes." She smoothed his collar and flattened her palm over the warm region of his heart. An urgency to speak her heart pushed her to keep going. "In a very short time, I've learned what a caring man you are—how you love with your entire being." She nibbled her bottom lip. "Lucy was one lucky woman." She dragged a breath through her constricted chest.

He shifted from one booted foot to the other. "Where are you going with this?"

She drew in her lips and wished she'd saved this conversation for later—after she'd bathed and changed into her dress—or sometime next week. "Rachel mentioned that when Lucy died, you lost yourself." She held up a palm. "I get it. Losing her had to be so difficult." She closed her eyes for a moment, then opened them to gaze into his. "Your dedication to her memory is one of the attributes that I admire most." She paused and drew a sharp breath. "Are you capable of loving again?" She hurried to add. "Rachel thinks so."

His pulse fluttered against his tanned throat. "So, you and Rachel were discussing me? Surprised my ears weren't buzzing." He glanced away and centered his gaze on the door.

He probably wanted to escape—hop on Sundance and chase stray cattle. She understood the impulse to run, but she'd started this. Now, she had to finish it and know the depth of his desire to please her. "Rachel's worried I'll break your heart. Are you?"

He raked his fingers through his dark, thick hair. "Rachel worries too much, but yeah, you've been on my mind a lot."

"Well, she adores you and only wants you to be happy." Chloe placed flattened palms over his defined pecs and plunged on. "She thinks I'm who you're interested in."

"I did ask you out for a date." Levi centered his gaze on hers. "Guess it's time to talk about Lucy." He shoved his hands into the back pockets of his jeans and shifted from boot to boot. "Losing Lucy…I didn't think I'd survive it, let alone love again." He tugged a hand free and ran it over his mouth. "Took me two years to realize I'd neglected the ranch. Rachel helped pull me from a dark place. She moved to Coeur d'Alene and advertised for the ranch hands." He shook his head. "Talk about providence—without their help, I might never have recovered."

Chloe followed his movements and rested her hands on his tanned, muscle-corded forearms, right below the roll of his shirtsleeves. "You're a man with strong convictions, but sometimes, we all need help finding our way."

"Seems like a lifetime ago." He flexed his lips. "When I first met you at the open house, something I never expected to feel again stirred inside me. Common sense told me a glamorous designer couldn't be romantically interested in a rancher." He touched her hair. "But over time, your care about Rachel's success, your sense of humor, and yeah—hey, I'm a man—your beauty and grace—made me willing to pursue you. That's when I started showing up on Friday afternoons—working up the nerve to ask you out."

Her heart fluttered, and her throat tightened. "Seems we've both struggled with misconceptions about who we should fall in love with." Emotion bubbled and escaped in a giggle. "You've completely rewritten my list of the ideal man." She tilted her head and smiled into his amber gaze. "Right down to the dusty jeans and wash-worn shirt." She slid her hands back to his shirt front.

He covered her hands with his. "Life doesn't offer guarantees, Chloe, but I'm ready to take the risk and see if our lives can mesh."

His nearness, his scent, and his warmth turned her brain to mush. She lowered her gaze to his tanned neck and breathed deep. "Are you sure you want to deal with my baggage? You've had four years to adjust to Lucy's passing, but I just went through a crazy time, and my relationship with my bio-dad is a complete unknown."

"Life is filled with challenges." He crooked a knee and brought his eyes level with hers. "Facing them together is much better." Levi skimmed calloused fingertips over her right cheek. "How long do we have before you leave?" He inched closer still, until the tips of his dusty cowboy boots bumped hers.

Chloe clutched his shirtfront. "Leave for town or for Sacramento?"

"Both." He placed his hands on her waist. "Fair warning—I plan to drop in at the studio more than one day a week. Ask you out for dinners and for drives. There's a viewpoint up north where you can see into Canada and three states. Overlook a lake that's even larger than Lake Coeur d'Alene."

"Sounds wonderful." Heat coursed through her. "When I'm not being forced off the road, I enjoy beautiful views of mountains and lakes." Excitement danced over her like a live wire. Maybe—just maybe—her dreams *could* weave through his.

He chuckled, then pressed his lips to her forehead. "You impressed me this morning by hanging onto Chocka and facing every type of terrain I led you through. You were completely out of your comfort zone, but your grit and determination made you refuse to quit." He brought his gaze even with hers and rolled his lips. "Lucy tolerated my rodeo dreams, but she stayed on course with her career at the University of Montana. She taught me that when you love enough, differences can become strengths." He swallowed hard.

"Oh, Levi, I'm so sorry." She swallowed hard and studied the array of emotions behind his amazing eyes.

"Until I met you, I never imagined falling in love again." He made a sound from deep in his chest. "Probably sounds crazy, but last night when the music paused during our final dance, I could have sworn I heard Lucy's laugh." Tears welled, and he blinked them away. "As if she's happy I found you." His voice went hoarse.

Chloe's heart twanged. She forked her fingers through his hair, framed his head, and brought his amazing, tear-filled gaze to meet hers. "Lucy can never be replaced, but maybe she found a way to assure you it's okay if you love again."

He swiped at his eyes and flashed a crooked smile. "Maybe I heard a memory, but I believe Lucy would have liked you." He raised a palm. "Look, this all happened fast, sort of like the moment the chute opens, and it's just you and the bull in that ring. We barely know each other, but I believe this is something special." He lifted his chin toward the door. "Monday when that shot fired, I panicked. Chloe, I refuse to lose you, even if it means letting you go."

Her breath hitched, and she tightened her hold on his shirtfront. Tears blurred her vision. and her thoughts floundered. "I didn't see this coming—this conversation—my feelings for you—but I don't want to give up what I've found in Idaho."

"Can a beautiful and successful designer fall for a simple rancher?" He cupped the back of her head and brought his mouth to hers.

"I don't know." She chuckled against his lips. "I haven't discussed us with Scotty. You know, I loop him in on all important matters."

He grinned against her lips. "I'll never come between you and Scotty." His amber eyes went intense, and he ended the conversation with a kiss.

A mind-blowing kiss—a kiss like nothing she'd ever experienced. Chloe slid her arms around him and molded against his lean body. She felt as if she'd come home. Challenges would happen, but they'd face them together. With the assurance of their love, she'd willingly remodel her preconceived future.

He withdrew a few inches and gazed into her eyes.

Something right settled deep inside—something that told her he'd never ask her to compromise her dreams or her career. She'd brave the long winters, and she'd already begun to conquer her fear of driving through the countryside. Destiny had used extreme measures to bring her to Coeur d'Alene—had taught her, she could build a life here and make new friends. Open her own studio, mentor a young designer, and most of all, meet the man of her dreams.

She rolled to her tiptoes and, with a fierceness that might have joined their souls, pressed her lips to his. *I'll take good care of him, Lucy.* The promise echoed through her mind.

Levi shifted, and his *RBR* belt buckle pressed against her stomach.

On impulse, she brought her *Design* buckle to match his brand.

"Hmm, uncomfortable?" Levi spoke against her lips.

"Not in the least." She smiled.

She still needed a hot bath and to discuss the studio with Rachel. Later, she'd take Gina to Coeur d'Alene to tour her building, but right now, she'd enjoy this time in Levi's arms. She paused and pulled away just enough to ask. "Uh, when should we tell everyone?"

He framed her face in both hands. "I don't think we'll need to say a thing."

Epilogue

September 12th, four months later…

A breeze lifted the early autumn leaves, already dropping from the towering maple tree to dot the manicured lawn. They whispered past the silver-bling of Chloe's cowboy boots and fluttered to rest against the cedar-sided house. The rich touches of orange and gold only added to the beauty of her wedding day.

She tightened her hold on the satin-ribbon-wrapped stems of the bouquet of mums, daisies, and trailing ivy—custom-made by Rachel—and gazed toward the two men who waited to escort her to the flower-strung arbor and the spot where Levi waited.

Dad shot her a grin and lifted his chin.

Will offered a halting smile.

He still didn't quite know his role in her life, but they'd figure it out. Months ago, she'd granted him forgiveness for disappearing from her life. Life was too short to harbor resentment that wouldn't change the past.

She'd immediately forgiven her mom for her extreme reaction to Will's betrayal and for causing hardships for herself and for Chloe. Those times had shaped both their characters and had opened the door for Mom to meet Zach.

Now, Chloe stood on the precipice of joining her

life with Levi's, the man destiny had introduced her to. She arranged her long, satin skirt and inhaled the rich scents of autumn. *Ah,* the perfect day to marry the man who'd helped reshape her idea of happiness, and to share it with her loved ones.

From under the maple, Clay drew the bow over his fiddle, signaling her entrance.

The fifty guests stood.

Will and Dad moved toward her.

Dad crooked his arm.

She rested her manicured hand on the sleeve of his black suit jacket.

Will moved close to her other side and cupped her elbow.

The song picked up tempo and, just like they'd practiced last night, Chloe stepped toward the aisle formed by the cloth-draped chairs.

Will's wife, Kathy, sat next to Mom. Jeff, Chloe's new half-brother, sat one row back. Her half-sister, Lana, stood next to Diane, beautiful in the dress Chloe had found at the last minute after Lana finally capitulated and agreed to be a bridesmaid. A breakthrough in the tension since Chloe and Levi visited the Mather home in July, in combination with the trip to Sacramento to organize shipping her few belongings to Coeur d'Alene.

Her stomach fluttered, and her breathing hitched, and as much as she'd schooled herself not to cry, her carefully made-up eyes welled with tears. She paused and, for a moment, took her hand off Dad's arm to dab her eyes with the small, lace-trimmed hankie Janice had loaned her. Stuffing the hankie back into the hidden side pocket of her dress, she again placed her hand on

Dad's arm and continued down the aisle.

Halfway to the arbor, and for the first time that day, Chloe met Levi's gaze. Dressed in a charcoal-gray, Western-style tux, he took her breath away—but then, he always did, no matter what he wore.

He widened his eyes for just a moment, then smiled, sending creases toward his temples and dimples in his cheeks.

Whoa. Her pace faltered. Was that satisfaction in his intense amber-brown eyes? Admiration? Whatever he felt right now, his expression heated her to the core. She smiled and held his gaze.

Clay changed tempo from the traditional wedding song to an orchestral rendition.

Chloe blinked, then laughed. They hadn't practiced with that version, but she loved it. She glanced over her left shoulder, past the rows of friends and toward the maple.

Clay grinned and lifted his chin.

Pure joy bubbled through her, and she returned his smile. Had Levi planned the change in music as another surprise? She turned back toward Levi and continued down the aisle.

Scotty walked beside her, then trotted toward Levi and sat next to Duke.

Gina had tied a tiny, satin pillow around Scotty's middle and attached Levi's gold wedding band.

Her boy was so handsome and looked proud to have an honored job at her wedding. *Her wedding.* The occasion hit her full force, and she paused to absorb the scene.

Her four attendants looked beautiful in their sage-green dresses.

Gina stood as her maid of honor.

Rachel, her arm free of the cast, stood next to Gina as an honorary maid of honor.

Diane and Lana were both bridesmaids.

Mike Parker moved around with his large digital camera, recording the occasion.

Chloe flashed a smile and ran her gaze over Levi's attendants. Riley, Carson, and Wade were all dressed in Western-cut tuxes, all very handsome. Travis was an usher.

Her attention back on Levi, the air whooshed from her lungs. She took the final steps to reach him, and once again, her emotions bubbled, and tears spilled over her cheeks.

Oh, my gosh, she was crying at her wedding.

Gina smiled and took the bouquet from her hands.

Chloe retrieved the hanky from her pocket and dabbed her face.

The music slowly faded.

Suddenly, everything but Levi disappeared from her notice.

This wasn't Levi's first rodeo. He must have recalled his wedding day with Lucy. Those memories would always be a part of him.

Will lifted her veil and kissed her forehead.

Dad kissed her cheek.

More tears fell, and the very modern, very trendy interior designer, Chloe Austin, hugged each of her fathers and threw a kiss at her mom. Last night's rehearsal hadn't prepared her for this level of emotion.

Levi accepted her hand from Dad and cupped her elbow. He guided her to stand under the arbor where Pastor Tibbetts waited with his well-used Bible.

Chloe turned to face Levi, and her heart overflowed with love. Trembling, she grasped both of his hands and drank in every angle of his face, from his high cheekbones and broad forehead, to his lips she'd never tire of kissing. He hadn't worn a cowboy hat to avoid bumping her when they kissed, and his freshly cut hair lay in dark curls over his head and still brushed the starched white shirt collar.

The fragrances of roses and morning glories filled the space under Wade Creighton's arbor and wrapped them in a private space.

Pastor Tibbetts opened with a prayer and led them through the traditional vows with patience and focus. He reached the end, closed with a prayer, and pronounced them husband and wife.

Chloe exhaled an *Amen,* and with all her being, she welcomed the next chapters of her life. Some filled with joy, others with sorrow—and many filled with the children they both wanted.

Levi drew her close, and with his lips, he sealed the vows.

The guests stood, cheered, and clapped.

Levi smiled against her lips, then cupped her elbows and led her through the back of the arbor.

"Wait! Where are we going? We have to walk back down the aisle."

"Riley and Gina know what we're doing." He chuckled and pulled her hand over his right arm. "We'll be right back, but first, I want to give you my wedding gift."

"Now?" Her feet tangled in her long skirt. Levi's mischievous grin and twinkling amber eyes made Chloe imagine their children. Would they have his eye color or hers? Probably curly hair, but would it be dark brown or reddish blonde? "Okay, lead on."

He led her across the freshly mown lawn.

Chloe laughed, then shrieked. "I'm glad I wore boots instead of three-inch heels." Like she'd always planned to wear on her wedding day—the wedding that would have taken place in a grand cathedral, with the reception at a country club, and a honeymoon in the Virgin Islands—yeah, yeah, yeah—that list had been rewritten.

Levi shortened his long stride and paused to kiss her with a fervor that shook her to her bling-covered boots. Then he pulled her toward the riverbank.

"Levi, slow down." She didn't have time to find her equilibrium and grasped at his right bicep.

"Sorry, guess I'm excited about you opening my gift first." His chest expanded under his vest and jacket. He lifted her left hand to his lips and kissed the joined rings. "Beautiful wife, get used to many surprises and gifts."

She shivered with delight over his old-fashioned gesture and glanced toward the riverbank where, since May, she and Levi had shared many evenings. She frowned. "Why are the chairs covered with a tarp?" She tugged free from his hold and moved to remove it.

"Wait." He stepped around her, grabbed an edge of the brown tarp, and with a flourish revealed the chairs.

"What?" Chloe opened and closed her mouth, her mind completely blown away. "The chairs! What happened with the red chairs?"

Lucy's red Adirondack chairs had been replaced with new ones, painted in Chloe's favorite shade of bright-teal and accented with colorful, beach-patterned cushions. Fresh tears welled and blurred her vision. "There's even an outdoor rug. Oh, Levi, they're beautiful!"

He slid a hand over her backless wedding dress and tucked her against his side. "Happy wedding day. A special place, uniquely your own, to make new memories." He again lifted her left hand to his lips.

"You're amazing." She touched his cheek and gazed into the amber eyes she looked forward to seeing every night before she went to sleep and every morning before she left their bed. "I love you so much."

He tilted his mouth into a soft smile. "I love you, and I plan to spend the rest of my life showing you how much." He pulled her close and moved his lips over hers.

Despite her overwhelming reactions to his touch, his kiss, and his thoughtfulness, Chloe pictured them sitting at this very spot through the seasons of their lives. Romantic evenings, then later holding babies, and reminiscing about their day. Their hair would gray, and time would line their faces, but Levi would always be the most handsome man she'd ever seen.

The earthy scent of the river rose around them, blending with the fresh-mown grass and the array of flowers in bloom. Close by, she caught the laughter and murmured conversations between their guests. A feminine laugh stood out.

Chloe glanced around. Her emotions were running high, but had Lucy given her blessing? *Rest in Peace, Lucy. I'll take good care of him.*

She framed Levi's handsome face with both hands and gazed into his eyes. "Thank you for the special gift. Now, Cowboy, it's time to return to our guests."

He chuckled and swept her into his arms. "I'll share you for now, but expect a very eventful wedding night." He strode toward the arbor and the milling guests.

Chloe's body heated from her face to the tips of her polished toenails.

"They're back!" Gina clapped her hands.

The guests went silent, then smiled and applauded.

Grinning, Levi carried Chloe down the aisle and turned at the end. "Sorry about the unexpected twist, but I wanted to be the first to present my wife with a wedding gift. Now, on to the dining hall for the party."

Chloe tightened her hold on his broad shoulders. "I suspect my life will be filled with spontaneous events." She pressed her face against his tanned neck and breathed in his spicy scent. "Lead on, Cowboy."

A word about the author...

Teresa Davis dreamed of becoming a published writer before she could write. Inspired by her great-grandmother who wrote bits of philosophy and poetry, she remembers holding those books and imaging her name on the covers.

Teresa lives in the Mountain Northwest, with her husband of over fifty years, and likes to joke, she ran away with him when he was a sailor. Their three daughters, sons-in-law, seven grandchildren and great-granddaughter are Teresa's joy.

Loving to travel, after leaving the Navy, Teresa and her husband managed small trips while raising their daughters, then began the big adventures where Teresa absorbed the locations and the people for future stories!

You can find Teresa Davis on her website, teresadavisauthor.com

Thank you for purchasing
this publication of The Wild Rose Press, Inc.

For questions or more information
contact us at
info@thewildrosepress.com.

The Wild Rose Press, Inc.
www.thewildrosepress.com